Settling
Down

Settling Down

June Barraclough

ROBERT HALE · LONDON

© June Barraclough 2005
First published in Great Britain 2005

ISBN 0 7090 7793 9

Robert Hale Limited
Clerkenwell House
Clerkenwell Green
London EC1R 0HT

2 4 6 8 10 9 7 5 3 1

Typeset in 11/13½ Sabon
Derek Doyle & Associates, Shaw Heath.
Printed in Great Britain by
St Edmundsbury Press Ltd, Bury St Edmunds, Suffolk.
Bound by Woolnough Bookbinding Ltd.

For Frances and Piers

Then be not coy, but use your time;
And while ye may, go marry:
For having lost but once your prime,
Ye may for ever tarry.

Robert Herrick: 1648
To the Virgins to Make Much of Time

Part One

TURNING POINTS

1

For years, Janet Walker had wanted to move from the London suburbs to the country – specifically to a beautiful grade two listed country mansion with woodland and a walled garden. She had a picture in her mind's eye of a many bed-roomed Regency or early Victorian house – centrally heated, of course, but with high ceilings and sash-windows and a pillared portico. Her husband pointed out that to exist with any modicum of comfort in such a house, would need the possession of a great deal of money.

'To pay for a fleet of servants – a housekeeper, a chauffeur – a cook,' he said, exaggerating, which was his way of teasing his wife. Tom knew she loathed domestic maintenance – and that he was hardly a DIY expert himself.

'Not to mention gardeners,' Janet added, playing along, knowing it was only a romantic dream that kept her going. She did not easily relinquish her vision of the ideal existence, but once their daughters had fled the nest, the idea of living in such a place was absurd. Her daughter Anna understood that day-dreaming had always kept her happy. At various times their mother had had the idea of moving to Suffolk, where several of her favourite painters had lived, or to some Dorset parsonage, or to Norfolk, where the tentacles of horrible giant motorways had not yet reached, or to the Welsh Marches, or to Cornwall – or even Northumberland. They all fascinated her. Her elder daughter, Emma, said it all depended on what she had just seen in *Country Life* in the dentist's waiting room. Janet was possibly relieved that she did not have to choose, being obviously constrained by lack of money and by a husband who refused to live in a more rural part of England, many of his activities since his retirement still taking place in London. It

11

was probably too late to settle down to a completely different way of life, but she had begun to feel dislocated: recently London had changed a good deal. It was perhaps the wrong *time* for Janet rather than the wrong *place*.

'*Tout passe, tout casse, tout lasse*,' she quoted sadly.

'Oh, really, Mother!' said Emma.

In 1990 Janet had not quite stopped imagining a new life in a beautiful place. *Someone* had to live in beautiful houses in lovely parts of England, so why not she and Tom?

What happened was not really surprising. Tom decided he would not mind living a little further out, and offered a compromise. In 1991 they sold their large but shabby family house in Blackwich, a pleasant leafy suburb in south London, pronounced 'Blackidge' by its inhabitants, and moved to a village in north Kent that was not quite a suburb, not far from the border with Surrey. Less than a dozen miles from their old home and only twenty miles from central London, it was an oasis between old roads and the motorway, the latter distant enough to forget about, though useful for people who liked moving around. The 'real' country was away from the Home Counties in places like Dorset or North Yorkshire but Janet was to find that Deepden House in Hookden was countrified enough for her, and near enough to London to be convenient for Tom. She realized it was London she had wanted to leave, as so many of her friends had already done.

The Walkers had lived in their last Blackwich house for twenty of the thirty-one years they had spent in the suburb, and it meant a certain amount of disruption, but Tom said: 'Now or Never!' and in the end his compromise was a great success. They bought the lease of the ground floor of one wing of a country house advertised as early Victorian. It was not cheap, but cheaper than London, and the disruption of the move was worth it to be able to walk across fields, or enter a small wood by the side of a lane, and for air that smelled fresh.

The whole of Deepden House was divided into apartments for separate occupiers; central heating and modern kitchens and bathrooms had been fitted, but to Janet's delight the high ceilings and sash-windows had been retained. It was not actually Early Victorian but had been solidly built in the eighteen-fifties and was quite handsome. The upkeep of the building and the grounds, and the repairs and charges were high but were fixed for 5 years. They were both relieved to be rid of such responsibilities. There would be no more need to think about gardening, although you could do some if you wanted, or outside painting, or the 'improvements' that a suburban house often appeared to need, and there was little noise of traffic. The roads and lanes were cleaner, and the pavements had fewer uneven paving stones. Janet might still enjoy imagining other existences, but now admitted that she would have had to be a quite different kind of woman to have enjoyed them in reality.

Neither of their daughters was married at the time they left London. The Walkers hoped that both Emma and Anna might soon find someone to settle down with, and Janet hoped one of them might one day produce a grandchild. Anna, the younger, did want children – after an interesting job, of course. Their elder daughter was more ambitious for what Janet still called a 'career'. If you were a woman, it still seemed difficult, if not impossible, to succeed in both. Emma had almost lost sight of her old friend, Catherine Hawkins, so different were her priorities. Catherine now lived in Staffordshire, had a large family and no job. On the other hand, both sisters were friends with Lucy Hall, now a single parent, working outside the home (in Tom's parlance) and her life enticed Emma even less.

Emma and Anna had sharply contrasting temperaments. Emma, the elder by two years, was regarded as the rational one, Anna, more extrovert, the talkative one. Tom thought Emma was more like his family and Anna more like her mother – or as her mother had been when she was young. Emma once said sardonically:

'We inherit our parents' problems in one way or another, I suppose.'

Anna added more sententiously: 'Well, we are all bound by the genes of our talents or temperaments,' which Tom thought was just the sort of thing his wife might have said, and probably had said.

Both daughters had been at university in the first half of the 1980s, a greedy and grabby decade which Janet, in spite of her romantic dreams of sudden wealth, had not liked at all. Neither Emma nor Anna had succumbed to a get-rich-quick career in the City, which meant they would probably not decline financial help

if it were ever offered. The profit from selling the parental suburban house was not large but gave their daughters something
towards buying flats, whether or not they ever 'settled down'.
Anna had been sharing a flat with a woman friend in a less salu-
brious area than Blackwich, but she was now able to afford a small
one back near the old home patch. Emma put the money towards
buying the lease of a maisonette in Pimlico, sharing a mortgage
with a woman colleague, Lydia Carter. Tom and Janet were
surprised and pleased that 'Anna', as they still thought of her, was
not averse to a return to her childhood haunts. 'Emmie' wanted to
be nearer her work in Westminster, even if property in SW1 was
almost as inordinately expensive as Notting Hill or Kensington.

The sisters were slow to 'settle down', which in their parents'
old-fashioned terms meant marriage. Janet felt slightly surprised at
herself when she admitted that she would like them to find steady
partners, even if husbands were not always the thing nowadays.
She really wanted them to find men who would be good fathers to
possible future grandchildren, and she admitted this to Tom.
Emma, conscientious and ambitious and extremely good at her
job, showed no inclination to find a partner of any kind. In 1994,
however, Anna, now working a mile or two away from Blackwich,
met Martin Macdonald who, after they had been going out
together for almost a year, proposed to her in the old-fashioned
way. They were married in the late spring of 1995. Martin was
already living quite near so they decided to look in Blackwich
'Village' for their first home.

Since the middle of the nineteenth century, City workers of all
sorts, clerks as well as professionals and businessmen, had found
the place, then part of North Kent, an ideal place to settle down in
and bring up their families. The railway had come in 1847 to what
had still in the eighteenth century been a small village, mostly the
property of several large landowners. The first houses were built
on land belonging to an old manor, or had been grouped around
a flat expanse of gravel pits and heathland that rose above the
Thames by the side of a Royal park.

Martin was working in a City office reached by train in less than
twenty minutes. His work description was as a sort of broker
concerned with English businesses that were connected with vineyards and vintners in France, necessitating several trips to

Bordeaux and south-west France.

'Explain to your parents, Anna, that I am not a rich City type,' he'd said to his future wife with a laugh before he was introduced to them. Anna didn't think this would be necessary, and Martin was amused by the mixed range of expressions on Janet's face when he told her where he worked: in the City, but neither as a conventional stockbroker – nor from a background of business studies. The Walkers enjoyed Anna's wedding. Emma put it in her scrapbook.

Macdonald – Walker. On Saturday 20 May 1995 at St Peter's Church, Blackwich, Anna, younger daughter of Mr and Mrs Thomas Walker to Martin Macdonald, younger son of the late Dr Christopher Macdonald and Mrs Cora Macdonald of Cambridge.

A week before his daughter's wedding, the postman had brought Tom an astonishing letter from his solicitor.

'Look at this, Jan!'

He went into the large, excellently but not over-modernized kitchen, where his wife was taking dry clothes out of the washing-machine, having put them in to wash the minute she got up. She liked to get unpleasant jobs done as quickly as possible, being impatient by nature. Even well away from the Great Wen the postman arrived later and later nowadays. Janet straightened up, sat down at the table, and quickly absorbed the contents of the letter her husband handed her.

An old uncle of Tom's, who had died not long before, had bequeathed him a house on the edge of Blackwich Heath.

'Good Lord! Hall House? When was it built?'

'About a hundred years ago, I'd think – I imagine it's very solid.'

'You must be his only surviving relative,' said Janet, taking another look at the letter.

'We'll have to go over and look at it.'

'Don't say anything yet to the children.'

It turned out to be the very house in which an older generation of Tom's family had lived before the Great War. Tom had quite forgotten that Blackwich was an old family stamping-ground. It had actually been Janet who, years ago, had suggested Blackwich as a pleasant place to live. She said that she must have 'telepathized' Tom's homing instinct. That was, however, too fancy an explanation. Tom had genuinely forgotten about the place. He had never taken much interest in his physical surroundings or in the byways of family history, while Janet counted this sort of history as one of her greatest interests.

A closer investigation in the company of a surveyor revealed that the house, one of an Edwardian pair, but detached, was in a basically sound condition. Two respectable middle-aged tenants, already about to retire, had been living in it, but had both separately expressed a wish to move away when the owner died. John Walker had never lived in the house himself. He'd let the whole house out to various tenants through the years, always retaining the freehold, which was to be passed on to his great-nephew. The house needed rewiring and repainting, and could do with some alterations, but once modern central heating was put in, other improvements could be seen to in time.

Nothing was said to Anna and Martin at the wedding about the house.

'Better get all this over with first,' Tom said.

The couple had not yet bought a house; Martin was selling his old flat in order to put the money down for a mortgage, and for the time being they were staying in Anna's flat. Emma was informed of the bequest whilst the others were in France on their honeymoon. Anna and Martin might like to live in Hall House themselves? It was quite a large house. Or it could be sold and some of the money divided between Emma and the Macdonalds? Or Emma might even like to share it with them? Emma expressed no interest in the last two possibilities and reiterated quite categorically that she had no desire to return to Blackwich.

'We'd have to make it up to you eventually as far as the money's concerned, if we leased it at a low rent to your sister,' said her father.

Emma said she was quite happy with that, so once the couple had returned from their honeymoon, Tom and Janet called a family conference where all was revealed. Would they like to lease it from Tom, and share it with one or two new tenants, perhaps friends of theirs? There was a more-or-less self-contained top floor, and a decent basement. It might be a good idea?

Anna and Martin were amazed and delighted, Anna almost speechless, an unusual state for her.

'It depends a bit on finding decent tenants,' said Janet.

'We *could* sell it,' said Tom. 'We've asked Emma, but she's really not interested in sharing it.'

Emma earned more than Anna, for she had a good salary from her position in the Civil Service. Things were not so promising for Anna; her interesting work in a nearby picture library was not very well paid. She had loved the work at the beginning and it had brought her luck, for it had been where she had come across Martin for the first time, when he'd been browsing around one afternoon.

Martin said the idea sounded very exciting. He was a sensible man, and did not wish to be too beholden to his in-laws.

'We'll think it over,' he added soberly.

It was clear to Anna what their decision would be. Living in her old flat was rather cramped and they were still searching for a suitable larger one. A house in this area would be extremely expensive.

'Do you think Emma would really mind?' Martin asked Anna that night.

'My parents would make it up to her later,' said his wife, not wishing to discuss their eventual demise, which she hoped was far away in the future.

'We'd only be leasing it from your father – he'll retain the freehold for the time being.'

'I know – and we must make sure we pay him a decent rent. Knowing him, it won't be anything excessive. But shall we – should we – be able to afford the upkeep?'

'I think so – we wouldn't be paying out anything like what a mortgage for just an ordinary house near here would cost. It's a very generous offer – think of the *space*!'

'Well, I'm sure they wouldn't want to live there themselves – they're both glad to have got out of London!'

'Let's go over and have a recce tomorrow evening, as your mother suggested. I know where it is. I often used to pass by it when I walked to the other station. How did they manage to keep it to themselves? They never said a word at the wedding,' Martin went on.

17

'They knew we had something even more important to think about than where to live. They've got their priorities right.'

'True.'

They both smiled, but Anna couldn't help wondering whether her father might have wanted the house for himself if it had been left to him a few years earlier. No, he would have sold it. From their description, Hall House would need youthful energy.

What the couple were not to know was that Tom would bank all the rent they paid him. With Janet's hearty agreement he intended to leave it one day, plus interest, divided between all their descendants.

'One way of saving up!' he'd said to Janet. 'That's if they want it.'

The next day, Anna and Martin went to see Hall House, along with Tom's surveyor, who had the key, and the following day they returned, accompanied by a builder. They would certainly like to live there.

Martin was practical, knew about property, and was already planning improvements. He made a long list of the most essential jobs: general survey, central heating, and repainting were the most important. He had many useful contacts, but now that they were both back at work all day, everything had to be organized in the evenings and at weekends. Tom and Janet could come over in an emergency but Anna was determined to save them the trouble. She put her own flat on the market, rather than let it out, which was always a bother. If they were lucky they would be able to pay for the alterations out of their joint sales. Fortunately, builders and painters and heating-contractors were quickly found – there had been a slump in the trade, with quite a few bankruptcies, and they were all glad of employment. Various estimates were compared, the best accepted, and work was started immediately whilst the weather was good.

It all made Anna feel she was really married.

'Well, don't feel you are married to a house,' said her mother. 'It's a mistake – houses, like some husbands, can be nuisances as well as blessings.'

'I suppose that's why you always enjoyed your imaginary ones,' replied Anna innocently.

After less than six months the house was actually ready for reoccupation. A few days before Christmas 1995, the couple made the move. During the months of preparation Anna had begun to love it more and more for what was left of its slightly faded grandeur. The first days and nights they spent there did not diminish her enthusiasm or Martin's. There were still further improvements to make, of course, but all this could be done bit by bit once they could afford it. They were very lucky indeed to be renting it for so little outlay. If Anna appreciated its period charm, Martin had enough realism to work out the future necessities for its preservation. Provided the house was warm and was not going to fall down, Anna was content. Martin had had a pipe-dream of living in France and owning a vineyard, but for the present he was more than satisfied.

2

Two hundred miles away from the Walkers and the Macdonalds, there lived, in Ilkgate, a pleasant semi-market, semi-dormitory town in Wharfedale, a young woman called Moira Emsley, who was a qualified librarian. She had recently parted from the married man with whom she had been having a love-affair for almost six years. He was an archivist, well-known in the town and in Woolsford, the nearest city. The affair had been both a torment and a guilty secret for Moira, who had never seen herself cut out to be a 'man's woman', never mind a 'mistress'. Her father had died while she was in her teens and her mother had remarried a few years later and departed to Australia. Moira had known for certain that Australia was not for her, so she had stayed on in Yorkshire, and met Dennis, or 'TD' as he was called by his friends, when she was twenty-four. Over five years later he finally decided to accept a post over the Pennines, urged on by his wife who had been completely cognizant of her husband's relationship with the younger woman.

Moira was by now over thirty, fair and slight and young-look-ing, her appearance belying her rather 'colourful' situation. Colourful for Ilkgate, if not unusual, she thought, knowing very well that such a love-affair as she had enjoyed, or rather suffered, was a commonplace in cities and other parts of the realm a little less traditional than Old Ilkgate. She had had no parents to scandalize, which had been a blessing, but had begun to realize during the last year or two that she would one day like to have a child. She accepted that Dennis did truly love her, but as long as she stayed with him this would be wrong, if not impossible.

I couldn't do that to his family, she thought, but then, a year later: *Do I really want to stay with him for ever?*

Moira did not look at all ruthless but the last five years had made her grow up. Suddenly, she made up her mind to leave her native county, and move south whenever a suitable post turned up. The field in which she was most interested, children's books and children's reading, was flourishing in certain parts of the country, in spite of public library cuts. She had finally determined to tell 'TD' she was going to break with him during the very week when he revealed that he too was making his own plans. He was to move to a better-paid post in Manchester, having decided that this promotion would be his last, and having also come to realize that he might be standing in the way of Moira's future. He was twenty-one years older than his beloved, and time would not wait for either of them. It was far too late to leave his wife Cynthia. He ought to have done that years earlier if he had been going to do it at all. He had sensed for some time, however, that Moira needed to leave him, or rather that she wanted him to make up her mind for her.

In January 1996, what sounded to Moira like an ideal post had turned up in a southern suburb of London. She applied for it. If her application succeeded she could be away from Ilkgate by late spring or early summer. She already felt quite dizzy and dislocated when she posted her letter in the pillar-box.

When Teresa Victoria Winterbon's divorce was finalized in 1989, she returned to live for a time with her also divorced and now widowed mother in rural Essex. Vicky was working near the Tower of London, arranging and cooking business lunches and dinners. Her long commute was wearisome. For some time she had very much wanted to found a little business of her own, perhaps making meals for well-off women who didn't know how to, or didn't want to cook, but for a year or two she chose the noble option of living with her mother. It gave her a break from her more recent past. When her mother died in 1993, Vicky had decided to apply for something a little different. At one time in her versatile youth she had learned to touch-type, and with the growth of computing she knew she might find this useful. In a magazine which she found lying around, a female psychologist and therapist in south London was advertising for a PA and secretary: must be a good typist, discreet, articulate, and able to drive, and she immediately knew this was for her. Her cooking might eventually come in useful as well, and she did possess a driving-licence. Armed with this, and her other skills, including her very distant past as a drama student, Vicky considered she would make the perfect assistant to a therapist.

Ms Winterbon – she had reverted to her maiden name – was just what Frieda Ingersoll was looking for. She had employed too many arts graduates with little knowledge of life, and fewer skills, and what she needed was an unshockable and experienced woman in her thirties. A less assertive woman might not have applied, but Vicky did. She was offered the job, and she took it.

After Christmas, the New Year of 1996 was upon them all. Janet Walker's most fervent wish was that time would stop. *Stop the World I Want to Get Off* had been the title of a musical the year Emma was born.

So much had accumulated in her mind that needed to be thought about. As well as the housework there was a great pile of newspapers and books she wished to read, new family photographs to sort out, and letters to write. Many of these tasks were pleasant. Tom kept telling her they were self-imposed. A pile of letters to answer lay on the table; she corresponded with many friends and relations, writing what some American friends had begun to call snail-mail. Recently, she had spent a lot of time and energy addressing Christmas cards and birthday cards. Many of her friends had winter birthdays. She did wish they all lived nearer, for one must not take friends for granted. The close family, and one or two cousins, had visited them over the Christmas week, and visitors had meant more housework. Janet needed time to herself. Tom helped with the chores, but usually managed to do what he wanted as well. Almost all men were able to put up with the kind of domestic squalor that irked most women of her generation, she thought, and men did not seem to be implicated in housework to quite the same degree. Domestic guilt had apparently been built into the female sex chromosome. Even young women who worked out in the world had their primitive impulses activated when children arrived. New chores were discovered to be necessary to keep life ticking over. Chores did not just invent themselves, as she often pointed out to her husband. Men had always worked out in the big world, which at the time when Janet became 'domesticated', most women had not. Teaching even part time – once her children were at nursery and primary school – had made her fairly unusual among her middle-class friends.

Tom said she should get out more after Christmas, perhaps go up to London to the sales. The railway halt at Hookden was very near – but she couldn't think of anything of which she was in desperate need, and she heartily disliked this kind of shopping. She did intend to visit two new exhibitions in London soon, and if she could persuade Tom to go with her, might even go to the cinema or theatre. But that meant she wouldn't have as much time to read, or write letters, not to speak of the unavoidable chores of tidying up, grocery shopping and preparing meals. She confessed to skipping the cleaning, for although Janet was not the worst housekeeper in the world, housekeeping took up so much precious time. As you grew older perhaps you got slower? When their daughters Emma and Anna were still children she had baked for Christmas, made parkin on Bonfire Night, given many birthday and Christmas parties, and written stories for them, which they had appeared to enjoy. Publishers, however, had not liked them enough to publish them.

She and Tom had as yet no grandchildren to whom she might read her stories, but once they moved to Hookden she had been offered a little job reviewing children's books for a recently founded magazine. She enjoyed the challenge of clarifying her reactions, and worked at her reviews conscientiously.

Janet had always been a great reader; her childhood ambition had been to be a poet. Some years ago she had begun to trace her family history, which was enthralling but very time-consuming. For many of the older inhabitants of Hookden village, and at Deepden Court itself, mornings and evenings were full of private, or sometimes local authority, groups following their own pursuits, and many older people – more women than men – became literary 'groupies', founding or joining reading-groups. Janet thought she had quite enough to read.

As a change from 'words, words, words', she would occasionally get out her paints or oil-pastels and produce vividly coloured daubs to please nobody but herself, or listen to piano music or opera. She often admonished herself for physical laziness. She had joined a yoga class for a year or two, held every Monday at the church hall, hoping it would keep her healthy. Tom could not be persuaded to accompany her. The yoga amounted to stretching exercises that she could carry on by herself – when she remembered – so now she did them at home instead. Her daughters went to gyms, but she had been too glad to leave the gymnasium behind her when she left school to try one again.

The Walkers usually took a holiday in May or late September, usually to the fairly sedate lakes of northern Italy, or to south west France, where Tom would not be called upon to drive. Their favourite spot was a small lake in Piedmont and they had already stayed there several times. Self-catering holidays had never appealed to Janet: they were too much like housework. She liked staying in French and Italian hotels, and now, with Eurostar so near, it was much easier to get to France. Not so much of horrible Heathrow.

Tom read many newspapers and journals, and world news was always running around Janet's head. It was a change from worrying about chores.

'My mind is a rag-bag,' she said to Tom once.

'You ought to go in for pub quizzes!' was his deadpan reply.

Nightly, television poured out what it regarded as important; daily, newspapers and opinion-formers claimed your attention. She had always been concerned about what was happening in the world of wars and of conflicts and politics – which were only a substitute for war, if not an extension of it. She scoured the papers looking for something cheerful. Did old people all become more pessimistic? What had become of the serenity of age? She tried to live in the present, but it seemed vague and weightless, without the solidity of the past, and there was always that unknown future round the corner. As you got older the future did not appear exciting so much as faintly menacing.

Janet did not feel 'old', in spite of creaky knees, and the big 'floaters' that had suddenly arrived in one eye with a flash of gold at its outside corner. There had also been the matter of a broken wrist when she had slipped on a cowpat on holiday. Worse by far had been giving up smoking. She didn't feel sure she had stopped for good; she had loved her cigarettes.

One got used to one's physical defects, and recognized one's

24

self-indulgent character, but might one be unaware of mental deterioration? Friends of her own age were always going on about 'losing their marbles'. A cheerful prospect indeed.

Today it was almost the end of the year and she piled up their many Christmas cards to reread. There had been no time over Christmas to digest the exploits of more distant members of family and friends far away, with their accounts of wonderful touring vacations or cruises, or of developments within their own families, continually augmented by grandsons and granddaughters. Well, not all, perhaps; there were spinsters and bachelors and some childless couples amongst them, and not everyone could afford to go, or would even want to go skiing in Colorado or wintering in Florida, or on safaris, or white-water rafting, whatever *that* was. It made her feel weary to think of it all. Exploring museums sounded more up her street. Neither Tom nor she wanted long holidays, and had no desire to travel to far-distant places on long-haul flights. Europe was quite enough and held so much that interested both of them.

Tom was fully occupied going up to London to attend the groups and meetings devoted to his various interests. World affairs, scientific developments, and learning Arabic were the ones he presently favoured, and he had decided to write a book, which he said was a 'satire', entitled *Disunited Kingdom*. As soon as he had retired he began research and planning for it, and he had now begun to write it. All he really needed her for, thought his wife, was to keep the place tidy and provide supper on the days he was at home. Tom was no cook, was happy to eat ham and cheese, or salad and bananas for his lunch. Once a week he helped Janet with the grocery shopping, which necessitated an expedition to the nearest town.

Janet had been busy the previous autumn coaching two children. Once a week Silas Ashcroft and Chloe Pearson had arrived, separately, to improve their prospects for entrance to a good secondary school. That was over now, as they had both succeeded in entering the school of their parents' choice. Now she had been asked if she would help Chloe's younger brother Jacob with his reading. She would most likely agree to help, but decided that he'd be her last pupil. She wanted more time for herself.

When she had reread the Christmas cards, she watered her

indoor plants, mostly at this season spider plants and flowering cacti. In summer she had geraniums and even orchids. As she watered them she thought about what she would like to study if she had the time. She had always wished she had learned Greek, but it was a bit too late for that now, so she had crossed that off her mental list. She did want, though, to learn more about the history of the locality, so that in the summer they might visit one or two interesting places.

The postman arrived – as usual rather late. He visited them frequently with junk mail that grew week by week. Tom never looked at it but she would glance at some of the catalogues before throwing them out. She was in the habit of arranging books and non-junk-mail items, along with her many notebooks, in little 'cairns', on various surfaces – tables and sofas and bedside tables. Every now and then she made a big sweep. Her daughter Emma told her she had a butterfly mind, which she feared was true.

She finished the watering and wiped up the usual drips spilt on the windowsills, deciding it was about time she made a little more social conversation with other inhabitants of the Court and with the people she now knew in the village from chatting in the post office: they were lucky still to have one. Then she'd look over the lesson for Chloe's brother Jacob next week, and she might telephone her only real friend in the village, Margot Denton, a retired doctor, who had been away for Christmas.

On her return from the post-office-cum-store, Janet decided, as she loaded the washing-machine once again, that when a reasonable domestic situation had been achieved, and the coaching sorted out, she would read the latest story that she had been sent for review.

She went into the sitting-room which looked out on to the communal garden, and found herself wondering whether the family might soon start to expand. It would be pleasant to become a grandmother, a new factor in life that needed no effort on her part to bring about.

The years seemed to be continually updating themselves, and she ought to make a few New Year resolutions soon . . . Would it be less trouble just to relax and go with the flow, rather than try to take stock as she got on with the multifarious duties and pleasures attendant upon being a woman, a mother, a wife, and an elderly person with an enquiring mind? How she loathed that euphemism, 'elderly'. Yet she must accept growing old and waiting for it all to happen to someone else, her duty being done, excitements being for others. People didn't change much inside, and she feared she would not either.

Places however did change. If you revisited a place you had known well years and years ago you still saw it as it had once been. Last year she had stood stock-still with her eyes shut on a traffic island in the city of Woolsford, which she had known well as a child, and half of which had been pulled down to be replaced by a ghastly 1960s shopping centre, and she had not seen it, but 'seen' instead solid old Victorian buildings.

People probably thought she was mad.

Did you 'see' yourself in the same way as if you had not changed at all?

Janet found Sunday evenings melancholy. New Year's Eve was no exception. Even Tom, who was not much given to moods of melancholy, said that the years went by too quickly now. Another new year made him feel a bit glum. 'A *new* year when I've scarcely registered the *old* one!'

Emma, and Anna and Martin had made their own arrangements for New Year celebrations. Tom had gone out to visit to his ninety-four-year-old aunt in a nursing home in Surrey, not too far away. Janet had visited before Christmas, so was absolved, and was look-ing forward to an afternoon and early evening by herself. She and Tom never celebrated the New Year with more than a glass of champagne. Telephone greetings at midnight were all that were necessary. Anna had offered them a stay in Hall House – 'There's a bedroom ready for visitors – and we've bought two new beds . . .' But the not-so-long-married pair would probably prefer an early night, to be celebrated in their own larger bed, and she and Tom had tactfully declined. The winter holiday which this year stretched over two weekends with the intervening week, had been quite long enough, and she was looking forward to giving herself a treat and settling down with a detective story.

Dusk had already fallen , although it was only four o'clock, and she had been standing for a moment at the window looking out at the dark shadows among the trees of their landscaped lawns. Their part of the old mansion faced south, and it was lovely having

27

sunlight in spring and summer when you wanted it, and drawing long curtains when you didn't. Beautiful objects, however, needed upkeep – you could never get away from the reality of 'things'. Sash-windows were large and lovely but tedious to clean.

Time to stand and stare . . . no need yet to think about supper. No need to wrap a present, do the shopping, and make any further 'arrangements'. The village shops would reopen after the break and then the business of quotidian life would begin again. Who had said: 'How *daily* life is'? Some French poet probably.

Two years earlier, Janet's mother had died in her nineties, never to know that one of her granddaughters had married. They had all been relatively late brides in her family, which was now quite usual. She remembered her parents returning north after a snowy Christmas visit. In those days, people had shorter breaks from work, the shops were not so crammed with consumer rubbish, and trains actually ran on Christmas Day. Emma was at that time the baby. You didn't get snow all that often in London even then, but it lasted longer than nowadays. She was always remembering the past. It showed you were elderly when you remembered your first forty years better than the last twenty-five, and the first fifteen even better. Young women were treated very differently nowadays. It was quite incredible that when she had gone for job interviews in the fifties, the interviewer, always a man, would come out with: 'Why is a pretty girl like you not married?' or, 'If we give you the job, what will you do if you get married?' Even at school parents' days, the fathers said; 'What's the use of educating Lynn? She'll only get married!'

A vanished world, and not all that long ago. Her daughters had had more choices. The year of the snow was before the real changes had come upon them all, before people had 'partners', or expected to own a personal computer, before central heating arrived for most people; when almost everyone smoked, and the poor and old ended their days in council homes. At the other end of life children's homes had been full. In the 1970s there had been one on their old road. Often, when she sat reading in a room at the front of the house, a sudden scream and bellow outside would mean that the children from the home were out for a supervised walk. Later, a girl inmate had tried to burn the home down.

Janet calculated the 1960s and 1970s by the ages of her daughters, and what they were wearing in old photographs. Did men remember clothes and dates in the same way?

'That was the year Emma was four and wore that crisp turquoise-cotton frock she called her "arranging frock", and copied her letters so beautifully at the little nursery group.' Or: 'That was the summer when Anna couldn't wait to join the infants at school and longed for her fifth birthday in April and insisted on wearing that pinafore dress she claimed was "uniform".'

Well, the swinging sixties had certainly swung for some people, but not for the mothers of young children.

Janet smiled now, drew the curtains, still longing to light a forbidden cigarette to help her both relax and concentrate. Could she ever have coped with two babies and bringing up two toddlers, and then two teenagers, without that delicious crutch?

She located the detective story.

A good two hours before she need rouse herself to make supper.

'Happy New 1996' she said out loud.

3

Emma Walker had kept her journal when she was a child and had begun to keep one again when she was thirty. She had once thought she might be a writer, and a diary was good practice. That ambition had faded but she enjoyed observing what was going on in the world. She tried hard to be objective about her own life, sometimes even referred to her diary to check past feelings.

Rereading it always made her realize that she possessed very decided opinions. She thought she had not always been like this. Only in the last two or three years had she felt more self-confident. When she reread what she had written a few years earlier she was irritated by her own limitations, but nevertheless she persisted with the diary.

'Emma is rather introspective,' Anna used to say when she was about ten, having just learned the word.

New Year 1996 was almost upon them all and Emma had taken a few days' leave to extend the Christmas break. She was planning to read a book of architectural history. It was useful for work but she also found it genuinely interesting.

'I shall potter and ponder,' was all she said to Lydia Carter, with whom she shared the maisonette. Lydia had now departed to stay with her parents in Somerset for a few days and Emma was luxuriating in solitude and privacy. She and Lydia got on reasonably well only by keeping a slight distance, and each enjoyed some time away from the other. How people ever managed to spend all their days and nights with a husband, Emma could not imagine. She thought of her sister, now married for over six months to Martin Macdonald. Anna seemed very happy. She was just more willing than she, Emma, was to subsume herself into the life of a 'wife'. Now that they had been given the tenancy of Hall House she'd have even more scope. A good thing Martin was practical. Emma wouldn't want to live in that house herself but it would suit Anna and her plans for a family.

Sunday 31 December
Tomorrow will be Monday 1 January 1996. Leap Year.
People wish to be settled: only as far as they are unsettled is there any hope for them. So wrote Emerson in his *Essays* of 1841.

No lucky man has received a proposal from *me*.

I haven't written this journal for months. I intended to make it a sort of commentary on how we lived at the end of the twentieth century so that one day I might find it interesting, but I seem to write more about the family than society. I think I shall just use it every 1 January as a 'summing up' sort of journal. But today I feel like summing us all up – I mean my family and myself.

I nearly went to Mother and Dad's for New Year's Eve, but after seeing all the family at Christmas decided I'd rather have a quiet time. So would Mother, I'm sure. Is it odd – middle-aged, even? – not to want to go out tonight? Most young people do, I suppose. I could have stayed at Anna's but they have quite enough to do and will enjoy a bit of peace alone. Mother and Dad rang at midnight to wish me a happy New Year. They were not going over to Anna's. Driving into London is more of a bore than Dad likes to admit, even at less than twenty miles' distance.

I intended to write down some New Year resolutions but when it comes to it I can't remember the specific ones I intended to make. I shall become as bad as Mother, always intending to add something really important to one of her famous lists and then forgetting what it was in the stress of trying to do too much at once. People might think I could be writing: 'Must make more of an effort to meet "suitable men". Suitable, though, is not a word I'd ever use. Nowadays everybody seems to think that if you are a woman of thirty-four you must be longing to 'settle down', i.e. get married, and be desperate if you have no partner – and therefore lonely. I might reply with: 'Don't worry – there's always Giles Ellis.' I think he's a second cousin – the son of a cousin of Mother's anyway, and I happen to know that he 'fancies' me. With a little encouragement he'd clearly propose. But I'm neither longing nor lonely. He's a nice man, but his love, if that is what it is, will have to remain unrequited. He thinks he knows me, but he doesn't. I'm not unrequitedly in love any longer with anybody, and I don't spend my days weighing myself, smoking

Marlboros and drinking large quantities of chardonnay. My weight has never been a problem; unlike Anna I have *never* smoked, and though I enjoy a glass or two of good wine now and then, I'm never over the limit. I sound priggish, but there's nothing special about me. The problem is rather the existence of a non-problem: that I don't want to get married – or have a baby. My sister has found Mr Right, and I am very pleased she has, but I am not envious. Martin is capable and decent and I feel sure he'll be good for my sister, not that she would be consciously thinking of that when she agreed to marry him.

I'd really rather write about other people than about myself. It's a change from the sort of writing I am obliged to do during the week. At work I have to be very precise and factual and it can become a bit deadening. If *I* were actually making the big decisions it might be exciting, but I'm too lowly at present to have much influence. I wonder how I'd be described on the jacket of a book I wrote:

Emma Harriet Walker lives in Pimlico where she has a secure post in a government office connected with the conservation of ancient buildings.

How would it sound to say I'm the Acting Deputy Head of a section that is part of a division of a department that has far too much in its remit and therefore the conservation bit gets neglected?

Well it *is* a good job, I suppose, and I do enjoy it. I know I couldn't be a writer. I want to keep my life to myself, and I fear that if I tried to make up a story using parts of it, truth would slip away both from my life *and* the story. I don't have an especially vivid imagination, unlike Anna.

It occurred to me the other day that in essentials Dad's work was once probably rather similar to mine. Once he was retired, he began to write this famous satire of his. He says it's called *Disunited Kingdom* and is set in the future, a sort of double dystopia. It sounds quite interesting. England has split into two. The Eastern Kingdom is 'green': anti-technology, a bit authoritarian perhaps but benignly old-fashioned, with a religion called Pragma. The Western side has become a republic: liberal, crime-ridden and anti all religion. That sounds rather like the present. Scotland has joined up with Ulster in Dad's book, and Wales is inhabited by rebels. Other rebels from the Eastern Kingdom have gone to swell the English in France – tired of not being able to use their cars. I think Father is assuming that women may have taken over, which the men don't like. There's piles more – he's got it all worked out but won't tell me how it ends till he's finished it. Perhaps he doesn't yet know himself. I've seen stacks of typescript. Mother says it keeps him happy – but I think she has high hopes of it really.

Both my parents are a bit otherworldly, Dad in a different way from Mother. I suppose writing a satire is one way of getting away from what you don't like about life in the present and having the opportunity to reveal what you hate about it through exaggeration. When he was frantically busy at work, he used to tell us about the ridiculous set-up there. It was all change at the time (still is). Mother used to say: 'You must write about it, Tom. Nobody would believe it.' He'd look sceptical and say; 'Perhaps one day I will.' Now that Dad is a free agent again, it's usually Mother who goes on and on about what is wrong with the country and the world.

She told me last month that she had finally applied for and received her bus pass. She showed it to me. *Janet Winifred Walker*. She hates her Christian names. Winifred was after an aunt and she said that at least it was better than Gertrude, who was another aunt of hers. Anyway, Mother now gets her fares reduced but if she had stayed in London she wouldn't need to pay for public transport at all – and she could actually have received that free pass before they left Blackwich. She said she preferred to wait until a *man* of her age would have been granted it – why should women be treated differently? It was the reverse side of Mother's feminism, and I rather admired her for it, though most people thought she was a bit daft.

Mother is not very practical, and Anna takes after her in this, but Anna is less obsessive, though just as expressive and romantic as Mother. Mother says – and I believe her – that she is still learning and is painfully aware of her areas of ignorance. She appears strong-minded, even tough-minded, and she can certainly be assertive, even aggressive. Dad is less possessive, less anxious, and slower than Mother. They both admit they have social and political prejudices, and Mother admits to being physically timid and physically lazy. Dad is much braver. Mother tries to conform on the surface – I don't think Dad cares or notices social niceties. Mother's always had a love-hate relationship with family life. She loves – and needs – time to herself. So does Dad, so that suits both of them, though it's easier for a man. He depends on Mother more than he realizes. They are both mentally active in very different ways. Dad doesn't worry so much about what he doesn't know but relies on what he does know. He's much milder-mannered than Mother. I'm not like him in that, I'm afraid. Underneath, though, Dad is really more tough-minded and critical than Mother.

She and Dad are, I suppose, in what people call 'reasonably good financial circumstances', now that he has his pension, and they have sold the family house. They're not great spenders. When he was left Hall House, which could easily be a white elephant, he could have sold it on and been in even better financial circumstances. I'm not against his leasing it to Martin and Anna because I know that Martin will improve it and thus increase its value.

Mother doesn't drive. It's her great secret, of which she is ashamed. She always walked or cycled when we were little. I wonder if she sometimes wishes they hadn't left London – she always longed to get away, but they're only about sixteen miles from Blackwich, as the crow flies. They're pleased Anna has stayed in Blackwich, not too far for them to lose touch – so long as Dad drives. I suppose it's better for them not to be *too* near either of us.

Mother is the sort of person who is easy going in some ways – the things other people's mothers used to be angry about didn't worry her, things like swearing, or smoking (not that I ever did the latter, and the former not much) but she hates laziness and procrastination. She never bothered much about hoovering carpets or rushing round with a duster, though she always *talked* about having to do it. She's the sort of person who always makes her own routine. I'm like her in that. She says she can't sit down and read a book until she knows she's done a few chores.

I remember, even on holiday when we were little, she used to erect a cage of 'jobs' around a room in a foreign hotel. She'd unpack everything, whilst Dad would live out of a suitcase. Perhaps having children makes women like that? She wants to make everywhere part of herself. Not that Dad often accompanied us on those little trips we took to nearby places in Brittany and Picardy.

When I come to think of it, Mother is a peculiar mixture. I think a lot to do with domestic life goes against her grain. She was a teacher, of course, and is always 'researching' something. She once taught German, and their literature is all misty romanticism and *Sehnsucht* and *Schwärmerei*, the grammar being the intellectual exercise. She enjoys tutoring children in a variety of subjects – it suits the butterfly mind she knows she has.

She's easy to tease, and I'm afraid I see her sometimes as slightly comic with her oft-enunciated despair about the times we live in. The thing is, she hates *change*. Once she's expressed it, she looks quite cheerful and gets on with looking after Father, all the time grumbling about men in general, and domesticity.

She has had various unpleasant intimations of old age – she has to wear specs not just for reading now, and her hair has faded. She broke her wrist on a country walk and now takes extra calcium. She kept trying to stop smoking and every time she stopped she got eczema. Last time, she said, looking up from some medical dictionary: 'They say that eczema on your *ankle* is a typical symptom of over-stressed businessmen.' But she *has* stopped smoking.

When she's secretly annoyed with me, she doesn't mean to be rude but she says things like: 'I married just before I was thirty – that was really on the shelf in those days!' On the other hand, she says: 'Marriage is a lottery,' or: 'Men get more out of it than women.' I know she was pleased, though, when Anna got married, and she'd like me to produce a partner.

A husband would be even better. She will drop into a conversation some remark about arranged marriages and how successful they can be if both partners 'work at making them work'. Yet she'd never have wanted anything whatever 'arranged' for her, and I'm sure she and Dad married for love, though I guess Dad wasn't Mother's first – or even seventh – love-object, but by the time she met him, experience had taught her what she really needed. Anna is like her in some ways but was never as interested in learning foreign languages as Mother and I are.

When she got married, Anna had been down ten years from university and myself twelve. To me it seemed ages, but the parents said it had all passed quickly. Anna went out with a large variety of young men over the years. Mother used to ask: 'Why say "go out with" when you really mean "stay in with"?'

Anna has had a variety of occupations too, chiefly in the publishing line. She couldn't seem to settle, but I was a bit surprised she'd wanted to go back to Blackwich two or three years ago. She said she was tired of what she called a 'rackety life' in London. She'd been buffeted by Fate – in the shape of several uncommitted or quite perverse young men, in two cases quite badly – and at one time I know she began to write a story called *Knaves and Hearts*, which I thought a terrifically good title, but I don't believe she ever finished it. At the back of her mind she always intended to settle down, get properly married, and above all have children. But of course the right man is not always there at the right time for that.

Blackwich always reminds me of childhood and I feel I've moved on since then. I was always quite ambitious, and perhaps Anna was less so. Subject of lecture: *Why do elder children always feel they must 'achieve'?* Anna had a bit too much of London 'freedom', and she never had any money. The ostensible reason for her move back to suburban respectability had been the offer of the job at Martha Hankinson's, the famous picture library founded in a neighbouring suburb. I think now she's got more than she bargained for. Recently, everything has begun to be 'digitalized' and you have to be an 'on line' researcher. Computers are revolutionizing the job. She remarked wistfully at Christmas when we were over at Deepden Court and talking in the kitchen, that everything about her work is changing. She says that getting hold of some things, especially photographs, should be easier now because of the computer, but that it has actually become, like everything else, more of a technical scramble. She'd done a short course, to prepare herself, and she's worked for lots of publishers, but I think she's a bit less keen on her work than she used to be.

Martin was the answer to a maiden's prayer, and Anna's more willing than I am to adapt to other people. She is quite old-fashioned, and I have the impression that now she's married she will certainly not aim for promotion. I couldn't ever be as outgoing as Anna, who gets on with most people, and my interests are different – not only languages and philosophy, which I studied for my first degree, but also architecture and chess. Anna would not want to have my present job; she never wanted to go into the Civil Service and really, in spite of appearances, she was always less single-minded about work than me.

When we were chatting about things at Christmas, Mother said, out of the blue: 'Well, thank God, so far, the one thing that *doesn't* change in life is a baby.' Then she looked guilty. I know she's dying for grandchildren, but she wouldn't mean to upset me, who have not provided any.

Martin Macdonald had gone over to the picture library one day to look for paintings and photographs of south-west France. He told Anna he was researching the acquisition of some land, connected with his work in the City. She gathered that he negotiated among other things the buying, shipping and storage of claret, at the same time as being a financial adviser to several English firms in the Bordeaux wine trade. His job also involved complicated historical research. He told me later that the great Châteaux vineyards were always at each other's throats, with as many league tables to argue over as our state schools. I discovered his own private sideline – which I suspect he'd have preferred to be his main job – was backing newer, less prestigious, small vineyards in Aquitaine owned by young English people. He's even written advertising copy for them. You can tell he's a man who loves his job.

He was in the library that afternoon looking for less well-known photographs or illustrations of the places he was interested in. I expect Anna would have been very helpful and enthusiastic. She always enjoys work that has what you might call 'human interest' – welcoming and being nice and helpful to visitors and researchers in the flesh. It would not be my cup of tea. Anna is much more sociable than I am. Sometimes the visitors to the library need illustrations for a book they say they are writing, or claim to have written. More often, it's a woman researching for a publisher.

The library has quite a lot of French material – I once spent an afternoon having a look round and found some excellent old reproductions of paintings of ancient villages, even some old wine labels. Martin's project was just up Anna's street and she found plenty to provide him with inspiration: some of the first postcards from the beginning of the twentieth century, and older engravings, as well as illustrations removed years ago from expensive old books by wicked dealers.

Martin invited my sister out that very evening. Perhaps at first it was because she appeared interested in *his* work and she may have expressed a liking for wine of somewhat humbler vintage than the *grands châteaux* that produce the great clarets, the Margaux and the Mouton Rothschilds and the Saint Emilions. Martin took her out to dinner to an Italian restaurant, not a French one, and not one of the trendy expensive establishments in the village, either. It would please my sister that he wasn't trying to impress her.

I suppose they got talking about life in general and found they were interested in the same things: history and walking and trees and amateur acting and, probably, reading detective stories – Anna is as much an addict of the last of these as Mother. She's easy to talk to and I expect she also found him a good listener. They even found they had friends in common. It turned out that Martin, who commuted to his City office job, lived only a mile or two away from Anna's flat, quite near our old house.

She told me that when she and Martin had each got over the shock of meeting such an unusually presentable member of the opposite sex on their own home patch, they both began to feel that fate must have been working on their behalf to bring them together. Anna has always been a great believer in Fate – I'm not sure whether Martin has. They were soon seeing rather a lot of each other, and eventually I was invited to meet him. I invited them both to dinner here one evening and after that it couldn't have been long before she took Martin home to meet the parents. I knew then that he must be in love with her. Most men aren't keen to meet their girlfriends' parents but Martin was.

Dad and Mother both liked him and were delighted when he proposed marriage. To be truthful, I think they were rather amazed that he had not only fallen in love with their daughter but also actually wanted to *marry* her. This is quite an unusual proceeding in some of the circles Anna moved in.

I thought Martin was nice-looking as well as intelligent and he was clearly good at his job – always a good sign to the parental generation. He told me that he'd found himself his first post through his knowledge of French, and vacations spent in France, so we all had something to talk about with him. All of us adore France, if for different reasons. I think he still nurses a secret ambition, but has put it on hold for the time being. He'd like to buy, or perhaps at first just sponsor, a small vineyard, and then go and *live* over there one day and own one. More and more English people are apparently doing this, though he told me it's punishingly hard work and very risky. He won't want to take that risk at present and I'm sure he's as keen on Hall House as Anna is. He doesn't look like a risk-taker but it's often the strong and quiet men who carry out exciting projects. He's very temperate, isn't a great drinker himself, enjoys wine and probably knows a lot about it, but I think he is the kind of person who prefers a clear head to alcoholic haze or exhilaration.

Well, these are my impressions of him. I wonder if – when – I reread this one day I shall have changed my mind. Its amazing how one does change – I find some of my earlier diary entries years ago very odd.

Mother telephoned me for a chat a day or two after their meeting him and I told her I liked him. So did she. 'He's a hard worker but not a workaholic,' she said approvingly.

I think Martin won't give up his early dreams but will just postpone them, and I feel sure he'll be a successful entrepreneur of some sort one day. But he'll concentrate on earning enough money for his family to exist in reasonable comfort, though he's not the sort who yearns for luxury. Anna is certainly more of a spendthrift than I am, and I feel certain he'll be a good money-manager. I've noticed even since she got married that she's begun to be more careful about things like money and clothes. She's always wanted to have children – it's the *mess* they make that puts *me* off the idea. Even in her early twenties Anna was never actually averse to marriage, even if she thought she was. She just met the wrong men. Martin is just right for her, and the die is now cast. Her heart was never for long in what Mother still persists in calling 'Bohemia' – where I imagine Mother's heart was once.

Some women want husbands and not children, but change their minds later, and other women, like our friend Lucy Hall, have children without a husband. Lucy should have married that man from Leeds who loved her and was a stable type. But she was an intellectual snob and had no idea how clever he would turn out to be. She fell in love with the wrong people and had her early thirties ruined by Edward's father, ending up being left with the baby. Lucy bartered her future for infatuation, seduced by a literary 'name'. She'd have been happier in the country with a nice solicitor.

Anna never got pregnant but she is a loving person, and wanted the old female solution – marriage and family. Having experienced the slings and arrows of romantic love from the men whom Mother – who is a terrific admirer of Jane Austen – calls the 'Willoughbys and Wickhams of this world', she has maybe settled for a younger version of Captain Wentworth. Jane Austen never got her Darcy in real life, but she was a genius, and I can't see her having a 'career' in novel writing if she had *married* such a man. Anna never wanted a lifetime Career with a capital 'C' of any sort.

People think I'm cold, but I'm not, just sensible, an 'old head on young shoulders', and glad now that Paul didn't pretend he loved me, and that I didn't continue to base my life on romantic love. So many of our friends have already been divorced. I now want the freedom of a well-paid job – ie a 'career'. A few women are, I expect, as uncommitted as many men are at our age, but not quite so many. Others fall in love with unavailable men who married someone else early on. Or they marry young and then discover it doesn't work. I believe most women depend too much for their happiness on men's feelings for them. Since my *grande passion* for P when I was twenty-two, I've never had romantic feelings. I must have absorbed Mother's going on about 'obsessive love'. She always used to say that people who wanted a successful marriage and family life should not marry primarily for that kind of love – which I take to mean sexual infatuation – and so I suppose it was a good thing P *didn't* want me. *I* was obsessed, even if he wasn't. Not that he was the kind to believe in marriage either. I was not obsessed with my 'career' at that time – and indeed I don't believe that a 'career' often prevents women from settling down: it's more often a man. Being desired by the wrong one, or loving an uncommitted one ... I've noticed how often after they are about thirty-five, people change their minds about getting married, and settle for second best – not that I believe my sister has done that. I don't think I shall. I know what suits me at present, and now it's my work. End of my diary seminar on love.

Mother and Dad seem happier since they went to live in Hookden at Deepden House. Martin says more and more of houses like theirs are being divided up into apartments, and the gardens landscaped. I expect success also depends on who is sharing the house. They share common expenses like roofs and external painting. Our old family house had been near one of a communal development planned by idealistic architects about ten years after the end of the war, and Mother always said that one day, when the nest was empty, she would persuade Dad to move to the country and find one like it. If Mother makes up her mind to something, Dad usually falls in with it, and so it has proved. She says she doesn't like London any more except little bits of it. I quoted Dr Johnson but she made a grimace. (How old was Johnson when he died? – must look it up)

Anna and I both went to school in Blackwich before we departed to universities, myself to Oxford, Anna to Leeds. I've written in an old diary about how I spent six months on a course in Paris before I went up. I was keen on the academic study of a language. Anna was more loquacious than me in *any* language. Unlike me, Anna didn't have a gap year, said she wanted to get on with her life. My time in Paris made me grow up a bit, and I've always been glad I had it, but Anna travelled more in long vacations than I did. I think, like Mother, I'm more addicted to old things than Anna, though she read history. I also enjoy trying to think in an 'abstract' way, not that I always succeed. It's always said that the elder or eldest child is more traditionally minded and I believe that's true. Anna is more of an extrovert, more gregarious. When she came back to London and we shared a flat for a time she was always out or on the phone with friends. I decided to buy the lease of a flat with Lydia, whom I had met at work, fortunately in a different government department, so we don't talk shop.

When Dad was suddenly and unexpectedly left Hall House last year he had already helped both of us a little financially. I agreed that his and Mother's wedding-present to Martin and Anna should be their occupying 'HH' and paying a fairly low rent. The happy couple will be spared the millstone of a mortgage, most unusual except for the stinkingly rich, which our family is certainly not. They will have to pay all the bills of course – maintenance and repairs and telephone and gas and electricity and council tax, and any 'improvements' that are needed, so they really will need tenants. As well as the usual living expenses, they'll have to spend money on gradually improving the house, which will take up most of two salaries. If Anna stops work, tenants will be even more necessary.

Dad is not good on knowing the market value of property. I said to him that in spite of recent stock market problems and the depreciation in the value of some London property, the house would eventually appreciate a good deal in value. Even Dad must realize the normal destiny of such houses in that part of London, so long as they are decently modernized. If Anna and Martin move in the future, the sale of the house, with all the improvements they envisage, will fetch a lot. I'm surprised the fairy god-uncle hadn't tried to make money on it, but none of Dad's family was very money-minded, perhaps because most of them had always had enough.

Dad's grandfather and this Uncle John had apparently lived in Hall House as children for some years at the beginning of the twentieth century. Then the family moved to Surrey before the Great War. Even so, I think if it had not been for Anna's imminent marriage Dad would have sold Hall House straight away and divided the money between him and Mother and the two of us. They have explained to me so many times that to be fair they will eventually leave me more cash. I have always earned more than Anna so I'm not bothered, as Mother would say, about Anna living in Hall House. Anna keeps on telling me how guilty she feels about their having been handed such a big house. I keep repeating wearily: 'I wouldn't want to live in Blackwich.' I think she now believes me. I hope Mother has realized that actually, I *am* happily 'settled down'. Giles Ellis looked at me soulfully in church, at Anna's wedding, but Mother was fortunately too occupied being polite to Martin's family to notice.

Anna got married in church because not long ago she became a fully fledged Christian. I know she would not have wanted that sort of wedding unless it meant something to her. At the wedding, Mother and I both talked to Kit, Martin's brother and best man. My mother agreed later that he was a fantastically good-looking man, reminding her of some actor, she said – probably the type she used to fall in love with. Not my type, though. I suppose I've always had the vague notion that if I ever did marry it would be when I was in my late forties.

Martin was good at finding builders and heating-engineers and check-ing damp-courses for the most essential renovations and refurbishments to HH and they actually moved in just before Christmas, much more quickly than we'd expected. It's now habitable, if not perfect. It's Edwardian, right on the edge of the heath, the kind of house Anna likes, in spite of what I said about her attitude to history, and Martin will have scope for his many skills. It's not as huge as some of the houses in Blackwich, but it really is too big for one couple, even when children arrive, which I feel sure they will. The partly self-contained two rooms on the top storey will be a great advantage when they come to finding a tenant, and another flatlet could be made in the basement.

Anna is now taking photographs of the house and garden as it is now. It's not the period I prefer myself, but when I first saw it I liked its pointy gable, and the long lawn at the back with a gate in the bottom wall, open-ing on to a narrow old lane that runs by the garden walls of the houses before turning into a minor road and looping back to the village. Inside the house, I imagine there was once early Edwardian splendour in the large, high-ceilinged rooms, and the airy tiled entrance hall. The title deeds show it was planned on the cusp of Victoria's and Edward's reigns. The kitchen is big and was obviously 'improved' after the last war, not a popular time for domestic architecture, so it will need more moderniza-tion eventually. The big kitchen window gives a sort of 'french window' effect with a door leading out to the garden. This paved area turns into the long lawn. There must once have been old-fashioned herbaceous borders on each side.

They plan another bathroom somewhere and a shower on the top floor and in the basement. I would convert one of the many bedrooms. Nowadays, people appear to need an *en suite* bathroom. Perhaps I should have been a land agent, which is a posh name for research I do on much older and larger houses. I think the couple should set about getting some responsible tenants as soon as possible if they are to live without finan-cial worries. It has passed through my mind that if one of our parents dies, the other could move into Anna and Martin's basement flat. But then, I don't think Mother would ever agree. She likes her independence. Dad might.

The flat on the top floor is quite a good size. It has one large attic room and one medium-sized one and a little kitchenette, and there's plenty of room to put in a shower. It's all a long way up the stairs though and has a sloping roof. It could be made completely self-contained if you added a door at the bottom of the stairs like those large houses that are divided up in some Kensington squares. Fortunately, the ex-tenant did up this flat a few years ago so it doesn't need quite so much attention. The basement and the main house need more.

I cannot understand why Dad's uncle never sold it. Perhaps in the 1930s he'd thought he might get married, and then the war came. The house escaped bomb damage – lots of houses nearby didn't. In the war some rooms had been used at one time as a sort of office by the high-ups in some ministry or other. It would be ironic if it turned out to have been the predecessor to my Department.

Anna will let out the top flatlet soon, and then do up the basement, or 'garden flat' as people call basements, to help pay for more alterations and improvements, in the event of the disappearance, temporary or permanent, of her income. I think they are being a little too sanguine about 'improvements', but perhaps they'll find tenants who would rather pay less and stay old-fashioned. I guess Anna fully intends to stop work, for a time at least, if she starts a family, as they say in women's magazines. She's seen too many women friends going mad trying to carry on work-ing full-time as well as looking after children.

Martin is earning a decent salary, and the windfall of the house, even if it's not their freehold, means that she needn't wait too long before having a baby. I know quite a few *men* who'd like to have part-time jobs and be house-husbands, and Martin could do that extremely well, but Anna will never earn as much as he does, though it's quite true that if Martin ran his own business he'd be good at working from home as well as doing his share of the chores. He's a real-life New Man, though Mother never stops telling us that men never do as much as women around the house, or with the children. I prefer my full-time job, am too much of a perfectionist not to be driven mad with domesticity if I were at home all day.

I have no doubt that Hall House will make a really pleasant family home. Anna isn't a 'House Beautiful' type any more than a 'good house-wife', but she has quite good, if slightly colourful, taste – like Mother.

It's children Anna wants, not cooking or interior decorating.

(Later): Reading all this through I wonder if I have given an honest picture of my family. I'm very fond of them but they can be infuriating sometimes, like all families, I suppose. It's easier to describe a house than to describe people and relationships.

Anna tells me she intends to advertise in some intellectual or literary magazine for sensible tenants, preferably female. I suppose there might be a faint possibility of finding a suitable person to take it on from among our friends and acquaintances. They will have to find someone soon.

Anna told me last night on the phone that they have just acquired a tabby cat they have named Dora. Of all the names for a cat! I suppose a cat-sitter-cum-(eventual)-baby-sitter might already be in my sister's mind. She's learning to plan ahead. Up till now, I have always been the practical one of the family, but Martin has his head screwed on right.

When they are settled into the house I wonder how much they'll really savour tenants. I should not, but alterations – and renovators and painters and decorators – cost money, even when spread out over time. Many of our friends are either settling down away from London, or prefer to live in north London, or on a tube line. I worry lest the Macdonalds may have taken on too much, the council tax being what it is in Blackwich.

I wonder how much marriage will change my sister. Like Mother, she's a less unconventional person than she thinks. She is a much nicer and kinder person than I am. Granny Lister always liked Anna better than she liked me. I think she thought I was a bit offhand, whereas actually I was shy. Granny Lister was a very down to earth sort of person, quite a modern woman for her time, but by the time she was eighty she didn't want to keep up with the present. Mother remembers her sniffing long ago with a sort of feigned horror over our second names: Charlotte and Harriet, and her saying to Mother:

'Fancy naming a daughter Charlotte! A name that hasn't been seen or heard of since Charlotte Brontë!'

Mother told me she herself added 'or since Charlotte Mary Yonge', but Granny Lister did not appreciate High Anglican novels. She had high standards but not Anglican ones. 'They're such old-fashioned names – people my own grandmother's age were called Emma and Harriet!' she said. That's why Mother liked the names, I suppose, and they were to come in again when we were little and become rather fashionable. That annoyed Mother who absolutely loathes fashion. Gran never realized they'd become newly chic. Well, at least Mother didn't call us Poppy or Daisy, like so many young women I've met since. Mother later discovered that an old friend of hers from school, Sonia Greenwood, had also given the name Anna to her daughter. 'You can't win!' she said.

I have written quite enough on and off for this New Year diary. I've enjoyed writing it with my Christmas present from Dad, a new 'old' pen from that shop in Burlington Arcade. I've been rereading what I've written and I realize I have said quite a lot about men and marriage. Perhaps I'm trying to sum up my present attitudes to them. If I ever read it over in future, shall I have changed too? I can look after myself, I think. I don't despise Anna for wanting babies. I just get annoyed when everyone assumes that all women do. Who said: 'Men love women and women love children and children love hamsters but hamsters just love other hamsters'?

Ah, well, back to the office and the world of work tomorrow. . . .

Part Two

CHANCES AND CHOICES

4

Ever since they had first met at London University forty-six years before and become friends, Bridget Banks and Janet Walker had kept in touch with each other, even if it had been only to write and exchange news once or twice a year. Their lives had been very different. Bridget still lived in the small town on the edge of Wharfedale where she had taught English at the same grammar school for twenty-five years. Unlike her friend Janet, she was still firmly rooted in the north, where she had spent almost all her life, and still saw some of her old pupils, though not many had stayed in the town. As she had never married she had always had time to keep up with her many friends elsewhere.

3 Moor Drive, Ilkgate.
12 3 96

Dear Janet
Sorry I only sent you a card at Christmas and didn't enclose my usual letter. Thanks for yours. I went away with Rita Ormondroyd (remember?) to Prague for Christmas. I may have mentioned on my card to you that I might. Then all through February I was busy – at my age! – helping out at a school a few miles away that was in dire straits. Thank God they have now found someone – I was exhausted! I shan't offer again. If they could have found anyone else they would have done, but I took the opportunity to disprove their clear opinion that I was too old to face modern youth. It wasn't the pupils I found hardest to put up with!
I am so pleased about Anna's marriage. You sound very happy about it. He sounds a remarkably sensible man, and

you say the two have a lot in common as well as being 'in love'. Nowadays one worries that a marriage won't last, but Anna is old enough to know her own mind and I feel sure she will have made a good choice. As has your son-in-law! She is such a lovely girl and from what you have told me in the past he sounds a different cup of tea from some of her previous 'boy friends'.

How is Emma? Still in the prestigious Civil Service job? No plans for matrimony? I sometimes see ex-pupils around the town here who have returned home after divorce or separation. I am always sorry for the children concerned. Some of the parents married very young. Of course plenty are still together – and one or two have never married.

It's about one of them I wanted to write, and put in a word for. You wrote that the happy couple are now living in the house Tom has unexpectedly inherited and that Anna is looking for a tenant for the upstairs flat. The other day I was chatting with a young woman I used to teach – Moira Emsley – I don't know if I've ever mentioned her before? – she's a qualified librarian working in Ilkgate. I had been surprised to hear from one of Moira's neighbours, whom I know quite well, that she'd decided to leave Ilkgate to try her luck elsewhere, had applied for a job in London and was on a short-list. It's a big step for a young woman who has lived all her life here. Her father died and her mother remarried when Moira was about twenty-one. Moira's name, by the way, gives no indication of her character or provenance. She's not a Scot, but I believe her mother was influenced by the film The Red Shoes *when she was a child and was thereafter determined to call her daughter, if she ever had one, after the ballerina in the film, Moira Shearer! Anyway, Moira decided to stay on in Ilkgate when her mother emigrated to Melbourne with her second husband. I had thought Moira was a fixture here, although I happened to hear some gossip in the summer that for some years she had been involved with an older married man but that they had parted. Whether she left him, or he her, I have no idea, and it isn't my business, though I have always liked the girl. However, perhaps ending this love-affair has made her decide to make another big change in her life. She must be about*

Anna's age, or perhaps a year younger.

I was talking yesterday to Moira's friend Aurelia Smith, whom I also taught – quite a different type, with a very silly mother, about Moira's move, and gathered that she has no idea where she will live if she does get the job she wants. They need to interview her quite soon for the post – something involved with children and their reading – in a library in a borough south of the Thames. I don't know how much Anna is asking for rent and I have of course said nothing to Moira herself but if Anna has still not found anyone – has she put in her advert? – I could have a word with Moira. I could certainly vouch for her. She rents part of a little terrace house here, and she would be an ideal tenant. She was always a very quiet and sensitive girl, a great reader, and rather old-fashioned for her generation in many ways. That was why I was surprised about the lover. I suspect she writes too – she produced very original essays when I taught her. Her life may have been rather sad, with her father, of whom she was very fond, dying suddenly and then her mother remarrying and going off to Australia. Moira is not at all the sort of young woman one might imagine having a fling with a married man, so I assume there was more to it than that.

It seems that she has made up her mind to get away. I have the suspicion that she'll take something temporary in London if she doesn't get this post. She told me it would start in the summer if she were to be offered it, but that she'd like to move earlier. I imagine she has a few savings. Now, would you make a few enquiries of your daughter? Moira could sort things out quite quickly and I'm sure she'd be willing to meet your daughter to be 'vetted' at the same time as she has her interview. If Anna has already found someone, would you let me know? I thought I'd better write straight away.

Moira is a very pleasant person, with hidden depths. I feel, as her one-time teacher, that I can say that. I assure you she is not a loner and in no way neurotic. She is always polite and cheerful – and a hard worker. Sorry if this is beginning to sound like a school report! She worked for our local Antiquarian Society in her free time, which is possibly where she met the chap, a dynamic kind of man, but quite difficult

51

by all accounts. I don't think many people knew what was going on – I certainly didn't, only heard the gossip just at the time he and his wife moved to Manchester (last September). They used to have a lovely house in Knaresborough. Moira doesn't know I know any of this, but I expect she will forgive Aurelia if I let slip anything about what I know.

Give my love to Tom and the girls – I still think of them as the girls though I know they don't like being called that nowadays.

In haste – with lots of love from –
Bridie

Moira Emsley was packing a case for her interview in London. She had been pondering the direction of her work and her life for months, feeling confident about her needs and more rash than usual. A big change in her life was demanded and the chance to move away had quickly become irresistible. She was naturally fearful lest she had made the wrong decision, and as worried about the interview with her possible landlords as about the interview for the library post. But if this Macdonald couple didn't like her, perhaps it wouldn't be too difficult to find somewhere else, though she suspected that the recommendation from Miss Banks to Mrs Macdonald's mother *might* mean they would not ask for as much rent as they could have done. Everyone said London was so expensive – but the London weighting meant she would be getting paid more, apart from the promotion.

Ten years ago, after her mother had remarried and she had decided to stay on alone in Ilkgate, everyone had thought she must be very self-sufficient. But she'd been *excited* to live alone. She loved her birthplace, and after the strain of living with her mother it had been a relief to be able to concentrate on her own inner life and dreams. She'd enjoyed working hard to pass the library examinations, and she'd liked her job, though it hadn't called upon all her resources. She had also enjoyed doing bits of research for the 'Antiq. and Phil. Now she felt less drawn to Ilkgate. There were other places in which she might one day be as happy.

It may have been too easy to go on living there when her mother left. She had stayed because a man told her he had fallen in love with her. It would be foolish to say she had remained against her will, but true that she been ready to move elsewhere just about the time he declared himself. Ilkgate was now inextricably connected with him. If only she hadn't embarked on a long love-affair just then. She had been twenty-five, old enough to know what she wanted? Did she regret what had happened? Not really. It had given a boost to her self-esteem at first but she doubted it would carry over to her feelings for other men in future.

Dennis had hardly been an ordinary sort of man. Last year, after they had parted, she'd been depressed for a time, wondering if he had set the course of her life. She was nearly thirty-two. Was it too late to change? She must make some sort of effort to take her life in her own hands. Leaving Ilkgate and going to London would be a wrench, but the first step towards a new life. She felt a bit as she had done after her mother had departed to Australia; sad, but also happy to be left in peace. What a confession! – and what a peculiar, even horrid feeling to have about the departure of a man who had truly loved you. It was true: he *had* loved her. But before Dennis, I wasn't actually lonely, she thought.

Outside, the sky had been heavy and grey all afternoon like a pregnant goose on the wing. It was not very springlike. She must go to the store for some luggage-labels before it closed. It was still wet underfoot, and going out of the house would mean that she'd have to change into her heavier shoes, and clean them again before she used them for the journey. It might also mean that she would be accosted by people who had heard on the grapevine that she was hoping – expecting? – to leave Ilkgate. Funny, in Spanish you used the same verb for 'expecting' as 'hoping'. What did that tell you about a country? If she met any of these interested acquaintances in town she would have no shortage of advice from them. She was fond of them, but the people of the place were typical of small towns, especially in the north, she imagined, always volunteering unsought advice.

'Oh, I wouldn't go out in those shoes! Still – please yourself.'

As she put on her shoes Moira smiled, in spite of her partly sombre, partly unsettled mood. Rain was more agreeable than Ilkgate's tearing winds which were like a carving knife slicing at your shoulders. It *would* be pleasant to live somewhere a little less cold – and where nobody knew you. Only her friend Aurelia knew her well, and Aurelia (who had been christened Audrey) had married an estate agent and was expecting a second baby.

At the birth of the first, eighteen months ago, her friend's habits had changed overnight. Instead of the tangle of underwear, cosmetics, and paperbacks that had usually greeted Aurelia's visiting friends, one big airy room had been made over into a nursery, and the rest of the house transformed. Aurelia would soon have even less time to see her. It had been a good idea of hers, though, to tell Miss Banks, their retired head of English, that Moira was thinking of a move. Kind of Miss Banks too to make such an effort on her behalf about what she referred to as 'digs'. Somebody would have told her a bit of her own past history as well, she didn't doubt, for she knew a few people had known about her and Dennis, but Miss Banks was discreet, more sophisticated than most people in the town. The thought reminded her to give back the out-of-print books of verse she had borrowed from her when she had been to her old mentor for tea, to hear the news from her friend Mrs Walker in London.

Moira opened the books and read some of the poems before getting up with a sigh and going to the window. She saw that the clouds had suddenly lifted. Now the sky was clear, and the sun, soon to set, was spreading light like orange tea-roses against a heavenly silver-blue. The weather could change so quickly. She would miss the skies over the moors, especially the night skies, more than she would miss the town itself. She still loved Ilkgate in so many ways, but it too was changing, as she was. For one thing, it was growing, getting more like everywhere else. Perhaps that was what was happening to her, too. She must leave it, to discover the truth. She put on her old tweed coat, and went out.

Moira passed the neat front gardens of the old stone terrace houses, gardens that sloped down to each garden gate. Everything here was on a slope. Would she find a garden in the Macdonald house? That is, she corrected herself mentally, if they want me at the library – as well as at Hall House. She loved growing things, and her landlady, Mrs Jackson, had encouraged her to choose some more roses for her garden.

'Why, they're ones I remember from years ago!' she'd exclaimed. 'I didn't know you could still get hold of these!'

The Ilkgate soil was good, if heavy, a mixture of clay and rich brown earth, because of the proximity of the river, but there was a south-facing wall at the back of the house and the roses had flourished on the trellis she'd put up in the yard. She'd miss them.

Moira walked down the path and opened the front gate. She saw the next-door cat leaping into the next door-but-one's garden. Cats always appeared to prefer other people's gardens. Oh, she did hope there was a garden at Hall House.

As she walked along, the rhythm of her footsteps accompanied her thoughts. She had begun to realize, and feel uncomfortable about it, that her Dennis, her 'TD' as people called him, referring to his initials, had been rather selfish. If he'd loved her unselfishly – as he'd always said he did – he would have left her alone, been a friend, and supported her, not needed to be her lover. She'd never dared to acknowledge that before to herself. He had made her grow up, but at what price? Had she been desperate for love? Or sex? No, she'd just needed experience, wanting to be like other women. Younger men hadn't appeared to want to give her that. Had there been something wrong with her? Her lover had not thought so, but after six months with him she could have chosen to move on to another way of life, even one day to someone else. She wasn't thinking of marriage at the time, but when she confessed her worries about the future, Dennis had fallen even more madly in love with her. Keeping the whole thing secret had been the worst thing about it all, but she felt sure that for the first year or two, apart from Aurelia, nobody had had any idea. Why had she accepted the whole arrangement? Was it only because of Anthony Vernon, with whom she'd been unrequitedly in love in her early twenties? After this, had she thought that perhaps she would be evading life if she didn't respond to a man who loved her?

As she passed the old library, now used for meetings of Ilkgate societies, she remembered how Dennis had at the very first persisted in attaching himself to her after meetings of the Antiq. and Phil. He'd been really kind, and then a few weeks later had declared he couldn't live without her. Nobody had ever said anything like that to her before.

She found the shop, which stayed open till half past six on a Saturday but was just about to close, bought the luggage labels and an evening paper, and walked slowly home as the sun prepared to set.

She folded a cardigan – you never knew what the weather would be like in London; here it was still chilly. She was thinking about her early days with Dennis. She'd tried to break it off so many times but had always given in to him. Had she taken pity on him? Was that why it had all started in the first place? At first she had thought that love like his should be accepted – even if he was married – and that she could just get to know a bit about men and love through him.

It wasn't ever that she had wanted to take him away from his wife.

'My wife has a lover,' he had said. Which was indeed the case at the time. It was their son Sebastian, twelve years old when his father had started the long-drawn-out affair with her, who had disturbed her and made her feel guilty. He was a nice boy – that was the trouble. Sebastian had just started at university. But if she had not embarked upon their affair, it might have been her last chance of love, and she might have come to see herself too as an emotional coward. Had it been brave to carry on? Accepting love had given her some sexual confidence, but had sapped her will.

'I never thought of marrying him, never,' Moira said aloud, making herself jump. Then she wondered if that was really true. It would certainly have been easier if he had ever been able to propose to her – then she might have been able to decline his proposal! In her present mood she imagined she would have done. Remembering what she had been like five or six years ago, however, she'd most likely have accepted him. That would have been a big mistake. Not being able to make that mistake had left her hanging in the air. Oh, it was no good thinking about ifs and whens. It was over. Yet she kept recalling how fearfully persistent he had been at first. Were all men so single-minded?

Moira toasted some bread and poached two eggs. She'd have had to learn to be a better cook if she'd married him. It was strange how in the end, after all the ups and downs, it had been he who had left her and got himself a new job. A promotion that would last him until retirement. She knew he had gone because he had eventually come to understand that she had been too much of a coward to confess she didn't love him enough, and had not wanted to hurt him. At first, he had thought he understood her well.

He had taken his wife and gone to live over the Pennines

because, he said, he was spoiling her life.

'Can you honestly promise that you want us to be together for ever?'

No, she could not. They were not 'together', and she was still young. So really it had been *her* decision, he said. Yet his wife had wanted a change. The last eighteen months or so had been a muddle, and she did not want to go on remembering them.

Had he ever understood that she might want a child one day, but that she knew that it would not be fair on any of them, especially the child? According to Aurelia, most men never really understood about babies. They were just made differently. Moira did still want a child – possibly more than she had ever wanted a husband. It was odd, because she felt sure nobody thought she was the sort of woman who would want to be a mother, yet neither would they have seen her as a feminist. It wasn't that she thought single parenthood always a bad idea, but in the last analysis (one of Dennis's favourite phrases) she would not have the courage to be a single mother in Ilkgate. Many women of her age did choose now to be single parents, though maybe not so many of those who were, had actually chosen. You would have to be very strongminded. She had been worried at first about getting pregnant but had not liked the idea of the pill. It was mucking about with your body, making it artificial, so she had gone to the family-planning centre in Leeds, enquired about, and been given, another method of avoiding motherhood. Later, she'd thought that the possibility of any kind of choice about maternity just made everything harder. She did not want always to have to *choose*. Moira was enough of a child of nature to dislike the imposition of choice, but at the same time rational and sensible enough not to leave that choice to another person.

Aurelia had once told her that people saw her as a dreamy oldfashioned girl. What did it matter how she thought others might see her? The main thing was, how did she see herself. She often thought that the best part of herself, the part that wrote or dreamed, would always be locked up inside her. Even a man who said he loved you, even a chosen husband, might not have the key. Failure all round? She was tired of such thoughts.

As she washed up, she found interesting words and phrases rolling round her head. Where did they come from? She didn't want to think about husbands at the moment, or about men at all, would rather write about the colours in the sky, or the strange way people said to you the very things you were about to say to them . . . all sorts of ideas. As an adolescent she had always thought how wonderful it would be to have a platonic lover to whom you could talk, who would be the same sort of person as yourself, have similar thoughts, who would understood you without your having to explain. It was much more important than sex. Being wanted physically was something quite different, and in her experience so far, these things did not coincide. Having a clandestine lover in her twenties had held up her ordinary life, if it had not exactly robbed her of a baby. It had not truly made any enormous difference to the inner life of her imagination. If she had loved him deeply, ought it not to have done?

As she weeded out her sponge-bag for her visit south, her thoughts reverted to children. She would certainly not be capable of having a large family. I am too selfish, she thought.

Miss Banks had once explained the word 'solipsistic' to her sixth form, and Moira had thought: I understand that. Miss Banks had also said that artists and writers, and even scholars, did not usually make good parents. But I don't want to die without the experience of giving birth to and bringing up a new human being, thought Moira. Was that selfish? Intuitively, she had always felt that the bearing of babies was better over and done with by the age of about thirty-seven. She had a few more years to fit a baby in. How cold-blooded it sounded. How much less trouble to be a father than a mother!

Moira had always been an imaginative girl but in the last year had from time to time felt her imagination fading like a radio with an exhausted battery, the delayed effect of the end of the affair. He had changed her; she was grateful for that. Before, she had seen herself as a kind of gauche mousy person, and now she did not. At least he had given her a sort of new confidence, but she feared he might have taken away something too. After she was left alone, she needed to return to herself to begin making patterns of words and phrases, to shape the world into words, to write a satisfactory poem or a short story. She had never wanted to write love poems to Dennis, whereas it was always said women wrote mainly about love. It was true she had written much secret verse, years ago, on the subject of Tony Vernon.

She turned her thoughts to Anna Macdonald and her husband. What would they be like? Anna had sounded friendly on the telephone. Would she get on with them? More to the point, would they like her? What if they didn't? She would cross that bridge when she came to it. At least she had made a start. She heard her father's voice when she was learning to ride a bike, shouting; 'Come on, Moira! You're nearly off – only one more big push on the pedals!'

She smiled at the sound of that memory in her head. It reminded her of Aurelia's graphic description of the birth of her son Jonathan.

Exhausted by all these thoughts and decisions, she fell quickly asleep that night, alone for the present, and perhaps for ever, in the cool, but not chilly, softness of the well-washed, well-ironed, sheets of her blessedly comfortable bed, which had been a present from her mother.

Before she dropped into dreamless sleep, she said to herself: You've been given a second chance to live in a different way, be another person – and go on writing.

When she woke up the morning she was to take the train to London from Leeds, Moira had no memory of dreaming. She set great store by her dreams, which appeared to come in clusters. For a few days she would dream every night – wonderful, subtle, intricate dreams about people, which were accompanied by strange 'atmospheres'. Quite often, the dreams had long, winding plots as if she were in a detective story. Then there would be a week with no memory of dreams at all. When they came, her dreams coloured the whole day, even when the details had begun to fade. No dream-feelings this morning. The world seemed flat, and a little frightening. She managed to swallow some breakfast.

Once she was in the train she tried to prepare herself for her afternoon interview at the Bickdon library by reading a book for children, and became so immersed in it that for an hour she forgot her worry that the train might be late in at King's Cross. She had been told to take a taxi then to Charing Cross station, followed by a train to the suburb of Bickdon where the library's administrative offices were situated. After the interview she could get a bus from there to Blackwich where she had booked herself into an hotel. That very evening – only a few hours away now – she would be walking over to Hall House to meet Martin and Anna Macdonald.

She looked up from her book. The Macdonalds, the library, seemed a little unreal at present.

'Oh, I expect you'll meet a man down south,' Aurelia had said in her dramatic way the last time they had met. 'And you'll get married.'

Northerners always called London 'down south', as though it was the Antarctic.

Most of the older women whom Moira knew appeared to think that women should marry – marriage was a sort of abstract heaven where you would be nicely sorted out and settled down, 'for good'. They forget, thought Moira, what a limbo a marriage can often become. Most people did marry though, if maybe fewer than in the past: the 'triumph of hope over experience'. . . .

She looked across the table where the beefy young man who had got into the train at Doncaster was now asleep, his ginger eyelashes stubby in the sun and his hands loose and grimy on the shared table. What sort of book, if any book at all, would *he* have read when he was a child?

She must concentrate on her job interview. Thinking about work was usually much more restful than thinking about life. She switched her mind on to her work and jotted down a few ideas that had apparently formed in her head concerning books and children. In Ilkgate she had pioneered the reading of stories to toddlers, and meetings with mothers to help with suggestions for reading to their own children, and even ideas for their own reading – if they ever had a moment to themselves. Of course, you usually spoke only to the converted. She had introduced suggestions boxes for the Ilkgate adult and junior citizens. As far as older children were concerned, it was boys who were the problem. You had to find them books about scientific facts or space or machines or sport if most of them were to carry on reading at all. She had founded a reading-group for boys in a remote village, and learned quite a lot about minds different from her own, and facts she would never have discovered for herself. Possibly all this had been easier to accomplish in a small place like Ilkgate than it would be in a London suburb, where people, according to what she had heard, spent most of their time travelling to and from work. There were cuts in library grants from local authorities everywhere, and what money there was went more and more on bureaucracy. Managers spent their time on committees, and their money on staff and buildings, and the gleam in their eye was for computers, not books. She'd just have to gauge the atmosphere when she faced her unknown interviewers, would have to acknowledge 'progress' – or she would not get the job.

Now her train was just about to arrive 'down south'. Moira dragged her case down from the rack, waited patiently with the others, mostly businessmen, for it to stop, and then, a slight figure in a blue coat, alighted, her fair hair shining in an unexpected ray of sunlight.

5

April had arrived. In March Emma Walker had been obliged to travel out of London to inspect various candidates for architectural 'grading.' On her return, there had been much paperwork and many committees. She had been extremely busy.

The weather had suddenly become springlike and so she had decided to go shopping in the St James's Market off Piccadilly during her first free lunch hour. Only last Sunday her mother had said on the phone how she now looked forward to spring even more than to summer, and how lovely it had been down in Deepden in February with the first snowdrops and crocuses and the birdsong. Well, thought Emma, it's nice in London too. She was used to her mother's rapturous accounts of the seasons. Valldemosa in May had been her favourite and had influenced Anna's school composition about spring flowers when she was seven. Anna had never actually been to Mallorca at the time.

Emma decided she would sit outside in the churchyard café with a bowl of soup and a book. When you could do that, you knew that spring had arrived.

Having half an hour to browse the market for a birthday present for Anna, she began to look at the rings and brooches and neck-laces, made from semi-precious stones, which were displayed on the many stalls. Her sister loved Victorian jewellery and she was thinking of giving her an amethyst or turquoise necklace or bracelet.

She was hovering uncertainly between an amethyst-and-pearl necklace and a topaz bracelet when she had the feeling that some-one was staring at her. She turned round to her right to see who might be there. It was a tall woman, holding a solid old-fashioned curved-handled basket, the sort older ladies once used for grocery-shopping. The woman was not old and she had quite long, dark, curly hair and crinkly brown eyes that seemed to be laughing. When Emma went on looking at her, she came up to her at the stall. Where on earth have I seen her before? I'm sure I know her, she was thinking, just as the stranger said:

'It *is* Emma isn't it?'

She had an expressive but husky voice as if she had smoked too many cigarettes. Suddenly Emma knew.

'It's Javotte, isn't it?' she said.

The woman looked astounded.

'I haven't been called that for a very long time. You *are* Emma then! You haven't changed. I'm Vicky – my real name was Tess in those days. It was only in France they used to call me Javotte. Fancy you remembering!'

Yes, Emma remembered having being told once in Paris, where she had gone on a course at the age of eighteen, that Tessa was the woman's real name. And now she was apparently Vicky. How odd – she had never wanted to call herself anything but Emma.

'You remember *me*!' she replied. 'Good gracious, it's a long time ago!'

'I certainly knew it was you straight away, when I saw you holding up the stones. They're pretty aren't they?' said Javotte or rather Tessa-Vicky.

Paris! It must be almost sixteen years since they had met. There had been students of many nationalities, and Emma had been thrown amongst the worldly-wise and cosmopolitan young. One of them was a glamorous young woman with long curly hair and a slightly swarthy skin that did not detract from her attractiveness. This 'Javotte' had had teasing eyes. Later, Emma learned from another friend that they were were called 'bedroom' eyes. She had overheard some tutor say she looked like Deanna Durbin, the Canadian singer and Hollywood heart throb of 'It Started With Eve.' Emma had considered Javotte extraordinarily sexy, over-flowing with what her father called 'it'. How would she have described her to someone who had not met her? A kind of *glamour* had appeared to exude from her pores. Self-confidence too?

She tried to remember her surname; it had been an appropri-ately Hardyesque one, to go with Tess. Winterbourne? Winter . . . something? It came to her as she looked at the woman again, now older and with tiny shadows around the dancing eyes. Yes, it had been *Winterbon*. A strange name. The people she mixed with, usually men, had called her 'Javotte', and this was certainly the same woman. She did look a little older, and was a little less plump than formerly. Well, naturally she would have changed; there was a world of difference between a woman of about nineteen and one in her mid-thirties. Had she changed more herself? Perhaps not, if she had been so instantly recognizable. Emma was recalling how she had been overwhelmed all those years ago by a mixture of bewilderment and envy, confronted with this glowingly 'sexy' girl. She suddenly recalled the violet-coloured *espadrilles* she had worn, the like of which she had never seen since.

'I would have thought you'd still be living in France?' she exclaimed a little distractedly.

Javotte didn't belong in London. But perhaps Vicky did? As far as Emma could remember, Javotte had gone around most with a strange, tall man who was said to be related to a famous novelist. Emma realized now that she had most likely shared his bed. What *was* his name? There'd been pot in the air, as well as cheap red wine, that she did remember, but Javotte had always looked in charge of herself. She hadn't really flirted with the men, or hung on their arms. Probably she smoked joints, but she didn't drink much and Emma couldn't remember her ever looking or behaving in a foolish way.

Emma herself hadn't even pretended to inhale – or drunk much of the rough wine in the student canteen. She had been scared to death of drugs, and rather frightened of some of the foreign male students. Javotte had given the impression – that was it – of being 'older'. All those young innocent English who had only just left their sixth forms had been thrown into the maw of the Cité Universitaire. In at the deep end. She supposed it had done her good.

When had she first noticed Javotte? It must have been in the student restaurant. She seemed to recall a man hunched over a 'yaourt', which word she hadn't realized meant 'yoghourt,' and another person, a girl, had come and sat next to him.

And now here she was: Tess – or Vicky – Winterbon, the 'Javotte' of old, looking a little careworn but still handsome.

'No. I came back to England eight years ago. I work here.'

'What do I call you – Tess or Vicky?'

'Everyone calls me Vicky now,' replied the woman. 'I was christened Teresa Victoria. What about you? Do you live in London?'

Vicky Winterbon put her basket down without waiting for an answer, and went on: 'You had fairer hair then – the same eyes, though.'

Emma blinked.

'Greeny-grey. Miguel – remember him? – wanted to sketch you. I remember you because you were always so self-contained and *poised* and clever. I bet you became an academic!'

She sounded a bit wistful.

Emma was astonished. She knew she had been reserved, not self-contained, in those days. Fancy being remembered for her poise. 'Javotte' had been miles above her in sophistication, always the tall, talkative, laughing girl in a crowd of young men. That first time in the restaurant, another man had come up to her and trilled, 'Hey Javotte!' the first time Emma had ever heard that name. He had peered under her chin when he got no response and then sat down on her other side. She remembered all that quite clearly – where had the recollection been all these years? She hadn't thought of the name Javotte for ages.

'No, I'm a Civil Servant,' she answered. 'What about you?'

'At present I'm secretary to a therapist. Quite interesting. I've been working for her for a year or two. You live in London, then? I'm sorry, I'm stopping you doing your shopping . . .'

'I have to buy a present for my sister but there's no urgency. I hadn't decided what to buy, I can come again soon.'

Suddenly she wanted to talk to Javotte, was no longer shy or intimidated.

'Let's have a snack – or coffee in that little café just behind us. I've got half an hour – must be back at work at two-fifteen.'

'Well, if you've time. I was going to have something to eat anyway, but then I saw you and I thought, I haven't seen anyone from that part of my life for yonks. See'f I'm right – it's Emma . . .'

She was friendly, approachable, not quite like the girl she remembered. They had both grown up.

They walked back through the churchyard and went into the café. A few tables were unoccupied indoors but as it was quite warm they decided to sit outside. After a tedious queue for food and coffee they sat down with their trays. People were coming back into the open air from a recital in the church, through the arch-like corridor which led to the space reserved for the market. There were advertisements for every form of religious and semi-religious New Age practices strewn on a table and pinned on notice-boards, various forms of 'therapy' amongst them. Emma had had a look at them on her way in from Jermyn Street. What kind of therapist was Javotte working for?

She glanced at the woman she supposed she must now call Vicky as she unburdened herself of her tray, and then stirred her lentil soup. That and some bread would be enough. She had firmly prevented herself indulging in the passion cake but saw that Vicky Winterbon had not resisted temptation. Vicky seemed more ordinary now. Was 'tamed' the better word? She had been notorious, really, among the other English girls, who were probably jealous. How could she ever have forgotten her? Well, she hadn't really forgotten, but she doubted she would have gone up to her if Vicky had not spoken first. This ordinary – thirty-six or -seven years old? woman was the famous Javotte, with the flashing dark eyes, who uttered with a giggle what had been judged by the more censorious as outrageous comments. She couldn't remember now what sort of comments. Emma had always imagined she was half-foreign, though she spoke English with a normal English accent.

'Tell me, are you married, Emma?' asked Vicky, looking up.

'No, I'm a spinster, though they don't exist any more, do they.' She almost said: But my sister is married. 'Are you?'

'Oh, spinsters probably exist in staider places. No, I'm not. I was – for a time – but it didn't work out. I hoped for – as somebody once said – the 'transformation of appetite into love'. It didn't happen. We went our separate ways ages ago.'

Did she mean the man just wanted sex or that she loved him and he didn't love her? Perhaps both. It was strange hearing her speak English, for she had more often heard her speak French in the past, in the same emphatic but husky voice.

Was Vicky what they called a reformed character? Why should she think there had been anything to reform? It must be her old, slightly censorious, self-uttering inside her head.

'Did you marry that tall dark man you used to go around with? Antoine, was it?'

'André? No. He died young. I married an Englishman, actually. But we weren't right for each other. I was too young – and he was too old.'

She said all this quite unselfconsciously. Perhaps working for a therapist made you talk in this way. But she had always been outspoken – a sort of wild child, thought Emma.

'I'd like to settle down again now,' Vicky went on. 'Perhaps have a child.'

For some reason this surprised Emma.

'Where are you living?'

'I'm renting a bedsit and kitchenette above a hairdresser's in Blackwich. It's not so bad, but expensive for the amount of space I get. I pay four hundred pounds a month for it. It's a pretty suburb – but what a lot to pay for rent. Even Paris is cheaper. Small unfurnished flatlets here you just have to *buy*. The English are mad about owning property. I've never yet saved enough for one – not in London anyway.'

Emma wondered whether she had once lived in a house with a husband, and what had happened to it.

'Blackwich is not as dear as central London,' she said, thinking that Anna had decided to charge only £300 a month for her top floor, obviously less than the market rate. 'It's a nice place. I was brought up there as a matter of fact,' she added.

'*Quelle coincidence!*' said Vicky dramatically.

'I don't live there any more – and my parents left to live further out. But my sister likes Blackwich and has gone back there. Where did *you* live as a child?' Emma asked, rather curious to know. Perhaps Vicky was not really English.

'Rural Essex – a real backwater. I liked it when I was little, though. I went back home for a time three or four years ago, but then my mother died.'

'I'm sorry,' said Emma. She waited a moment and then went on: 'I've never seen you around in the village, but then, I'm only there on visits to my sister now and again.'

'I've never seen you there either. I jog sometimes on the heath or in the park.'

'Thinking of doing the marathon?'

'No, it's just for the exercise. Where *do* you live, then?'

'In Pimlico. I share a flat off Warwick Square – not so healthy, I suppose, but handy for theatres and concerts and galleries.'

Emma wouldn't tell her that her sister was looking for a tenant. Anyway, one might be enough for the present if this Moira Emsley her mother had mentioned, who was coming to see Anna tomorrow, filled the bill. People got the wrong idea whenever you mentioned you knew of a flat anywhere. She'd better be careful. Vicky, the Javotte of the old days, might still not be the sort of girl you'd be keen to have as a tenant. Then she thought, how *bourgeoise* I have become. The woman sitting across from her looked quite respectable and a little weary.

'You know, I thought you weren't brought up in England – you were very exotic,' Emma said instead.

'Well, that's one word for it,' said Vicky with a laugh. 'No, I came from that county they all affect to despise – Essex.'

It was the last place Emma would have imagined as Javotte's habitat. You'd have imagined a Spanish gypsy in Seville, or at a pinch a sort of Dorelia John in Bloomsbury. The idea of Javotte coming from Essex was hardly plausible. But this woman both was and was not the girl she had once – if the truth were known – been impressed by, but had also slightly disapproved of when she was eighteen. Her sister Anna would not have disapproved of her. She saw 'Javotte's' eyes crinkle and look naughty again.

'The *very* rural part of the county,' she added. She changed the subject. 'Did you go on with your French? You spoke it very correctly – that's one of the reasons I remember you. Most of the English consignment weren't good at expressing themselves in French.'

Emma noticed she still didn't seem to see herself as one of the English contingent, despite the Essex connection. 'You knew your way around didn't you? We were only eighteen – you seemed older,' she replied.

'I was twenty, but I'd left school – and home – three years before. I was a drama student on a grant to begin with, but I didn't like their way of teaching, so after a time I borrowed some dosh and decamped to Paris. I think it was after reading Zola. I had a fantasy that I'd go to work in a laundry, be a sort of 'Nana'. Or I'd study painting, meet artists. An aunt sent me some money – not much – and I did enrol at an *atelier* – that's how I knew some of the older students. I'd been in Paris for a few months when your lot came over. I only went to the Cité to eat because it was cheap.'

How had she afforded even that? So she hadn't really belonged to the group of English young ladies spending part of their gap year on a French course. Her knowing older students must have accounted for her 'foreignness', and the reason for her French being so fluent. She must have lived with a Frenchman.

'In the end,' said Vicky, scooping up her cake and cream, 'after realizing that I was not as good an actor as I had imagined, I also discovered I'd never make a painter. But I *was* a very good cook, and so later I cooked meals for rich people who didn't know how to boil an egg. I learned to drive too – and to type. A girl can keep afloat if she can type – or could, anyway, till computers came in. Now you need qualifications in IT.'

She seemed to have managed her life quite well – apart from the failed 'partnership'. Emma was intrigued. 'Next time you come over to see your family drop in and see me – or we could have a drink in the village,' Vicky suggested when the time came to leave.

'Thanks, I'd like to. But you could come to see me after work one evening before you go back—' she was about to say 'to the suburbs' but it sounded rather high and mighty, 'home,' she said instead.

They exchanged phone numbers and parted with smiles on both sides. Emma wondered whether to mention the meeting to Anna when she next telephoned her. If the Northern girl coming for an interview was not approved of, wasn't 'suitable', would they advertise? They were not under any obligation to have Moira Emsley as tenant. Mother's friend would be disappointed, though, if they didn't.

After a frugal supper of omelette and fruit, when she was drinking coffee with Lydia Carter, her co-mortgagee, who was 'in' for once, Emma told her a little about the lunch-time meeting, and the impression she had had of 'Javotte', or Vicky, ex Tessa, Winterbon, as she must now call her. The more she thought about her, the more she seemed to remember about herself too.

'I suppose she was what my father called "sexy" – when the word meant just what it said – not interesting or exciting, just plain attractive to the opposite sex.'

'What did you say she used to be called – Joëlle?'

'No, Javotte. It *is* a real name. I think it's a pet name for Geneviève – sort of Breton – but she didn't come from Brittany. She told me today she came from Essex.'

'A sort of Saint Tess of the D'Urbervilles then?'

'Well, no. She used to look more like a Flamenco dancer – all twirly skirts and long curly hair – sort of gypsy. I do remember her well. She had the most wicked eyes and smile. We all thought she was a real dare-devil. She laughed a lot with a sort of throaty purry sound and she always had so many men around her, it was amazing! Then today, here was this quite ordinary woman – I mean it *was* she, but it wasn't. She seemed keen to talk. In the old days I scarcely realized she'd even noticed me – or anyone of the female sex.'

'She obviously made an impression,' said Lydia drily. Emma was not usually so forthcoming, did not go into such detail about her encounters.

'She's had a partner – a husband, I think, but is alone now . . . Guess what she does and where she lives.'

'She's a prison officer and lives in Holloway,' suggested Lydia sarcastically.

'No, she's the secretary to a therapist and lives in – Blackwich.'

'Well, perhaps your sister will invite her round – she sounds more Anna's sort than yours.'

'I did say she might like to come over for supper with me one evening, and she said she'd like to see me when next I went to see Anna.'

'You find her fascinating?'

'No. Well, a bit – not as much as I once did. It's just made me wonder how far people can ever really change.'

Yes, that was it, she thought in bed later. How the years went on, and when you were perhaps half-way through your life you wondered what you had been really like when you were young – although perhaps you weren't half-way through, so many people now living on into their nineties, and you were still what your parents' generation called young . . . She fell asleep.

The next part of the journey happened quite smoothly with no bother of missed trains or lost bearings. Moira was pleased with herself; it was ages since she had made a long journey alone. The interview, though not inspiring, was manageable. She found what she hoped were adequate answers to the quite searching questions of one of the interviewing committee of six, four of them local councillors. There were no longer any chief librarians. They had become 'managers'. Her heart always sank when she thought about this, for she knew about books not spread sheets. Ah well, if they don't like me I can at least appear knowledgeable, which I am, she thought.

She had been called into the rather too large committee room, which was furnished with a large table and the enlarged photograph of a mayor from long before. The library was in a Tory borough, but was almost, if not quite, inner city. Just in time, she remembered to bring in what they called the multi-ethnic dimensions of reading, which really meant stories for children about people like themselves. There had not been many black or brown children in Ilkgate, only a few Indians from the professional classes, so she expatiated on what children had in common: fairy-tales and fantasy, and the difficulty of getting boys to read fiction that was not concerned with sport or space. She hoped they found her suitably politically correct.

She would not know until the following week whether she had got the job, but saw no other candidate that afternoon. She took a train to Blackwich after they had dismissed her. Now the ordeal was over she felt a bit tired. Had it been a foolish idea to arrange to call in at Hall House the same day as the interview? She located the hotel in Blackwich; the Clarence looked more imposing from the outside than she had imagined, but inside she saw that it was less so, and in fact smelled rather dusty. She booked in, tidied herself up, deposited her small suitcase in her room and emerged into the evening.

First she must cross over a corner of the heath by a Victorian church, walk over to a road that skirted the other side and turn down it. Several rows of houses of different periods were jumbled up here on the edge of the heath and she found a narrow road that led behind them, lit by old-fashioned lamps. She had been told that Hall House was on the left, not far down this road, one of several houses, some detached, some in pairs, all with large long windows and a genuine Edwardian look.

She found it easily, and stood for a moment. It was very quiet and was now getting dark. No moon was visible. Her watch said seven o'clock. She rang the bell.

She heard steps behind the door and then a cheerful-looking, brown-haired, snub-nosed young woman opened it. Behind her there walked a pretty little tabby cat who obviously liked to inspect guests. Instinctively, Moira bent to stroke her.

'Hello,' said the young woman. 'You've found us then! I'm Anna Macdonald, and this is Dora.'

Moira followed them both down a long hall with a floor of blue-and-brown-patterned tiles. There were bookcases stuffed with books all along one side. Oh, good, they're *readers*, she thought. If she was stumped for polite conversation she could always talk about books.

'We're in the kitchen. Martin is cooking supper,' Anna continued. 'You won't have eaten? Come and join us. No, Dora, you've had your supper.'

The cat turned tail and rapidly disappeared up the stairs at the end of the corridor.

Anna opened a door on the left with a flourish. Moira had only had a sandwich and a cup of coffee between train and interview, and was longing more than anything for a cup of tea. She followed her possible future landlady meekly. Anna didn't look at all like a landlady and was about her own age. They had the love of reading and a liking for cats in common, thought Moira. This augured well.

'We need better lighting here,' Anna said. 'There's still a lot to do. We usually eat here.' She led her into the room on the left, a large kitchen. Moira saw a teapot on the table.

A man with wavy dark hair, slim and of medium height was standing at the stove. He turned and held out a hand. The other hand was holding an oven-glove.

'I'm Martin Macdonald. How was your ordeal at the library?'

'It wasn't too bad,' said Moira, at last able to get a word in edgeways. 'I shan't know for certain till next week or the week after.'

Anna was looking at her, registering the delicate face and the fair, slightly wavy long hair and thinking: she's nice; I hope she gets the job.

'Sit down, and Martin will bring you his speciality – if you're not allergic to scrambled eggs.'

'Lovely,' murmured Moira.

'Would you like a cup of tea? It's just made.'

'I'd love a cup of tea.'

Anna smiled and poured, saying: 'It's drinks time, really, but we were both late home and felt like tea.'

Martin turned round again and began a swift buttering of toast.

The Macdonalds were not on ceremony, were so openly friendly that Moira found herself immediately warming to them.

'We only got back at half past six – I was terrified you'd be waiting on the doorstep. We thought we'd not bother with anything complicated,' Anna went on. 'I'm glad you like tea – so do we. Some people round here drink nothing but coffee.'

She lapsed into silence for a moment and drank her own tea. Scrambled eggs on buttered toast, thought Moira, my favourite meal. She still had simple tastes in spite of her experience of the Midland Hotel in Woolsford and, less often, a fantastically good restaurant in Wharfedale, where she had been taken by TD about once a month in the past that now seemed so distant.

'We'll show you round when we've all finished,' said Anna.

Moira, who had not been able to see much of the outside of the house in the dusk, looked round the warm cosy room. Was that an Aga? No, an ordinary-looking stove. The kitchen must be right at the back of the house. She wondered what it overlooked. Was there a large garden?

'I do like the tiles in your hall,' she ventured after a few swallows of deliciously hot strong tea. 'I think blue and brown go well together.' She noticed the kitchen curtains were of the same mixture of hues.

In her letter Anna had explained that the rooms to let, including the little kitchenette for the use of a tenant, were all on the top floor, so Moira thought that perhaps she had better not enthuse too much about downstairs. A tenant would not see so much of that part of the house. It might be bare boards upstairs for all she knew. But Anna replied, 'Oh, they *do*. The tiles aren't William Morris or anything, but they are old – and so pretty. I'm glad nobody did too much alteration to the place.' Martin smiled. Perhaps he was more practical than his wife.

They all munched away and Martin made second helpings of toast.

73

'Anna had better show you round.' he said. 'She can explain it all.' He was not as talkative as his wife.

Anna told Moira more about the house as they walked up to the next floor. Moira noticed high ceilings and old-fashioned doorknobs.

'The ceilings are terrible to clean,' said her guide. There was unusual stained glass in the long landing-window. 'We haven't decided whether to get rid of that or not. Do you like it?' Moira did.

Then the bathroom:

'We think the bath is an antique.'

Martin Macdonald joined them at the bottom of the steeper stairs to the top floor and led them all up.

'I'm soon going to put in a shower,' he explained, opening the door to the proposed flatlet. Suddenly the cat Dora reappeared.

'She likes coming up here,' said Anna. 'You'll have to shoo her down if she's a nuisance.'

'I love cats – especially tabbies.'

They all looked round the two partly furnished rooms. There were no bare boards, just a felt-like carpet that you could put rugs over. There was the smell of something like coal-tar and English lavender mixed up together hovering in the air. The incense of love, thought Moira a little wildly, as she noticed the couple holding hands as they looked out of the attic window.

'Once, you could see stars from here, I expect,' Anna said. 'Nothing but London now, the sky's rarely clear enough.'

'I can see the stars from where I live,' Moira said, suddenly wondering whether she was willing to give them up. But she had fallen in love with the house. What was good about this top floor was that little by little she could buy bits of furniture to add to the bed and desk she was bringing. She would need a new, or rather second-hand table.

'You'll find heaps of second-hand furniture shops not far away,' Anna said.

'I don't own much furniture except for my bed and desk, but that's all to the good. Less to bring.'

Martin said they'd be pleased for the tenant to furnish it however she wanted but they had a table they didn't need in another room if she couldn't find what she liked. 'We had two lots of old furniture,' he explained. 'Anna had a small flat and I had a semi-furnished one, so we brought all our furniture here. Not very stylish, but we have enough.'

That was if she liked the place, he was thinking. They needn't worry about stylish furniture, thought Moira. She wasn't a great follower of fashion.

'I do like it here – it's lovely,' she said.

They trooped downstairs, and it was arranged that if she were still interested Moira would telephone them once she knew her fate at the library. In the evening would be best, or at the weekend.

'If I haven't been given the post, you'll be wanting to find someone else.'

She did hope she would be offered the job.

'My mother-in-law had the impression that you'd go on looking for a job in London in any case,' suggested Martin.

'I'm definitely coming to London,' replied Moira firmly.

'We'll telephone you if we don't hear from you within a fortnight – we've got your number – but you can write to us too if you prefer. That is – if you get the job and want to come – to sort out – er – terms,' said Anna. 'If you do want the rooms there'll be a three-month decision period on either side in case it doesn't work,' added Martin, sounding more businesslike.

Anna smiled at her. They both appeared to want her. Who would be the first to communicate? The library had said she'd know within two weeks, but she knew all about bureaucratic delays. Whether the job was hers or not, she had already decided that if the Macdonalds wanted her she would certainly like to be their tenant at Hall House.

'She's nice isn't she?' Anna said to her husband when she had gone.

'Very!' he replied, 'but not as lovely as you!'

Oh she did love him! She did *love* him! thought Anna. She was the luckiest woman in the world.

'I am the luckiest man in the world,' said Martin Macdonald.

The washing-up was left for the time being.

6

Janet had been miles away in the Balkans in her thoughts when her telephone bell rang ten days after Moira's visit.

It had been last summer, mid-July, not long after Anna's wedding, when she, in common with so many others, had agonized over Srebrenica and the failure of the United Nations Dutch delegation to prevent the massacre. There had been terrible pictures on television of women and children being herded away in buses from their villages, their animals left unfed, fields untended and unharvested. Somehow, she had found those scenes and the reports of what was happening to the fields and the animals the most painful. It was always the innocent who paid – animals and children, even a natural object like a field of corn. She had felt exactly the same when she read *Black Beauty* as a child. Six-year-old Anna had cried over the desecration of the faun's house in Narnia by the White Witch even though the faun in the story seemed half-human. But the poor horses, dogs and unmilked cows of Srebrenica would not understand why they were being abandoned.

People had been shocked but not surprised by the later discoveries of the massacre of boys and men. Anyone who had been an adolescent, as Janet Walker had been, at the time of the opening of Buchenwald and Belsen, could hardly be surprised at the evidence of man's inhumanity to man. She was thinking, how quickly, each time, people forgot, and how ignorant everyone was of all that had led up to each international horror story. How long would it take for other European nations to intervene in Bosnia?

She jerked herself back to the domestic present and its more manageable problems. On the telephone was her daughter Anna, wanting to tell her mother about Moira's visit to Hall House.

'She's very nice. A quiet sort of person, but not distant,' she began. 'You both liked her?' asked Janet.

'Oh, yes, we both felt sure she'd fit into the household if she came to live at Hall House – she's very fond of cats too . . .'

'I was sure that if Bridie Banks approved of her, she'd be OK.'

'Anyway, she's written to say that if she's offered the library job, she'd definitely like to be our tenant,' her daughter went on. 'We can only wait and see. We really liked her, and we had made it clear we wanted her to come. I do hope she gets the job. She seemed to like us too – and approved of the flat – even the top stairs! You must meet her when – if – she comes.'

'Your father insists she'd be a lodger' said Jane. 'But I told him that lodgers expect meals, and tenants don't.'

'Oh, Dad is so unworldly. Tenants don't expect meals! Martin is about to test-cook the Baby Belling up there tonight. I shall never be a "real" landlady. Oh – sorry, Mother – a client's just come in – must ring off. 'Bye.'

Janet put the telephone down and did not immediately return to thinking about Balkan horrors. Anna always cheered her up; she was the sort of girl who deserved a happy life. Well, she'd found her man, and he was lucky too, as Bridie Banks had said. Anna was now wholly absorbed in living her life with Martin. She was kind and tender-hearted, and she agonized about the horrors of the world as her mother did, but it did not seem to interfere with her belief in humanity – or God. It was pleasant to have a daughter who was like and yet not like yourself and whom you need not worry about – at present.

Janet could never remain content for long. It seemed to her sometimes that every time she turned on the radio or opened a newspaper, the whole of the outside world was overflowing with horrors, including the unpleasant crimes perpetrated in a fortunate country like England. She went into the kitchen to prepare a meal. Thinking about what was happening all over the world only made you depressed about it all, and depressed about London and English vandals and hooligans. Should that be 'British' she wondered, as she peeled potatoes? She'd never felt British except when they asked for her passport. The French called them all *Anglais*, even the Scots, whom they called 'Scotch'.

What could you do, if you read newspapers or listened to the radio or watched television? Was it a kind of superstition that told you if you didn't bother with any of it, everything would be worse for you in the end? She ought to stop reading or listening to news. You gave money to charity and there were a few heroes and heroines who went out to face danger. Martin's brother Kit had been in many dangerous places working for a medical charity, and she admired him. Such a *good* man . . . Tom and the girls did sometimes get as despondent over the state of the world as she did, but those over thirty years younger tended to look on the bright side, see the glass half-full, not half-empty.

Was it better to be too busy to have time to concentrate for long on the world's miseries and iniquities? She knew Emma gave regular donations to overseas aid, whilst Anna, more generous with her time, helped with her local church branch of Christian Aid. Anna had once fervently believed that political action would transform the world. Emma, more pessimistic, had always been more sceptical and spoken less about the sorrows of the world, preferring to keep her feelings to herself. As a child she had once accused her sister of being a 'greedy giver' of presents. Both of them had evinced the same characteristics as children as they did now, thought their mother. Emma had never panicked over examinations, or else she was too proud to show her emotions, but it was only a succession of uncaring young men that had ever depressed Anna. Not for long though, and now that she had Martin, her sunny nature had reasserted itself.

If only Emma could find a man like Martin. It was no good dwelling on the possibility. Emma wouldn't have wanted to marry a Martin, and in any case you could hardly expect a child to marry for the sake of your own peace of mind, though that was probably what it really amounted to for most mothers. She told herself sternly that Emma was just not the marrying kind, and that she did not appear to feel any doubts about her future.

Janet found that creative ideas often came whilst she was doing the ironing, or polishing one of the little pieces of silver that Granny Lister had left her two years ago. She would find herself making phrases or inventing characters. She should write her ideas down, for making up stories had always been an enjoyable exercise. When she was a child her mother had complained that she always embroidered reality when retelling some incident. If so, was it because reality – the enormous variety of existence – was almost too much to comprehend, so that to convey her excitement she had to embroider? Well, she realized her own faults. To be free of self-deception was perhaps the best one could hope for.

More sombre thoughts usually came to Janet in the middle of the night, or if she woke early. She would fall asleep quite cheerfully, not worried about herself, or Tom, or even the wider world, looking forward to some small treat – a letter from a friend, a book waiting for her at the library. Then, hey presto, she would find herself awake after about two hours, unaccountably anxious. She knew the difference between the dead misery of depression that was almost like some alien chemical in the brain, and the lively melancholy of some of her daytime thoughts. The mind – or was it the brain? – was a Jekyll and Hyde. Did the ageing process account for it?

Janet had agonized over the world in her youth – she'd been worried about overpopulation and of course the Bomb, and had worn a CND badge, but this new anxiety was not objective, more like a pain on the brain. Yet some of her dreams were amazing, with many plot lines and intricate psychological dramas. Most of all, she enjoyed the half-asleep early-morning thoughts that came on the edge of a fading dream. In most of these dreams, Anna or Emma were about five or six years old, or even a little younger, dressed in clothes she would not have thought she remembered but which proved accurate when she looked at old photographs.

These dreams were a joy, made her blissful. But in other dreams – nightmares – their old house stood neglected, or had its doors flung open wide, neighbours running in and out, piles of clothes for her to pack, lurking dangers, a gigantic task to undertake . . . Where had this whole phantasmagoria been lurking in the years since her children grew up? Where did it go during the day, or before she fell asleep? What was she frightened of? Why did it come back to plague her? The workings of the mind through time were very odd. The daughters in her dreams were still infants, little children, once or twice babies, occasionally primary-school juniors, but never more than about nine years old. How she would love to have her children back for a time as children. Were these dreams wish-fulfilments?

The passage of time saddened her. Twenty years between the first baby's birth and the last 'baby' leaving home for university . . . Where had all those long years gone that she had lived through alongside them? Into photographs and school reports, letters and diaries, and a few old toys? The years were strata that had solidified, as they became adults, concertinaed now into a slab of time.

Life truly was too short.

Had Emma and Anna felt the pressure of the world outside as they struggled out of the blacks and whites of childhood and the security of home, towards adolescence, to find they would be expected to propel themselves up in the morning, be in charge of their own bodies, read, train their minds, keep sane, and jump over examination hurdles to university.

All *she* had wanted when she was young was to grow up – to be sixteen, then eighteen, and, at last, twenty-one. She could still recall her old longings, could fix the dates of her own adolescence quite precisely, before she had gone to university at eighteen, and to work at twenty-one. Her friend Margot said that the past bulked more and more in the minds of people as they grew old. At least it was better than forgetting and having no memories inside oneself, a void waiting to be filled.

An active but not now 'embroidered' imagination furnished Janet's mind and made her feel whole again, especially when she was alone. There was always too much happening in external life in their own changing country in a changing world. She tried to be useful in the world, writing letters to newspapers, or helping some child who had fallen behind in his school work – it was usually a he – or who had never caught up at all.

She enjoyed, too, poring over maps, more intrigued really by the town and countryside she had known as a child than by Blackwich or Kent, though they had a long history. Blackwich was now the Knightsbridge of south London, its delicatessens a sort of minor Harrods, its restaurants fashionable as they had never been when they first lived there.

She was the one who had known the Blackwich neighbours, and now knew the new ones, enjoying a chat with Greta Allott who lived across the court, or with the really old about their ailments, wondering when they might become hers. It was women, whose houses had become for them places of sanctuary, if also traps, who kept a place going. Her own mother had been much the same, but her community had been in the north. You inherited a whole way of being from your mother. Even though the world had changed, old habits died hard; you were friendly to neighbours, interested in their children. . . . She wondered what Anna would inherit from her in an even more fractured world.

Tom did not often speak of his own dreams, and if he suffered from nightmares, never said. If, unusually, he was at home in the morning he worked happily in his study, a corner room on the ground floor of the old converted country house. Here, he would write his 'satire' – or claim to be doing research for it, or would carefully read his newspapers. Two days a week he went up to town to libraries or regular afternoon meetings, for he kept up his membership of various professional bodies. She had to make more of an effort to get out of the house and make for a London gallery or museum, but once she did, she enjoyed the congenial solitude of the London Library, or being amongst a crowd of art-lovers who acknowledged your existence but allowed you to observe them at a distance.

Emma had impulsively asked Vicky Winterbon over for supper after work, one evening when Lydia Carter was out. It was unlike Emma to act spontaneously; she liked her routine and disliked surprises and, unlike Anna, was never quick to make new friends, savouring time to herself after work. But there was something about Vicky that still intrigued her.

They were sitting talking over coffee, remembering Paris. In the past week or so Emma had found countless memories of 'Javotte' lurking in her head; she had never actually forgotten her, just chosen not to recall her. Had she omitted to do so on purpose? Memories were treacherous, later memories sometimes ousting or altering earlier ones. Had the younger Javotte been too much for her to take in when she was eighteen? Now that she had seen her again quite by chance, she realized that years ago Vicky had made more of an impression than she had imagined. That part of her youth had held so many new experiences, but once she had started at Oxford she had concentrated on the present. Vicky had been so utterly unlike her other friends.

Vicky, alias Javotte, was being extremely forthcoming tonight. Years ago Emma had been shyer than her present self and it was most likely that her present relative ease of manner was allowing Vicky to become more expansive, making her more willing to talk about herself. The old Javotte had been more mysterious, if never shy.

Had she even been a little afraid of her? They must both have

81

changed a good deal, for now she found herself feeling a little sorry for her.

'Do you remember that student restaurant?' Vicky was asking.

'I certainly do. We took a tin tray already scooped out in sections so the staff could dump your food in it. They didn't want the washing-up of plates, I suppose.'

'I didn't think much of the food,' Vicky went on. 'But it saved slaving over a gas-ring. I used to cook on a gas-ring in the studios for the men. They were always so hungry and they never had enough francs for a proper meal.'

'Funny – we were supposed to be liberated by nineteen seventy-nine, and there you were cooking for men,' said Emma ironically. 'They lived on those tooth-breaking baguettes, apart from the Cité meals to which they were not really entitled, and the Boulevard Jourdain was really too far to go if you lived nearer the centre of the Left Bank. I was always urging them to eat bananas.'

'Where exactly did you live? I remember a friend and myself were asked after lunch one day by one of your friends, a Spaniard, I think, to go by Métro to some studio or other.'

Emma was recalling a rather ugly gangling, sharp-nosed man who had been obviously in love with Javotte.

'I'd never seen any room like it before,' she went on. 'A big oil-stove and a sort of upper deck in the room with bunk-beds, and above them a rope hammock slung high across the ceiling. Did anyone actually sleep in it?' She had almost forgotten that hammock until now.

'Oh, sure – I did myself. I used the place now and then for what my Uncle Jim used to call a 'kip'. I had all my worldly goods in a sort of basket – do you remember?'

'No, you always looked very settled. I had no idea what was in your basket.'

'Things got better for me later – but we all lived pretty hand to mouth. Pablo – he was Mexican, not Spanish – was a good painter but he never really amounted to much in the end in the art world. His style wasn't in vogue – rather old-fashioned. He liked what he called the 'bony structure' of English women's features – did he ever tell you?'

'Good heavens, no!'

'Well, he probably said it in Spanish.'

'There was that man – André – as well,' Emma pursued. 'The one you told me died young.'

'Ah yes . . .' murmured Vicky reminiscently, but did not elaborate.

'The studios were very beautiful, weren't they? I remember thinking they were sort of Art Nouveau – decorative tiles and enormous windows.'

'They were all that was left from the destruction of the quarter when the new Tour Montparnasse went up. Even they've all gone now. Haven't you been back since?'

'Not to that particular district. I remember that studio though. The ceiling seemed to reach up to the sky.'

'That was because they were purpose-built to get the north light – a bit like some of the Chelsea ones, though I expect Chelsea copied the French. Before the Tour Montparnasse was built, most of the older painters and perpetual students I knew had lived in the streets behind the boulevard. By the time you and I arrived in Paris most of their studios had been pulled down.'

'That horrible tower. Do you know, long before you or I were there, my own mother was a student living on the edge of Montparnasse – it was not long after the war.'

'Before the old station was pulled down and the tower built? What did she tell you about it? I'm interested. I got very nostalgic at second hand from the people I knew then. Perhaps your mother even saw in the street – when they were young – some of the very people I knew later.'

'She said to me that any baby she saw in a pram, or child going to school, when she was there, would now be middle-aged – at least half a generation older then me.'

'That would be the same anywhere for someone her age.'

'Yes, but I suppose that if one bit of your life is cut out and separate, you are more impressed by it. She remembered being perpetually hungry at English tea-time, and perpetually pursued by young men. It's all bathed in a golden glow for her now.'

'Paris hasn't changed as much as most places. I'd love to have seen Montparnasse in the forties, but it would have been past its best by then. Even in the nineteen twenties the real French bohemia had disappeared.'

'I suppose it all began in the nineteenth century and went on before the Great War. According to my mother, it still had atmos-

phere, even after the last war – she tends to glamorize places a bit
– 'glamorous nights' and all that. According to her, the backdrop
of her life there was like an old French film – I can't remember
which. Probably *Quai des Brumes* – though she didn't live near a
river or a canal. When she first saw that part of Paris again after
the later changes, she just couldn't believe it. She loathes what's
been done to the whole area – especially that ghastly tower.'

'She sounds to be a woman of very strong opinions.'

'When we were little she came back from having a short holiday
without us and she was furious. I remember her telling us about
Montparnasse. I think it was because of what they had done to a sort
of monument of her imagination. That would have been about ten
years before I went to Paris for the first time and met you. I wonder
if *we* shall prefer things as they used to be when *we* are old?'

It was easy to talk to Vicky. Her mother would like her too.

'I'm *already* nostalgic,' said Vicky. 'You know, when I was
young, I was very radical, wanted to break the system – that was
very old-fashioned of me in nineteen seventy-nine, I suppose.
Now, I have every sympathy with your mother.'

Emma felt sceptical. She had thought of Vicky as an eternal
rebel. Was she not still one at heart in spite of external appearances? Had she become a reactionary? People always went to
extremes.

'It must be nice to have a parent concerned with the fate of old
parts of Paris,' Vicky went on. 'Most of the people I knew there
were a lot older than me. I used to sit for various ancient artists
and got to know all about the *quartier*. I never heard the end of it.
Some of them were a bit younger, like the man whose dinners I
was cooking – Pierre. I'm sure you must have met him. Now *he*
lived in the past, always going on about the old days and how the
whole area had been ruined.'

'Did any of them remember those famous expatriate Americans
of the nineteen twenties whom I've read about?'

'They'd have had to be children at the time – by nineteen
seventy-nine they'd be a bit old even for me!'

'You felt you really belonged there?'

Vicky had had such a different sort of life from hers.

'Seventeen years ago,' Vicky went on, 'it seems an age – I *loved*
living in what was still there – much more fun than where I

worked in posh parts like Auteuil or Passy. But I don't quite feel that now, not really. Montparnasse had always been a bit tatty but those studios *were* fantastic – the old ones... Nah, I'm a Londoner now!'

'You ought to go and live in Hackney or Deptford.'

'I'm not trying to be an artist – not that there's much figurative painting going on at present. Where did your mother live in Paris?'

'I think it was on the other side of the boulevard, off the rue Vaugirard – in the direction of the Luxembourg Gardens.'

'All that's posh boutiques now. Dear dead days. Places are always somebody's past aren't they? I don't want to go back. I suppose I grew up, and don't want to remember all the mistakes I made around the place. But one part *is* still worth seeking out if you ever do go back, Emma, and that's the cemetery. Practically every writer and painter and musician of the nineteenth century is buried there: Maupassant and Baudelaire and César Franck and Saint-Saëns and Fantin-Latour – *all* of 'em, along with one or two of the old gents I got to know the years I was living there. They're not in Père Lachaise.' Emma poured them both another glass. The claret had been given to her for Christmas by her new brother-in-law. Vicky took another mouthful.

'This is good,' she said,

Vicky might be what Lydia was wont to call a culture vulture, thought Emma. She had first wanted to be an actress, (but you had to say 'actor' now, as she had recently corrected her mother) then she'd wanted to be an artist, and had sat for artists, before becoming a cook!

She was certainly versatile. Had she quarrelled with her parents and never gone back home after France? Emma did not like to ask. If she understood this new Javotte at all, it might all come out eventually.

'You make *me* want to go there again – as a student, not a tourist – but I'm too old for that now,' she said, sounding rather prim. 'I'm more interested in English buildings and old towns and churches.'

'We have all become tourists,' said Vicky gloomily. Then: 'Why did your mother call both of you by the names of nineteenth-century heroines who committed suicide?'

'Did she? Well, yes I suppose she did! *Anna* and *Emma* – it hadn't occurred to me before . . . of course it could have been Jane

Austen's *Emma*, I suppose?'

'No – Bovary and Karenina,' said Vicky.

'Were you called after St Teresa or Queen Victoria, then?' asked Emma, getting her own back.

'The saint for my mother and the queen for my father's father. My mother was originally Irish, so I was christened Teresa. I insisted on using Vicky when I was older, having been Tess at school. I had read Hardy, unlike Mum, but that wasn't why I wanted to be called Vicky. It was sheer dislike of having a saint's name! Just not me. I changed to Victoria for a time, and then I became Vicky.'

'A good thing she *didn't* read Hardy – you might have been called Eustacia. But you didn't mind being called Javotte?'

'I was flattered when a chap called Yves gave me such an original new name. It showed he cared. "It means a white stream", he said. He was a Breton. Said it was short for Geneviève.'

'You can't get away from saints,' said Emma.

Vicky looked wistful. 'I was brought up to believe in them. My mother still did, though my father was an absolute pig.'

'You were very popular with men,' said Emma, after a silence. Maybe Vicky had gone to bed with them *all*. Why not? That censorious younger self that called girls 'fast' was still lurking somewhere. Where did it come from? Her own parents were not judgemental.

'I often used to wish I were the sort of person who sits quietly in a room reading. Like Pascal,' said Vicky.

'Go on. I don't believe you.'

'No, it's true.' Vicky stood up and stretched.

'Do you think therapy does any good? I don't know much about it,' asked Emma.

'Oh, I'm sceptical about "therapy talk", but lots of people seem to need someone to talk to. Lucky you – never feeling the need. Look, I've to get up in good time to catch the bus to work, so I'd better get a move on.'

'Where exactly do you work?'

'The opposite direction to all the other lemmings. I work in London occasionally but in Beckington in the Kent suburbs most of the week. I can take a bus there all the way from Blackwich. Trouble is, the gaps between them are a bit long in the rush hours.

I'm used to being at the bus-stop by about eight-fifteen. I've promised myself to buy a car soon.'

'Anna says she still misses her student days when she could lie in bed if she wanted. It seems a long time ago. I don't mind getting up fairly early myself.'

'There's always the weekend, but I bet *you* go to bed early,' riposted Vicky, putting on her long black coat. She's summed me up as puritanical, thought Emma.

'Do keep in touch,' she said.

'Perhaps we could all meet over in Blackwich one day when you're at your sister's. I'll treat you to a drink at one of the many watering holes.'

'I'll certainly mention it. I'll be over there again one weekend to see their new house again. Anna and Martin are still busy sorting it out.'

'I expect they're very busy, newly married and all. Love's young dream.'

The two women parted on the doorstep, both sincere when they said they didn't want to lose touch.

Emma's rooms overlooked the gardens at one corner of the square. Vicky sniffed the air.

'At least you get trees here,' she shouted, and waved goodbye, to walk to the 24 bus stop to go to Charing Cross, She was thinking it must need a good income to pay for half the mortgage on a maisonette in a Pimlico house. Not as dear as Kensington, but still well beyond her own means. She wondered what Emma's friend Lydia was like. Judging by the paintings and the furniture, which Emma had told her were mostly Lydia's, she was a conservative kind of person. But so must I try to be now, thought Vicky, hoicking up her shoulder-bag and swinging her basket in the other hand.

After she had shut the outside door Emma went back upstairs to get ready for bed. She felt sure that Vicky would intrigue Anna. Lydia wouldn't like her. She heard her arrive home a few minutes later, but did not go down to say good night. She had talked quite enough about Vicky Winterbon to Lydia already, and did not intend to go into further details about her. Lydia never said much about her own friends or their doings. She would find it 'amusing', to meet Vicky one day but would not take her seriously. Emma could not imagine two more different women. Lydia liked a comfortable surface life of shining tiles, agreeable rooms, quickly whipped-up sponge-cakes, clean towels, flower prints, fresh curtains, one pristine book on her bedside table, pleasant dinner parties, efficiency, oiled wheels – and also 'fun', meaning clothes and theatre-going, as reward for all her hard work. She did work hard, and insisted upon a cleaner once a week to keep Emma up to the mark.

Emma was clean and tidy but did not care for cakes or flower prints, and put up quite different pictures in her own room. Lydia was good for her, though. One day Lydia might want a flat of her own, but in the meantime it was pleasant to share with such a paragon. She would be the ideal wife for someone, and Emma was surprised no man had yet scooped her up. Neither Anna nor her mother liked Lydia very much, but as they hardly ever saw her, Emma visiting the family more often than they visited her, it did not matter. She and Lydia had decided early on in their flat-sharing that they must lead separate existences, so did not burden each other very often with such things as the details of their families' lives.

Now Vicky lived so near to Anna she must arrange a meeting. Anna would want to meet her, and their mother might like her too. But Emma was busy at work during the next few days and decided there was plenty of time to arrange something. If Vicky wanted to contact her, the ball was in her court.

On her way home on the train from Charing Cross Vicky was still remembering the smell of the Métro and Montparnasse, and the people she had known so well there. In Paris she had experimented with perfumes as well as men. She must be getting old if a whiff of *L'air du Temps* brought back Paris. She considered Emma Walker. Was she really as self-sufficient as she appeared, or did she just want to give that impression? Had she had any men friends? In her work as secretary to Ms Ingersoll Vicky had heard quite a lot about repressions, but Emma did not appear repressed, just cool. Sometimes people were just as they appeared. She decided that Emma was a very rational person. As she fell asleep that night she saw in her mind's eye the rather posh Pimlico apartment she had been sitting in all evening. She had enjoyed the visit.

7

Janet was on the phone a few days later to Emma with the news that Moira Emsley had secured the job she wanted. It was to start in late August. It would take her two and a half months to work out her contract in Ilkgate, to give them time to appoint a new assistant librarian, and for her to help him or her in their first week or two. She'd have a lot to get ready, too, for her new life 'down south', but would like to move to London sometime in early July.

'She told Anna she was looking forward enormously to coming to live at Hall House. There's still plenty of work to be done on the top floor – get it all shipshape, give it a lick of paint,' said Janet. 'Moira's interested in the garden, by the way. She's willing to help out with that.'

'Anna has no idea about gardening,' said Emma. 'I don't know about Martin.'

'Well, I expect he knows how to mow a lawn and plant a few shrubs,' replied her mother.

After a few more remarks from her mother about Hall House, and her new pupil, a boy of fourteen who was brilliant at science but had no idea how to write a paragraph of reasonable English; and Tom's cold and the world news (bad), Emma got another word in.

'Did I ever tell you about that extraordinary arty girl I met years ago in Paris that time I was there during the summer before Oxford?'

'No, I don't think so.'

'Well, I met her again quite by chance two or three weeks ago. She's called Vicky Winterbon, though they used to call her Javotte in Paris. The thing is, she lives in Blackwich. If Anna and Martin ever decided they'd need another tenant, she'd be OK. I gather she's an experienced cook – and she can drive.'

Janet was surprised. Emma did not usually talk quite so much about the people she met.

'Well, they're not looking for a housekeeper, love. She sounds just what I need myself. You'd better tell your sister – she'd want to see her first. You haven't said anything yet to the girl, have you?'

'Oh no. I just mentioned it because I think they will need more money and I have the feeling Vicky would like a nicer place to live.'

'I think they're going to wait till autumn before deciding. Arty, you say? I don't remember your saying anything about her.'

'Oh well, it's a long time ago.'

'You and Anna used to meet so many people, I could never keep up with them all. How did you meet her again?'

'Whilst I was shopping at the St James's Market. But when I knew her in Paris I thought she was the sort of girl who corresponded with what you used to tell us about women belonging to *"la vie de bohème"*.'

'A sort of Mimi?'

'Oh no! Do you remember telling us about your time in Montparnasse when you came back from Paris that year you left us with Auntie?'

'Did I? You must have been about eight . . .'

'Well, when I was on that course I met one or two artists who ate with us who were friends of Vicky, and I remembered what you'd said.'

'I'm surprised you remembered. Each time I go now, Paris seems less like itself – everything changes.' Janet did still harbour romantic memories of her youth.

When Emma was young, had her mother been a little bit like Vicky Winterbon? No, her mother had belonged to a more repressed generation, had often said her youth had been constricted and constricting, though Emma had her suspicions. Her mother might well have been in studios like those of Vicky's friends.

'Vicky was never a drop-out. I think she's had a hard life since Paris. She works for a therapist. She isn't lodged very happily in Blackwich. Somewhere over a hairdressers.' She paused.

'You tell Anna about her then. Anna's looking forward to

getting Moira ensconced. Very busy at work, too.'

Married life must take some getting used to, thought Emma, but she did not venture such a comment to her parent.

'Do come over to see us soon, love, if you have time. Perhaps one Sunday soon? I could ask Anna and Martin around the same afternoon.'

Their mother liked to see all her family together. All mothers were much the same, whether they had had comparatively 'wild' youths or not.

She would go over one day soon to see her sister in married bliss.

When she put down the telephone, Janet was thinking about what Emma had said. Meeting an old acquaintance when you were thirty-five was not quite like seeing one after over fifty years, which had happened to her the year before when she went up north for her aunt's funeral. It was the same feeling with long lost friends or colleagues who turned up at conferences or old girls' reunions. She wanted to ask them: Who are you now, when once I knew you? Where have you been and what have you done to alter those chubby cheeks and wings of black hair to pale fine-lined skin and grey mop? What world have you lived in? Who has loved you, what have you lost? People fascinated her. Even Emma appeared a little fascinated by this woman she'd met again.

The passage of time was quite upsetting. She knew the mood and distrusted it. She ought to be having a serene old age.

Once Moira knew that she was going to leave Ilkgate, the beauty of her everyday surroundings was borne in on her. She must give herself time to savour her existence in the place, since it was about to become her past. That hardly seemed credible even now, but she would have to stop thinking about it.

She had loved so much in Ilkgate: the litmus-coloured light of winter dusks, and in April, through Mrs Jackson's landing window at the back of the house, the view of a copse on a hill in the middle distance. In winter the further hills were bare and brown, often with a darker hue on their ridges; misty when it was raining, or white with snow. Then, in early spring, other trees began to give the suggestion of a faint greenish veil. In summer, there were many early mornings when she watched the way that light infiltrated the skies. If it had been raining in the night (which was often the case), especially after what she hoped were only the two or three chilly days that sometimes occured in June, the air after dawn was rinsed out with rain and light. Once or twice she had seen dawn itself giving the whole earth a rosy glow, and later the air would be very still and opaline. She would lose all this.

There must be beautiful skies in London too, even if Anna said you could no longer see the stars because of light pollution. Well, that was often the case in cities of the North too. She had been spoilt in Ilkgate.

One day she might go back to the provinces to live, even return to the North, and then Ilkgate and the hills might seem different. A line from a poem: *The light of other days*, came into her head, and made her think more about her dead father than her lost lover. Whether she returned or not, she would always remember moments up here which had been suffused with tranquillity. One day, she might even see her first thirty or so years in a new light. For the present, she needed a change, a challenge. She could always return from time to time to the moors on holiday, to the places where she had tramped years ago with her father, or where she had walked more recently by herself.

Her friend Aurelia Smith, now Hinchliffe, was insistent that she must visit her whenever she felt like it, but solitary walks were not easy if you stayed with a family. Walking had been a solace to Moira in her adolescence. Being quite alone 'up on 't tops' had made her feel a peace, an almost physical sensation of completion, an opening out of her whole self to the sky and the wind and the great rolling mauve-and-brown expanse, and the green fields beyond in the valley. That sort of feeling had happened only when she was by herself, not even when she was with friends and walking on ahead of them, and it came less often now.

She hoped there would be places not too far away from Blackwich where she might wander. Parks? Kew Gardens? Solitude would naturally be harder to find. That was one of the reasons for her move. She loved solitude but needed new friends, new experiences. If she found she could not bear to be away from open country she could always change her job again, but at present she felt it was important to make an effort to alter her ways. She was still young, after all. Thirty-two was hardly old. She must learn to be more sociable when she was not at work.

Her father had always said: Just be yourself, Moira, but how was she to know what she would become if she went on enjoying being a hermit? A reading hermit, true, but closed to the wider world. Aurelia had continued to urge change – for the wrong reasons, but her heart was in the right place. Now that Aurelia had a young family to bring up, Moira did not want to intrude upon them. She'd never tried to explain her deepest thoughts to Aurelia since about the age of fifteen, and she was an unusual sort of person for her to remain friends with. But she felt that Aurelia liked her, and she returned her affection.

Moira had never tried very hard, after the first few months of their affair, to explain herself to Dennis either. She had come to the conclusion that he actually loved her more when she was silent. Then she could remain a mystery, and men liked mysteries, not 'mystical' young women.

We were all mysteries to others, she thought, sometimes even to ourselves, and unlike many women she did not find that maintaining a 'mysterious silence' was difficult. Her mother, Sylvia Emsley, had been a busy, talkative woman, who had done her best by her daughter, according to her lights, often expressing the opinion, both in his lifetime and later, that Moira was very like her father Charles. Moira had never tried to discuss her inmost feelings with her mother, and her mother had not attempted to discover Moira's. If her father had lived, he would have understood her, because they were similar kinds of people. Moira marvelled at how her parents had ever got together. Sylvia, now Mrs Carruthers, had not in truth expected her daughter to accompany her to the Antipodes, and Moira suspected she had been quite relieved that she showed no inclination to do so. Her mother's remarriage had made her glad for her mother's sake, but after this, until she had been 'claimed', her life had continued on the surface in a mildly happy way; she had not been discontented.

Before the man Aurelia called 'the archivist' came on the scene her friend had urged her to make more of an effort to be sociable and go out with young men. Moira remembered saying to her:

'I'm just not the sort of girl men want to marry.'

She had not known then that she might be at all the sort of girl a middle-aged man might have an affair with, and even fall in love with. She still felt that she wasn't that sort. She had had the wrong part in the wrong play. As a member of the 'Antiq. and Phil.', busy with her work, keeping body and soul together, reading, writing her verse, walking, she had not actually felt the need for a man until Dennis had created one. Perhaps everyone was self-contained, and even physical love only sent you back into your own mind eventually.

Moira wondered about the Macdonalds. They seemed well suited, and she would take care not to intrude upon them. She must just be friendly enough to keep on good terms, without being standoffish. Being yourself did not always find favour with other people. It would be wonderful if she could be herself with them. Her father's quoting: *to thine own self be true*, had had a big effect upon her. She liked outgoing people such as Anna Macdonald because they took you for granted. They had plenty going on in their own lives and did not expect you to make a big effort to fit in or give pondered answers to questions.

Moira did not believe that she had exactly compromised her integrity, only that she ought to have left Dennis earlier, once she had known in her bones that he did not accept her at her own valuation, thought he knew her better than she did herself. She had tried to accept herself as he appeared to see her, but it was far from her own estimate. He had not even known of the effort, even when she had confessed that she did not feel natural with him. What she had really meant was that she was not truly in love with him.

How would the world appear when she moved away from her little town? Aurelia used to say that Ilkgate was a 'dump'.

'*Honestly*, Moira' – Aurelia's favourite expression – 'We're too good for it!'

At the time Moira, who could not help recalling an apt quotation, had remembered Milton's words: that *the mind is its own place*, and in itself could make *a heaven of hell, a hell of heaven*. Now, of course, Aurelia was happily reconciled to the 'dump', and she herself would be challenged in a different way in Blackwich. She hoped she would be able to retain her integrity; she had always imagined that each person had an inner core which did not fundamentally change. Not that she always approved of herself, or thought she was special, but she knew she did cling to some ideal.

Not even Australia might have changed her real self, she decided, so she supposed she could have gone there and remained the same Moira inside. She had been convinced that it had not been the right time for her to leave Yorkshire then, or to make any sort of move. Maybe she had just been waiting for her fate – except that it had turned out that Dennis was not it, although he had thought he was.

'Nobody will love you as I do,' he had said.

She felt ready now for change, open to it: new people, new dreams – even new men, though she thought that unlikely. She must expand from inside outwards trusting that the little kernel of self would still be there.

She smiled at this image as she sat looking out of the window, knowing she must rouse herself soon to give instructions to the removal men who were soon to come and look over the job to see what she wanted.

Next Wednesday the big move would take place. The removal firm would keep her goods overnight and deliver them the next day in London. On the Thursday she would travel to Kings Cross on the train, arriving in Blackwich, she hoped, before the removal van. Anna Macdonald had offered for her mother, Mrs Walker, to be there to receive the van and contents in case of its too early arrival, but thought it unlikely they would arrive before she did.

Was she expecting to be happy in Blackwich? What did make her happy, apart from nature and art? Well, she liked a good part of her work. Conversations with some of the children at the, library were rewarding, and so was gardening, and wandering along in an apparently aimless way observing life. This big new upheaval in her life would rearrange, not change, the pieces of the kaleidoscope that was her own mind.

That was her hope. One day she might be able to write at least one poem that satisfied her, whether anyone else ever saw it or not. Just a few words could turn the world around.

She knew she appeared shy. At school she had been bullied at first, but as she never cried or reacted, they had given up, and at the grammar school she had been accepted. Whatever people thought about her, other people's opinions did interest her, even if they did not always engage her deeply.

Literature was the other element that had given her life meaning. Moira is bookish; Moira is a literary girl, had appeared count-less times on her reports and she had never been sure whether this was praise or criticism. She found in stories experiences and feelings that paralleled her own.

When she had been taken into a church or into York Minster as a child she had seen herself as one small atom looking up to what she had assumed was God. God, she felt later – if he existed – would know everything about her there was to know, so she could leave part of herself in trust with him, although that would not stop her later asking him for a few explanations. This early idea of God was something static, whereas living nature moved in 'spots of time' that might or might not have religious significance. Wordsworth conveyed all that, and she had been delighted to discover him. That had been in Miss Banks's class, though she had heard a lot about his poetry before that, and had visited Westmorland. For a long time it had seemed to suffice that she experienced her own 'timeless moments' and let them penetrate her.

Memories were shaped by such moments. Her lover was a scholarly atheist who had had great hopes of improving her under-standing, liking to argue with her about philosophical and religious matters. Moira, he said, too easily 'spurned the contin-gent'. At first she had no idea what he meant until she looked up the word in a philosophical dictionary at the library. But he has no 'spots of time' in his life, she thought, no 'moments of being', except perhaps sexual love, and she could not help feeling that that belonged to a different kind of understanding.

'I don't spurn ordinary life,' she had eventually replied, after studying the dictionary, 'nor places, nor people. It's just that what I need to take away from them is a certain feeling.'

She was remembering the 'snowy feeling' she had had as a child. Snow was cold, snow was dangerous, and snow could kill. She did not discount these realities, but they did not detract from the beauty of the snow and the feeling which that beauty aroused. Through the particular, the artist, the poet, *remade* the world.

She said this to him.

'Oh, you are so romantic, darling,' he would say, and she would feel herself thus described and made allowances for, but subtly depreciated. Feelings were not enough, she knew that, certainly not enough for poems, and 'reason' was important. But she wanted to make something out of her experiences and feeling, out of cathedrals, flowers, children, states of mind. Words words words . . . .

Her mother had once told her that her friend, Moira's Auntie Doris, had said: 'Oh, Moira is *one on her own*,' and it had disturbed Mrs Emsley, who was worried lest Moira was too unconventional. That was not really the right word, her mother decided, but she could not discover a better one.

'Do you mean I am "detached" or "indifferent?" Moira had asked, and her mother had looked puzzled. Only Miss Banks had said:

'You are perfectly all right, Moira, don't let anyone tell you otherwise. You're not Emily Brontë, but you know that. You'll grow into yourself – and you write very well.'

It was July, time to go, and Moira saw the removal van coming up the lane to take all her bits and pieces, mostly books, and the bed her mother had given her as a farewell present before she went to Melbourne.

She'd sleep on Mrs Jackson's divan tonight. That would mean she had really left. The men would take all her things up to the top floor of Hall House and she was a bit worried about the bed.

'We're used to beds, lass!' leered one of the men, after she had explained about the top floor and the rather narrow top stairs of Hall House. There was her desk too, where she often sat and wrote. It had been a present from her father the year before he died.

She felt like going to sleep on the bed now, to be put in the van along with it. So much less bother. She had packed all her clothes in three suitcases, two of them to go with the van. Boxes contained the rest of her life: books in a special set of tea-chests, with papers, small ornaments, a teapot, cups and plates, saucers, three pans, photographs in albums and in a few frames, and some small reproduction paintings and prints. Anna had said there were heaps of bookshelves already there and she could buy more as she needed them. She had remembered clothes only when all her other possessions had been packed.

Moira felt a sudden shiver go through her, remembering when

one of their neighbours, an old retired teacher, who had lived at the house up the lane, had died. Men had delivered a coffin in the dusk and taken it out in the darkness. She had thought: 'carrying coffins out, hunking fridges in', as though there wasn't much difference, and been appalled.

She mustn't be morbid. All this removal was her doing. Leaving *was* like a little death; she must believe in her rebirth into some sort of new life.

'I am "removing",' she said to herself the way they all said it in Ilkgate. It sounded odd: 'Moira is being "removed".'

They would all be waiting at Hall House for her. She would see Anna's mother tomorrow afternoon, and Anna was coming back early from work too to welcome her. There would be so much to be getting on with. She felt like a character in a story called *The First Tenant*.

8

Janet left Deepden early on the morning of Moira's arrival. Tom was going on to London and dropped her at Hall House. Anna telephoned when she arrived telling her to make herself at home. She would have liked to welcome Moira herself, but work called. The van men had not been able to come at the weekend.

Anna looked forward to the day when she could stay at home and sort things out and have the day to herself. Only a baby allowed you to do that nowadays. Even with a baby, however, people often expected you to go back to work and leave him or her with someone else. She and Martin would be able to manage on one salary only because of her father letting this house to them. She knew how lucky they were. She must be old-fashioned, for she was sure she'd never be so desperately fond of any work as to want to go back to it after the birth of a baby, unless, like so many women now, she needed the money. You never knew, though; perhaps she would find a baby harder work than she imagined and would long for freedom. She was very well aware of all the arguments for and against, and sometimes felt quite exhausted by having to give reasons to some of her women friends for a decision that after all did not yet need to be taken. She still met her old friends now and again in wine bars in the village or in London but really preferred to get home and talk to them on the phone.

All Anna wanted now, once tenants were sorted out and settled in, was to have some time alone with Martin, and then have a baby.

Janet arrived in good time and was roaming round her daughter's large house, followed by Dora, checking that all was ready so that the removal men could take the contents of the van up to the top

floor. Moira Emsley should be arriving any minute. There was no
sign of the van yet. She wondered what the girl would be like. She
mentally corrected herself again. You were just not allowed to call
young women 'girls' nowadays. In her mother's generation any
women younger than themselves were 'girls'.

Would Martin and Anna like Moira? If Emma and Lydia were
anything to go by, not really sharing their lives, only a maisonette,
that wouldn't really matter. Moira would be even less in evidence
up at the top if she wanted to keep herself to herself. Her daughter Anna liked most people and would certainly be friendly. It
would be Martin who might find tenants intrusive, but he really
couldn't complain since Tom had solved their present housing
problem for them. She often asked Tom if he thought they might
have preferred to buy a modern flat like their own first flat in
Blackwich, but Tom said 'Anna's always liked houses with character, you know,' and it was an expensive area now for a flat like the
one they had bought years ago. Janet thought: well, we could have
sold Hall House and given them the money for a mortgage. It
would certainly have been beyond their means to buy it, even with
a mortgage and two incomes.

Anna must have changed recently for she said that now she
really *preferred* older buildings.

Luck was so important in life; in her letter of thanks, Bridie
Banks had said that Moira knew she was lucky, too. When Janet
thought of the bed-sitters she had inhabited herself, before she was
married, in the centre of London and in far-flung north London
suburbs, she could not suppress the thought that her children's
generation didn't really understand how well off they were. When
she was in her teens she had probably felt it would be romantic to
starve in a garret in the cause of art, though probably more fun in
Montparnasse than Edgware. Once she'd arrived in London in her
twenties she'd had to undertake many uncongenial jobs, had
learned the hard way that if you didn't live at home, the basic
necessities of food, and money to pay the rent were not come by
without much toil. With her daughters she had always tried –
nobly – to suppress feelings of 'I had it harder than you'. She
would certainly not want to be their age now in the 1990s. The
times were not auspicious, but the 'girls' did not realize it, and
imagined everything must have improved since their parents'

youth. After all, it was partly because she and Tom had lived quite simply after their marriage, and worked their way a little bit up the property ladder that their children had initially been able to take over from where they had left off. Both Emma and Anna – and Martin too of course – had good jobs, even if Anna's did not pay as well as Emma's. Work itself appeared to matter more than it used to; certainly everyone spent far too many hours at work.

She must try to stop believing that the world was getting worse, though she was convinced that it was: incorrect grammar in letters from the bank, children forbidden to 'play out' because of traffic, or other children's bullying, or possible paedophiles. One day she felt sure everything would collapse, and she found the thought of anarchy very frightening. The civilized world was a weird mixture already of crime, vandalism, brutality, and official gobbledygook: vacuous admin-speak that meant nothing and appeared to be written by robots. Everyone was supposed to be better educated but you knew that was not true. The world certainly knew little about and cared less for the matters *she* cared about . . .

She made herself a cup of the Earl Grey she found in the kitchen cupboard and sat down to peruse the newspaper on the kitchen table. There were certainly more violent incidents than formerly, reported as a matter of course on television and in the papers. She and Tom had never possessed a television until the year after they were married. She read on, thinking: when we were young, much of what is now called sexual harassment would have been described as seduction. Violence and sex appeared to sell newspapers. Were more small children really being abducted and murdered, or did we just hear more about it? Certainly there were more crimes than fifty years ago, and much more of what had once been called juvenile delinquency, and far, far worse conditions of total indiscipline in schools. You were not allowed to say any of this in progressive circles, and now there were the dispossessed from old Communist empires, or anarchic African states, wandering jobless and hopeless all over the place. Old wars had been in a way safe: you had known where you were with them, but now there were madmen who could bomb anyone anywhere. Nowhere was safe. . . .

She was aroused from these gloomy conclusions by the ring of a doorbell.

She got up as quickly as she could from her chair in the kitchen and went into the hall. The van or the girl? It was the girl.

'Moira! Do come in. I'm Janet Walker – just holding the fort.' She smiled.

Moira saw a small woman in her mid-sixties who looked a little like Anna. Her hair was coloured about the same shade as Anna's.

'Oh, thank you.'

Moira put down her large suitcase and they shook hands.

'I do so *hate* carrying luggage, don't you? They should be here soon with your other things. Leave your case in the hall and I'll help you carry it up in a minute. It's all ready for you up there. What about a cup of tea?' At least Mrs Walker didn't ask her how the journey had been but said instead; 'I used to travel from home to London by Kings Cross until my father died – such a cold, dark old station it was then. Now it's all been modernized.'

As she was found a chair and given a cup of tea, Moira had time to register how like her daughter this lady also was in her rapid conversation.

'The last time I got the train from there was for the funeral of an old aunt a year or two ago,' Mrs Walker went on.

It had been when she was going north to Woolsford for Aunt Lily's funeral, and she was remembering the smart new front clapped on to the old station in the late 1970s, the station that had been her first glimpse of London. The glossy chemists and ranks of magazines of today made her feel that the trains no longer went to real places. They should be steam-trains lurking there, about to explore an unknown country, sliding out through dim north London stations up to Lincolnshire and beyond.

She said something of this to Moira as they sat in the kitchen.

'Of course they're all the same now just like trains from Paddington or Victoria, not going anywhere specially distant and different.'

Moira had not realized that this Mrs Walker, Miss Banks's friend from university, was from the North. She could tell from the inflection of her voice as well as her knowledge of the station's destinations.

'I always felt the North was different . . . there was a novel called *To the North* . . . the trains only take half the time to get there now. They don't seem *real*.'

Moira smiled. She knew just want she meant.

'I've read that novel,' she said shyly.

At the station Moira had actually felt that the crowded concourse was like a gigantic congested chessboard with hundreds of people trying to make bishop's moves, involving mistakes, and a sudden checkmate. She did not offer this conceit to Mrs Walker. Mrs Walker was voluble but might consider it a pretentious observation.

'Did you live near Ilkgate then?' she ventured as she drank her tea.

'Oh no – not in such a lovely place as yours – I know it of course – we used to go youth hostelling nearby. No, I lived in a more industrial part, but there were plenty of woods and fields around.'

'Did you miss them when you left them?' asked Moira boldly. It seemed you could say anything to Anna Macdonald's mother.

'Yes, I suppose I did. But down here I've got used to feeling warmer, and you can come across lovely country not too far from London, though it's not so easy to get there as it was from my home village – and we had no car.'

They both heard the bell at the same time and Janet jumped up.

'It'll be the men. I'll show them where to take everything and then we'll leave them to it. You go up later if you like, and show them where to put things. I should have taken you up straight away, I suppose, but they're in good time.'

She bustled off into the hall and Moira followed her. Yes, it was the van, large and red with gold letters, and already the driver had jumped down to check the parking. Once the front door was opened and they had ascertained they were at the right house, the men got on with it.

'Will they be able to take the bed up?' whispered Moira.

'Oh, I'm sure they're used to it.'

A third man had appeared to help.

'Have you enough for tips?' Janet said in a low voice to Moira. 'Did my daughter remind you?'

'Yes,' she thought, 'twenty-five pounds – for them all.'

'That's *quite* enough,' answered the older woman 'You see to the paperwork when they're finished. It's not like a full house-move. I shall make them some tea. They'll want to get away as soon as they can. Go up and have a look.'

It was rather soothing to be told what to do, thought Moira, and began to mount the stairs with her case, which Mrs Walker had forgotten to take up.

The man behind her said: 'Put it dahn Miss and I'll take it up for you.'

Moira found her rooms actually larger than she remembered. It took rather a long time steering the bed up the stairs but eventually it rested where she wanted it. What a business moving was. She felt she would never want to move again for the rest of her life.

She sat down in the wicker armchair provided by Martin. She must buy some colourful cushions for it. Before the men brought up the tea-chests of books and her own bookcase she got up to look out of the window. Her room was at the front of the house and the dormer window now revealed a daytime view of the road and a glimpse of the heath. The cases of books arrived and she looked forward to unpacking them.

Mrs Walker came up and stood at the door.

'I see Dora has made herself at home,' she observed, seeing the curled up figure on the unmade bed. 'It won't take too long once you've got your books sorted and made up the bed,' she said comfortingly. 'I always feel once the books have arrived you can begin to live in a place. They've finished unpacking. Did you go through your list?'

'All of it,' replied Moira. 'I'll come down, then, and write a cheque.'

'Tea and biscuits in the kitchen,' said Mrs Walker to a man on the stairs who was bringing up Moira's last possession, an Anglepoise lamp. He winked at Moira on her way down. Dora stayed upstairs.

'She's a nice looking young woman – slender with big blue eyes and slightly wavy fair hair,' said Janet to her husband as they ate their supper back at home. Tom had collected his wife in the car and they had left Moira to Anna and Martin. Martin was upstairs showing her how the little oven worked, and helping her move a few things around.

'I think she's settled in – it didn't take long. She's very polite. Reminds me of someone, though I can't think who. Nice voice, low and clear. I enjoy hearing that Yorkshire sound. I liked her. She gives an impression of thoughtfulness.'

'Tell her to come and see us sometime,' said Tom, who had only glimpsed the paragon in the hall.

Anna and Martin were at last tucked up in bed. Moira had gone back up to her flat after the supper they had insisted on sharing with her, along with a glass of wine to wish her well at Hall House. Once she had replied to their hearty 'good-night', they heard nothing more from upstairs; the thick Edwardian walls were solidly soundproof.

There'd be time at the weekend to go shopping, thought Moira. She wanted to buy an old wall mirror and add to her list of necessities, once she had sorted everything else out. She was a tidy if not house-proud girl and there was ample room for her things. One room of Hall House equalled two of Mrs Jackson's in size, and the sloping roof gave her room character.

She was too excited at first to be sleepy. Anna had given her a spare duvet, just in case, for it was at present cold for July, and she had made up the bed and was lying in the darkness. Blackwich darkness. Dora had disappeared in search of food.

She must soon practise using the Baby Belling, and sort out more books, and write to her mother. She had already telephoned Mrs Jackson and tomorrow she would phone Aurelia. She would keep a list of non-local calls so that her landlords were not out of pocket. There was so much to do.

She set her alarm for eight and fell asleep to the sound of a faint murmur of traffic. That must be from all the cars and lorries and buses crossing the heath.

Twenty miles away, Janet was having her recurring dream of the old Yorkshire manor house which she had been recalling when she had mentioned her last visit to Woolsford for Great Aunt Lily's funeral.

In the dream she was in a bus that was toiling up a hill past low stone cottages, now fronted with incongruous doors. In one bay window, far too large for the house, a Christmas tree looked out in a maze of fairy lights. They reached the top of the hill, past a church and a chapel on opposite sides of the road, facing each other like the old enemies they had once been. Then the bus swung to the right and she heard the wind keening away over the snowy fields.

Low, black dry-stone walls separated the smallholdings and now the bus was nearly at the manor house stop. She had only to get off, turn down the lane, walk about a quarter of a mile and there would be the gates and the lodge at the top of the drive with the mid-Victorian house just visible.

She got off the bus and it chugged stodgily away. Now she was alone, and all the weight of the years lifted for a moment, as she seemed to glide down the lane to the liver-coloured drive, trees on each side.

'Just ruins,' she heard herself say, but before she could see these ruins she woke up. The feeling of the dream was still with her the next morning: the winter and the snow and the old bus, darkness coming on with the wuthering of the wind, and someone in the ruins whom she was going to meet.

Part Three

HALL HOUSE

9

In high summer Emma Walker had not yet taken her holiday entitlement and was still pursuing her tidy life in Pimlico. Lydia Carter
was in Tuscany. Martin and Anna were living slightly less tidy lives
at Hall House and Moira was savouring Blackwich whilst she
could, occasionally going up to London on the train to a prom or
an art gallery. Anna and Martin had quickly got used to hearing
Moira's footsteps on the stairs and her quiet greeting if they passed
each other coming in or going out.

At the beginning of July the Macdonalds had celebrated the
second anniversary of their meeting by eating in the restaurant that
they had patronized the evening of the day they had met. Emma,
who always did the right thing, had already paid a visit to Hall
House to meet Moira. She worked long hours and did not often
go out in the evening, and she had not tried to see Vicky
Winterbon in Blackwich, having received a postcard from her from
Edinburgh where a conference of therapists was taking place,
attended by Vicky as secretary to Ms Ingersoll.

'They are all mad,' she had written cheerfully. Emma wondered
if Vicky ever told her employer her opinions of therapists. Possibly
she did not really believe they were mad but liked a striking phrase.

By now Tom had spoken to 'the tenant', Moira. He had dubbed
the house 'Wildfell Hall' in honour of its new Yorkshire associa-
tion. Martin's brother Kit, who had been his best man, had come
over later that evening from a neighbouring suburb, bearing a large
potted orchid as a present to the house. Moira, who was there only
to be introduced to Tom saw Kit's back as she looked down from
the landing.

Janet had said to Anna: 'Your father must have a look upstairs
and at the basement sometime when we're not in such a rush.'

Moira knew that the house belonged to Anna and Martin only

because Tom Walker had leased it to them.

'You are welcome to have a look round,' she said quickly, 'but I haven't quite finished furnishing it yet.'

'You could do with a larger cooker – or a microwave perhaps, one day?'

Tom seemed in no hurry to inspect his property and, respecting her privacy, did not come upstairs but turned his attention to Kit Macdonald, a qualified doctor who had been working in trouble spots abroad for several years for some medical charity. He was at present on some sort of leave in London.

'She's got it really shipshape,' said Anna to her mother.

'I wouldn't mind living there myself,' said Janet. Maybe she regretted the days of youthful freedom in such attics or 'top room backs'.

'We must soon find someone to live in the basement,' said Martin to his mother-in-law. 'When I've done some more painting and fixed the skirting boards. They were a bit bodged.'

Kit had come on his motorbike from Brickley and therefore refused a second drink before leaving. Moira wondered about him later when she saw a literary journal she recognized, which must have been left by him, lying next to the orchid pot on the hall table, an unusual journal for a doctor who worked for an international charity.

Tom and Janet soon said they must go too.

'They're all so busy,' Janet said to Tom in the car on their way back. 'Having to cram most of the shopping and housework into the weekend.'

'You used to do the same,' replied Tom, remembering their own young working days, before children arrived. It seemed a long time ago to him too.

Vicky Winterbon, returned from Scotland, had not yet met any of the Hall House inhabitants but had walked past the house and seen the name on a faded plaque on the back gate. She was hoping she might soon see Emma again, and meet her sister.

Anna rang Janet up regularly every week, and her mother relayed her news to Emma. The sisters did not communicate very frequently by telephone, both having enough of it in their working hours, but Anna did telephone Emma the following Saturday.

'You must come round soon and meet Moira. Mother and Dad have been. When are you taking a holiday?'

'Lydia is away for three weeks,' said Emma, circling round her answer.

'Aren't *you* going away, then?'

'Yes, I'm going walking in the Lake District with some people from work in August. In September I might just pop over to Italy with Paula for a week or two. What about you?'

Paula Talbot, with whom Emma had been at school, had cousins who lived near Stresa.

'We ought not to go anywhere ourselves, really,' sighed Anna. 'There's still so much to do. But Moira seems settled in and that means we could leave the house for a bit as she's still officially on holiday. We shall go to Bordeaux before the end of August – not the best time, but Martin's busy at work. He wants to revisit his vineyards.'

'Does he actually *own* any?'

'Not yet – he oversees these particular ones for various English people. Before too long, I suspect he'd like to invest in a small one himself a bit further from Bordeaux, but it would have to be one that grows grapes for a cheaper variety of wine than the ones whose finances he looks after for clients in the Margaux district. More of a 'villagey' kind – not one that really counts as 'Bordeaux'. Châteaux vineyards are costing millions. I don't know exactly what he'll decide to do in the end.'

'The English call all the wine 'claret', anyhow. At least you'll have a change if you go over and look round.'

'It's all been so hectic ever since we were married. You knew Mother and Dad were going to Orta later on in autumn?'

'After I've got back. They like their holidays when most of the foreign families have gone home. I *would* like to meet your tenant. How do you find her? Is she liveable with?'

'She's gone to an exhibition at the Royal Academy this afternoon so I can say what I think, and that is that she's very nice.'

'Did Mother tell you about Javotte, the woman – well, she was a girl then – whom I met years ago in Paris? I think you'd like her. I promised her I'd see her sometime in Blackwich. When might we get together?'

'Why not bring her round here before we all go away? Come over for a cup of coffee or something next Sunday – a week tomorrow. Ask your friend if she can come too. I won't promise a meal – I'm still the world's worst cook.'

'We could meet for a drink Sunday morning and have a bite in the village later. Save you cooking at all.'

'Invite her whatever time you prefer but let me know, will you. Sunday afternoon perhaps.'

Emma thought: they want a long lie-in on Sunday morning.

'Next week then. That would be nice. I'll give her a ring and let you know. Will your Moira be there too?'

'I'll ask her if she's free. She might have a concert or an exhibition planned. She says she ought to go out now she's near London. I told her, when she starts the new job, getting back here in the evenings on weekdays and going out again up to London, especially without a car, is a real pain.'

Martin had expressed a wish to stay at home on Sunday as they would have been out visiting some friends of his in Wimbledon the evening before, and he wanted to continue his basement labours after getting up late on Sunday. Anna was quite relieved. She much preferred having friends round for tea and talk. It was soothing before the next working day of the week began. Like her mother she had always disliked the possibility of a melancholy Sunday. The pubs in Blackwich were all very well, and some of the restaurants excellent, but she disliked dressing up, or at least trying to look less messy than usual.

Emma telephoned later to say she would come over after lunch, and reported that Vicky Winterbon would meet her at the station and they would walk over to Hall House. Moira, when asked if she'd like to come down in the afternoon to meet Emma and another friend, looked pleased but a little scared.

'Martin can get on with his painting and leave us all to talk,' Anna explained.

At three o'clock on Sunday Anna opened the door to her sister and a tall, curly-haired young woman.

'This is Vicky,' said Emma.

Just then Moira, who had been hesitating on the stairs, came into the hall.

'And this is Moira,' said Anna. Moira wondered which one was Anna's sister, but seeing a woman of approximately the same height as Anna, guessed correctly that the other one, the tall one, was Vicky. They all laughed as they acknowledged each other. Moira and Emma, and then Anna and Vicky. Moira and Vicky shook hands rather formally. Emma had not met 'the tenant' before and was curious. Anna led them into the sitting-room and found everyone somewhere to sit, thinking it was like a tea-party out of Jane Austen: four girls, but no man.

Moira looked at Emma as they sat down. Anna looked more like her mother but Emma's oval face had a look of her father, whom Moira had only recently met. Emma looked very intellectual and efficient.

Vicky's painter's eye picked up details immediately.

'I do like the colour of your double doors – do they lead into a dining-room?'

At the same time, she had taken in Anna and seen a rounder-faced, rather plumper woman than Emma, with brown eyes, slightly darker hair in a half-fringe, and stockier legs. She turned her attention to Moira and registered quite a different kind of person: light eyes, thin wrists, fair wavy hair and a slightly faraway look. The nose was aquiline, the ears small, and the whole impression that of someone deep and serious, with a secret inner life. Vicky admonished herself: she knew she was given to sudden first impressions but ever since she'd started working for Ms Ingersoll she had tried to avoid labelling people too soon after meeting them.

Anna had taken in the twinkling eyes and upright but relaxed gait of this old friend of Emma's. The olive skin and curly locks assorted strangely with the woman's height. You wouldn't usually find a tall Spaniard. But then, of course, Vicky wasn't Spanish, was she?

'Martin, my husband, is busy doing some painting,' she explained to Vicky, 'but he'll be up for some tea soon, I expect.'

'Painting?' enquired Vicky, sliding into a deep armchair and putting down her capacious bag.

'It's only the walls,' explained Anna laughing. 'We're thinking of letting the basement.'

Oh dear, she ought not to have said that, since Emma had explained to her that Vicky wasn't very well housed over the hairdresser on Prince's Parade in the village, and might hope to be offered the basement flat. But Vicky, who could be tactful and had guessed the lie of the land, looked only mildly interested.

'I'll help you bring in the tea,' said Emma. They must let Moira meet one new woman before she had to talk to her landlady's sister.

'Oh, let me,' said Moira, a little intimidated by the obvious free

113

and easiness of the tall Vicky, and happy to cover shyness with activity.

'No, you have a rest. I know where everything will be,' said Emma, who seemed to have taken charge.

'I live on the top floor,' Moira said to Vicky. 'I came only two or three weeks ago.'

'How do you like London – or rather Blackwich?' asked Vicky.

'I've decided to say that I live in Blackwich, not London,' replied Moira in her gentle voice. 'I've made an effort and been to a prom and the V and A and an art exhibition at the Royal Academy but I ought to get to know round here better. There seems a lot going on.'

'There's plenty to do in Blackwich,' said Vicky. 'I have to travel to Beckington most days – and sometimes to London at other times, so by Saturday all I feel like doing is walk or run in the park. There's a concert hall here, you know, and a cinema over the other side of the heath, and several little galleries. Did they tell you about our local amenities?'

'Are you from here yourself, then?'

'No. I was brought up about sixty miles away from Blackwich. Can you believe I never visited London till I was twelve,' Vicky remarked wryly. There had been people in Spire who had only once been to London, but her first visit had been after her father deserted her mother. Her mother and aunt had wanted to give her a treat. She had not minded her father's going away. He had been a bully and she knew her mother was secretly relieved. Auntie Orla had a good job and would support them whilst they in return let her share the old village house.

'People from *my* home town think anyone living in the south-east is a cockney,' Moira said.

Anna heard them chatting as she and Emma came in with trays on which were balanced somewhat precariously, a teapot, cups, saucers, sugar bowl and plates of biscuits.

'Earl Grey,' said Anna, 'to please my sister. And we have lapsang souchong for our mother. I hope nobody is on a diet because there are piles of things to eat on the table in the kitchen.'

'Oh, I forgot,' said Vicky. 'I baked you a cake.' She dived into her big bag.

'Goodness – how kind!'

'I hope you don't mind. I bake a little now and then. I find it soothing, but I can't eat all I produce. It's only a sort of simnel-cake. Wrong time of year for it, really.' Emma wondered how on earth Vicky could cook in what according to her amounted to a bed-sitting-room and a minute kitchenette. She went into Anna's large kitchen for another plate, feeling slightly annoyed.

'How sweet of you,' Anna said. 'I love home-baked things, I never have time myself.'

Moira was thinking it was like Ilkgate, people arriving with the products of their baking.

Well, I suppose it's only like bringing wine to a party, thought Emma in the kitchen. Vicky was clearly determined Anna should approve of her.

'Moira has been doing some gardening,' offered Anna.

'The flower-beds at the back are all overgrown, and she's persuaded me to order some rambler roses for the garden walls.' She smiled at Moira. 'I just wouldn't know where to begin with weeding and hoeing and raking and clearing.'

'Not quite in that order! Martin will mow the lawn, I suppose,' said Emma drily, hearing her. She had seen a long expanse of jungle through the kitchen window. The talk turned from gardens to cars, which none of the women yet owned. Surprisingly, Moira turned out to be able to drive, but said she would never drive in London, not knowing her way around.

'I'm going to buy a little old car soon – I like driving,' declared Vicky.

'In all, a car costs about £1000 a year to run,' said Emma severely. Lydia had grumbled a lot about the cost of a car in London. What with parking-permits and fines, she now left her car at home in Somerset.

Anna was feeling useless, having to rely on a husband to ferry her round. Like her mother she had never managed to pass the test. Hopeless driver and hopeless cook. Emma had passed but did not need to drive in London. Oh well, Anna found herself thinking, a little ashamedly, surprising herself, I've got a good chauffeur. She guessed her sister thought it was one good reason for having a husband.

'Mother and Dad are coming over and Mother will be here any minute,' she said to Emma. 'Dad's going to some friend in London – he'll leave the car at the station to collect on his way back. He

115

likes a few hours to himself, though I told him he'd be welcome.'

'Will she walk from the station?' asked Vicky politely.

'It's only ten minutes, even at her pace. She's always saying she needs more exercise. He can bring the car round here later this evening on his way back.'

'You have a parking place here?' asked Vicky.

'For the time being – on the lane at the back. The council will probably impose more restrictions soon.'

'I saw quite an old lady jogging yesterday,' said Moira.

'Some really old people run the marathon,' said Emma, adding: 'Vicky jogs too – don't you, Vicky?'

They began to talk about London traffic and work. Moira was a good listener but was glad she would be able to go by train to her library job. She noticed that Vicky often joked with a solemn face or said serious things with a grin, which had puzzled her at first. She soon cottoned on to the mixture of drama and irony in the young woman' s manner of conversation, thinking that she reminded her a little of Aurelia. Vicky looked saucy even when she was silent.

Suddenly Moira missed her old friend. She was a stranger here and felt a little out of it. Emma turned to her.

'You'll soon enjoy getting out around here. Some people never go to London unless it's for work, and you don't need a car to go over to Greenwich – in fact it's easier without one.'

Anna thought she had better say something to Vicky, the newcomer. Conversation between four women, two of whom knew only one of the other two, could be a bit sticky. She didn't want her guests to be bored.

'I always intended to jog but I never found time,' she stated.

'Oh, I'm not a serious jogger. I do it just to breathe some fresh air,' said Vicky.

'Do you ride?'

'Years ago I used to. There was a riding-school where I lived as a child. Not recently.' She looked a bit sad when she was talking about her childhood, Moira thought. 'Do *you* ride? Is it like a bike or a car – once you can do it, you never forget?' Moira asked Anna.

'Not quite. I learned when I lived in London, not as a child. Mother wasn't keen on what she called trendy exercise. Half the girls I went to school with were having riding-lessons and the other half ballet. We had neither.'

'Thank goodness,' said her sister.

'Riding was my only exercise apart from swimming when I lived in London,' pursued Anna, 'You know you can go swimming down near the river, Moira, in the new sports complex.'

'It's odd you like riding and swimming but hate driving, Anna,' said Emma who occasionally went to a gym.

'Perhaps they are more . . . natural?' offered Moira.

'Mother used to ride her bike round here,' said Anna, 'It was an extension of her personality.'

'Mother's one and only example of exercise,' added Janet's other daughter.

'Till we told her she'd have to buy a hard hat, or she'd get killed.'

'I'd like to get a bike,' Moira said.

'The traffic has got a lot worse in the last five years or so. Mother cycled everywhere for over thirty years – did all her shopping on her bike. Martin's brother has a moped,' Anna said.

Martin poked his head around the door.

'I've put the kettle on,' he said.

'Which means he's ready for tea now,' said his wife. She went out to the kitchen.

Moira found she was still quite hungry and ate another large piece of Vicky's cake, which was really good. She had not yet got used to eating her main meal in the evening. They heard the bell ring.

'It'll be Mother,' said Emma and left the room to greet her.

Vicky was thinking, what a very 'family' atmosphere it is. Moira is very much OK here. Would they mention again this other flatlet they were thinking of letting in the basement? The husband was still painting it, so she assumed it was not quite ready for occupation. Both sisters came in with their mother, who was carrying a large canvas bag. Moira got up to help pour more tea.

'Lapsang souchong for Mother in the little pot,' Anna said.

'Well, Ma,' said Emma, 'What have you in that enormous bag of yours?'

'Oh, some books and things,' Janet answered vaguely. 'Anna left some behind last time she was down with us.'

'This is Vicky. I think I mentioned to you we'd met years ago in Paris,' said Emma, producing Vicky rather like a trophy. Anna

poured her mother a cup of the delicious smoky liquid. Janet
shook hands with Vicky, sat down and turned to Moira.

'How are you getting on? Have you started work?' she asked.
'Missing your old job?'

'Not properly. I've just been in twice to observe but I start properly next week. It's quite complicated; getting used to it will need
a lot of thinking about.'

She had felt she would never get accustomed to the amount of
'admin' she had been shown, and the forms that seemed to be
connected to it, and would have to feel her way carefully.

'You look well,' Janet went on.

Moira did look cheerful, but then she hadn't done any commut-
ing yet.

'They'll throw me in at the deep end. I'll be fine with the work
with children. I'm still not very good on a computer, but fortunately I've been told that one of the others just loves spread sheets.'
She took a breath. They were all so friendly: she felt a little less shy.

Anna groaned. 'It's the same everywhere,' she began.

'But you'll have an assistant, Moira, won't you?' asked Janet.
'They'll probably try to make things seem complicated at first.'

'People are always like that with a new person,' said Vicky
consolingly.

Anna began to tell her mother about her own work-load and
Vicky listened, drank her tea, munched the biscuits and then it was
her turn to tell them a bit about the sort of people her employer
worked with. It might be rather indiscreet but they wouldn't ever
know the clients. She made them laugh a lot.

Moira thought how she would not want Vicky's job. She had
not been paid for going to the library to 'look round' so that she
could start with a little background knowledge. Emma sat and said
nothing; she rarely discussed her own work. She thought it was
time to turn the subject to holidays.

Anna was happy to tell them about their plans.

Janet listened to them all as she savoured her favourite tea.
Sweet of Anna always to remember to have it in. It was pleasant to
see her happy daughter and her helpful husband, she thought,
when Martin came in and listened to Emma describing places in
France where they might stay. It was going to be a happy marriage
. . . but how is my other daughter really, who, as far as I know, has

never met a 'suitable partner' as they say? She turned to look at Moira, feeling a good deal of sympathy for her. Had her life been blighted by a married man? Perhaps girls should have babies in their twenties, before they settled down with a partner. But then the whole basis of Christian marriage would collapse, she thought, as she munched Vicky's cake. Once you separated babies from fathers' responsibilities, you had a different kind of society. There was no easy answer to the question of what women needed, what they wanted. Independence?

Men? Babies? Nobody consulted babies . . . I'd have been hopeless with a baby in my twenties, I was vehement and muddled and gave my heart away too easily. . . . .

She turned her attention to the other young woman, Vicky. Now she was quite a different kettle of fish, reminded her of someone but she could not for the life of her remember whom . . . Tall, a bit blowsy, but jolly and handsome, she was possibly a bit older than the others. Emma had told her Vicky had one failed marriage behind her. No children. Had it been the case of the wrong man at the right time? Janet was eventually roused from all her speculation, which had not stopped her joining in the various conversations going on.

'How's Dad?' asked Emma.

All yesterday Tom had been, as he often was, immersed in his own thoughts. She was used to it. What some women might have seen as neglect, Janet saw as opportunity for time to herself. Tom would not let her read anything he had written until it was finished, which might be next year or in another ten years. . . .

Well, she had her own thoughts to get on with, not that they ever appeared to lead her to any firm conclusions. Her generation had been very serious.

'Oh he's fine. Needs new glasses, though,' she answered briskly.

'Moira has been looking at the garden and giving us ideas,' said Martin.

'Yes, Anna said something about it.'

'This year it will have to be dug over and weeded, and the shrubs cut down in autumn,' said Moira quietly.

'And we have to think about what to beg, borrow or steal – or buy. It all sounds daunting,' said Anna with a shudder. Martin laughed.

119

'We shall need a compost-heap,' he said severely. 'I shall start on that – and something to get rid of slugs and snails.'

'You could try beer for the snails,' suggested Vicky.

'I bought some bags of compost-reducer yesterday and some green tubs,' said Martin, adding: 'Anna suggested we improve the so-called patio in front of the kitchen.'

'You could get someone to lay a few paving-stones when you've finished the basement,' said his mother-in-law, who believed in expert help if possible.

'We could put a table and chairs out there before next summer,' said Anna enthusiastically.

'The next-door garden is very regimented,' said Moira.

'I envisage masses of old rambler roses and a cottagey patch – delphiniums and hollyhocks and larkspur . . .' Anna went on. Martin looked at her fondly.

'She's off,' said Emma. 'But do you really want a *patio*? You'll be having a barbecue next. I hope Martin is prepared.'

'We used to have a barbecue,' said Vicky rather wistfully. 'In the end I thought it was more bother than it was worth.'

Did she mean at home in Essex or with the unnamed husband, Emma wondered. Janet was speculating how many times this Vicky had reinvented herself. How much, underneath, did people really change?

'I'm not a good gardener,' she confessed. 'I'm lucky not to have to bother any more about it now, except indoors, and a few tubs, and still enjoy a lovely garden.' She explained how each household paid their share down at Deepden and it was organized for them by the management committee, who also employed gardening help.

'Which consists of committed gardeners like you, Moira,' she added.

'I'm sorry, I shall have to get back,' said Emma to Vicky, getting up to go. She had done her duty introducing them all. It had all gone quite well. She knew she'd be leaving her in good hands. She wondered what they made of *her*. Gatherings of friends, when they were younger, had often ended with everyone analysing the one who had just left.

'I had to take some work home on Friday,' she explained to her mother. 'Statistics.'

'You work too hard, love,' said Janet. Emma never stayed long.

120

She was now wondering why Vicky's marriage, or whatever it was, had collapsed. So many did. It was sad, but not the end of the world, if you were still young and had no offspring, she thought.

'Give Dad my love.'

'Would you like to come up and see my room?' Moira asked Vicky, hearing Janet making rapid family arrangements with her daughters about their father's birthday. Martin and Anna were going away for a short holiday towards the end of August just after Tom's sixty-eighth. Janet wrote the dates down in her diary.

'Oh, do show me!' said Vicky, and Moira led the way to her eyrie. She remembered that she had not yet shown it properly to Mr Walker; she'd better offer, when Anna's father arrived. She wanted to show Mrs Walker, too, what she had bought yesterday, feeling she would like the older woman's approval.

By the time Tom called for her Janet was quite ready to be driven back to Kent. Moira came up as they were leaving to ask if they might like to have a look. Vicky had thought it 'super' and was coming down to meet Mr Walker.

'Just a quick look,' said Tom. 'Traffic on Sunday is worse than weekdays so we mustn't be long – the world and his wife make trips on Sundays.'

'That's you and Mother,' said Anna.

Her parents went up and she heard approving noises when they came down; accompanied by Vicky.

Vicky and Moira were apparently getting on well, she thought, though they were so different in their personalities. She always wanted people to like each other, felt responsible. Moira could have fitted well into a literary story about a shy young provincial coming to London, whereas Vicky looked more dashing, even if she were, in spite of her sister's descriptions of the old 'Javotte' originally only another provincial girl. Emma had wanted her and Martin to 'look over' Vicky to gauge her suitability for the basement flat. Anna's own impression was favourable.

She said this to Martin later that evening, when they had all left, except for Moira who lived her noiseless existence upstairs. Martin had been out to collect more paint from the DIY shop, also now open on Sundays. 'Emma brought her, then? Are they friends? She seemed very nice – she likes cars,' was his reply. Men never remembered personal details. She was sure she'd mentioned that

Vicky had been in Paris at the same time as her sister. He added: 'Very unlike Moira, who sometimes makes me think of a nun!'

'Shh. She might hear you!'

'Really, Sundays are getting just like any other day,' said Janet on the way back. When the children were little in the 1960s all the shops had been closed on a Sunday and the place had been quiet, almost deserted. Almost universal car-ownership had made all the difference to Blackwich and the roads were choked and noisy. Restaurants did their best trade at the weekend and some shops stayed open too, even sometimes the bookshop. Was it 'progress'? It didn't seem like it, and yet she remembered that in her twenties she had wanted London Sundays to be more 'continental' and for big bookshops to have shift systems. Would even Deepden be like this one day?

Everything had changed since Emma and Anna were children, including of course themselves and her. 'I like Moira Emsley,' she said to Tom when they got back. 'She reminds me a little of myself when young.'

'She doesn't look a bit like you!' exclaimed Tom.

'I didn't mean her *looks*.'

'You weren't a librarian either,' he said, literal-minded as usual.

'She likes children and knows a lot about books. But I have the feeling she might be a writer herself.'

'She's made it nice up there in the loft,' he said. 'That other girl was a flashy one, wasn't she!'

'Flashy?'

'Well, you know – sexy!' he said, which made her laugh.

'I don't know about her, but I feel sure little Moira will concentrate better than I was ever able to do,' she went on. 'And one day she might publish something. Poetry perhaps.'

'How do you know?' he asked.

'Oh, just intuition,' replied Janet.

122

10

In her long-ago youth Janet had wanted to restrict her activities to three things: Love, of course, and the life of art, dedicated to books and music and painting, and – unavoidably – work, to earn just enough money to be independent. She still saw these things in capital letters, but knew that something to do with love had got in the way of the last.

Anna appeared to manage all right but Anna was a different sort of person. It was always assumed that women of her age must have settled into themselves, and no longer had any ambition, but it wasn't true. All that many acquaintances of theirs could talk about now was their computer and how something new called the Spider's Web or Fish Net, or something, was going to revolutionize everybody's lives. Moira would have to understand all this new stuff and she hoped it would not faze her. She felt sure that Moira's true ambitions were quite like her own old ones.

She should feel lucky that she had a family, and was still needed, even if it did involve putting washing into the machine, which she was doing this very minute as there had been no time before they left for Blackwich, and sorting out ironing from the last lot, and watering her orchid and getting a late supper for them both.

That was what she always did on a Sunday evening before settling down with a contented sigh to the Sunday papers.

As Moira had already explained to the gathering on Sunday afternoon, her work at the library in Bickdon would turn out to involve a good deal of paperwork. She was busy trying to work it all out. Getting used to a new place and new people was, not unexpectedly, tiring, and she felt a little at sea during the first two or three weeks. After two weekend afternoons spent in the garden, 'tidying up', she felt more refreshed. She had the run of Hall House whilst Martin and Anna were in France but they would soon be back from their holiday. She had nothing to do in the house but look after herself and Dora, sort out the Macdonald post, take phone messages, and plan the garden. A long telephone call with Aurelia had made her realize that she was not actually missing Ilkgate, even if she rather missed a comfortable, face-to-face conversation with her friend, who was deprived of sleep on account of the baby's latest teething.

'I do envy you your freedom,' Aurelia had groaned, which did not sound at all like her. Moira attempted to cheer her up, and sent messages to Miss Banks and Mrs Jackson.

'You sound quite settled,' Aurelia went on in a surprised voice.

Moira did not see Vicky Winterbon again until one Saturday at the beginning of September. That morning she had received a late card from Bordeaux, signed by both Anna and Martin, who would now be on their way home.

'I like the old town here,' Anna had written, 'though Martin has a yen for the classic rural idyll. You get into the country pretty quickly from her and one could have the best of both worlds.'

Moira had some groceries to buy and wanted another look at the second-hand bookshop where she had so far avoided spending too much time browsing. Books were very important, but she must soon make an effort to cherish new people as well as old books. She did not yet know many Blackwichans, and had not wanted to presume upon the friendliness of her landlord and landlady, who were blissfully in love as well as fully occupied with the house. More house improvements awaited their return.

Moira fed Dora. It was good that her mistress would never have to send her to a cattery. She decided as she walked to the shops that she could not see Anna as the proprietor of some ancient ruin in Aquitaine. Hall House was quite enough to be getting on with. After she had bought an expensive pack of dark coffee from the specialist delicatessen, and two croissants, feeling guilty at her choice – but after all she was now earning the wherewithal to pay for them – she had some time to browse in the second-hand book-shop. Whom did she come upon outside it but Vicky, looking through the table of cheap paperbacks. Cheap moneywise, but not in quality, for the village did not sell rubbish, even second-hand rubbish, as Moira had already noticed in the charity shops. She felt a little wary of greeting her, knowing her own need in bookshops for peace and quiet, but Vicky looked up and smiled.

'Hello, Moira. How's life with computers?'

'Slightly better this week than last, thanks. The others will be back tonight or early tomorrow.'

'I'm still saving up for the car. I hope you're enjoying taking literature to tots in the outer suburbs.'

Vicky always spoke a bit as if she was on stage, thought Moira, but she was friendly, and it was pleasant to be greeted by a friend in this place that was, in spite of everything, a little alien.

'You want to browse, I can see,' Vicky went on. 'Will you have time for a cup of coffee before lunch?'

'Yes, thank you. I was just . . .' Moira indicated the shop.

'Why don't we meet when you've finished? But don't worry if you haven't time. I'll be in the coffee-shop down on the left – past Oxfam.'

Vicky departed, having made no purchase, and Moira entered the large old shop. There was one whole wall of valuable anti-quarian books near the entrance and ranks and ranks of old fiction at the back, with old children's books, some of which were rare, on window-sills and tables. She made a beeline towards those. She could not afford the ones she'd love to own but must have a look at what had been put out since she had first discovered the place.

As far as first editions were concerned, there was a *King of the Golden River* no, she didn't want that, and a *Coral Island*. On another table, some 1940s adventure stories and two Nesbits, not first editions but about seventy years old, an annual or two, several collectors' items of schoolgirl stories from the same decade, several Arthur Ransomes, some quite old, but not first editions, and a first of *Tom's Midnight Garden*, her favourite book as a child. Quite an eclectic collection, but difficult to choose betweeen them, and not yet within her price range. She moved on to a wall of poetry and essays: what Miss Banks used to call *belles lettres*, and found she felt at home there. She'd most likely buy a very slim volume of verse, for she was determined, having once, though unwillingly, winnowed – she preferred the word to 'culled' – her books in Ilkgate, not to accumulate too much. This shop was more inter-

esting than any in Ilkgate. The proprietor must make his profits
from mail order, unless Blackwichans were all voracious readers as
well as being specialist ones. She would like to have a chat with
Vicky, for she had been too tired in the evenings to do more than
relax in the Hall House garden, and after all if she were to begin
to cherish some new people she'd better begin with her.

She bought an old and inexpensive copy of a book she had used
at school, an anthology of what had been 'modern' poetry in Miss
Banks's day, but it had quite a lot of Thomas Hardy, then she
wandered down towards the coffee shop. An early London
autumn was still summery, certainly warmer than in the north, and
a few people were sitting outside at the pavement café. Vicky was
one of them; she waved.

'I thought I might as well sit here. Soon it'll be too cold, but if
you want to go in . . .'

'No.' Moira would have preferred to sit down more comfortably inside, but Vicky obviously preferred outside.

'Have you met anyone nice at work?' Vicky asked, when they
were both sipping their lattes.

Moira guessed she meant 'a man'. The only man she had talked
to so far was a middle-aged peripatetic manager. The girls who
worked under her at the library on the high street, where the children's branch was to be found, were difficult to talk to. One was
a keen reader but confessed she preferred children's books because
she liked fantasy: indeed her favourite word was '*funtas*tic,' and
the other was a certain Jean, a slightly older woman who wore
horn-rimmed specs and pink cardigans, and who also loved other
worlds and knew many chapters of Tolkien by heart. Apart from
these two, she hardly ever spoke to anyone. Moira wondered
whether she had expected to get the job of supervisor herself.

'Have you seen Emma?' Vicky went on, having received no
answer from Moira but a small smile.

Moira gathered up her thoughts.

'No, Anna said Emma would be out of London walking in the
Lake District. When they come back, the others will still be busy
with the house. Martin showed me the basement before they left.
He's finished painting the walls but he says it needs new vinyl and
more cupboards and some power-points. He asked me if I'd rather
live there than upstairs, but I like my eyrie.'

'It's a lovely house, isn't it. You must come and see *my* room. It's not far from here.'

Moira had understood that Vicky wanted very much to be a tenant at Hall House.

Vicky was still talking. 'They seemed a very happily married couple, I must say.'

'They are. I hope they have some children,' said Moira, and then wondered why she had said that. It sounded a bit intrusive.

'I expect they will. Don't you think that's the best reason for getting married?'

Moira wouldn't have imagined that Vicky would come out with that, but decided to agree, and said so.

'I've been married,' Vicky went on. 'If I'd had a baby I suppose I might still be married. But then – poor baby! After a year or two my husband and I just didn't get on.' She stirred her coffee.

How very outspoken. Moira didn't quite know what to say. Emma had told Anna, who had told her, that Vicky had been really 'married', not just had a partner, as many middle-class people did down here – unlike the circles she'd moved in up north. Ilkgate was of course full of quite rich businessmen and their families who went in for big weddings. The so-called working classes saved up for a similar over-the-top wedding, very like those of the rich. A few professional people got married in register offices. She had had a partner herself, she supposed, if not a husband, though she had always considered her TD a lover, not a partner. What was the difference? Perhaps a partner wasn't usually married to someone else, even amongst the middle-class young of Blackwich. Ought she to reveal her own past to Vicky? Not yet. She felt Vicky would be astonished, had marked her down for a virginal spinster.

'I'd like to see your room,' she said instead, 'but I have to get back to mine with my groceries.'

'Come tomorrow, then – if you're not doing anything. It's just round the corner up the hill past the bookshop.'

'Well, er – thank you.'

They parted, Vicky with a merry wave. Moira crossed the road and, lugging her shopping, walked across the narrow strip of heath back to Hall House.

In spite of a faint sense of guilt, Anna was savouring life in Hall

127

House, still very much enjoying being married after almost a year and a half.

However hard they'd both worked they'd never have been able to afford this nice house without parental help. People talked about women having it all, but it was money, either earned or inherited, that allowed them to do so. Unlike men, women not as lucky as herself could only 'have it all' – provided, like her sister they loved their jobs but employed others to look after their children.

More repairs and alterations had been carried out by Martin in the house and she felt quite settled.

It was out of this feeling of being settled that Anna became pregnant. She would be a mother around the time of her second wedding anniversary! So far, she had not once felt sick, and people said it was in the first three months that you did if you were going to. Everyone said she was very lucky. Luck appeared to accompany Martin and her. Martin, who did not usually go into ecstasies, was thrilled about the future infant. Anna knew he was speaking the truth when he said meeting her was the best thing that had ever happened to him.

'But will I be a *housewife*?' she asked him one dark afternoon in November two months after the official confirmation of the future human being. 'Now, I am a wife, which is pleasant, but next year shall I change into a housewife – just a housewife?'

As unlike many men might have done, Martin did not grunt an uninterested or non-committal answer. He was a paragon, her friends said, who always listened to her, even if he was immersed at the time on a book or a job. If on occasion he betrayed a certain amount of scepticism towards her enthusiasms, Martin would consider her questions seriously and give well-pondered answers.

Today he was reading the paper, which he regarded as a relaxation.

'Not "*just* a housewife",' he replied. 'Housewife is what philosophers call a "boo" word for people who think that women who look after a house and a baby don't have a proper job.'

'I do have what they'd call a proper job at the moment as well. What about when I haven't, though, and am just at home with the Bean?'

This was their name for their future baby, the prospective

human being. Anna had looked it all up in an enormous medical dictionary and informed Martin that after two months an embryo became a foetus. 'Foetus sounds faintly disgusting,' she said, 'Like fetid or fungus, a sort of smelly parasite.' *Bean* reminded her of growing one on blotting paper – the only scientific experiment, she claimed, that she had ever done with success. 'Bean fits all the ages and stages – and it sounds natural.'

So they had named 'it' Bean. Anna didn't want to know its sex – she liked surprises.

'If *I* am going to be a "housewife", will *you* ever be a house-husband?'

Martin had an answer to this too. He liked splitting verbal hairs.

' "House-band" leads to "hus-band", so husband already has the meaning of "house".'

'Thank you, *mon professeur*. So "wife" by itself doesn't?' She often called Martin her 'man', which was rather more exciting than 'husband'.

'*Weib* is just a word for a woman in German.'

'So you would only be a "house-husband" if you stayed at home and didn't have a job outside the house in the big world? Would you ever want to do that?'

'I wouldn't mind,' said Martin heroically. 'I *like* looking after the house.'

This was quite true, though he had less time than he'd have liked. He was very busy at work. More and more vineyards were expanding commercially.

Anna was still not sure if she wanted to be called a housewife. 'Mother' was rather different.

'I can't believe it's really going to happen,' she had said to her own mother. "Housewife and mother", sounds odd. We never say "woman and mother", do we. Are housewives a different sex from other women?'

'Women only stay at home now if they have children,' her mother had said. 'Most women of my generation used to be *glad* to stay at home – I did myself after eight years' hard graft.'

Even working part-time, Janet had been unusual forty years ago in middle-class Blackwich.

'It's the feminist revolution,' said Martin, now returning to the crossword.

'Giving women two jobs instead of one! Most couples need two!' said Anna indignantly. She felt a mixture of guilt towards other women and piety towards the family. She was actually looking forward very much to being at home. She might look for a part-time job later. They had discussed all this many times but Anna kept reassuring herself. She often chatted to Moira about leaving the job and going on maternity leave. But she had absolutely no plans to go back straight after that leave. Was she letting the side down?

Moira had agreed with her.

'It would be different if you adored your career,' she said, 'or were very poor.'

Moira wouldn't mind having a baby herself, thought Anna.

Moira described Anna's feelings to Aurelia when she next wrote to her. Aurelia, who had just had another child, a girl, wrote back, to say there was far too much to do at home – a job was easier than twenty-four-hour baby and toddler duty.

Vicky Winterbon had now been round a few times and had offered heartfelt congratulations to Anna when her news was imparted. Anna encouraged Moira to invite her. She was the sort of woman who might know a few men and it was Anna's opinion that more male company might do Moira good. She had not yet made any other close friends in Blackwich and told Anna there was nobody at the library whom she wanted to see outside it. Vicky did not overdo her visits, knowing that Moira, like Emma, also enjoyed her own company.

The afternoons were darker day by day as November dragged on, and the news was all of terrorists in Paris. At the beginning of December Vicky volunteered to help Moira cook supper for all at Hall House one evening soon. Moira had mentioned that she wanted to entertain her landlord and his wife, and asked for advice about a suitable dish. She also owed Vicky a meal, but was a bit worried about what to give her, wanting to kill two birds with one supper: return the hospitality and invite Anna and Martin up to her quarters for it. So far, she had experimented with omelettes and pasta, but thought she should offer something a little more exciting.

'I'm a rotten cook,' she confessed. What she had sampled of

Vicky's cooking had been delicious.

'Well, why don't you ask them up one Saturday evening and let me help with the cooking? I really enjoy it, honestly.'

Moira mentioned an evening to Anna. Unfortunately, Martin's brother Kit had already been invited for the evening she had planned, and Anna was in a slight quandary. She did not really feel like cooking. She had still not felt sick, and was in fact quite hungry, but looked forward to the weekends when she could have a rest.

'Kit can eat bread and cheese,' Martin said cheerfully, but when Moira's scheme was put before him, he told Anna to take her up on it. If Moira would like to invite his brother as well as Vicky the cook, they could all eat downstairs. They could go up to Moira's afterwards for coffee if they wanted. Anna thought that cooking for five people might be asking a bit too much of a tenant's guest, but informed Moira of the suggestion.

'You might like to use our oven. It's quite a good size. What about it?'

Vicky did *offer* to help, thought Moira.

'Shall I ask Vicky if she'd help me cook a supper for five, then?'

'That would be wonderful!'

Anna had heard of Vicky's prowess with food. 'Let's make a joint effort,' she went on. 'We can all be both guests and hosts. We lend you the big kitchen and then sit back and let you both do the hard work.'

Vicky was delighted to agree, especially as she had liked the look of Kit one Sunday when she had glimpsed him coming out of Hall House as she was jogging by. Moira had told her who it had been.

Moira was relieved that Vicky would take over the meal. Next time she would cook it all by herself, but was eager to learn from Vicky first.

On the Saturday evening the downstairs household and the upstairs one, along with the guest-cook gathered in the dining-room next to the kitchen to consume a meal of wild mushroom, chestnut and sage pasta followed by what Vicky called an 'easy' lemon chicken with olives, which had been Moira's choice. Vicky was an expert with herbs and spices. Moira had at first thought beef would be nice, like that meal in *To the Lighthouse*. She'd have to try that another day.

The heavenly scent of cooking greeted Kit Macdonald when he arrived. Vicky, looking up from adding the olives to the chicken, thought again what a good-looker he was, even better-looking than his brother. Not superlatively tall, he had darkish wavy hair, and the most gorgeous grey eyes.

Moira had set the table and was carrying and stirring and watching Vicky do her stuff. She looked up at the newcomer and was immediately struck by his quiet presence. She too saw his beautiful eyes. Their expression was, she thought, as she surreptitiously glanced at him again when he was talking to his brother, quite unconsciously intense. She tried to remember the name of an actor who looked a bit like him. But Kit wasn't an actor, and he appeared unpretentious, and friendly towards everyone. Perhaps he looked more in Vicky's direction than in anyone else's. Goodness, any man would be bound to fall for Vicky, who was so easy-going yet sophisticated, and had such a commanding presence.

Magisterial in a blue-and-white striped apron, Vicky was looking as cool as a cucumber, whereas Moira felt hot and bothered and useless. She had done her bit by providing the bottles of wine Martin had advised her to buy.

'If we need any more I shall bring some up from my cellar,' he'd offered.

The first course was ready when they were, the Parmesan ready to sprinkle on. Kit was now formally introduced to Moira in case he had forgotten who she was. He had appeared to believe at first that Vicky was a professional cook employed by his brother. Moira was allowed to sit down for a moment.

'Vicky *is* a professional,' Anna said, having heard from her sister more of Vicky's versatile career.

'You must take it up professionally again then,' said Kit. Moira thought: perhaps it doesn't pay very well, and Vicky would really rather be a secretary. She wished she had so many useful talents herself. 'As a matter of fact,' said Vicky, about to echo her thoughts, 'nowadays if you have a little business of your own, doing dinners can earn you a decent sum, but it's the large business functions that pay most in England. I prefer cooking for a small number.'

'The return of the domestic servant?' said Martin as they began

132

their wild mushrooms which Vicky had found at the farmers' market.

Perhaps Vicky would think they should be paying her?

'Vicky is a guest at her own dinner party!' Anna said hurriedly.

'Moira's guest too,' said Martin and Kit looked closely at Moira for the first time.

Was he finding it all rather confusing? He might not be sure which woman lived upstairs, Moira thought; he's probably wondering why I'm here.

'Its Moira's party,' said Anna. 'Vicky's a guest too.'

'She's showing me how to cook!' said Moira.

'I don't cook as much as I'd like in my own flatlet,' Vicky added. 'It's a treat to have such a large amount of space in which to operate.'

'You like doing it too much for pleasure to want it as a career?' asked Kit. They were all eating with many expressions of delight, and the cabernet sauvignon had been opened, which would also go with the next course.

'I'd rather operate a word processor at work and escape at half past five,' Vicky explained. 'Cooking should be a joy, not a chore.'

Both Anna and Moira looked sceptical but said nothing, and the conversation turned to exploiting one's talents and living off what one liked doing.

Martin described his idea of one day buying and working a small French vineyard – or even perhaps one in England. There were several less than sixty miles from London, in both Kent and Essex.

Kit, who had appeared a little abstracted, though he had looked · closely at Vicky as she was speaking, obviously made an effort and turned to Moira.

'I hear you are a librarian?'

'A children's librarian.'

'I didn't know they had special librarians for children.'

'It's a big growth industry: "Books for Kids",' said Martin.

Moira plucked up her courage.

'Sometimes,' she said, 'I wish I could just write books for them rather than spend my time encouraging them to read.'

It was sufficiently unusual for Moira to voice a definite opinion or feeling, that her companions regarded her with serious faces.

'Then they could read *your* books!' exclaimed Anna. 'My mother reads heaps of children's books. She reviews them for some parents' magazine.'

Mrs Walker was just the kind of person who would be a reader of children's books, thought Moira. I must ask her to come to my next dinner-party if I ever dare to do the cooking myself upstairs.

Of all the new people she had met since arriving in London, Moira thought she probably had most in common with Janet Walker. More than with people of her own age, even with Anna and Emma and their friends. She'd always got on well with older people. This brought back sudden memories of Dennis, and she made an effort to banish them by explaining more about children's reading to Kit Macdonald. He really had the most beautiful eyes, and they had a kind expression. She wondered if he was aware of their effect. TD had had a different sort of charm, perhaps to do with his mental rather than his physical equipment. But Kit must be clever, too.

Kit was now politely asking Vicky where she had found the fresh herbs and she was being pleased to inform him that Moira had found some in the garden here which would do for next year, but that the mushrooms and sage today were from the local farm market, held each Sunday morning.

Moira thought how very down to earth Vicky Winterbon was, and imagined Anna still did not quite know what to make of her. She and Martin had been told that Vicky would love to have the basement flat, but Anna was worried about what rent to ask for it. If Vicky could contemplate running a car she might be financially better off than Moira, who paid £300 a month. Her mother had been amazed that this was actually less than the going rate in Blackwich for a room, plus kitchenette and tiny bathroom.

'When I was first in London I paid *two guineas* a week for my bed-sitter,' Janet had told her daughters.

'*Oh, Mother!*' Their usual response.

'That was forty years ago,' Emma had said, and Martin had added: 'You can get six hundred pounds a month for a small flat-let round here.'

Anna knew she and Martin would need the money when she gave up work, and hoped Moira's finances were in a satisfactory state. She liked her more and more as time went by. Such a restful person. Whenever she met her on the stairs, or going in or out, she felt it incumbent upon her to say 'Hello', and usually to ask if she had all she needed. Being an extrovert, conversation came as easily to Anna as breathing. Janet had not revealed the whole story of Moira's long affair, but had hinted at something unsatisfactory. It was not necessary for them to know the whole story. Moira would probably open up to Anna one day. People usually did to her younger daughter.

'Moira is so quiet it makes me feel a bit guilty that she might be lonely,' Anna had said only yesterday to Martin.

'You're being over-sensitive, darling,' he replied. 'She'll make a life for herself.'

'But I've never been a landlady before.' She was thinking about all this now; pregnancy seemed to sharpen all your impressions of other people and your reactions to them. If Vicky Winterbon did come to live in their the basement, *she* wouldn't need to be worried about. Vicky was obviously capable and was making an impression on beautiful Kit this very moment, for she saw his eyes following her when they brought in the pudding. How stupid men could be. Not Vicky but Moira would be just the right woman for him!

The party went off very well. They stayed downstairs in the sitting room for coffee and Kit went back on his motor scooter to his digs in Brickley after midnight. Moira had noticed that he took only two glasses of wine.

'Next time you are doing the honours,' he said to Moira and Vicky, 'I shall book a taxi in advance.'

In bed that night Anna told Martin more of her thoughts about Moira.

'Darling, you are as bad as Emma,' said her husband.

'Emma? I don't think my sister cares about matchmaking.'

'I mean the novel, love. Jane Austen's *Emma*!'

'My wits have slowed down,' she said. 'Vicky is a bit mysterious,' she went on 'What do you really think of her? I'm sure your brother is smitten.'

'It must be her cooking,' said Martin, who was used to all the young women he had ever met, except for his wife, falling for his handsome older brother.

135

11

The New Year came and went. Anna gave more thoughts on her tenants to her mother one Saturday afternoon in January. Martin had had to go into work for some unforeseen emergency and after she had done the shopping she went home for a cup of tea and a piece of cake and then telephoned Janet, wishing she could just pop in to their old home.

She was always hungry now. After answering her mother's questions about the state of her health and how soon she could go on maternity leave, Anna changed the subject to that of Moira and Vicky.

'You *must* invite Moira to Deepden. We told her you reviewed children's books and I'm sure she'd like to have a long talk with you.'

'I talked to her quite a bit in the summer,' Janet reminded her. 'As a matter of fact I had already thought of asking her over for the day in spring. I guess she'll miss the countryside more then. I meant to ask her but forgot. I've been trying to tidy up a bit recently.'

Her mother was always in the process of tidying up; it seemed to solve some atavistic need to start afresh every season or so.

'Has she said anything to you about wanting to get out of London?'

'No. She went to Yorkshire for Christmas, but not for long. I think she's still getting acclimatized. I'm sure she'd love a day out in better weather,' replied Anna, feeling she wouldn't mind a day away herself. Now that Christmas had passed, she also wanted her parents' honest opinion about letting their basement to Vicky Winterbon. After all, in theory the house still belonged to Tom. It was clear that Vicky would still very much like to rent it, but no offer had as yet been made. Moira reported that Vicky would need to give at least a month's notice to the owner of the hairdressing salon who also owned the two bed-sitting rooms above.

Martin said that as far as he was concerned they could eventually offer her the basement when he had finished improving it. There were still a few matters to attend to. He thought it had previously been a mixture of kitchen and storeroom. Vicky had, perhaps deliberately, not yet asked directly whether it was available.

After a few days back in Blackwich, her short visit north over Christmas to stay with Aurelia and her husband and children seemed like a dream to Moira. She had let slip to Anna that she had spent most of the time helping to amuse Aurelia's toddler, as well as baby-sitting on two evenings, wanting to help her old friend.

'I'm fond of the little boy but it's a very exhausting age!' she said. Anna thought she looked tired – it had scarcely been a holiday. Moira did not tell her that she had felt a bit of an outsider in Ilkgate. Strange how quickly you got used to a new way of life.

'I found it a lot colder up there,' she said. 'I must be getting spoilt by soft southern ways.'

Anna introduced the subject of Vicky and the basement to her father on the phone.

'The main thing is, do you like her?' Tom said. 'You can't expect to know someone's habits well unless you live in the same house – and not even then.'

'Well I didn't know much about Moira before either but it's working well.'

'Your mother knew Miss Banks's judgement was to be trusted,' he said. 'Your Miss Winterbon seems a jolly sort of girl.'

'Emma thinks she is a very practical woman who always lands on her feet,' his daughter replied.

Janet came on the line.

'Is the basement quite ready for a tenant?'

'Nearly, and I'm sure Vicky would be a help to us when the baby comes – especially if the rent were lower than usual. She's just bought a little car, so when Martin is away Emma thinks she might collect groceries for us – that sort of thing – and might even enjoy doing a bit of cooking. But that may be Emma's idea of my future incompetence with an infant.'

'I don't think you should mention *anything* to Vicky about reducing the rent in exchange for help!' exclaimed Janet. 'Emma is rather inclined to make assumptions about willing helpers. Just look on her as a tenant. Does Moira get on with her? Not that they need to be thrown together.'

'Oh, they already know each other quite well.'

'What does Martin think?'

'He's quite agreeable. We do *know* her now.'

'What are you worried about?'

'Nothing, really. I just had the idea that things had gone so well so far that . . . I didn't want to do anything that might spoil the set-up. It's probably just being pregnant that's making me a bit anxious – perhaps I am too contented.'

'You think this young woman might be a cuckoo in the nest?'

'She seems so *capable*. Too good to be true.'

'It's nothing to worry about! But don't expect her to be a sort of au pair. The basement has its own entrance – and you needn't be all that matey so long as she pays the rent. Have a three-month trial period on both sides; it's what you suggested to Moira, isn't it?'

Anna relied on the whole on her mother's judgement, unlike her sister who thought their mother worried about all the wrong things, like air crashes.

'Have a chat with Moira, will you? You could just ask her how she's getting on and bring in the subject of Vicky quite casually,' suggested Anna.

'I'd love to have Moira over for the day,' replied Janet. 'I'll give her a ring tonight if you think she'll be in. I told you I intended for ages to ask her. If you think she'd like that – she's probably too busy.'

'She'd love to, I should think. She doesn't go out a lot especially at night, and she misses trees and fields.'

I bet that Vicky will go out more, thought Janet.

In this she was not quite correct. Vicky did not visit London theatres or galleries very much, preferring to exercise. She had a little car now for her work journey, which, fortunately, was against the tide of the traffic. Whether she had a boyfriend was unknown.

'*You* must make the most of getting out to theatres and concerts with Martin before you have the baby, Anna. You'll find it much harder later.'

Not if I have two willing sitters, thought her daughter.

Little did she realize what living with a baby was like, thought Janet when she had put the phone down. If she had been anything to go by herself, new mothers were very reluctant at first to entrust their baby to anyone but themselves. It had been five months before she and Tom had had an evening away from the house after Emma was born. They had been more relaxed with their second baby. But some mothers now had no choice, and had to put their babies into crèches the minute they could. Some newspapers crusading against child neglect implied they were doing their children a disservice whilst others trumpeted the value of 'social interaction'. The use of crèches for tiny babies must often be against their mothers' inclinations. Childminders, though, who often had children of their own and were more experienced, were useful for part-time workers. She was secretly glad that these alternatives had not been so readily available thirty-five years ago.

Janet was as good as her word and telephoned Moira, feeling she owed Moira a day in the country indirectly to thank Bridie Banks for putting them in touch with each other. Bridie had not been able to see Moira on her flying visit north at Christmas as she had been away, and she would be pleased to hear news of her.

'In my opinion she's settled in really well,' she said to Tom. Perhaps Moira had already written to her old teacher. She telephoned Moira.

'Tom and I would love you to come over to Deepden, any Saturday or Sunday, whenever you feel like getting out of London. Tom can meet you in the car at the station halt, it's only a mile away.' They chatted for a time and then Moira said suddenly, surprising Janet:

'When I left from King's Cross at Christmas and when I came back, I remembered your description of coming back from the north long ago. It didn't feel *different* enough to be returning from another world. I can just imagine how steam-trains made people feel. Yorkshire still is a different country, though I suppose not as different as it used to be.'

Janet had forgotten what she had said about the old station and the old journey, and was surprised that Moira had remembered. She seemed to understand how in the last twenty years an older person found that everywhere had become like everywhere else.

'Real journeys are always into the past,' she said now, quite surprising herself.

Janet found Sunday afternoons less melancholy than Sunday

139

evenings. The evening feeling must have come from long ago, before she was married, or before she had the children, when she had dreaded the inevitable next day's return to the difficult teaching-post that she was not enjoying. Afternoon melancholy had dissipated once she was busy looking after her children, or had returned to temporary and part-time teaching-posts, off and on in various establishments, until she was sixty. Now that there was less compulsion to be busy, Sundays seemed an irrelevance, and yet she still wanted them to be different from other days.

'You ought to go to church,' said Tom, a little unsympathetically.

'Or for a walk,' she answered.

This they sometimes did if it were not raining. If it were, she tried to remember to accomplish some mild yoga stretches. She ought to have more free time now than in days gone by, but the Protestant work ethic, not the Sabbatarianism of her childhood, insisted she did the washing, tidied the apartment, wrote letters, and cooked one decent meal on that day. Ironing appeared to have become a Sunday job too, like the short walk.

When they had had a garden of their own, Sunday was the day for mowing the lawn. Tom had grumbled that he was nothing but a suburban husband, yet there was something comforting about Sunday rituals when melancholy was banished until evening. Reading was for both of them an everyday pleasure, but the plethora of Sunday journalism was now off-putting. How could people ever say they were bored? Melancholy was not *ennui*. Even without television and radio and newspapers there was so much to fit in. Pottering around her indoor plants or sketching with her oil-pastels were, she supposed, Sunday activities too.

Life had resolved itself into routine as it did for most people. Emma always telephoned them dutifully on a Sunday. Greta Allot and the other retired couple, and the middle-aged family who lived at Deepden Court did not make a cult of sociability, which suited Tom. In summer, they might exchange a few words from strategically placed deckchairs. There was no communal sitting-room, except for the lawn in summer. Every three months, an old billiard-room was used for meetings of the tenants with the managing agent of the ground landlord, when complaints or suggestions for repairs were voiced to him. They all had long leases of their well-restored house.

So far all had gone well; there had been problems about the roof before the Walkers had moved in, but recently, there had been no property headaches. A retired villager, Herbert Wood, kept up the gardens with the help of volunteers, of whom Janet was not usually one unless her conscience pricked.

Sunday was also a good day for listening to their compact discs or to the radio, and now and then watching an evening television programme. Janet had recently discovered that the best concerts on the radio were in the middle of the night. She had listened to the new classical music station at its inception in 1995 when the wavelengths had been full of birdsong, but then become irritated by its one-movement-only-rule, and its advertisements. Her more technical or up-to-date friends still enthused over the fascination of computers, and this 'spider's web' idea, or whatever it was. Tom had an Apple Macintosh to which he transferred ideas for his satire, but Janet had never found machines of any sort at all friendly. But she did not like to fail to understand anything and intended to enrol at the village hall for computer classes. Good intentions, however, had not yet been realized. Others from Deepden House might play bridge in the same hall. Neither she nor Tom was a card player.

A fortnight after Janet had invited her, Moira was to come to spend Sunday with them.

'It'll be a nice change for you,' Anna said.

That morning there had been a sudden burst of sunshine and almost springlike weather. The journey was not a long one and Moira had looked forward to getting out of London. She knew she would feel comfortable with Mrs Walker.

Tom met her and drove her through Hookden village to Deepden Court set back at the far end of a lane off the main street. He pointed out a little wood in the distance.

'Next village – lovely churchyard – nice in summer,' he said, before handing her over to Janet, who said when she arrived:

'Do call me Janet – everybody does,' and deposited her with a tray of coffee in the large sitting-room. Tom disappeared to his small corner room at the back which he called his study, but which had been originally intended for a dining-room. He thought his wife would prefer to talk to Moira alone before lunch. The meal of home-made soup, cold chicken and salad, Gruyère and fruit, was ready in the kitchen, where they usually ate. Janet liked to prepare even cold meals in good time; she was not one of those women who like to cook whilst chatting to a guest; it made her far too flustered. Tom brought up from his wine cupboard in the communal basement one of the bottles of claret that Martin had given him.

A nice girl, Moira Emsley, he was thinking, then remembered Janet was always telling him girls did not like to be called girls nowadays, it was not politically correct. All nonsense, he thought. There were 'boys and girls' and 'youths and girls' as well as 'men and women' and 'old boys' and 'ladies and gentlemen.' Changing the habits of a lifetime, being ordered to call people by new names was one of the things that had made him want to write his satire. . . .

Moira did remind him of his wife years ago. Not the personality, more the occasional remark about a book or some idea, and his feeling that inside the nunlike demeanour she must have had a 'past'. Not that Janet had appeared nunlike. Janet said she was an original, but Moira did not say anything odd or pretentious to him on the way. He liked her lack of pretension, shared it himself.

'I hope you feel completely settled at Hall House,' Janet remarked as she poured the coffee out. Without waiting for an answer she went on, as was her wont: 'I was interested in what you said about the station. How did you find Yorkshire at Christmas? Did it make you feel sad to have left?'

Janet was very like Anna, thought Moira; she was 'taking an interest'.

'A little, I suppose. My friend Aurelia – Miss Banks taught her too – was very busy with her family, and it all felt different – not 'belonging' any more. I mean, I do belong there and always will in a way, but it made me realise my *home* isn't up there any longer.'

She was happy, then, at Hall House.

'I went to see my old landlady, but Miss Banks was away. I've just had a letter from her. She sent her love to you; I forgot to tell you on the phone. Other people my age had mostly already left long before I did, so apart from my friend Aurelia there's nobody to miss. I feel I belong now to a past place. Even in the time since I came to London, things have altered. I suppose you notice them more when you've been away for a bit.'

'I know. When I go "home" now I find some things so different that they aren't home any more.'

'Some places don't change so much though, do they. Moors and woods – although they must change over a century or so?'

'The M62 cut a swath through *my* landscape – children now won't remember its being any different. Did you go into your old library?'

'No, it was closed till the twenty-ninth. I never knew the assistant I worked with very well. I was told they'd got a new man to take over my old post. He's not a specialist.'

'How are you finding Bickdon?'

'Under-funded as far as books are concerned and too many forms and red tape, but the children are fine. *They* are much the same everywhere, aren't they.'

'I suppose they all see the same TV programmes and are bought the same toys as in Ilkgate. But the country air up there must make a difference.'

'Yes, they do look a bit less healthy down here. Children come for books from quite well-off families, but their mothers are less talkative. I have to arrange school visits to encourage the less well-off to join the library. So far only the children from private prep schools are taken there by their teachers. Isn't that a shame!'

'Too busy doing the new national curriculum, I expect.'

'I've rearranged the stock. I've always thought good picture-books are enjoyed by older children as well as babies and toddlers.'

'You can get through to the reluctant readers with good illustrations,' said Janet.

They were well away, talking shop, comparing opinions on the plethora of new 'books for kids'.

'I do wish I could get a few volunteers to sit and read with some of the older children,' said Moira, 'but there isn't the space. We have a toddlers' group and the babies are always well catered for.'

'I don't believe we have that in the village library here, or I'd offer to read. What about your male 'over twelves'?'

Moira groaned.

'A lot of the cash is spent on new videos. They'd never displayed books that might attract boys. It'll be a long haul.'

'Do you never wish you'd trained to be a teacher?'

'I'm not cut out for telling people what to do. I don't mind suggesting and encouraging in my own province, and you get fond of some of the children.' She plucked up her courage and added, 'If you really want to influence society, you can do it more through an individual reading a book than through schools.'

This was so much Janet's own opinion that she warmed even more to Moira.

'I often feel that even if children learn to read, nobody gives them the idea that reading is a *pleasure*,' she said.

'I'd feel too that my wings were clipped in a school. I learned more from books myself than teachers, really. In a library you can smuggle in your own ideas. Even there, though, changes are bound to happen. There's a rumour that in a few years they'll fill the place with computers.'

'Computers. Well, you can't profit from them if you can't read, can you. Or do they intend children to play these games with them that I've read about? Where will most children find stuff to feed the imagination when they grow up?'

'On the other hand we have really old people who take out lots of books – people who left school at fourteen, most likely. Don't you – didn't you – feel when you taught that whatever you did there would always be some people who would have imagination – not always the cleverest – and others for whom, whatever you did, it seemed to make no difference?'

'Yes I did – I do – feel that. Limits exist to what we can do for others. I'm old-fashioned!'

Moira was thinking, like me, but *she* has every reason, being a generation older. . . .

'I wish I could have a poetry evening for the children,' she said. 'I mean, poetry in schools depends on enthusiasts, and some children will never have heard a nursery rhyme, never mind a poem.'

'And no learning by heart much nowadays, either. Let's have a drink.'

What a pleasure it was to talk to such a serious-minded young woman.

She went into the kitchen while Moira looked at the crammed bookshelves. Janet came back with two glasses and a chilled bottle of white wine.

'Do you drive around much to other parts of Kent?' Moira asked.

'Tom drives me. I did have hundreds of lessons but I never sat the test, never mind passed it. My instructor still didn't trust me enough to put me in for it; he said he'd never had a failure yet and didn't intend to start. I've probably forgotten how to drive. I rely on Tom. He isn't a keen driver himself, he thinks cars are just useful, not an end in themselves, but we go on short drives to neighbouring villages in summer.'

Moira was silent, thinking, then she said:

'My father taught me to drive just before he died.'

'Anna really must learn: I don't want her to emulate my incompetence. As Martin is so competent, she might just do that.'

'I was told by Anna that your husband is writing a book,' Moira ventured after a pause.

The statement invited an answer.

'Well, not what you or I might call a *novel* – more a fantasy, or satire. He's motivated by political considerations: he admires Orwell above all. Do *you* write?'

This was the question Janet had been wanting to ask her ever since she had first met Moira on the day of her arrival at Hall House last year.

'Not novels – poems. I mean, I try. Like lots of people, I suppose. I'd be no good at novels. I like developing one thought, playing with words, you know. I've no narrative gifts.'

'I thought you might be a writer. I used to write myself till I found I was no good. I did try children's books but you have to be more . . . childlike, less self-conscious, I suppose, than I am, to do that. Have you sometimes thought of writing for children?'

'Yes, I have thought of it, but so far I haven't discovered the right tone. It's harder than people think.' Moira will succeed one day, thought Janet. Poets often do write well for children. She would love to see some of her work but knew better than to ask. If Moira wanted her to show her anything, she would.

Moira, however, had no false modesty for she answered Janet's unspoken thought.

'I used to write reams but I've only written one or two poems recently that are any good – that I'd want to show anyone, I mean.' Perhaps she couldn't write when she was involved with that man. Moira was probably not the sort of woman who wrote love poems.

'Did the move hold your writing up – worrying about whether to come south or not?' Janet asked.

'I suppose so. I couldn't concentrate enough to get the right words down. I had ideas but they seemed vaporous, even to me. I think the change has been good for me though. London has turned me inward. Isn't that odd? No more hills and dales to look at, so I'm

145

cast on my own resources. I wrote too many 'nature' poems years
ago. I shall write them again one day, but at a distance. Now I'm
thinking more about . . . I don't know exactly . . . little things that
please me or interest me. Like the robin singing every morning this
month in Hall House garden – sometimes all through the night!
Perhaps he thinks the street lamp is dawn – and we have a blackbird
at dusk. I'm quite inspired by the faces of commuters as well. I mean,
extraordinarily ordinary people are really ordinarily *extraordinary*!'

Janet laughed and Moira looked away, feeling a little awkward
over her own eloquence.

The girl had the gift of seeing ordinary things afresh. Just what
she needed, grumbling her life away about her routine and her
chores . . .

'Has Anna said much about the baby?' she asked.

'Oh, yes! I'm so glad for them.'

'Only five more months now. That will be a big subject.'

They laughed.

Now was the time to ask her about Vicky. Janet plunged in.

'I think they will be glad to let the basement now it's finished, and
as the baby will be here in summer . . .'

'Yes. I think Vicky Winterbon wants to rent it. You met her, I
think.'

'Do you think she could afford it?'

'I think so. Of course Martin and Anna could ask more – for my
room too – but I think they want someone they know. I've seen
Vicky's room on the Parade and it's terribly expensive for what it is.
She's really desperate to move, from what she's told me. Of course
it's up to them. Vicky is a very interesting unusual person. She's
done all sorts of jobs.'

'Full of beans, I imagine!'

'Absolutely.'

So that was settled. Janet had done her duty.

Tom came in, and over their late lunch the talk turned to a topic
that might have touched upon Moira's past and the man she called
what sounded like 'Teedee'. Janet noticed that this appellation came
into Moira's description of a walk in the Lake District. No mention
of another name, just 'TD'. Janet was not sure how much Miss
Banks had revealed to her ex-pupil of what she had told her old
friend, so tried not to look too interested.

Moira was actually thinking just then that she wished she could tell Mrs Walker about him; she would not be shocked. Dennis ('TD' was after his initials and he was called that by some of his friends) had said such things to her – outlandish, when she thought about them now here in this haven of calm, and in a household she thought of as 'civilized'.

After lunch they all walked round the garden, noticing the crocuses straggling through the lawn. There was a statue by a red-brick wall which Janet said was a copy of Peter Pan in Kensington Gardens. Moira thought how Dennis had once told her he would like to have a sculptor make a statue of her.

'You are almost as slim as a boy,' he'd said, 'but I'm glad you're not a boy.' She had thought at the time: had he wanted to put her in the garden, like Peter Pan? It had made her shiver; she did not like the notion of having a memento of a past self in such a concrete form. She had even wondered if he had once preferred boys; she didn't think he had, at least not after he had left his boarding-school, but he had not liked older women. She had been only about twenty-four when he'd talked about his sculpture idea.

She did not think about Dennis so much now when she was at Hall House, but in this garden he came back into her mind. She made an effort to discuss Hall House and Yorkshire, and books, and her work, and to try to draw Tom Walker out about his 'satire', but he was not to be drawn.

Dusk came and Moira was taken back after tea by Tom in the car, and dropped at the station. Before her husband returned, Janet sat on the sofa and thought what an extremely pleasant day it had been. Not at all a melancholy Sunday. Moira *was* like her younger self in some ways, more in those ways than either of her daughters. Not at all physically, for Moira was fair and small-boned and her nose was aquiline, her eyes a lighter blue. Anna, with her heart-shaped face and dark-brown hair, looked more like her. Emma was not quite so dark – a 'dark blonde' she had once been called – and she resembled Tom, who had a much thinner face than her own. It was just that Moira's expressed thoughts often seemed to parallel hers. Maybe that was just her imagination. They certainly had similar interests.

She considered Moira and her life in Ilkgate, and what she had been told by Bridie Banks. Moira brought back her own young days. She had often been 'in love' in adolescence and after, but never, before she was twenty-one, had any man been truly in love with her. Some men had lusted after her and she had found some of them attractive, but they were never the ones with whom she fell in love – or was infatuated by. They had never been her heart's desire, and she doubted whether she had been theirs. She had wondered if there was some kind of rule: if you fell in love with – or were infatuated by – someone, that person would never fall in love with you. Infatuation was like wine: it worked for a time, but love made you believe in a constant compatibility.

She had looked around her and seen women friends who appeared to have found their heart's desire in a mutual relationship. How had they managed to find the 'right' man so *quickly* – and one who was also attracted to them? She had asked herself then: how did it work? Were these friends easily satisfied, or did they wait for a man to fall in love with them and then decide to reciprocate? There was a certain injustice in relations between the sexes. Only men were expected – allowed? – to make the first advance in those days, and perhaps even now? It was up to the woman to say yes or no. But *she* had wanted a simultaneous, mutual falling in love. Had she connected it at the time with marriage? She must have done – it was the way they had all been brought up.

A little later she had come to the conclusion that you might not have both together, and that it would be better if people did not marry too young, 'for love'. A pretty face, or a handsome one was a trap, for they did not reveal inner selves, which could then be betrayed. It was a dilemma. A man must have the same problem. When she was almost twenty-two, after an infatuation of the early summer had gone abroad, she had been a bit lonely. It was then that had begun, in late summer, the saga of Neville, all of which Moira had brought back to her.

Neville, to her mingled incredulity and even amusement at first, had declared himself, told her she was remarkable, wonderful, unique. He appeared anguished, perfectly sincere, although he tried to protect this sincerity with a slight irony. That in itself should have told her this was not the first time it had happened to him, and might not be the last. But how could she not have succumbed? Would most young women have declined his advances? He was married of course, over twenty years older. She knew already that something in her appealed to older men. Neville was not the kind of man for whom she had ever entertained romantic yearnings, but she decided she did need experience, and who better than Neville?

For once the boot was on the other foot. Should she decline this amazing opportunity? No, she was impatient, and so she had allowed herself to be claimed. It was not an equal relationship. Neither, she felt sure, had Moira's been with her 'TD'. Four years later Neville was still passionately in love with her and she began to wonder how she could ever free herself. She had tried twice to escape, with men not usually quite as clever as Neville, but more her sort, and younger. Each time she had returned to him, for the young men were certainly not 'in love' with her. Must Neville, in some mysterious fateful way, be meant for her? He certainly thought so.

She had even tried to be the person she thought Neville believed she was. You could not help acting up to someone else's idea of you, as children often ended up doing in their families. Neville's passionate projection of her was of a young ebullient enthusiastic woman. No younger men of her acquaintance had been capable of such projection. Neville told her that young men did not know how to love. He was intense, must always have been so, and always 'in love'. The woman's name might change, but his projection did not change. He was in love with love and with his own feelings, she thought now. Eventually she had wished he were less devoted and slowly she began to find it hard to live up to his idea of her.

Those friends who had found devotion from young men in their early twenties had married them, and must now be grandparents of adolescents. She and Neville could see each other only once or twice a month, though they did take holidays together abroad. It kept love on the boil, but it was a curiously artificial way of living and loving, making sex more important when they did meet, an ideal arrangement for a serially polygamous man, which, she later realized, many but not all men were. Neville was also a romantic, which complicated things for him. In spite of many reservations, she had sometimes wished they *could* marry, to make an end to dependency and the concealments and the mutual agonies. It was impossible; you could not divorce children, and she liked his wife, who was aware of Janet's existence and was prepared to condone it. Neville said he admired his wife, and so therefore must she!

At last she decided to act, and had applied for work abroad. Before she was even interviewed, Neville confronted her yet again.

He had found a prestigious post for himself, this time nearer her. Now he was offering to stay with his family at weekends, and to live with her for the rest of the week. He would buy a flat and they would share it, live together. What would have seemed an exciting solution four years earlier no longer thrilled her. It was not the 'living in sin' that worried her. Her parents were ignorant of the whole affair and she would never tell them; the truth would be more hurtful for them than ignorance. Far from contenting her, a 'married' life that was neither one thing nor the other, had satisfied her not at all. Slowly, with more time together they became slightly estranged; she found some of his opinions and attitudes inimical, and longed for an impossible 'freedom'. No more lovers for her, as long as she lived with Neville. It was the domesticity she liked best, the very thing that had once put her off the idea of marrying for love. But she wanted a child, and Neville did not, had had enough of 'all that'. Men could enjoy themselves for years, did not need to 'settle down'.

She had realized ruefully that she was no longer in love with him. Had she ever been? Had she just been flattered to have a member of the Royal Society in her bed? 'You don't want my child, in any case,' he once said to her brutally, 'You just want your own!' She realized the truth of this.

Eventually they had parted, with pain on both sides, but more on Neville's. She found herself another post, tried to change her habits, felt for a few weeks (what was not then so termed) depressed, when even a hot bath or the taste of a peach no longer filled her with delight. But she also felt relieved, gave herself no time to rest from entanglements, but jumped headlong into one affair after another, none of them serious. She did not think Moira had done that.

Still young, she had decided to renounce for a time the complications of love. Then, quite serendipitously, not long after, she met the man who was to become her husband, Tom Walker, whose key she now heard in the door.

Moira's lover had gone back to his wife. Would he be faithful to her? When Neville died, twenty-five years later, he was 'in love' with yet another young woman.

These old memories were no longer painful. Moira had brought them back. She hoped Moira would recover her own life too.

12

The following week, Moira and Anna had a chat of a different sort from the one Moira had enjoyed with Janet. Martin had had to go to France for a few days, but before he left he and Anna decided to ask Vicky if she would like to rent the basement. Anna invited Moira down for a drink on the second evening of Martin's absence. Dora gave a welcoming mew.

'We've definitely decided to offer the basement to Vicky,' said Moira. 'It's a good idea to have someone we know a little.'

That was just what everyone said.

'It must be thrilling to be expecting a baby,' said Moira, trying not to sound envious.

'Thrilling and terrifying. Martin says people talk about "a baby" but really it's just carrying on the human race.'

'That's true,' said Moira firmly. 'Just what I think too.'

Anna had still not been told all of Moira's story, but she began to wonder whether her recent past might be connected with the loss of a baby, since she spoke so enthusiastically about babies.

'They say a baby makes the biggest change you can ever have in your life,' Anna went on. 'I just wonder how I shall cope. At the moment I'm too busy, rushing round finishing off work and show-ing the temporary assistant what to do. I just can't think coherently. I shall make a big list like mother does the minute I'm free. Next week, though, I want to do something definite – buy a changing mattress and a carrycot . . .'

'Aurelia bought scores of Babygros,' said Moira.

Anna had heard quite a lot about the famous Aurelia.

'Hasn't your friend a lovely name,' she said.

'Have *you* thought about names?' asked Moira politely, but with a secret smile, remembering Aurelia's secret.

151

'Your mother seems to believe it will be a girl.'

'They can easily let us know the sex, but we'd both rather wait and see – have a surprise.'

'Your mother is very interested in names, isn't she.'

'It's one of her hobbies. She didn't know any Annas when they named me until she discovered that two of her old friends had also called their daughters Anna! Mother was rather annoyed – the name must have been in the wind, and there's nothing she dislikes more than being in the fashion. Anyway, *we* thought that if it *is* a girl we might call her Christina. Mother is at present keen on Tatiana, one of the very late lamented Tsar's daughters.' She laughed.

Emma, knowing their mother's tastes, would have said 'Typical', but Moira only looked intrigued.

'Christina goes well with Macdonald,' she said.

'Or Nicholas for a boy,' Anna went on. 'Nick. All rather Russian, I suppose.'

'Aurelia's daughter is Alexandra, but they shorten it to Alix.'

'We mustn't shorten Christina to Tina or Chris. Chrissie would do, I suppose. Martin's brother was always called Kit, though he's a Christopher.'

Moira's heart gave a sudden jump.

'Is it a family name?'

'I don't think so. Unless it was his grandfather. *My* mother says: "Not *Janet*, I beg you – or only over my dead body!" Jane would be OK, though.'

It did not escape Anna's notice that Moira had looked away for a moment when she had heard her mention Kit.

Vicky Winterbon moved into the Hall House basement in March, just three months before Anna's baby was expected. Before Anna left work in April she would find tempting little snacks in her fridge concocted by her new tenant. Later, when she had only a month to wait, Martin said what a good idea it had been for Vicky to come. Their two tenants could hardly be more different, but they appeared to have struck lucky with both of them. If Vicky were going into London on some of her working days she would always ask if there was anything she might get for them, or would drive Anna to the clinic if Martin was at work. Moira was now, with Martin's agreement, planning the garden according to Anna's notions. Daffodils had suddenly appeared and she had discovered many plants still alive under the piles of greenery that she had cleared. She and Anna were happy to see that the rambler and climbing roses they had planted up the back wall of the house and over the garden fences were beginning begin to show dark red and green at the tips of their branches and twigs.

'Next year they'll be in full bud,' Moira said, 'Like your baby!'. She had planted bright pink Zephyrines and pale pinky-orange Cornelias, once grown by her father when she was a child, and trained them round the long french window of the kitchen. Along one side of the garden and over the high fence she had put Gloire de Dijon, wanting the effect of an old-fashioned hedge. Hall House was detached, but built very close to its almost identical twin, a house now split into flats. They hoped the tenants would not mind roses growing over the dividing hedge, and that the owner, a city gent, would be pleased when he next inspected his property. Moira had shown Anna and Martin descriptions and photographs of many other 'old' roses from books she had found that were about to be discarded from the library, as were so many old reference books, to make place for videos and eventually computers. Martin had sent for garden catalogues and had already had planted tall Queen Elizabeths and Icebergs at the bottom of the garden to cover the wall on the lane.

'They grow so tall,' he said.

'Sleeping Beauty thicket,' said Moira.

Anna felt a fraud. She knew very little about gardening though she was determined to learn, and had chosen some newer ramblers – pale pink New Dawn – to go round a pergola which Martin said he was going to build. In the garden proper there were to be Buff Beauties and a glorious old pink rose called Celestial. In a year or two they would all be blooming. Blackwich soil was not rich, but roses did well. Tom had not been a keen gardener; Anna remembered his mowing the lawns of her childhood under complaint. It had been her mother, helped occasionally by Emma, who had done their best in their last, much too large, garden in Blackwich. She had had great success with easy childish flowers like nasturtiums and marguerites, and had always grown roses, and nurtured indoor plants. The Gloire de Dijon was a favourite of her mother.

153

Emma knew more about trees and plants than her sister did but no longer felt she should advise, now that Anna had a husband to do the digging, and tenants to help. She considered Anna rather lazy, but Anna was very much hoping that bringing up a baby would not be as tricky as being a gardener, never mind a good one, for she could not help feeling there might be similarities.

There was so much to learn and you could learn only by doing. In other words, hard graft.

Part Four

CONSEQUENCES

13

When the voices of children are heard on the green
And laughing is heard on the hill
                    William Blake: Songs of Innocence (1789)

That May a Labour government had been elected. Anna did vote
but not one of her close friends or family had that enormous optimism over political change burbled about by the media and found
in some Blackwich activists. She and Martin were awaiting their
own more personal change.

It was a lovely morning in June. It was almost a month since
their second wedding anniversary and the baby was four days
overdue. Anna had very much wanted to have the birth at home
but had been dissuaded – it was no longer encouraged in the
district. There were not enough midwives to go round in the
hospitals, never mind in people's homes, although private
midwives were already beginning to make an appearance. She did
not feel knowledgeable enough to make a fuss and hold out over
a home birth, knowing she was not what they called the Earth
Mother type. Janet said to Tom that she hadn't been that either,
thirty-six years earlier but, as things turned out, could easily have
had Emma at home. They wisely refrained from interfering. They
would have offered a private midwife if necessary.

'In those days, as far as I remember,' said Tom, who had been
with her for Emma's arrival in the world, 'the health service ran
almost hotel standard maternity wards!'

All that had changed, in Janet's view for the worse. 'Like most
other things – except coffee,' she said to Tom. The hospital in the
nearest town centre to Hall House had a reasonably good reputa-

tion and had recently been given a new name. You could even return home the same day if you were so minded.

'Most people stay just one night,' Anna told them.

Forty-eight hours appeared to be the longest any new mother stayed. Tom explained that if you wanted to stay a bit longer, or if there was any problem, you could pay for an amenity bed.

Janet was dismayed to hear how many women returned home within twenty-four hours of delivery. How could they get any rest to prepare them for the onslaught of a full-time and unremitting job, in her own experience much harder labour than giving birth? She remembered ward attendants who arranged flowers, and nurses to instruct in bathing the infant, free nappies, even baby nightdresses provided, stitched with the hospital monogram, and a capable sister in charge.

'You mean people actually arranged and watered your flowers?' Anna was incredulous. 'You must have gone private?'

'Certainly not. It was all on the NHS – admittedly a teaching hospital. They spent a lot of time and patience showing you how to bathe the infant, and weighed the babies every day, sometimes more if there had been any problems. There was a special lady called a lactation officer who called round every day to see if any mothers had problems over feeding!'

Anna giggled over the phone but her mother added: 'I really *enjoyed* the week I was there.'

'*My* friends told me they just wanted to get home!' said Anna.

'Young people never believe what the old tell them about the past,' said Tom soothingly.

Martin was to take a week off.

'He'll ask us if there's anything we can do. After all, two other young women live in the house if they need help,' said Tom.

He had recently changed the name of Hall House from 'Wildfell Hall' to 'The Convent of the Sisterhood' when Martin was away on business in France.

'Soon it will be The Nursery,' he said.

Janet knew full well that a trained nurse was ten times more use than well-intentioned friends, unless they knew about babies, but only the very rich, or women who returned to prestigious jobs, could afford such nannies. 'Of course,' Anna said, 'we don't want a nanny!'

Neither did she want her mother to stay for a few days. 'You know I'll come if you need me,' said Janet, and left it at that. She was quite determined not to be an interfering mother or mother-in-law, and had certainly not wanted Granny Lister taking over when she was Anna's age, not that her own mother had ever offered.

'It was never at all likely,' said Tom. 'Your mother hated any sort of nursing. When she did come to see Emma she was amazed how well you managed!'

Martin and Anna religiously attended natural childbirth classes, which encouraged Janet. The similar movement in England had scarcely begun when Emma was born, so all those years ago she had followed a French system of breathing and coping, and it had worked extremely well. They would wait at home for Martin to let them know when labour started, and when the baby arrived, they'd visit straight away.

'It worries me that so many women are obliged to go back to work so soon after a birth,' Janet observed to Emma.

'Anna won't be one of them – but many women just long to get back to their work.'

'They must be mad.' Janet was always sharper with Emma than with Anna.

With all this baby talk, Emma might feel excluded or neglected but she said she was just relieved not to be involved and liked the idea of being an aunt.

'The world isn't kind to ordinary women,' she added.

Anna was one of the lucky ones with a good husband who had a decently paid job.

Anna spent an ideal late pregnancy basking on her grandly named 'terrace'. Some roses planted there long ago by some previous tenant, or even Great Uncle John, had made an appearance in June, released from years of overgrown jasmine. Dora enjoyed stalking through the garden and leaping in the air after butterflies, or sitting, teeth chattering, when a pigeon ventured to alight. She never caught one. The bell thoughtfully attached by Martin prevented any slaughter. She did demolish a few flies.

'I'd like to add Rose to my baby names, if it's a girl,' Anna told Martin.

'If it's a boy I suppose we could call him Thorn,' said Martin.

As they sat outside their window at Deepden, Janet said to her husband. 'Summer gets earlier every year. Soon we'll be having spring in December.'

'We already do,' Tom said. 'I mention the weather in my satire: global warming, no more seasons – but then *suddenly* the cold returns . . .'

Janet shivered. 'Everything's topsy-turvy. If we had known when we had the children what sort of world it was going to be, would we have wanted them?'

'Well, *you* would,' said Tom.

The imminent birth gave the future grandmother a lot to think about. Martin's mother already had grandchildren. Martin's sister in Norfolk had married young and had two boys.

'In a curious way a daughter's baby seems different from a son's,' she told the Walkers on the telephone. Janet said she would-n't know that. Cora Macdonald had meant it kindly. Grandmothers were stale old news. One of her old friends was already a *great*-grandmother. How had she come to this so late? She knew why.

Never the kind of person who could be relied on to knit exquis-ite baby garments, Janet did remember spending weeks before Emma was born knitting a bright scarlet-and-white pram cover in extremely thick wool on enormous needles, and two pairs of bootees in thick yellow wool. Tom had said she looked so concen-trated that she appeared to be knitting a baby, not a pair of socks. Apart from childhood kettle-holders and egg-cosies, having a baby had been the only impetus for Janet's knitting. She did not feel like adding to her efforts and Anna had no intention whatever of doing so.

Like Emma, when she was a young woman Janet had thought that life with children must be like a perpetual nervous break-down. She remembered telling her mother when she was about twelve that she did not intend to have any offspring. Nora Lister would never admit in so many words that she did not enjoy her life of domestic work and self-sacrifice, but she continually grumbled about it. For her there had been Duty, and there had been Pleasure; the former was motherhood, the latter carefree days in her twen-ties teaching singing, at which she had excelled.

Emma wondered what kind of mother her sister would be. Their own mother had been impatient and quick-tempered but, if they could believe her, certainly less strict, and more indulgent than Granny Lister had been with her. Emma told her sister that children nowadays were allowed even more of their own way than when they were little.

'In shops their parents either deny them nothing, or continuously bawl at them.'

'Emma's getting really spinsterish!' Anna told her husband. It was unusual for her to criticize her sister. Janet was rather amused, for she realized some of the truth of her own mother's old strictures, although Granny Lister's remembered and horrendous puritanism still did not appeal.

'Emma's probably speaking the truth about some children,' said Tom, 'but she won't have to deal with them, will she.'

Janet was looking forward to having a grandchild, and still wished Emma would one day produce. But Emma did not intend to settle down.

'My own grandparents spoiled me,' she said, with a sigh. 'Perhaps it's worth having children just to have grandchildren.'

That summer, for as long as there was sun and not much wind Janet put up a deckchair in the side garden at the Court. Each tenant had a small space at the back or side of the house and sometimes sat under their own window if, like the Walkers, they had a ground floor apartment. The grand sweep of communal grass – the lawns of the old house – was at the front. As she sat in the sun with a book, she found herself again pondering past time as well as thinking about the coming baby. A mixture of Moira's arrival and Anna's imminent future had led her mind back to her own old life. Birth and death concentrated the mind. When her mother died she had had similar thoughts. How differently women might turn out if they had been lucky enough to have an easy-going female parent. Anna's child would be luckier than Anna, as Anna had possibly been luckier than she had been herself. She could not imagine how Emma might cope, but she had chosen not to risk the common fate of many women. Nowadays Emma didn't even need to call herself a feminist. Janet had always suspected that modern feminists were childless.

Now, Vicky Winterbon might have had a casual mother, but in

her case it was her marriage that had failed. So had her friend
Margot's marriage, possibly for a different reason. She had
recently said something about mothers to Margot.

'Oh, my mother was very casual,' said Margot, 'which made me
want to be different, and gave me the ambition to be a doctor like
my father. Fathers have just as much influence in my opinion.'

'Yes, of course they have.' But Janet felt it something of an
achievement to have brought up two women who were not afraid
to do what they wanted. How she would have managed with a son
she would never know. Her generation had not used parental
authority in the way Granny Lister and hers had used it. At every
turn of her own life Janet had had to consider her mother's happiness, which meant never confiding in her. Nora Lister had not
been a happy woman; far back in her childhood Janet had felt
responsible for her happiness. She hoped that neither Emma or
Anna had felt quite so responsible for *her*. She had been ready to
be on her children's side if they had lovers, became pregnant by
accident, but she may have affected them in other ways.
Sometimes she felt mothers couldn't win. 'Mummy is the root of
all evil!' teased Margot.

There were still many young women in this new world of choice
and 'free' sex who did not realize how much their youthful actions
might change the course of their lives. However free young
women thought they were today, they could not release themselves
from making decisions to do with bearing children – or avoiding
them; nor free themselves from the disappointment of wanting
children and not being able to have them. Few had the firmness of
mind to reject all that. It was quite impossible to know all this and
decide the direction of your life when you were still in your twenties.

'Having no choice at all was what had ruined women in the
past,' Margot said.

Yet some had survived, even if they were not all Florence
Nightingale, and had paid for their survival by doing without the
kind of existence they really wished for. Money widened choice,
and a different kind of freedom was in the possession of smart rich
women who had the tails of their last affairs tucked neatly behind
them; these were the kind of women she could never have been.

Janet lay back in her deckchair in the sun pondering these

jumbled impressions. Finding Mr Right – or Mrs Right, for the same might apply with lesser force to men – was not the answer to all life's problems. She thought of Margot again, who lived alone in a small house in Hookden. Deserted by her husband in late middle age, and subsequently divorced, she had formerly had a good career in medicine, but in Janet's opinion still felt guilty that her marriage had failed. Like perpetual mourners, many divorced people, who would formerly have been named as the innocent party, appeared to feel obscurely guilty, as well as angry. Why should this be so? Was it an early induction into the religion she herself had rejected, but which Anna had quite freely espoused?

Why am I so sorry for Margot? she wondered. Is it because she was a man's woman in spite of her professional qualifications, and should be basking in a satisfactory, if unexciting, married life. Gillian, another friend of her youth, had been another 'man's woman', of the kind she herself had never been. She had succeeded in a career at the Bar, but she had never married and had confessed that being admired by men did not preclude repeated romantic disappointments. In the end they became inoculated against love and did not fear to stand alone. Maybe Emma would be like that. It was not a cheerful thought.

Now Anna always made her feel more cheerful. Lucky Anna, and lucky Martin too. But men's lives were not balanced on a narrow ledge, depending upon who was going to throw them a rope. They either took pleasure where it was offered – as some, perhaps many, women did nowadays – or they married late, and were still able to have offspring. Margot had married young, and Janet remembered that her own mother had approved of her. Gillian had not been approved of. Neither had Janet herself until she had married Tom, a 'suitable man', and thus taken the route to approval. Without Tom, would she be an independent, single, retired, pensioner, rather than the epitome of respectability – a future grandmother? If she had been more talented, as she imagined Moira was, would she have risked becoming a single parent, thus breaking her mother's heart – and already have become a great-grandmother? She sat on in her deckchair, her book open on her lap but ignored. Well, if you will ask yourself silly questions you'll get silly answers, and you don't need answers to questions in your life when your life has already decided for you. It was just that you wished you could pass on some of your experience to others. But Tom said: 'You can't learn from other people's experience!' Tom had never thought it worthwhile to invest too much thought in other people's personal problems. Changing society was more important.

At the moment of Anna's marriage in church she had been glad, pleased for Anna, and relieved. If Anna was happy, then so was she, if human beings could ever draw a line under their lives and call themselves happy.

She would try to devote her thoughts in future to the next generation. The baby could not choose not to be born; the household over at Hall House would irrevocably change; the next generation and the next would inevitably take over. A baby would grow up to be both sad and happy.

'In my beginning is my end,' she quoted to herself, except it isn't mine now, but someone else's. T.S. Eliot, the poet who had written that time present and time past were both present in time future, and that the future was contained in time past, was probably not thinking about the result of youthful decisions. He sounded as if there had never been any 'choice'. Neither had he had any children in the real world to prove or disprove his words in the physical reality of lives.

14

Margot Denton had gone to live in Hookden before the Walkers had made the decision to leave Blackwich, and this had been one of the reasons for Janet suggesting that a move to Deepden Court might be a good idea. The two women would meet from time to time over a mug of coffee, and Janet was at Margot's the morning after her long day of wasteful introspection. It was the very week the new baby was expected, and she was enjoying a gossip with her.

Margot had lived alone for the past ten years. Her son and his family lived in Edinburgh at present but she had many friends. Being a most public-spirited woman, she had done various kinds of voluntary work after her retirement.

This morning Janet had left Tom trundling along to the general store, pushing his shopping trolley, what a friend's grandchild called the 'old ladies' pram'. Tom insisted he needed the exercise every day even if it was only to buy a packet of matches for his pipe. When Janet went shopping in the nearest town it was always with a long list; she did not trust herself to remember every essential item. There was no shopping for her today and so she was calling on Margot, who was looking rather drawn when she opened her door.

'I'm very much in favour of babies,' Margot said. 'Keep your fingers crossed – James tells me he may be 'relocated' in Croydon! I'd see a lot more of Toby!'

'How old is he now?'

'Nearly five, and every time I see him he's changed. You forget how quickly they grow up. Of course you can't wait for them to grow up when they're toddlers, but . . .'

'Yes. I know exactly what you mean.'

'People forget a baby isn't just a baby but immediately a new member of the human race. If you're, on balance, in favour of *that*, you must be in favour of babies.'

'I'm on the whole, as you say, in favour of the human race, though I must say I do wonder sometimes whether the Christians aren't perhaps right about original sin. I suppose we do deserve to continue?' said Janet, taking off her distance glasses which she was trying to get used to when out for a walk.

'Twentieth-century developments have rather dented my own faith in progress too,' said Margot. 'Except for improvements in medicine.'

'We thought the last war was the one to end all wars, but then, our parents thought the Great War was that.'

'Agreed. But as far as medicine is concerned, I was going to tell you. I had a mammogram a fortnight ago, even though they don't call you up after sixty-five. They've just told me I have to go in again for another look.'

'They think there may be something wrong?'

'Possibly. They call it 'calcification', but I know what that usually means. There might be a small cancer there.'

'Oh, I am sorry. But if you catch it early . . .'

'Yes, I know, just when I had the good news from James.'

No wonder she'd been looking worried.

'Well, I certainly think *you* deserve to continue,' said Janet, feeling indignant on behalf of her friend. 'Please let me know how you go on. When do you go in for them to have another look?'

'Tomorrow. It's only outpatients.'

Janet went home in a sombre mood. Yet hadn't a cynical Frenchman once said that we may find something even in the misfortune of friends that does not entirely displease us? Did he mean we are so glad it is not ourselves to whom it has happened? As we are superstitious however, we reject the thought as ignoble.

The following day, Janet was sitting in the sun again when she heard the telephone suddenly shrill from inside the house. She staggered to her feet in a daze and dashed inside to the cool room where it was still ringing. Tom was out at the library. When she heard Martin's voice, she felt suddenly calm.

'It started early this morning about five o'clock. We came in by car. They say the baby should be here by teatime.' He sounded breathless.

'Is she all right?'

'Yes. We'll let you know as soon as it's over.'

'Give her my love.'

Let present time hurry on into the future and little Anna be safe. Janet remembered her own labours, which she had felt were miracles. All the women she knew had warned her about pain . . . and although it had not been exactly painless it had been so exciting. Only eleven hours from first twinge to: 'It's a girl'.

She hurried around waiting for Tom to return, and packed an overnight bag for them. It had been arranged for them to stay for the night at Hall House. Then she sat down, willing things to be as easy for Anna as they had been for her the day Emma was born. Tom had been there the whole time. So much for the people who stated that in the early nineteen sixties, fathers had not been allowed to be with their wives at the birth of their children. Tom had timed everything and they had studied the pages of the French breathing charts, which traced lines that looked like humpy hills on the first page and high Everests on the last. Much later, she had thought that the two of them must have looked rather sweetly earnest and comical to the old-fashioned and rather posh obstetrician, a Mr Fox who poked his head in once or twice to say: 'Labour means pain,' looking slightly disappointed not to be needed. The breathing exercises worked excellently and kept her mind from thinking about the next upheaval.

She had soon found herself wheeled into the delivery room where she chatted away to a young doctor whose fourth attendance at birth it had been. The second stage had taken its time. The midwife was a sort of cheerleader, which she remembered thinking at the time was not really necessary. Exactly one hour and twenty minutes after entering the green walled delivery room there was a real baby in her arms, a little body covered in white waxy stuff. The child gave a few yells, then calmed down and went to sleep.

'A miracle birth,' they had said later in the nurses' home, reported excitedly by a neighbour's cousin who worked there. A whole week then to receive friends and eat grapes, smell the flowers brought by visitors and read the telegrams. She fed Emma with no trouble at all, and had been amazed. After this, she had decided that perhaps she was rather good at giving birth. She had expected to be extremely bad at it, as bad as she she was at ballet and riding and swimming and skating. Barely two years later, she enjoyed doing it again, even more quickly, the day little Anna arrived. Such reserves of patience you had to draw upon if you were not a 'natural' mother, that patience she had been thinking about the other afternoon. Reserves you never believed you had, and which nobody else would notice if they did not know how impatient you usually were.

She made some tea, still thinking about her daughters' arrival in the world, and welcomed Tom back with the news.

They waited. And waited and waited.

When the phone had still not rung again and it was already six o'clock she began to worry. Martin was very reliable. There must have been a hitch. By this time the baby should have arrived. She was in a fever of apprehension with a migraine building up, far more nervous than when it had happened to her. She wore Tom out saying. 'He should have telephoned by now.' At seven o'clock the phone rang. She seized it. 'It's OK,' Martin said, 'took a bit longer than they thought – the cord was round the neck, but all's well. By the way it's a girl – eight pounds one ounce. Do come over as soon as you can – stay over at Hall House tonight as we arranged. Anna's having a wash – she's going to spend the night here.'

It took less than an hour to get into south London by car at this time of the evening. They were lucky with the traffic and arrived before half-past eight.

There were three people in the recovery room: Anna sitting up in bed, Martin hovering around with a camera, and in a little cot at the end of the bed a white bundle with pristine white mittens.

Janet went straight up to Anna and kissed her, then went to look at the infant who was asleep.

'They nearly had to give me an epidural,' said Anna, 'but it was too late. God, it was pretty hairy!'

'She's a lot bigger than you were,' said Janet, as Martin went into a long explanation of unprepared midwives and nobody realizing why the baby was stuck.

'But he was very calm and held my hand,' added his wife. The baby appeared to have woken up for she was now kicking her legs vigorously under the cot cover.

Janet took several photographs.

'Does she look all right?' asked Anna

'Perfect. Enormous!'

'Christina Rose Jane!' said Anna. Anna had insisted that 'Jane' stood in for 'Janet'.

'Pluperfect!' said Martin.

'She looks very strong and active,' Tom said. He was a grandfather. He looked pleased.

'I am married to a grandfather!' said Janet.

At two or three hours old Christina was certainly energetic. She was moving her legs vigorously as though she were on a bicycle. No wonder the cord had wound itself round her neck!

Janet could not remember if Emma had kicked like that. She thought not. But Emma had always been the quiet one.

'She's a very active personality, you can see that already,' she said fondly. 'You must have a really good rest now.' I told her there was nothing to it, she thought, but each birth, like each individual, is different. 'I'm sorry you had such a hard time.'

'If they'd known what was happening they'd have done something,' said Anna. 'Martin had to fetch the consultant. He took one look and gave me an injection. I ought to have guessed – she turned somersaults all last week.'

'They're very understaffed,' said Martin. 'The baby's heart was just beginning to show signs of strain when they got her born with the *ventouse*. Out she came and all was well.'

'The tests they did a quarter of an hour after she was born were all normal,' added Anna.

'Anna decided she'd stay the night and morning in a private room,' said Martin, looking up from opening a bottle of champagne in the sink. 'We both thought that would be a good idea.'

Glasses were handed round.

'Everything seems a bit muddly here – and I was told by a woman I was at classes with that the wards are terribly noisy,' said Anna. 'I want to get home tomorrow, but at present I feel like I've been in a battle.'

'They used to take the babies away to the next room,' said Janet.

'Well nowadays they leave them in a cot next to you all night. I keep thinking, is there something I should be doing?'

'Relax,' said Janet, guessing how she must feel after a difficult birth – relieved but a little in limbo.

After a telephone call to Emma who expressed her delight that 'it' was a girl – and more kisses and drinks and photos and talk,

Janet and Tom decided to leave them all in peace. As they went out, two nurses came in to take the baby and its parents up to a private ward.

Tom and Janet stayed overnight at Hall House and Martin, having returned home after midnight, left again early next morning to organize the return of his wife and daughter. Janet had slept well, she felt both excited and exhausted. She remembered not getting a wink of sleep the night her babies were born and wanting to sit up and write about it all.

She and Tom left everything ready at Hall House, the fridge full, the cradle standing in the big bedroom, the garden looking lovely in the sun through the windows. If Anna needed any help on her return it would be forthcoming. Janet understood her own daughter well enough to know she would not be too proud to ask. But Martin was a confident sort of person and already appeared as much in charge as Anna needed him to be.

Moira had been told the news by Janet, and came into the kitchen with some flowers to ask if there was anything else she could do to help. Vicky had gone off to work leaving a message on the hall table: *Write list of any groceries etc you need and I'll buy them.* After a hurried breakfast they arrived back at the hospital at half-past ten and went up in the lift to the private wing. The room was pleasant, long windows looking out over flowerbeds and a carpark.

Anna was sitting on the bed looking a little pink-nosed and an elderly midwife was walking up and down holding the baby over her shoulder.

'Mrs Andrews has been very helpful,' said Anna. 'She's shown me how to put on disposable nappies.'

'No terry towelling provided,' Janet said to the lady, 'and no washing. Aren't they lucky.'

She suppressed a lurking conviction that these easier contraptions might not be an ideal answer as far as the environment was concerned. Then she remembered that she'd used a nappy service and thus escaped the worst. Mrs Andrews smiled.

'Baby and mother are going home this afternoon after lunch!' she said.

'She's had hers,' added Anna pointing to the infant, and looking more cheerful. 'I've begun to feed her – she seems to know what's what.'

'No milk yet though,' said the midwife. 'Plenty tomorrow.'

Christina burped out a peculiar yellowy fluid, which worried Janet a bit.

'It's what she swallowed yesterday,' said the midwife sagely. It must be one result of the long labour. Anna was obviously still concerned with the previous day's events for she said, with a catch in her voice:

'Honestly, I thought she would never get born.'

Janet embraced her daughter.

Anna turned to the maternity nurse.

'The baby seems all right though, doesn't she?' she asked.

Janet saw that she needed reassurance.

'All this morning's tests were fine,' Mrs Andrews replied. 'No damage done from the long wait. You've a fine, healthy, big girl.'

Martin came in just then from the accounts office and began to pack up various things in a box, and to shut a suitcase. He looked up. 'Anna had twinges all the evening and night before,' he said, 'so really it was nearly twenty-four hours in all.'

Mrs Andrews turned to face Janet, the baby comfortably slung over her broad back.

'I heard all about it,' she said. 'She couldn't push because the bairn was stuck.'

The baby was looking over at her grandmother. The mittens were off and you could see an almost bald head with just a fine grazing of fair hair on the crown.

'In the old days they'd have seen to that,' Mrs Andrews went on, 'not go on telling her to push. But if you don't complain they leave it be. We're very short of midwives and many of them are agency ones.'

'At least I didn't have to have a caesar,' said Anna. 'Only a *ventouse.*'

'She didn't make a fuss,' said Martin, sounding proud of her and more concerned with his wife than his daughter. 'Anna's strong, but the little one was struggling with the blasted cord round her neck.'

They meant the infant was nearly strangled.

'Let me take her,' said Janet.

'Go to your grandma then,' said the midwife, startling her a little.

She took Christina and held her against her left shoulder, her

171

palm cupping her head in the same way she had once held her own babies, and sat down in a comfortable wicker chair to cuddle the fair, big-eyed quite heavy child. She stroked the baby's wrist. They said babies responded to touch immediately from day one. She could not remember doing that with Emma at first. It had all been new to her then. They had put the babies into an adjoining nursery for the first night, to give the mothers a rest, and she had heard that they fed them on sugar-water if they yelled.

She felt quite at home holding her granddaughter and for a few moments it was as if she had never gone though the intervening years and was young again. Still, she could not help feeling relieved she would not herself have to devote every minute of the next weeks and months to the new arrival. She had not forgotten how, and could undertake it if it were necessary – but she hoped that being a grandmother was going to be rather less like penal servitude than some aspects of motherhood.

Just then, Emma arrived, having taken a morning off work. Janet handed her the baby for a moment. Emma held her gingerly, exclaiming: 'Fascinating but terrifying!' before handing her back. But she kissed her sister, who was looking happier. She had brought presents, a changing mat, several pink Babygros, and a bottle of Veuve Clicquot, which she instructed Martin to open.

'I took our glasses home,' he said.

Mrs Andrews went to a little cupboard over a washbasin and brought out five glasses. This was certainly the private wing. Janet wondered how much it would cost – it seemed a pity you could no longer have for free what she had had with no extra payment at all for more than a week after her own babies' arrivals.

The atmosphere was relaxed. The champagne cork gave a satisfying pop.

'Uncle Kit called in really early,' said Anna, 'And we telephoned Martin's mother last night.'

'We shall be home by three,' said Martin.

There was a knock at the door. It was Tom, who had been doing a little shopping, since they were to return to Kent later that afternoon.

He was handed a glass. 'It's better than after the last Schools exam,' he said. 'Cheers!'

They drank again to Christina, who had fallen asleep. 'Have you got those bits of things I left in the car?' asked his wife. 'I found them in an old suitcase a few weeks ago and remembered I once knitted them for Emma.'

He produced a brown-paper bag. Janet opened it and held up a pair of bootees.

'They're a museum piece,' she said.

'Whenever did you knit those?' asked Emma. 'I didn't know you even knew how to knit.'

'Before you were born. I was reminded the other day that I used to look as if I was knitting a person. I hadn't forgotten.'

'You always grimaced as if it was a really hard job!' said Tom.

'Well, I haven't knitted anything,' said Anna. 'I should have done, but there never seemed to be any time.'

'You forget I wasn't at work the year before Emma was born. I had all the time in the world to read and do my exercises. A bit of knitting seemed appropriate.'

'She made them yellow, so they'd do for either sex.'

Janet was touched that Tom had remembered. When she looked at the bootees it did seem an awfully long time ago. They were even more lumpy than she remembered.

'I did intend to make a patchwork quilt,' said Anna.

'Ragbags can make good patchwork quilts,' said Emma, quoting something she had once heard her mother say. She was getting ready to leave and go back to work that afternoon. Christina opened her eyes and Emma kissed her and held her tiny finger.

'I can't believe it's all over,' said Anna when her sister had gone. She looked both elated and anxious, if that were possible.

Janet thought it was time for them to go and leave the new family to themselves. Mrs Andrews came in again, wrapped Christina tightly in a small cot sheet and placed her in the little carrycot which was ready for her first journey into the outside world. She did not protest.

Anna and Christina had to get to know each other, needed time alone with the infant and Martin. Nobody else could really teach you how to cope. Here lay Anna's new 'work', her labour of love.

It *was* a shame the way they turfed them out of hospital. Poor girl, she still looked a little shell-shocked, but she'd manage, as almost everybody did in the end. Janet had no desire to take over. She'd be there to be consulted on the telephone, but Martin's leave would allow him to learn how to deal with the baby. Tom had not stayed away from work at all, if she remembered rightly. But of course she'd had a week on the ward.

Christina already looked as if she would be very active – and noisier, in old-fashioned terms a less 'good' baby, than her own first child had been. Anna had been noisier, but had suffered from 'colic' – till she was four months old. They had all that to come. The child's temperament made all the difference.

A personality was there waiting to unfold. . . .

She left with Tom soon afterwards, half-reluctantly, but confident that things would now go well. Anna had dressed in her 'pre-birth-day' clothes, and the carrycot, the packs of nappies and other new impedimenta brought by Tom were all ready and waiting. Martin would have the car ready in the carpark to take them all back home after lunch. Anna might still feel a little awkward holding her, might be inclined to weep for a day or so – but that would be normal.

A new way of life had begun.

'They will telephone us soon,' Tom said in the car, perhaps feeling a little as she did, or guessing her thoughts.

Janet imagined the life of her baby's baby and felt a little bereft.

'That baby will be an extremely hungry one,' she said.

Once she was back home, Janet found she was thinking less about her own past life and less about boring domestic routine. The demands of a baby or of children had always effectively prevented too much introspection. She was concerned now with that new little head, which would one day contain feelings of happiness and misery, and would slowly learn to know the big world outside. A baby who would be there perhaps towards the end of the next century! Anna had not just had a baby; they had, as Margot had said, created a human being, vulnerable yet tough, young and new, even if mortal, a small person with so much to learn.

'It seems such a pity we can't all start off from where our mothers and fathers left off,' said its grandmother.

This kind of love was part of the inner core of life in time and time was what she and Tom would not have for ever. The baby had years of time ahead with nothing just now to think about, save for satisfying hunger. All the wearisome ins and outs of thought would be hers one day, nevertheless.

15

Christina turned out, as predicted, to be an extremely hungry and therefore noisy baby, and poor Anna was to feel she did nothing for weeks and weeks but feed her, change her, and wait for the next yell, sometimes not even that. Life would settle into a routine only little by little.

'I might as well wrap her like a papoose and carry her everywhere,' she said. 'Or lie down for months and resign myself to being a milk machine.'

'It might be more than months,' said Lucy Hall, whose own infant had continued noisy, hungry and sleepless for over a year.

'Why do some women always feel they must offer gloomy anecdotes?' Janet asked Tom, after Anna had reported this comment to her mother on the telephone.

'Some people feel they must make others suffer as much as they have themselves,' he replied.

'I fed Emma, and burped her and she went back to sleep like clockwork most of the time!'

'Oh, I do remember some yells !' Tom riposted.

Janet did remember some crying, but after the first week or two life had been rather peaceful, if busy, hadn't it ? She remembered that she had not found bathing a baby every day to be really necessary, and that she had refused to put little Emma in a pram out in the communal garden during her first weeks of life, wanting to keep her under her own roof. Of course Anna had a lovely big garden of her own away from the public gaze.

She was certain of her daughter's devotion to the infant; Christina would wind herself round her heart, strand by strand. It was like being in love. It *was* being in love.

'It's like having an extension to yourself – a sort of third arm,' Anna said to Martin. She hardly recognized her old self. 'I'd cut off my hand, or jump off the Eiffel Tower if it were necessary to save Christina's life,' she said.

Moira noted the new Anna. When she got back from work Anna would often ask her into the kitchen.

Christina had begun to scream in the afternoons. The visiting community midwife said it was colic, so Anna would bring the baby down, put her in her pram and wheel her around. The pram was an old-fashioned one, bought at a church sale, of the kind nobody used any longer, but it often did the trick. Moira would make tea. In spite of knowing that the new mother was often both anxious and sleep-deprived, even if she relished a moment's chat, Moira was not surprised to find herself still feeling envious. She would hold Christina and walk up and down with her to give Anna a respite from responsibility. Vicky offered to take her in the car if Martin was away.

'Babies like the movement. It might send her to sleep.'

'The responsibility is the worst thing about it all,' Anna said right at the beginning, but as time went on and the baby was obviously thriving and putting on a good deal of weight in spite of the yells, she relaxed a little.

'I can never keep her front clean,' she complained. 'It's what they call "possetting". Looks more like Niagara to me.'

She was still continually feeding the hungry baby.

When Martin returned home in the evening, Christina was usually quieter until later, when Moira would hear her in the night from her upstairs eyrie.

There was a sort of mutuality, Moira thought – she could not think of a better word – between Martin and his wife. They shared a good deal, even if Martin had had to return to work after a week of broken nights, stoically endured by Anna. She had insisted he must not lose sleep; he was the one who had to be up to work. It was a good relationship. Moira was far from thinking that marriage should be the be-all and end-all of people's lives but in Anna's and Martin's case it seemed to work.

At the end of July, Christina was to be christened, which sounded appropriate, but had rather surprised Moira. She would not have thought of the Walker family as conventionally religious, and so many people now dispensed with the offices of the Church. Martin enlightened her one Sunday afternoon when they were both working in the garden and Anna was having a well-earned rest whilst Baby Christina slept – for once – in the afternoon.

There was the scent of newly mown lawn in the air and it was a heavenly day.

Martin was nailing up a fence and Moira was weeding a flower-bed. She hoped the phlox they had planted earlier would come up next year, for she loved the powerful musty peppery smell of it – such a useful plant, since it lasted for ages. It belonged to late summer, smelled old even when it was young.

She had just asked Martin when and where the baptism would take place.

'Anna decided to join the Anglicans the year before I met her. I don't mind one way or the other myself. The church here is very "bells and smells", but I am told they do a nice christening,' he said, laughing.

'It's a good idea to have some kind of a ceremony,' Moira said, 'My parents had me christened.'

'So did mine, but our parents belonged to a more conventional generation. Anna and her sister were not "done" as babies.'

Moira felt this was interesting. Dennis's son had not been 'done' either and she remembered him waxing indignant over his mother-in-law's expectations.

'Their parents left them to make up their own minds later,' added Martin. 'Which Anna did.'

Moira did not suppose that Emma had turned into a believer. It would not assort with her personality. Anna, though, would be sincere if she had made that leap of faith they always talked about.

'Did you know Vicky was a Catholic?' Martin asked.

'No, but I suppose with an Irish mother she would be.'

Vicky had gone out for the day.

'I was told by Kit that she was a Roman,' Martin added casually just as Moira got up to fetch the wheelbarrow to collect her pile of weeds and some superfluous pebbles. The land here was very pebbly, doubtless because it had once been scoured by the Thames. They now had a compost-heap, and the green garden wheelie-bin full of useless greenery was left at the bottom of the garden, where the council van emptied it every Monday on the back lane.

Moira's heart gave a little jump. Had Martin mentioned his brother on purpose? He was not looking at her. Kit must already know Vicky better than she had imagined. Perhaps he was out with her this very afternoon. Vicky had not said where she was going before she had tootled off in her little car, which she usually left at the station carpark. But why on earth should she say where she was going? Vicky and she still chatted when they met and were friendly to each other, though their hours of work were different. They were both careful not to get in the way of the new parents at weekends unless Moira was doing some gardening.

Moira suddenly felt unexpectedly miserable. Not that Kit had visited Hall House very often but each time she had seen him his image had haunted her afterwards. She had felt strangely uneasy when one day they had been together for a moment in the hall. It had been as if she was balanced on the edge of something and must quickly find someone else to join them in their conversation. He too, she thought, had looked nervous.

Ah well, as most men would, he had chosen to get to know Vicky rather than herself. But it was only a guess that he was out with Vicky, the sort of surmise people she did not approve of were likely to make. Vicky had said nothing about him. She and Vicky were too old and seasoned, she supposed, to tell each other their secrets like little girls. She was determined never to reveal to anyone how she knew she could feel about Kit Macdonald if she allowed herself. It was too absurd, a sort of crush, ever since that dinner party she and Vicky had given. There was no sense at present or in the future for her to spend precious time mooning about unrequitedly as if she were an adolescent. Too much time in the past had been spent on a glittering firework that had fizzled out in the end. She ought to know better – and did, and admonished herself over that sudden quite unbidden sense of jealousy his name in conjunction with Vicky's had unexpectedly aroused in her. It was a different kind of feeling from her envy of Anna's motherhood. She had always known that Vicky was what Aurelia called 'on the prowl'.

Well, *she* was not, and Kit did not know her at all, had no idea what sort of woman she was. Why should he? But his eyes . . . they made her feel strange. Must they not make all women feel heady and romantic? She would certainly not be the only one. Strangely enough, she had never been made to feel that in the past. It wasn't just a physical yearning either, more like a recognition. How could he ever feel like that about her? She compared it with listening to a tenor's top C.

She would so like to get to know him – but if she did, the eyes might change and mean nothing any more . . .

'Oh – I am not anti-Catholic,' she replied a little wildly and stupidly. Martin looked at her in a faintly astonished way, so she added: 'Cradle Catholics are quite different from converts. I'm sure if I converted it would be to Buddhism.'

'Anna likes the Quakers too,' he said, and then; 'I must go in for the secateurs – prune those bushes a bit. Next thing is to build a garden hut. There used to be one here but we took it down, it was so dilapidated.' Moira made her escape and heard the baby wailing as she went in, up the two flights of stairs. She knew nothing whatever about Kit, or whether he had taken Vicky out, and if he had it was none of her business, and she would stop thinking about it.

Vicky was in fact meeting Kit Macdonald in London that afternoon. He had telephoned in the middle of the week to ask her if she would like to go to a new Japanese film with him. She had not been surprised, for they had had a pleasant chat during the week of Christina's homecoming. He had come round to see the baby, clutching a large bouquet of pink roses, and he had just been saying goodbye to his brother when she had rather barged into them as she came up the stairs from the basement. After this she had seen him shopping in the village and he had invited her to drink a cup of coffee in one of the many chic coffee-shops. They had not spent long there, but later he had telephoned her at work.

In spite of his looks, her original opinion had been that he was 'deep', certainly shyer than his younger brother. As she grew older, shy men seemed to like her more. When she was young it had been the saturnine beasts of Bohemia who had found her attractive. She'd learned a lot from them, but after her divorce she was more wary of the commitment she yearned for. The trouble with Kit was that he might give the wrong impression to a younger girl who'd find his looks a lure. She on the other hand would be encouraging if he showed interest in her, but must be careful not to frighten him off. Vicky knew that even at her age she need never be without a man, and a man could usually be worked upon if she liked him enough to bother. She had a good idea of what women thought of her. Emma's mother showed interest in her. Mrs Walker perhaps imagined she had had the courage to live in Paris in a way the older woman had not been able to live almost half a century ago.

Vicky knew she had been rash in her youth, if not as invulnerable as some people might think. She had been taken advantage of, she realized later, by men who then abandoned her, but had been unhappy with the man she had married. She thought it likely that Janet Walker had once been no angel either. Men had essentially changed little since Mrs Walker's youth. In Paris Vicky had found Frenchmen more 'sexist' than Englishmen. 'Free sex' was always practised in France but it was usually to the advantage of men. That was the case in general, but fewer nicely brought-up French girls were really wild unless they were already married. She had not been 'nicely brought-up' herself, not at home anyway, in spite of the convent, and her later rebelliousness had rather terrified well brought-up Englishmen of the kind who believed in marriage. Well, she had changed. In the nineteen nineties intelligent Englishmen now expected you to be what they called a 'feminist': strong-minded, which she was a little tired of being. She had never been a feminist herself, even when she was young. She knew she needed an old-fashioned strong man, who was also reasonably well-off and ambitious.

Frieda Ingersoll had an extensive circle of friends who telephoned or dropped in now and again. Ms Ingersoll sometimes introduced her secretary to these people but Vicky drew the line at socializing with clients, would not touch men with problems with the proverbial bargepole, having too lively a sense of self-protection. Her husband had been enough to teach her that. Of course not all the men she met through Frieda Ingersoll were patients. Vicky realized that like most women of her age she wanted to meet a 'really nice man' who was not self-obsessed, and that she needed the ballast of a solid professional man. Did such men even exist? Would the handsome but introspective Dr Macdonald fill the bill? He was 'deep', and she liked him, whilst thinking at the same time that he might be too good to be true. Vicky was well aware of her own surface charms but he might not be the sort of man who noticed such things.

Anyway, she would make the most of Kit's company.

Moira was puzzled at herself. Martin's brother was a man she'd like to get to know as a person, as a friend to exchange thoughts with, but she found herself in thrall to his looks, which she told herself was wrong. He can't help having those eyes, she said to herself. Were eyes really the windows of the soul? TD had had a certain authority and a great deal of will-power but she realized that he had never been her ideal. Why should people always seek for their Ideal? Psychologists would say the feeling had probably as much to do with a childhood family 'constellation' as with the present. That must be the same for everyone, even men. Some people, men or women, might be more realistic and eventually be happy with something less than their dreams. The essence of men, as of women, had to do with a personhood that was neither male nor female. In other ways they were naturally different, but not as spiritual beings – and her dreams had been as much to do with the spiritual as the physical.

Moira had been told that serious-mindedness was not something men usually looked for in women.

According to Dennis, he was the exception. It was because he was older, she decided. He said he loved her because he thought she was different from most women and he said he valued her personality. Moira was very well aware that you might live in more than one world at once, and everyone had their own dream world, to which the real world could perhaps never match up. She knew she was self-sufficient, and yet she admitted she did yearn for someone like herself, with whom she might proceed, hand in hand, towards the same horizon, a person to whom she need never explain herself. Did that just mean a friend?

She had dreamed several times of standing in the darkness close to a person she knew was a man and there had been no need for either of them to speak. In a dream you are able to 'know' what the other 'characters' are thinking, and sense how much they know of you. In these recent dreams she had truly 'known' – not just believed – that the other person, whoever he was, felt as she did. They clasped hands in the deep dream darkness and then put their arms around each other, and it was quite blissful. There were no unanswered questions and this stranger, who did not feel strange, understood her. Could that ever happen in waking life? She did wonder whether this sense of security had come from her early childhood when she had been held in her father's arms. It was the same as her frequently dreaming of a most beautiful building, more beautiful than anything she had ever seen in real life. She thought: I am not, like Vicky, a man's woman. Standing hand in hand *was* as much like having a friend as a passionate lover.

Dennis, who had wanted her physically, was typical of men, yet the man in her dream had wanted all of her and she had wanted exactly what he wanted, which was another way of saying that love was a shared gift, each to each. In these dreams there was complete trust between them, and it had been such a relief not to have to *say* anything. Naturally you could never know in real life what another person was thinking, however much you loved them. But it had not felt like that whilst she was dreaming. The trust must have been in the dream, because she had created the dream herself, although you did not need an act of will to create a dream. Unlike a day-dream, it was miraculously involuntary. The nearest sensation to this particular dream that she could remember in real life was when she had her arms round a child who trusted *her*.

Moira depended a good deal on these inner reserves but was not yet completely resigned to live by herself, in the deepest sense, nor resigned to a complete lack of hope that such a love as she had dreamed of would ever be reciprocated. So many people dispensed with the ideal of mutual eternal love. It must be rare, depending as it did upon simultaneous emotion. Who usually fell in love first?

Her mother had always said: 'Wait for Mr Right – you will know when he comes along!' and she could not deny the attraction of such an idea. This ideal person would magically appear, though she happened to know that her father had fallen in love with her mother without really knowing her at all. Moira suspected her mother's second husband to be a much more suitable choice. Jim Carruthers was as different as a man could be from Moira's dead father Charles Emsley. Her mother had conceded that here indeed was a second Mr Right. Moira had been relieved, sure they were suited to each other. Her mother had never gone so far as to deny her past feelings for her first husband, but how likely was it that a man like her father had found a soul mate in his wife? Even so, he had always been loyal to her, a good husband and father, and she did miss him.

She sat in her eyrie reading about famous literary marriages. Had Mary Godwin fallen in love with Shelley because Shelley had fallen in love with her? Part of the reason must have been that Mary had only been about eighteen at the time and nature had done the rest. Good heavens, Mary had written *Frankenstein* by the age of nineteen, and Shelley too had been an exceptional person. Would their marriage have lasted? On Mary's part, perhaps, after all those dead children.

Wordsworth had been fond of his wife, but not in the same way as he had loved his Annette. Keats had died before he had really known Fanny Brawne. As for Byron, well . . . Moira firmly avoided any further contemplation of poets – all men – and their marriages, and thought about women writers. Emily Brontë had lived in her head, and invented Heathcliff. Charlotte had suffered from unrequited love for a married man, but eventually accommodated herself to the solid reality of Mr Nichols. . . .

And here *she* was! Over thirty, and in a more enlightened age, and unsure whether she wanted any more romantic passion. Not that you met a Shelley every day, and she did think Kit Macdonald was a beautiful man whose nature she imagined to be as beautiful as his lovely eyes. . . .

16

Christina Rose Jane Macdonald was baptized one Sunday morning in late July after matins in the mid-Victorian church that Moira thought sat on the heath like a squat dowager. The baby's maternal grandparents had come over earlier that morning, Janet having presented her daughter with a family christening-robe of nineteenth-century cotton covered in lace and with a knot of pink ribbon, all carefully conserved by Granny Lister, but never actually used by the Walkers for their own children. Most of the members of the two families were present that morning: Emma of course, and three grandparents and the new father's brother and many many friends. Anna loved the idea of all her friends meeting together, which could not happen often.

All those here in church were smiling and well-disposed. Moira had accepted the invitation, but Vicky had volunteered to see to the catering; there was to be a buffet for the guests at Hall House after the service, much to the relief of Anna's mind. Vicky could be relied upon for good food, and Martin had several bottles of best champagne and Chardonnay chilling to accompany it.

Sitting next to Emma, who had declined godmotherhood, Moira was surprised to see how full the church was. London suburbs were obviously not yet a lost cause to the Church of England in this particular one of its many varieties. She had long ago deserted her mother's nonconformist chapel in Ilkgate. Anna's church was 'high', candlelit and ceremonious, the choir was good, and Moira enjoyed the formal ritual. Kit Macdonald was sitting in front of her next to his mother, the baby's other grandmother. Her husband had left her a widow several years earlier. Martin's sister was on holiday in Barbados with her husband and family so was not here today.

What was Kit thinking about? Probably Vicky, or the coming feast! Moira applied herself to reading the service from the prayer book in front of her. It was couched in a different language from the one she remembered from her childhood reading of the old Book of Common Prayer that her father had owned, though he had been an agnostic. Strange that even in a traditionally high church they used one of the newer service books.

Janet was thinking much the same thing, but she had often been taxed with aestheticism by Anna who said that what mattered was not the form but the meaning, and that more modern versions appealed to more people. Janet knew this was true, but to her religion was part of the past, of her childhood, and she was still moved by its sonorous and beautiful phrases and sentences.

Martin, looking slightly bemused, held his sleeping daughter for most of the service, allowing Anna to concentrate upon the ceremony. Then Janet took her as yet officially unnamed granddaughter for a time whilst Anna went up to receive communion. Two baptisms had been announced to take place after the end of the service proper, and eventually some of the worshippers made their way out of the church whilst others stayed in their pews for a few minutes. Granny Macdonald bent her head in prayer and Tom Walker stared up at the very much decorated ceiling of the nave.

The principal godmother was Anna's friend Lucy Hall, accompanied by her little son Edward, aged three. Tom Walker was thinking there were really no single parents – only a truly cloned baby could have only one. Edward was sitting between his mother and Tom, and was clutching one of his *Thomas the Tank Engine* books and a model of the Fat Controller.

Eventually Tom looked down and whispered something to him, and the child regarded him with big eyes.

The whole party of Macdonalds and their guests eventually got up and wound round to the back of the church where stood the font. The other baby, a large boy, was christened first and given the name Jack. Then Christina suddenly woke up, and was put in the charge of her mother. She gave a few preparatory squeaks but did not rise to full voice until it was her turn for the officiating priest to extract their promises from the godparents, utter the prayers, wet her head and pronounce her names. Father Knight wore his white vestments for one of these many Sundays after Trinity, and was clearly enjoying himself. He had a rich deep voice and the thought passed through Janet's head that it must be a very satisfying kind of job, especially if you had once wanted to be an actor.

The tension was relieved as soon as the christening ceremony was over. Anna disappeared to give her daughter a quick 'refresher', but soon returned and joined the rest of the company in front of the church in dazzling sunlight. The rite now fulfilled, the reception beckoned. They were near enough to Hall House for some younger members of the party to walk back. Janet, Cora Macdonald and Anna and Christina went in Tom's and Martin's cars. If you took baptismal promises seriously you needed to relax afterwards, as you did after a wedding. Even after a funeral, as Moira well remembered, it had been necessary for the adults to eat and drink. Wine helped, though she'd not wanted to drink so much as a thimbleful of wine herself after her father's funeral. She had not been offered one in any case, as she was only fifteen, and the ham had felt like dry sand in her mouth.

She could not help wishing that these various aspects of the Christian life meant as much to her as they obviously did to Anna. She liked attending church ceremonies, not because a wedding or a baptism were the done thing, though many English people appeared to do it for this reason, but because tribes needed rituals, and rituals needed words. Moira needed words too. She had always been exercised by questions of good and evil, and why good existed at all.

This morning as she let the cold champagne make its way down her throat she was thinking that for Anna the christening service had been illuminated by the gift of faith. Anna had once said to her, in the course of one of their chats in the kitchen that Christianity was a matter not of certainty but of faith and trust. Moira felt sure this was right, but today she had felt a mixture of elevation suddenly followed by low-spiritedness from her lack of this trust. Kit was a good man; did *he* have a special faith? Perhaps in humanity?

They all stood in little groups, balancing full glasses, by the loaded table in the Hall House dining-room. Kit had been talking to Janet, but then he turned and spoke to Moira. The others were chattering animatedly, Vicky laughing away with Tom who was clearly enjoying himself.

'You are looking very serious, Moira,' he said. 'How are the children's books?'

'I'm reading one at the moment,' she answered. He was polite. Did he really care about her?

'I was looking at *Thomas the Tank Engine* just now,' he said. 'Do you approve?'

'Very exciting,' said Moira, 'if you like crashes.'

'As most little boys do. I don't think I would have done myself. I never read them as a child, but I hated destroying things, even toppling bricks I'd built – well, perhaps I enjoyed it up till I was about four.' He smiled.

Martin came up just then with Cora Macdonald and Kit introduced her to Moira.

Where did Kit get his looks from? Cora was more like Martin in facial features; she did not have those eyes.

Nobody else had them.

'Such lovely food!' Cora said.

'Vicky did the cake. I'm her co-tenant – here she is!' said Moira in a rush as Vicky came up. She decided to say nothing to Kit's mother about her son's early tastes in stories.

'My dear I *know* – so clever!' murmured Cora to Vicky. Moira thought that Kit exchanged a quick glance with Vicky, and so she deliberately looked away from them.

The dining-room table was covered with a starched tablecloth of white linen and at its centre stood an enormous cake with pink icing and an angel with a trumpet. Where had Vicky got that from? Edward was rushing round now, released from sitting still, and Anna was moving from one guest to another, holding the infant Christina who was being admired by them all with possibly varying degrees of sincerity. Janet was beaming and everyone was happy, except possibly her own ridiculous self, thought Moira. She moved away to talk to one of the other guests, Paula Talbot, a woman who had been at school with Emma and Anna. There were several others who had not been at the service in the church.

Janet was happy; it was pleasant to be an ordinary grandmother with nothing more expected of one, and the baby was thriving in spite of her demanding wails and yells.

'I'm still relieved it's not my turn to care for a little baby,' she whispered to her husband. 'I'm looking forward to her being about two or three when I can read stories to her!'

Tom agreed, though he had never had to cope with two young children, having been a father in the days when it was on the whole regarded as women's work. He had helped, indeed he had, but the health worries had been hers: the enlarged tonsils and the colds and the teething and the chicken-pox and mumps and 'headaches', and all those early feeding schedules, and later the nutritious lunches and teatimes, and walking out in the afternoon with a baby and a toddler and the endless tea-parties with other mothers.

No, she did not envy Anna. She might still have the shopping and bed-making and washing and ironing and cooking and washing-up and tidying and vacuuming and putting out rubbish – so did most people. Babies were of a different order, more important than housework.

She took another glass of champagne and smiled at Emma, aware that Emma thought she had not been ideally suited to motherhood. But she would probably concede that she had done her best. Anna would be a more successful housewife and mother than she had been, Anna with her sociable nature and her practical husband.

Vicky had really enjoyed making the cake, and sorting out the caterers. She had had another drink with the beautiful Kit whom she admired but was a little wary of. He had told her a bit about his work for a medical charity and how promotion had led him back to an administrative job in London which he did not enjoy. 'They mainly need more management consultants now,' he'd said. 'I'm not trained for that. I went as a doctor. Médicins Sans Frontières is the sort of set-up I'd like to work for, but I'm no longer willing to undertake the sort of dangerous work I did in the eighties in Central America, for a medical mission. Now they need more people in Africa for the anti-AIDS campaign.'

She had wondered at first whether he might be gay himself, handsome men often were. He had been friendly but quite sexually reserved towards her. It was a nice change, thought Vicky grimly, but she was probably happier with a more ordinary man. She guessed Moira's feelings for him, though Moira had said nothing. Moira was as complicated as he was, which was quite a lot. Now that Anna had married his capable younger brother, Kit might have been feeling a little left out in his family, and she had been quite willing to encourage him at first, but as her employer Frieda Ingersoll often said, women must learn not to see men as 'projects'.

Vicky had learned a lot from Ms Ingersoll, which did not alter the fact that she would like to have a married life again. Hall House was lovely, and she was lucky to live there, but she did not have the ambition that she guessed lurked in Moira and was in some way to do with literary endeavour. She sensed a similar ambition in Kit Macdonald. They might be too alike. 'Moira is very clever, I think,' she had confided to Kit over a drink at the Cavern in Blackwich. 'But she had some long affair that held her up – I mean held up her life as well as her writing. She writes, you know.'

In spite of her own early interest in Kit, Vicky did not want to be ungenerous to Moira, and she noted that Kit was listening carefully to what she said. In spite of his looks, or perhaps because of them, he was, in ways which she was not quite used to, a diffident man.

Charming, but, she thought, unfocused. He had not confided his own plans to her and she still did not understand him very well, apart from the way in which most men resembled each other. She imagined he needed an intense relationship, one of which she was probably no longer capable, if she ever had been. It was not her style. The ball was in his court.

Janet was invited by Margot Denton for coffee one Saturday morning in late August. Margot was still being treated for what had turned out to be a small cancer. She had not had to wait very long for a lumpectomy, followed by radiotherapy.

As a grandmother, relieved that her daughter was coping and the baby doing well, Janet was happy to return to her own friendships and interests.

'You're not really *old*, Mother,' Emma had said last year.

She wrote many letters to friends about the new baby, read many library books, visited a local gallery in the town which had some surprisingly good watercolours, and the big Royal Academy exhibition in London as well, full of colourful flower paintings by women and sombre landscapes by men. She even had time to visit her favourite little gallery in Cork Street.

'We could take an extra little holiday soon,' Tom said. It was unusual for him to suggest a holiday, so she supposed he thought she needed a change. They would go on holiday to southern Ireland next month. The baby remained her chief preoccupation. Anna telephoned her frequently.

Now she was sitting on Margot's sofa, prepared to listen. So many friends had had medical problems and she did not imagine she would be spared them herself. Whatever Emma said, that was what growing older often meant.

'It's a bore,' Margot was saying, 'but they got it very early. I feel very relieved. They'll finish this part of the treatment next week and then keep me under observation.'

'What exactly does radiotherapy entail? I thought they gave women chemotherapy.'

'No, not for this, that's for invasive cancers, often in younger people. Mine hadn't spread. I knew what to expect – I used to describe it to patients often enough. It's all got a bit more refined nowadays, even if they don't have enough linear accelerators in the NHS, so you have to queue at the nearest teaching hospital, or cancer centre.'

'What's a linear accelerator?'

'It's the name for a sort of machine that sends charged particles in straight paths to a certain chosen spot. They use alternating high-frequency voltages.'

'Sounds fearsome!'

'Like most things to do with high tech medicine, it sounds more frightening than it is.'

Margot seemed to want to describe her experience in detail so Janet sat back to listen. She supposed it was not the sort of experience you wanted to describe to your son, and Margot had no partner with whom to share her thoughts.

'They refer to the mammogram, measure you to get the exact spot and then put a tattoo mark on the breast bone. Each time they do the daily radiotherapy in the special accelerator chamber, they measure you anew to make sure the rays go only into the exact spot. Then you lie back with your arms at a curious angle, sort of exposed, with your hands round two rests, and wait for it to begin.'

'Does it hurt?'

'Oh no – it's just weird. The radiographers all go out and you hear the door clang. Then the *bleep – bleep* sound starts. I counted the first lot of bleeps the first time so I'd know exactly what to expect, and there were twenty-nine. Then you hear a hissing noise – for about seventeen seconds, but one always counts too quickly and you can't see your watch or a clock. The necessary particles – call them rays – go into the target from one side. There's a pause then and about four more bleeps, and then I guess another thirty seconds of the rays again. Then you wait.'

'What exactly are these "rays"?'

'The ordinary ones are protons but next week I have the last one, the booster, and that's more powerful – electrons, I think. I have to go to another hospital for that.'

'Is that it then?'

Margot sipped her coffee.

'Well, what I've described is the first part of the session over, but then the radiographers come back and readjust the machine to the other side. Then out they go again! The safety gate clangs again and the bleeps go on again. I counted twenty-five bleeps the second time so I suppose it's just a warning, not an exact period of time. Then there's another seventeen seconds of protons, then a pause and a hiss, and then a short bleeping and the twenty-nine seconds again.'

'It sounds very complicated.'

'Well that's it, each time. They come back again when it's all over and you get down from the sort of sloping seat you've been lying on. Not as bad as the dentist, really.'

'So it doesn't hurt?' Janet asked again.

'Any discomfort is because your arm on the side where they operated has to hold a sort of stirrup and your wrist is twisted. I've had two ganglia in the right arm – from wrist strain, I think.'

She showed Janet the raised humps.

'I've had four weeks of it now and the area's reddish-brown and tender – obviously full of water or something.'

She sounded vague for a doctor.

'What do you think about whilst they're doing it? Do you think "positive thinking" helps? It did in childbirth – for me anyway.'

'I'm not a radiologist, but I like to imagine the good cells – the

191

white corpuscles – are being regimented to attack the bad ones.
Not that there are any more bad cells left, according to my surgeon
who says he is convinced he has removed them all.'

'None under your arm, then?' Janet remembered reading an
article in a woman's magazine about lymph glands.

'No, that's when you get chemotherapy. He says there were no
bad cells among the lymph nodes, so I was clear once he'd
removed the few millimetres of malignancy. Of course nobody
knows how long it would have taken for me to notice anything at
all – there was no lump. Radiotherapy's just a safeguard, a sort of
belt and braces along with the op – and then there's Tamoxifen,
which you have to take for some time to prevent it happening
again. The tricky part of the op is the removal of the lymph nodes.
You can't feel the back of your arm at the top any more after that
– they never warn you to expect that! Perhaps one day they'll be
able to tell by removing just one node, not all of them – they have
to cut through a nerve.'

'You look perfectly well,' said Janet, which was true.

Margot looked quite relaxed and healthy.

'It's been so time-consuming though, going up to bloody
London almost every day. As I once worked up there they took me
in the teaching hospital.'

'I suppose going there's become a habit.'

'I shan't miss it! I suppose after the final dose I might feel a bit
uneasy when nothing more's being done, but I have to make
appointments with the physiotherapist and the surgeon for reap-
praisal then another mammogram!'

'It must drain your reserves of energy.'

'Radiotherapy makes some people feel tired, but I can't say it
has me. I expect it's like giving birth – some people get more
exhausted than others. "Chemo" is worse, they say. Some of the
specialists sounded a bit too dramatic. I suppose they're used to
younger women with husbands who think they own bits of their
wives' bodies! Me, I don't care what my bosom looks like, so long
as I'm healthy. One said: "Your breast" and she meant *me* – "will
never be the same again after the trauma", and then she added very
sternly: "Be careful not to get stung in the garden". Well, you don't
go round looking for wasp-stings, do you. Another one said: "Just
carry on with normal life after treatment. You are *better*". Very

comforting! I must say I never realized how much difference an optimistic doctor makes to a patient – if there are good grounds for optimism, of course.'

'Your two sounded a bit contradictory.'

'They made me realize how carefully you have to choose your vocabulary when you're a doctor. Patients hang on every word and analyse it – along with your expression. Well, that's me done! Tell me about your granddaughter.' She poured another cup of coffee for each of them.

Janet was happy to oblige with descriptions of the christening and Christina's general wonderfulness.

After leaving Margot, Janet called on Greta Allott, their nearest neighbour at Deepden Court, said to have once been an actress but living now in reduced circumstances. Well, they cannot be very reduced if she can afford to live here, thought Janet, but Greta had recently asked for her advice about a friend's child who, she said, was eight and could not yet read. Fortunately the child lived in Devon, so Janet would not be called upon for active help. Once the parents of the neighbourhood discovered you had been a teacher, however long ago – it did not appear to matter what you had taught – they wanted advice. Usually they were worried that their younger children worked too hard, or terrified that their adolescent children were not doing any work.

Greta, a tall, rake-thin woman in her fifties, with stern grey fringe and bobbed hair lived alone as a first-floor tenant. Janet knew little about her present existence except that she played bridge and had unsuccessfully tried to get her and Tom to join the set in the neighbouring town, the one in the village hall not being quite up to her mark. Greta was however out today. Janet, feeling she had at least made an effort, thankfully went back down to her own ground-floor door on the other side of the house.

Tom was up in London and there was nothing she liked better than an afternoon to herself. She hoped nobody would telephone, for she intended to finish reading a new book for children before writing about it for the *Journal*. If it were any good she might mention it to Moira, though Moira had probably heard of it already. Janet did not enjoy fantasy fiction and remembered that Moira was not so keen on it either. Right from childhood, people were different.

193

June Barraclough

*

Moira hurriedly folded the letter she had received that morning and stuffed it in its envelope. It was from Dennis, from whom she had heard nothing since she had left Ilkgate. He must have asked for her address from Aurelia or a neighbour. On second thoughts, it was more likely he had asked the secretary of the Antiq. and Phil. for Aurelia would have told her and asked whether she wanted him to have it.

She went off to work feeling annoyed and obscurely threatened. Why should she feel that? He had hardly been stalking her. All through the day she tried to ignore her reaction. The day was a busy one; a consignment of new *Tracks for Reading* for seven-to-nine-year olds had been sent to the wrong branch, and one of the junior assistants was away with an unseasonable cold. When she eventually returned to High House her room was just as she had left it and she did not open the letter until she had boiled a quick 'fish in a bag' on the Belling stove.

It was rather a sad missive, not telling her much about his new work but hoping she was happy in hers. He would never forget her . . . and so on . . . and if she ever came up to Manchester . . . Did he want her to feel sorry for him? Probably. He signed it: *Affectionately TD.*

She knew she would eventually reply, though she'd need to think carefully what to tell him. She would describe her life in Blackwich, except for her most important non-experience, which was being under the secret spell of a pair of eyes belonging to a man who had no idea of the entrancement he had caused. She would tell him that no, she did not miss him, and that she did not regret the past, which was not entirely true. She would wish him well. She might see him again one day in some distant future, when she had settled down, whatever that meant. It certainly included having a collection of her poems published, which might be never. She would not rush a reply but would try to remember their early, happier, days. Those years seemed to have happened centuries ago; you tended to forget your old feelings, muddied as they were by subsequent ones. She had changed, but she did not believe he had.

Reading between the lines of his letter she realized he was miss-

194

ing her. She sincerely hoped he might feel happier in a year or two; best if he accepted the past as past and made a new future with his wife. That was not something she could tell him so baldly. It was no longer her affair, in more senses than one, though she could not disclaim her own responsibility for the past. All she might write to him could be made to sound hypocritical or self-serving, but he knew she was no longer in love with him, no longer even loved him. He was the one who had set in motion all that he had now lost. It would be easier for her to find someone, because she was so much younger. That made her feel guilty, and was perhaps the reason for her fear that he might come after her to claim her? And she didn't want to find just anyone, only Kit Macdonald.

She had recovered from Dennis, but she did not want to hurt him more than was necessary by telling him so. She'd tell him about Hall House and her new friends and subtly hint that she was fine, without mentioning the name of any male acquaintance, for he would be sure to seize on it. She hoped her reply would not encourage further correspondence. In the meantime she could look forward to Kit's occasional visits to Hall House, probably to see Vicky. She had given Vicky no hint of her secret feelings for Kit and Vicky had not mentioned him either.

Moira tried not to speculate whether they were still going out together. Anna had said they hoped he would stay with them this year for Christmas, and with that she had to be satisfied for the time being. She would let life carry her on; 'let the future slowly invade her' as some Frenchman had once said.

Part Five

LIFE GOES ON

17

Moira was to hear nothing further from Dennis 'TD' Whittaker until Christmas, when a card arrived from him: *With fondest regards.* Not: fondest love, thank goodness, she thought. Kit Macdonald was to be away at a conference until 21 December but would come to celebrate Christmas at Hall House after he'd visited his mother, who had her own plans for the festive season with his sister and her family. He would return to his rented flat in Brickley and come over to Hall House from there. Vicky too had decided to stay in London for Christmas. Anna and Martin had invited Janet and Tom to celebrate as many of the days of Christmas at Hall House as they chose, and Moira and Vicky were invited for Christmas Day dinner. Martin said: 'The more the merrier.'

Anna explained to Moira that she would have liked her mother-in-law to come to stay too, but she always spent Christmas in Norfolk and had plenty of her own friends in Cambridge as well. Martin did not appear to mind very much that he saw more of his own in-laws than he did of his mother. Cora didn't like London.

Hall House was a busy household nowadays with many comings and goings, chiefly centred upon Christina who at six months was already a character. Moira observed how much the baby noticed. A big smile would suddenly light up her little face when Dora the cat came into the room. There was a subtle recognition, she thought, between babies and animals, which for a time belonged in the same sphere. Christina lorded it in her baby-chair and the cat accepted her dominion, knowing quite well there were things a cat could do that a baby could not. Dora's favourite place was on people's beds and she sometimes made her way to the top floor to snuggle down with Moira. Vicky was more of a person to be followed, tail up, in search of titbits.

Christmas Day was on a Thursday that year and Christmas Eve was to be no ordinary Wednesday, for Anna was to give her babies' and toddlers' tea-party at half-past three. She had made so many new friends, new mothers like herself, and everyone agreed that Christmases with babies were bound to be more meaningful, if more chaotic, than childless ones. Janet and Tom were to arrive on Christmas Eve and stay until the evening of the 25th. Drinks for the family and a few adult friends had been planned after Christina's bedtime. Anna wanted to go to midnight mass on Christmas Eve, so the ever helpful Vicky offered to aid Martin in the preparation of vegetables and sauces for the next day's big meal. Anna might then concentrate on putting Christina to bed, joining the drinks party and putting her feet up before church. Moira thought it was all like a military operation but the part she was concerned with was the arrival of Kit. Emma was coming on Christmas Day but had declined an invitation to attend the children's party on the eve. She and Lydia would be at work that morning and would themselves be entertaining a few people for drinks on Christmas Eve in Pimlico.

Moira thought she had better offer to help with some of the festival preparations and with the children's party. Kit might come to that. She had already put up decorations downstairs on the household's behalf. Both holly and ivy grew in the garden and Anna wanted her to gather even more greenery, to accompany the giant red and green candles she had bought, for their appearance rather than their usefulness, and had accepted with alacrity Moira's offer to help dress the tree. A few days before Christmas, Martin came back from the village with a tall Christmas tree which they could replant in the garden afterwards, and Anna brought out the baubles she had kept from the year before. It seemed an eternity since last Christmas, before there was a Christina. Martin called that time, rather irreligiously, 'BC'.

The tree was so large that more gold and silver and green stars and lanterns and baubles had to be bought from the town market. It all reminded Moira of her own childhood in Ilkgate. When she remembered it, her northern Christmas seemed to have been full of lights: the Christmas tree in the town square with gold and silver and emerald baubles, crystal stars glittering over the hills and moors in the distance.

Presents were a problem. Anna insisted that only Christina was to be given a proper present from the tenants, so Moira bought various books suitable for six-month-old babies, to the later amazement of Martin who had not realize that babies' reading tastes were now specially catered for. She also bought Janet an Edwardian novel from the second-hand bookshop.

She and Vicky would leave the family to themselves after Christmas dinner. Vicky had arranged to drive over to her old aunt Orla near Colchester on Boxing Day.

'She's my only relative,' she said.

Moira looked forward to a good read every day until it was time to return to work, unless it was suggested they went for walks in the Park.

'Kit always likes a walk there,' Anna had told her.

Writing and addressing cards, and shopping for food and presents preoccupied Anna for weeks, but in the end she found she was in the usual rush, not sure if everything had been prepared.

'Mother always made a big fuss about Christmas when we were little,' she said, not adding that her mother would then complain of the burden that fell principally on women at this season.

'I'm so lucky, having so many willing helpers this year,' she kept saying. Tom's latest name for the house was 'The Commune'. Anna spent one whole afternoon preparing a bedroom for her parents, and a little one for Kit. All Moira could think about was that Kit was going to stay in the house over Christmas. Last year she had spent the festive season at Aurelia's in Ilkgate; now, she had begun to feel she was in her own home, almost part of the family. She couldn't help hoping for some sort of conversation with Kit, if she could manage to talk to him without appearing stupid or, worse, pretentious.

This conversation was to come about sooner than she expected. On Christmas Eve, before the children arrived with their mothers, she had gone down to the big sitting-room to try to fix the white-and-gold angel which had fallen down that morning from the top of the tree. The collapsed angel was one of the old decorations and Anna had her hands full. There was no time to buy another; three times Moira attempted and failed to anchor it. Martin had spent his first free day sorting out wine in the newly swept cellar next to Vicky's kitchen where he had recently installed a wall of bottle-holders. Now he had already gone out to collect the goose that he had ordered at Vicky's suggestion.

'It's better than a turkey,' she'd said. If I supervise its cooking, she thought.

Moira found a stepladder and had just begun to manipulate it near to the tree for one more attempt when she heard Kit's voice in the hall. She had not seen him come in at the front. The sitting-room door opened but she did not turn straight away when she heard him say:

'How can I help?' After a pause, she looked round. He must have put his motor scooter round by the garden gate at the back and come in through the kitchen where Vicky and Anna were making last minute preparations for the toddlers' and babies' tea.

'Martin's gone to the shop for the bird,' she said.

'Let me do that, you're not tall enough. Happy Christmas, Moira!'

The last time she had seen him had been just before he had gone abroad again, a few weeks ago. She had such a rush of pleasure seeing him there in the room beside her that she felt quite dizzy.

'What a lovely angel! They want me to be Father Christmas!' he said. 'You get down from that ladder!' He climbed up two steps and fixed the angel carefully on the top.

She gathered herself together.

'Have you a red suit?' she asked.

'Just the red cap and my red dressing-gown, and I bought a long white beard at the toyshop on the way. I'm told that only babies and very little children are coming, so I don't think I need anything more exotic!' He sounded light-hearted, as if he had been released from a burden.

'You can have these sleigh-bells,' Moira said, diving into the bag of baubles among which was a sort of large curved handle adorned with several small jangling bells.

'Perfect! I must practise. I'll have to robe in the cloakroom when Anna gives the go-ahead. Got my sack!' He produced a large bag. 'No time to wrap the presents though. I thought a sort of lucky dip.'

'Their mothers will do the dipping,' she replied, smiling.

'Are you invited or is it just Anna and her gang?'

She laughed. 'I said I'd help if I was needed. It's lovely having so much room for entertaining. But I must go up and get dressed.'

She was still in her old trousers. He thought she looked nice in them, and with her hair tied back.

'You go and titivate yourself then. Vicky is in the kitchen devising something for toddler stomachs. It looked so palatable she let me have a taste.'

Oh well, Vicky had seen him first, after all. But Moira desperately needed to say something.

'When we have the drinks tonight we're having home-made quiche and a Swaledale cheese which I bought,' she said.

'I was given the full programme by Anna. Swaledale goat cheese is my top favourite.'

'It comes from not far from Ilkgate – where I used to live.'

'Will you be here tomorrow for Christmas dinner?'

Was he being just polite? She told him: yes, she was, she was staying at Hall House for the whole of Christmas.

'Tell me what else I can do to help,' he said. 'I know men are usually seen as being in the way.'

Both he and his brother were awfully kind people, she thought. Practical too. Most men would just subside and let the women do the work.

'How are *you*?' she asked.

'One small part of my burden has been removed from me – administratively speaking. I still have to sort out the other at HQ in Europe, but I'm back for a short time.' So he was going away again soon.

Moira decided to go up to her room to change into her new scarlet-satin top and black trousers, which the boutique girl had said were just right for a fair-haired woman. She had never worn that colour before and was still dubious. Still, it was Christmassy!

It was to be the only time that afternoon she could speak to him alone. Later, she hoped she'd find him in the kitchen, but then Vicky would be there too.

Once the mothers and children arrived it was chaos. Dora the cat took one look at the noisy guests arriving and disappeared upstairs to lie under one of the beds until order and peace should be restored. Father Christmas and his sleigh-bells were, however, a great success. Kit sorted the children out, greeted each mother and child and saw that each toddler was given a suitable present. The babies, of whom there were four, most no older than the baby of the house, crawled round and variously screamed or went to sleep. One baby, only three weeks old, slept in the hall throughout the party. Kit appeared used to the chaos of children; she supposed he had been dealing with much less fortunate people.

'A great success,' said Martin when it was all over and the last overburdened mother had departed to prepare 'Christmas' for family in her own home. By the time Janet and Tom arrived, tea for the Walkers was being served round the fire in the adjoining dining-room with slices of home-baked cake. Janet was full of admiration for her daughter's giving a toddlers' party. Moira, doing the washing up in the kitchen overheard her say to Kit:

'I found bringing up toddlers far more exhausting than child-birth.'

Moira found it pleasantly relaxing to be occupied doing something ordinary that hundreds of thousands of other women were probably doing. Kit and Vicky were getting out the drinks and nibbles for later and Vicky was checking the food to prepare for tomorrow. 'Did your family celebrate Christmas Eve like this in the North?' Kit asked, taking a tea-towel and rapidly stacking cups and saucers. 'I thought it was more of a continental thing to have presents and the tree in the evening.'

Moira thought back to the quiet small Christmases of her child-hood. To bed with your stocking, and to listen to the town band playing 'Christians Awake' early next morning. Yet it had had its magic.

'No, it was all crammed into the twenty-fifth. We only had a little tree.'

'My mother went to midnight mass,' offered Vicky. 'I suppose that's more continental – or Irish.'

'Our midnight mass is absolutely packed,' said Anna, overhear-ing as she came in from putting Christina to bed. The baby had just graduated to a cot in a room of her own. 'Perhaps I shouldn't go tonight but I thought I'd be too busy tomorrow. I've really enjoyed having the little ones round this afternoon. It's all been so much easier with you all helping.'

'Anything to do with children can be tiring,' said Kit, 'You feel it afterwards when the work's done.'

'Are they ready for a drink – shall we take them in?' Vicky asked. 'Cheese straws are to hand,' she added, taking a tray from the oven with a flourish. How did she always manage to have everything ready at the right time? What would Anna do without her if, as Moira now once more gloomily assumed, Vicky married Kit and concentrated her culinary efforts on a husband? She dried her hands and childishly wondered where the mistletoe had been put and who might contrive to be under it. She must be going soft in the head. She had had her little chat with Kit, though, and she could enjoy his proximity. But family life could be quite exhausting for reasons other than the mechanics of domestic existence.

The rest of the festivities the following day went according to plan. Dora was given a red bow and skulked around smelling goose. It would soon be dark, but after the satisfying meal, which had started punctually, everyone but Janet, who declined, saying she would help to clear the food away, went out for a quick walk in the almost twilight on the heath with Christina in the pram. The infant was now sitting up without support and taking notice of the world. Next Christmas she would doubtless notice even more.

'Let's walk in the park tomorrow morning,' suggested Anna.

'You say that every year,' said Emma, who had not spoken very much in all this domestic hullabaloo, 'but you are never ready in time!'

Moira managed a conversation with Kit about the dates of the various houses that edged the heath, and how different they were from the houses in Ilkgate. Was she boring him?

In bed, the night before she returned to work, Moira was asking herself, what do I really want? Just to talk to Kit, to have him as a friend, to know he is in the world ? Or to have more of him – a part of him that may already be committed to someone else? To Vicky, perhaps? Am I returning to how I felt years ago, suffering from unrequited love, before I knew TD? I'm too old for that, she told herself. But probably nobody was ever too old to fall in love. Was it because she was older that she connected it with settling down? She wanted other things just as much: to finish her new poem about inner and outer life, to carry on doing her job as well as she could, to have friends, and to belong, in a new way, to life.

After Christmas she felt curiously dislocated, more than when she arrived in London eighteen months before. She knew why. It was precisely because Christmas was such a family affair and because she had been included and accepted by the Macdonalds and so had joined in with them. But it would never be enough. Was it enough for Vicky, to be needed? Didn't Vicky also need a centre, not to be on the periphery of someone else's life? Well, *she* was not exactly needed quite in the same way as the capable Vicky. Vicky might also have times when she wanted a home of her own, enjoying helping, but maybe with some hidden agenda. This was neither a kind thought nor the kind of thought Moira found herself comfortable with, and she tried to get back to sleep. In the meantime, for them both, Hall House was a good place to be, and Anna and Martin had given them some of their own good fortune.

One thing was sure. She would not reply to any further letters from Dennis. She wished she had the courage to ask Vicky about her relationship with Kit. Over Christmas, she hadn't noticed anything that might suggest a more than usual intimacy between the two of them but then *she* didn't want to show her feelings publicly either. She might have revealed them too much already. Her face probably lit up when Kit was in the room.

It was Kit whom she did not quite understand. If he was attracted to either of them, wouldn't he make some sign? He had, it was true, taken Vicky out more than once, and herself never, but he was going abroad again, apparently to see off, some of what he called unfinished business in the Balkans. Not for too long, he'd said.

When he had said goodbye to them all, he had smiled at her and taken her hand. He could not possibly guess her own feelings; she had never said anything untoward, just chatting about Christmas and childhood and old houses. Moira was a little at sea. Women were not supposed to *begin* anything; they were supposed only to reveal their feelings discreetly if a man made the first step. It had been like that with Dennis, except that *he* had taken her feelings for granted, which she now realized was a bit of a presumption.

She did wish she had someone to advise her, or just someone to talk to. Aurelia might have listened, but Aurelia was far away and there was a gulf between them now that Aurelia had her children to worry about. It even sounded stupid to need to talk to someone; she had usually been so self-sufficient. It was not exactly an agony aunt that she needed, for really nothing had happened! That was the trouble. All her agonies, if that was what they were, were private. She could hardly talk to his brother about Kit, or even to Anna, who was always so busy, and certainly not to Vicky. Unlike Anna too, she could hardly pray for divine guidance.

Then it occurred to her that on leaving after Christmas Janet Wood had said:

'Do come again soon to see us at Deepden Court! Promise!'

She would hint to Janet how she felt, and Janet, she knew, would listen. She'd make a definite date to visit Hookden in the New Year, at a time when the others were not visiting, for she knew Anna and Martin went over quite often with Christina. Having made this decision Moira found that she felt more serene. Another New Year: 1998. *Ah the years, the years!* she quoted to herself, Thomas Hardy being her favourite poet.

She and Vicky and Emma all returned to work in the New Year. Anna was just as busy in a different way from them. Christina caught a cold and began to teethe at the same time. Anna asked herself how, without much sleep, and worried about a child, any mother could have a full-time job.

'I suppose you have to let the nanny or the au pair see to the baby at night?' she said to Martin. 'I just *couldn't*.'

Some women had to get up at night and then go out afterwards in the morning to work, so the next time she was woken by cries and wails, she told herself how extremely lucky she was.

18

Moira went to Hookden to see Janet one Saturday afternoon in the middle of January. Tom was at a meeting in London. As she walked from the little halt down the lane past the small cottages and the larger new houses, she appreciated the peace and quiet that was so near yet so far from London. How long could it stay like this? No police sirens, no graffiti, no litter. All these were even beginning to invade Blackwich and the traffic was getting worse and worse, taking over the place. Well, she couldn't be blamed for that, since she had no intention of buying a car, unlike Vicky. Like the old and poor, and the young and poor, and the non-driving mothers with babies in pushchairs, she still used public transport.

Blackwich was not yet entirely given over to urban blight. There were still many species of birds around, as well as less welcome squirrels over from the park, and urban foxes, but the thuggish magpies were beginning to take over, and there were colonies of crows on the heath, mixed with seagulls brought downriver.

She found herself on the lane to the Court with the gate of the old house before her. How could she start to explain what she felt? Had she been a little mad to want to confide in Anna's mother?

Janet was welcoming, and appeared very pleased to see her. There was a fire in the hearth and there would be tea and crumpets later, she said.

'I'm thinking of getting another cat. I miss having one. I realized at Christmas when I saw Dora at my daughter's.'

'It's so cosy here,' said Moira. 'A cat would be very at home.'

'We both enjoyed Christmas,' Janet went on. 'It's such a relief not to have to do it any more!'

'You must have done it for years.'

'One of the penalties of domesticity. Did you hear from your mother? Does she miss England?'

'Oh, yes, she wrote at Christmas, and I telephoned her on Boxing Day. I don't think she really misses home – though she still calls it home.'

'And are you missing the north?'

'It's the country I miss really. I feel quite at home at Hall House; they are all so kind.'

'How was Christina this morning?' pursued Janet, 'Anna won't have had time to telephone. Is the tooth through?'

'She says the cold is getting better and she will ring you tomorrow,' replied Moira dutifully, suddenly remembering.

'Anna is not so much of a worrier as I was,' said Janet. 'Of course, Martin takes a lot off her shoulders. Men are expected nowadays to help more. My husband was never there – always "working for the family living" as he used to tell us. I know Martin has to go away from time to time but he's very practical when he is at home.'

'You worked too though, didn't you?'

'I began after the girls went to primary school, but not full time. I should not like to do it now. Schools have become battlegrounds in one way or another. Still, I suppose we must be thankful we have not been overrun by neighbouring tribes and are not at war.'

Moira saw her opportunity and grasped it.

'Martin's brother was telling us a bit about the former Yugoslavia,' she began. 'But he didn't go into many details about the violence and the horrors he must have seen.'

'I believe not only seen but also been involved in mopping up. You knew he studied medicine and worked in a London hospital before going out as a doctor to Central America and Africa, and then Bosnia for the Mother and Children charity?'

'Yes, he told me a bit, but he didn't give many details except to say it was a perilous world and television journalists could only show a tiny fraction of the terrifying reality. Anna was asking him about it after you had gone home. He said journalists got "burn out" but that doctors couldn't allow themselves that.'

'I think Kit has had enough now. He started off full of idealism but the world of international conflicts and internecine warfare has leached his hopes away. Conflicts have built up again in Europe, especially in the former Yugoslavia, and man's inhumanity to man can no longer be ignored.'

Moira had sensed a certain beginning of despair in Kit. She knew that power politics disgusted him from whatever quarter they came.

'He worked for a time in London helping to organize an Aids campaign in Central Africa, but I think he's ashamed of his decision to do something different – what, I'm not sure. That's my reading of him anyway.'

'You must lose your faith in humanity when you see enough horrors.'

'Yes. Some of his co-workers were killed, you know. Nowhere is safe I was terribly upset myself by Srebrenica – and all that long-drawn-out business in Sarajevo. It was because it was our own continent, and I could imagine it better than I could Somalia or Rwanda. But I know one should be able to empathize with one place as well as another. I expect Kit will go on working for the charity at home in an administrative post.'

'He didn't seem too happy about that at Christmas, did he?'

'I think he might go back to medicine. He's tougher than he looks.'

Moira was not sure about that.

Janet had noticed Moira's intense interest in Kit's welfare and drawn her own conclusions. Anna had mentioned months ago that Moira 'liked' him. 'He's so very handsome, isn't he!' she said now, craftily.

Moira hesitated and then said in a small voice:

'I believe he took Vicky out a few times. I suppose she's just the right sort of woman for a man who needs cheering up.'

I was right, thought Janet. The child cannot dissimulate and is consumed with love for the handsome Christopher. But she replied:

'Well, Vicky has sterling qualities. Many men's ideal, I expect.'

'I do like her. She's so capable – and worldly—'

'And such a good cook,' added Janet mischievously.

Moira smiled at her tone of voice.

'Kit is an interesting person,' Janet went on. 'I met him when Anna decided to marry Martin and found him quite an enigma at first, even if he's easy to talk to. Because he *listens*, I suppose. We discovered a shared interest in children. I had taught some and he had saved some. You must tell him about whether you've found any stories written specially for refugee children. There must be some in your library.'

Here am I, prattling on, she thought and I ought to confess that if I were forty years younger I might easily feel romantic about beautiful Kit, who is also quite a wise person. But it's not the kind of remark I'd be sensible to come out with. Anyway, she had never felt the slightest desire for a 'toy-boy'! Better talk about library books. Her thoughts ran ahead, whilst Moira too was silent.

Janet studied her as she gazed into the fire, and wondered how much of Moira's life went on in her imagination. When you were young, an enthusiasm for a man's mind and personality often started with his surface attractions. Experience had taught her they were often no indication to the real person. She thought again how so manifestly unfair it was that looks mattered so much. Beautiful eyes could often be a snare; they did not always betoken inner depth. In Kit's case she thought that they did. A complicated man might very well find, initially at least, that a woman like Vicky Winterbon was a relaxing presence. Men were notoriously bad at knowing what they really needed, and most did not enjoy challenges. It depended what they wanted from women. Vicky did not look like a challenge, though she might possibly be one. Moira was highly intelligent and would certainly be more mentally stimulating, if she did not entirely take the man's mind off tragedies and disasters.

If Kit had actually had what they now called a relationship with Vicky, Janet felt sure he would eventually have realized that *he* was not the right person for *her*, never mind the other way round. But the supposition that there had been a relationship at all was only what she had gathered from Moira and might have arisen from her imagination. This kind of speculation was none of her business.

She changed the subject, as she thought.

'Do you still hear from all your friends up in the north? I owe Miss Banks a letter – time passes so quickly.'

'Well,' said Moira nervously, but it was easier than talking about Kit Macdonald, 'I heard from the friend I may have mentioned – the one I went on a walking holiday in Westmorland with – Dennis. I used to go out with him, and he would like to see me

211

again. But I feel completely cut off now from all my old life and I could never go back to it.'

Janet wished she could confess she knew a bit about the girl's old life, and what Bridie Banks had revealed. She could not help being curious, but must not be a busybody. What she guessed about Moira's Dennis was so like her own experience with Neville nearly fifty years before.

Moira now seemed to want to say more.

'I've enjoyed being free of entanglements,' she went on, looking up from the fire. 'Yet it's hard to give up completely the idea of . . . love.'

'Why should you? Gracious me, you're only Anna's age!'

'I'm even a little younger than Anna!' said Moira.

Just the age, thought Janet, that a third child would have been if we had decided to have another. Tom had said, in the end, that he thought two were quite enough in the world as it was. She had imagined he might want a son but had been relieved to stop at two, knowing that three would have been almost beyond her capabilities, quite apart from leaving her less time for herself – and for husband, overworked as Tom had always been.

'TD – Dennis – misses me, I know,' said Moira, 'but I find I see things differently now. Is it true that doing the right thing makes one feel ruthless?'

'Often,' replied Janet. 'I'm sure you don't find ruthlessness comes easy. Why do you call him Teedee?'

'Oh, they were his initials. He specially detested his first name so was always called by his second, which he didn't like much either. Some people who knew him well called him TD. I thought of him as Dennis.'

Had she said too much ? She changed the subject.

'Anna says you think names are important. So do I. Do you like your granddaughter's name?'

'Yes. Christina was one of my own favourites but I felt one could scarcely give such a christian name to a child who wasn't baptized.'

'I am really, I suppose, Mary,' said Moira. Janet wondered if Moira would tell her what TD stood for, and waited. Moira said nothing.

'My second name is Florence, after an aunt,' Janet added. 'I believe it's back in fashion. I hated it, but I suppose it was better than being called after Aunts Gertrude and Winifred. Moira is a nice name.'

'That's getting popular too.'

'Why did your parents choose it?'

'It was my mother – after a ballerina she saw in a film.'

'Let's have some tea.'

Janet had intended to walk with Moira to the station-halt but Tom arrived home just as they were about to leave and took Moira back in the car. After they had gone, she sat for a time in the dark in the glow of the fire. She ought to have asked Moira, she could have asked her, but some *délicatesse* had stopped her. The girl had clearly made up her mind about her past, and had been happy to hear about Kit . . . but if Janet was right, the coincidence was quite amazing.

She made supper and ate it with Tom, and when he went into his study to check the reference books he had borrowed that very afternoon, she began a letter to her old friend Bridie Banks.

Moira was glad she had told Janet about hearing from Dennis, who was no longer 'her' TD, and that she had not said too much about Kit and Vicky. It was unlike her to talk about her private affairs with anyone. Talking to the older woman had relieved her a little, even if she had found at the last moment that she could not really ask for advice about Kit.

When she got back, quite late, to Blackwich, it was raining and there was Kit Macdonald just leaving Hall House!

'I've been saying goodbye again before getting off at last for several weeks abroad. I was delayed – administrative mopping up to do,' he said. He turned as he went down the path that Moira had just walked up, and seeing her under the outside lamp, her fair hair pearled with raindrops, returned to say: 'I *am* sorry to have missed you, but I shall be back quite soon – in the spring.'

In the spring! That was months away! Had he visited Vicky, she wondered, but did not enquire. He had bothered to tell her when he would be back. She treasured these few words he had spoken to her.

Vicky had that afternoon been out with Graydon Wilbraham, one

213

of Ms Ingersoll's American friends. She had continued to sense
complications in Kit Macdonald and come to the same conclusion
as before. She was not the woman who could truly understand
them or him. She had left him to decide whether they might get to
know each other better. This meant, she knew, that she was not in
love with him. Not that she thought passionate love was all that
important for 'settling down'; it had not worked in the past. What
she needed was someone kind and practical to look after her. Kit
was both, but she sensed she would never get below his surface.
This realization made her feel rather fed up with herself. Why
should she want to pry into a man's mind? On the other hand
she'd grown up, and seen too much introspective misery in the
people treated by Frieda Ingersoll.

'I got sick to death of "me" ages ago,' she had once confessed to
Frieda, 'and the myths I wove on my own behalf around myself.
When I knew this I could move on.'

Frieda had laughed. 'You are very clear-eyed, Victoria,' she'd
replied – she always called her Victoria. 'I don't think you need
therapy.'

She guessed, though she had never been told, that the girl had
not had an easy childhood, but was resilient and fundamentally
not self-deceived. This was the only time Vicky had ever
mentioned anything personal.

It was time now for Vicky to move on. She would do nothing
about Kit, and she would not tell Moira anything about him, or
about her recent realization. If Kit liked Moira enough, it was up
to him to get on with it. Men, though, could often be blind and
some would run a mile from a woman who might be serious about
them. If she had not done so already, Moira was certainly ready to
fall in love with him and Vicky was convinced he must now have
some faint notion of her feelings. But it was not yet her job to tell
her friend Moira that, as far as she was concerned, the field was
clear.

When Graydon Wilbraham said one evening, during a little
meal in Charlotte Street:

'Well, I guess I ought to take some vacations in your little country. I've gotten too used to London,' her heart rather sank. She
knew he had spent last summer in Tuscany and was due to return
to the States at the end of the year. He was on some mysterious

'attachment' for his business, part of which had to do with the promotion of his firm's series of *How to Live Better Lives* books. Frieda Ingersoll had contributed a chapter to the latest one, with the title *Turning Round Your Emotional Life*. Vicky had typed this chapter for her.

'Once the weather picks up, why don't we have a week away in some place?' he continued. 'You must tell me which parts of your countryside you can recommend. I've done the Cotswolds and Stratford and Scotland.' She cheered up considerably.

'You could go to Herefordshire and Shropshire,' she replied after a pause for thought, careful not to say 'we'. 'I hear there are some wonderful restaurants there, and it's unspoilt country.'

She had always wanted to go there but did not know it at all. One of her old boyfriends had come from Ludlow.

Graydon took her hand.

'I'll need you to guide me!' he said. He was a really nice man, simple but kind, and also, apparently, very successful.

After two paragraphs in which she had thanked Bridie for her last letter and apologized for the lateness of her reply, discussed the weather, her old friend's health , the world situation, Christina's latest doings, and the books she had recently read, Janet had continued:

> *Moira Emsley was here today for tea and mentioned that man she used to know. She calls him Dennis or 'TD', which she says are the initials of his first names. I'd be interested to know both his first name and his surname – Moira never mentioned either of them. Don't worry, she's over him, and between you and me she is, if I am right, now in love with my daughter's brother-in-law! I'd like to know his full name though. I'll tell you why later – I may be wrong.*

The dead months of January and February and the first half of March had passed and Kit was still away. Moira and Vicky were both extremely busy at work. Even Emma complained that she was getting fed up with the winter and wished she could take a holiday out of London. Parts of the capital seemed less and less pleasant.

'Now I am getting like Mother!' she said to her sister.

Anna hardly ever went up to town now at night, and Martin had enough of it every day. But Anna was content with her life.

'Mother keeps saying she wishes time would have a stop, but I'm happy for it to trundle on,' she replied. She was enjoying watching Christina change and grow. Every day there was some small but exciting milestone in her baby life.

'Do you remember Granny Lister saying she wished Nothing More Would Ever Happen?' Emma went on.

'Why, do you feel that?'

'Oh no. It's just that I think Mother does feel it now. Something to do with growing older.'

'But Mother has always been a hopeful person,' replied Anna. 'She just doesn't like the present day very much.'

Perhaps, thought Emma, the more optimistic you were, the more you disliked it when things didn't turn out the way you'd hoped. She had never been an optimist herself. Neither had Granny Lister, who had been a puritan of the old school. It was the weather and the noise and the traffic that got her down sometimes, not her work. She was conscientious and good at her job; there were rumours she might be asked soon to apply for an attachment to another division in the department.

She was seeing even less of Lydia who was hardly ever in at night and away for many weekends, staying with friends. Lydia was always either being collected by some man, or arriving home in a taxi. She was extremely well organized.

By March, Anna suspected she was pregnant again. Christina was only ten months old. At Easter, which was celebrated during the first half of April that year, Christina was crawling all over the place, and Martin took his family in the car on what his mother had always called 'a little jaunt'. On Easter Saturday the jaunt was to the Walkers in north Kent and was less of a jaunt than an expedition. Once out of London they were surprisingly soon in lanes that were just beginning to sprout green, with little woods on each side and one or two real villages. They were unspoilt because they had no railway station for commuters. Those with cars could easily reach the nearest station only a few miles away, but real countryside was an illusion. On account of its vineyards, Martin knew the lie of the land a little further south and had explored it.

Janet and Tom had been warned that their granddaughter was now an inveterate explorer herself and put anything she came across into her mouth. Janet had been busy making sure there was nothing the crawler could damage, or damage herself upon. As it happened, that Saturday was the very day Janet had at last received a reply from Bridie Banks. Bridie had been in Greece on holiday and had sent a card, which she said would probably take weeks to arrive, but she'd got very behind-hand with all her correspondence, and apologized.

After a rhapsodic description of her spring sojourn, the long description of the illness of a friend in Ilkgate, and the recounting of a dream of teaching forty years ago, 'and it was so lovely with the desks and all the bright faces', Bridie went on:

'I'm glad that you see Moira from time to time and that she is happy. You ask about her archivist friend 'TD' Whittaker. I believe most people called him that but that a few close friends called him Dennis. I never knew his first name! Being used to research I looked him up in a university list. I knew he'd been at Newcastle and guessed he'd be born about 1944. I found an old university yearbook in the reference library in Leeds. How about that? I can't imagine why you want to know – it sounds very mysterious, but his first name was Tristram! No wonder he didn't like it, though I gather it's become quite fashionable in the last few years, with people going in for medieval romance. I remember someone telling me years ago that our borough archivist had never got on with his father, though how that came up I forget – maybe it was at a staff meeting when we were discussing examples of people with 'difficult' parents growing up perfectly OK. Perhaps incompatible tastes in Christian names may have been one of the reasons for a lack of harmony! Are you going to return to that idea you once had about writing a monograph on first names?'

It was exactly as she had imagined had been the case, and Janet found her heart thumping.

She could have asked Moira her old lover's surname, but had wanted to be certain. . . .

Moira had more in common with her than either had ever imagined. They had both found that the excitement of first love had

217

made them feel that a man's love was compatible with their deepest selves, but it had not turned out to be true . . . never mind who 'Tristram' was.

Janet was distracted from her preparations for the Easter tea and arranging the Easter eggs she'd bought for the baby's visit, but pulled herself together, saying nothing to Tom.

Then Christina arrived with her fond parents and as Martin parked the car in the yard at the back of the house, Anna made her announcement.

This news crowded out Janet's earlier thoughts, and she concentrated on the present. How she loved this little granddaughter! One almost forgot the special closeness felt for very young children who depended on you, at an age when they could be cuddled by anyone who loved them. As she took Christina up in her arms and took her into their part of the house, the close, intense physical love she had felt for her own little children came back. Tom had enjoyed holding and caressing them too, until the age when children pulled away, having other things to do, unless they needed comforting for a fall or a fright.

As with most women, one part of Janet wished little children would never grow up. Practically, of course, she would have gone mad with years and years of the tasks necessary for their welfare. Life was such a mixture; baby-bliss did not last for ever. Tom had understood this too, and as he loved his daughters had never been jealous of their demands, or resented the time taken to amuse them.

'I haven't been to the doctor to check but I feel sure I am!' Anna was saying now.

Janet made rapid calculations.

'Christina will only be eighteen months old, if you are right and you have another baby by Christmas.'

'Yes. They say it's better than waiting till the first is over two. What do you think?'

'It's a good idea to have them close together. You and Emma had less than two years between you. Emma was an extraordinarily helpful and quiet child.'

Anna knew that for her mother the past was always clothed in the light of other days, and that she probably forgot the worst times, remembering only the best. Christina might not be quiet but she would be helpful!

'It's a frantically busy time with a tiny baby and a toddler, even a fairly biddable one,' Janet added. 'I don't know how women with more than two children ever survive!'

Anna was wondering how you even fitted in a new baby at all with an extremely demanding and active child like her first-born. She was still feeding Christina herself but hoped soon to stop, for the baby had already shown interest in a bright yellow mug from which she was slurping juice, and was beginning to enjoy some solid food.

Christina was at the age when anyone in the same room could scarcely concentrate upon anything but her. Janet had borrowed a high-chair from Margot, who no longer needed it since her grandson had outgrown such items, and they went into the kitchen-diner for tea where Christina was barricaded in it and presented with an Easter bunny, a teething-ring and some wrapping paper to play with.

'How's the writing, Dad?' Anna was asking her father.

'Not bad. Things are slowly making sense,' he replied. He was writing of a not too distant future, of a world Christina would inherit and which he hoped she would understand better than he and Janet's generation would or could, even if they lived so long. He knew his wife feared this new world of climate change and possible new conflicts, and what she saw as unnecessary technological inventions. His own attempt to satirize features that were often already in existence, in his opinion unfortunately, afforded him some satisfaction, but would not alter the direction of change. Martin would understand this possible future better than he could and be better adapted to it. But even Martin and his own daughters would be middle-aged in fifteen years and it would be Christina and this coming baby, if Anna's surmise was right, who would have to deal with it.

'You ought to talk to my brother,' said Martin, thinking: Kit too is a pessimist, but he has probably seen more of the dark side of the present than my father-in-law.

Janet was talking to Christina, attempting to interest her in a wooden toy. Christina, however, had glimpsed a sieve hanging on a hook on the wall and was trying to reach it. Tears threatened, so her grandmother reached it down to her and the baby banged it, tried to put its handle in her mouth, then threw it on the floor. Such was family life.

They all left at six o'clock, burdened by nappies, baby-wipes, toys and dummies. Anna had not forsworn dummies as the baby's yells had not always been for nourishment and she was immediately pacified when one was put in her mouth, her eyes crossed in a betokening of heavenly bliss.

Before they eventually arranged the car seat, and were almost ready to leave, Janet, with Bridie's letter on her mind's back-burner during the busy afternoon, remembered to ask how Moira and Vicky were getting on.

'Moira's baby-sitting for us tonight,' replied Martin. 'And we think Vicky has a new boy friend!'

This was good news indeed. Janet forbore to ask when Kit was returning to London, but Anna replied to her unspoken question.

'Kit should be back by early summer.'

'His return was postponed because of some admin muddle,' Martin added.

Janet had a lot to think about. She would like very much to see Moira again, but only if she were asked for advice would she venture any.

19

Before her first birthday in June, Christina was standing on her own two feet, holding on to low tables and taking great delight in pulling their contents on to the floor. Very soon after that she was walking. The next few months were to be tiring for Anna. What Janet called 'toddlerdom' was bad enough, but to be pregnant at the same time . . .

'You wait till you have a toddler *and* a new baby!' said sympathetic friends.

Moira did not dare look forward too much to the return of Kit Macdonald. He was now to be in London for some time but she was not sure exactly what work he intended to take up. She had heard Anna and Martin occasionally discussing him when she was sitting in the garden and they were playing with Christina who needed constant supervision, and she knew that he had now left the Mothers and Children charity for good, as well as the administrative work that had kept him busy, but he had not yet visited Hall House. At least he was no longer doing anything dangerous, but she sensed he would be in two minds about what he might see as his dereliction.

One Saturday afternoon in June, Martin being away on business, Anna had her friend Lucy Hall round in the garden. There was the sound of both laughter and screams coming through the open window in the kitchen where Moira was arranging some flowers for Anna. Lucy's little boy Edward was pretending to chase Christina, and there were many motherly interventions. Vicky came into the kitchen to put away some goods for Anna which she had picked up whilst she did her own shopping. Moira decided to pluck up her courage. She took a big breath, thinking it better to get it over with.

'Have you seen Kit since he came back?' she began.

'Just once. I think Anna said he'd be coming round soon. He's been in Birmingham about a job.'

Moira had not dared to ask any details of his movements from Anna. But Birmingham! Was he then to leave London?

'She told me he'd left the Mothers and Children charity,' Moira said, amazed at her own calm tones, thinking, oh, I do hope he doesn't go to Birmingham! In spite of her measured voice her consternation must have showed on her face for Vicky added kindly:

'I think he plans to do a bit of temping for a GP in London whilst he decides what to do. They're very short of GPs here, so he said.'

Moira concentrated on arranging the Celestial roses she had gathered from the garden. Vicky made up her mind.

'I hadn't gone out with him for ages you know, Moira,' she said, 'though I did for a time. We're not an item!'

Moira started and just prevented herself from dropping the bloom she was holding.

Had they ever been one?

'Oh – I see,' she mumbled.

'Well, anyway,' said Vicky, 'I'm sure he'll be around soon.' She smiled and was out of the room before Moira could say anything more.

He probably still needs a cheerful capable woman like Vicky, thought Moira, as she went back into the garden. But Vicky couldn't really love him if she looked so carefree. Just as Vicky had realized some time ago, Moira now knew it was all up to Kit himself, and he had not tried to get in touch with her since she had seen him last.

When Vicky disappeared for a short holiday the following week, Moira was not exactly surprised, for she'd heard Anna say to Martin:

'I met Vicky's American. I saw them in Vicky's car when I was out with the push-chair.'

A few days later a postcard arrived from Ludlow from Vicky. She said she was enjoying the food.

Moira had booked a few days off work during the week Vicky was away. June was usually a good month for sunshine and she had decided to take her leave in short bursts that summer. One afternoon, when Anna was out visiting another mother and toddler, Moira brought a book and her notebook down to the garden, and went to sit in a chair on the lawn. It was warm and sunny, even a little humid, and she feared a storm. After about half an hour she heard a voice call:

'Anyone at home?' and looked round to see Kit at the door that led from the kitchen to the grandly named terrace. She knew he had a key to the house but Anna had not mentioned that he might call.

She stood up clutching her book.

'Don't get up – I don't want to interrupt your reading. I know it's your holiday!' he said.

He had called partly on the off-chance that she might be there, and partly from a mixture of dissatisfactions over his own indecision about his future life and line of work. Also, he told himself he wanted to sit somewhere pleasant, and Anna had always said he'd be welcome to sit in their garden.

Moira drew up a chair for him.

'I'm afraid they're out for tea. Would you like a glass of home-made lemonade? I have some in my fridge.'

'It's thirsty weather – don't bother going upstairs. I'll make you a cup of lemon tea. Would you like that?'

She saw that he too was carrying a book and a writing-pad.

'Yes, that would be lovely.'

'Carry on reading!' he said and disappeared into the house.

Moira had with her a collection of late nineteenth-century essays describing the English countryside, its villages, churches and meadows. It was written by one of her father's favourite writers, was one of the books she had kept from those that Charles Emsley had left her when he died. It had seemed suitable for a summer afternoon, and she had been reading a description of clouds. In the notebook she had brought down with her there were the many times scribbled over and reworked lines of the verses she had been working on for weeks without success. She had begun them after she last visited Janet and Tom in Hookden and had just been thinking how she would like to spend summer afternoons like today's down there. Janet would welcome her, she was sure, but she did not want to presume upon her open invitation.

Kit brought out a tray with teapot, cups, sugar and a plate of sliced lemon.

'I thought lemon was better today than milk.'

'How nice,' she murmured.

'I'm sorry I haven't been round earlier,' he said. 'I had so much to do but now I'm free for a time. I have to decide what to do next.'

223

She poured the tea and they floated the lemon slices.

'I take sugar – very wrong of me, I know,' he said. 'But sugar is good with lemon.' She smiled at him.

'What do you really *want* to do?' she asked. It was easier to talk in the sun in this domestic setting when at any minute Anna and Christina might return.

'Well, what I want to do is to write about my experiences,' he answered after a pause. 'Does that sound pretentious?'

'No, why should it?'

'I suppose we can't change very much in the political world, except slowly, through ideas, especially as far as the rights of some Third World women are concerned, but I was trained for medicine, and I'm afraid I've become cynical about political motivations.' He looked very serious.

'Rich countries always want to hang on to their money and power,' she said.

'Yes. I've come to the conclusion that poverty is the principal cause of misery and starvation. Yet our earth is *so* rich in resources. They are shared very unfairly.'

'How would you start to make things better?'

'Oh, I think if I were starting all over again I'd begin with a clean water campaign. But the trouble is, there's always a new area of conflict turning up, with more emergencies. Charities are like sticking-plasters on deep wounds.'

'But you saved lives?'

'Some, perhaps, but for what kind of future existence?'

She was silent, thinking.

'Can anything be done without violence – without wars?'

'It will have to be if our world is to survive, but the new priority is to bring it about that the people who organize the charities come from the actual country that needs the aid.'

'Charities are really pressure groups, aren't they. I mean, in the past I suppose the anti-slavery people were a sort of charity. But they were political, weren't they. Anna belongs to a local church group that calls itself partner to a Christian charity. I think I've more faith in that sort of pressure.'

'Do you know there are almost a hundred thousand charities! Now we've got a new government we're hoping for better liaison with it. I may go back to work for another good cause eventually, but last year I just felt too tired – spiritually, I mean – to go on. What I *want* to do is analyse the problems, including what I've seen myself, and try to write a general book for the educated reader, an analysis of priorities. I'd like to make some difference, have some influence in that way.'

'People do feel confused; there are so many calls on them, especially when they see starving children on the television. I suppose in the past the general public just didn't know about all the misery in the world. But some television reporters have written books too.'

'Yes, but they tend to be ephemeral and only about the places they know personally. The experiences need to be seen as a whole, so that comparisons may be made, and something learned about how to deal with future conflicts.'

'General ideas about the future of the world, but linked with your own work in the past – that's what you want to describe?'

'Exactly. I have begun to write it, after months of indecision, but I shall need to find an agent to believe in it. It would be *easier* just to go back and be what my mother calls a hero! Last year I was lazy. It needs a great deal of effort, a lot of reading round and background research, to have the confidence to put forward one's own ideas.'

'Politicians do it all the time!'

'Yes, sometimes with unfortunate consequences. Many doctors fear sounding subjective and we're not trained to write, but it was always something I wanted to do.'

'Perhaps you have to decide what your own philosophy is before you work out the aims of international aid and development. Would *you* have chosen to develop the way we have in the last years?'

'A rhetorical question, as I believe you know I would not. Things change all the time: new wars, new presidents, new scourges, but you are right that everyone needs to be more philosophical. I'm not a journalist and neither am I an academic in this area. There have been plenty of those but what influence have they had? I'm probably crazy; it might take *years* to write something useful, and I have to earn my living in the meantime, though I shan't mind a drop in income.'

They had both been so absorbed in their long conversation that they were surprised when a shadow appeared on the lawn in the shape of Anna with Christina in her arms.

'Well, hello stranger!' said Anna. 'Say hello to Uncle Kit, darling!'

225

Kit got up and kissed his niece and then his sister-in-law.

'No, stay there and I'll bring out some more tea for us all if you'll keep an eye on Chris.'

Moira took the child's hand.

'Let's look at the flowers,' she said.

She was happy that Kit had shared his ideas with her and it had made her thoughtful. For the moment, though, a small child, a real little girl, was more important than agonizing over the world. Kit's line of thought was similar for he said:

'I'll go and help Anna.'

As he went back into the house, he was thinking that what his purpose amounted to in the end was to make a world where all children had the chance of the sort of life young Christina would have. Had all the decisions by the powers that be, all the plans continually made by the great and the good, all the help given by the ordinary person led to a better world? He must not be too pessimistic. They *had* made a difference, but it was like Sisyphus continually rolling his stone up the hill and watching it roll down again. Maybe he just wasn't suited to large endeavours, but he could at least write about what he saw as the priorities. It had been helpful talking to Moira. He never said much to family or friends about his ideas. Only once had he hinted about his doubts and that was to Martin's mother-in-law, Janet Walker. Like Moira she was genuinely concerned, though Moira was the better listener.

As she held a bright marigold in front of Christina, Moira was thinking too that there was so much wrong even in their own country which politics could not solve. Perhaps it needed Anna's kind of religious faith to make sense of it all and change things. Some hope. I am thinking like Vicky! she thought.

This time Kit held her hand in his for a long time when he said goodbye. Then he said:

'We need a change from "thinking". What about a visit to a gallery tomorrow, and perhaps a concert? Will you be free?'

'Thank you, I'd love to.'

The whole earth was bathed in celestial light when Moira went upstairs. Later in the evening she roused herself and returned to her book and her poem. A few lines of verse might connect the world as it was today with the world she had been reading about,

if it were all set in a sleepy village in a never-never-land of the past
– which, however, existed in the same world of danger and terror
and exploitation – and delight – as the one today. I am not really
a political person, she thought, and suspected that Kit was not
either. But how could you live without taking into account that
world outside?

Moira and Kit visited the Summer Exhibition the next afternoon.
Kit laughed when Moira told him Janet Walker had said the
summer exhibition was meant to be for philistines but that she
always found something good in it. They did find a few paintings
they both liked, especially one of *Lord Burleigh's Lake*, and some
Cornish landscapes. Moira said she was always a sucker for pictures
of snow, and paintings by women, and today was no exception.

'I wonder why women so often paint flowers?' mused Kit. 'I'd
rather look at them than nudes by people who have never studied
anatomy. Yes, I know paintings today are not meant to be natural-
istic.'

'Artists always used to have anatomy lessons, like medical
students,' said Moira. 'Vicky told me that. As far as flowers are
concerned, I suppose women like small objects.'

'They have often been the best botanists too,' observed Kit.

It was a pleasant afternoon and in the evening, after a quick
supper at a small Italian restaurant in Piccadilly, they attended a
concert of chamber music at St James's. This time they did not
allow the world to intrude. It was to be only the first of their many
meetings that summer and autumn.

Kit had found work helping out at a local surgery at the same
time as continuing what he now referred to as his project, so on
some occasions he had time only to call in for an hour or two at
Hall House to see her. It was clear to Martin and Anna that it was
Moira he had come to see. The combination of the urgency of his
need to write and Moira's busy life at the library, with the slow but
steady development of their friendship was a good one, for each
had their own concerns and yet each looked forward most to time
together. By the time Moira next saw Janet, who was about to go
off for a short holiday with Tom – to the Bernese Oberland this
time for a change – the word 'love' had not been uttered by either
Kit or herself.

Janet had come to see her granddaughter and her pregnant daughter before leaving.

'I shall go upstairs to see Moira,' she said. 'She telephoned me last week and was disappointed not to be able to come over to Deepden before August. I told her I'd pop in next time I came to see you.'

She had been longing to have a word with Moira for weeks. When she arrived, a little out of breath at the top of the stairs, Moira was just finishing arranging her next date with Kit on the telephone. An extension had been installed for both tenants but at present Vicky, who had returned from her Shropshire holiday in great form, and was planning another sortie, was hardly ever in, so did not use it very much.

Moira had her door open and saw her visitor, before she knocked. She said a rapid 'Ciao' to Kit.

'Do come in. How lovely to see you,' she began. 'Let me make you my special pot of lapsang souchong.'

'How do you think Anna is?' Janet began as she sat in the rock-ing-chair under the dormer window and sipped the delicate smoky brew.

Moira wondered whether to tell her that Anna had recently had an unpleasant experience with a woman who had told her that only rich women could afford to stay at home with their children. Martin was not rich, and Anna *did* feel guilty about not being forced to go out to work and being able to afford Hall House, and the remark had upset her.

'With a mortgage and a smaller house you might still manage on one income. Easier out of London, of course,' Moira had told her. She suspected Martin still harboured his dream of a vineyard in France, or an ambition to live a simpler life one day and live in the country. He'd work hard whatever he did, but Anna might then have to earn some money too. Moira did not go into any of this conversation but replied diplomatically to Janet:

'She's fine. Martin often tells her to take things easier, but how can anyone do that with a toddler?'

'I'm sure she doesn't get enough rest. I well remember how tired I became before Anna was born. All that extra weight . . .'

'Oh, she's all right. We help a bit too with Chrissie, and Martin gets Kit to keep an eye on Anna.'

228

'Oh my dear, I know. You and Vicky are better than au pair girls. In the old days we used to have to go every month to hospital for our check-ups. Lucky Martin's brother's a trained doctor.'

Anna had said nothing to her mother about Kit and Moira but Janet remarked Moira's easy introduction of Kit's name and wondered now whether she ought to keep her own titbit to herself.

Then Moira said: 'I never heard again from TD. I was telling you about it last Christmas, wasn't I.'

'I'm glad that's settled, then.'

'Well, I suppose I'm just feeling more settled myself. I've got very interested in a book Martin's brother wants to write. Did Anna tell you about it?'

'No, she hasn't said anything. Is it about international aid?'

'In a way. He thinks things have got in a muddle as far as charities are concerned . . .'

'Yes, he told me something about the "Mothers and Children" problem the first time we met. He's a very serious-minded man, isn't he. How's Vicky?'

Moira smiled. 'She has a new boyfriend.'

'Is it serious?'

'I don't know. How is one to know how serious anything is?'

Janet looked closely at her happy face, but then Moira added: 'She hinted to me that she wasn't going out with Kit any more. He did take her out a few times, and he liked her, but I think perhaps she's not the sort of woman who wants a man just as a friend.'

So perhaps he hadn't even made a pass at Vicky, thought Janet. Did Moira need the man 'just as a friend'? She felt sure the she would not want Kit only in this role, in spite of her previous sorrows over Dennis Whittaker, who had not wished to be 'just a friend'. Did Kit presume she did want just that? Many young people – Janet regarded Moira and Kit as 'young' – did conduct deep friendships nowadays, whilst in her day it had been quite hard to accept the opposite sex as friendly equals. She must keep most of her thoughts to herself, but there were things she'd like to say to Moira. She must not make it sound as if she was giving advice.

'I think Kit is rather a shy person,' she said. 'We – Tom and I – always found him easy to talk to but I expect when they get to know him he's a bit too intellectual for many women.'

229

'Yes, I think his friends have more often than not been older people – rather academic ones, too.'

'Men like that are often glad to be encouraged by women,' said Janet, adding inconsequentially: 'It's always difficult to manage an unequal relationship.'

Moira got the point. What an old matchmaker Anna's mother was. It was true that Kit's eyes might in a way belie his serious nature.

Janet could see that Moira was no longer so concerned about whatever had happened to her in Ilkgate, but persisted regardless.

'I wanted to tell you something else – a queer coincidence,' she added, allowing Moira to refill her cup. 'Your Miss Banks happened – er – to mention the surname of your 'TD'. You never mentioned it yourself and I just thought you'd be interested to know that I once met his father, Neville Whittaker. His son was called Tristram!'

'You *knew* him? What was he like?'

'Difficult and clever and argumentative, as far as I recall. Probably very like his son, as far as you described him. I'm glad that's all over now for you.'

'Yes it is,' replied Moira simply. She almost said that meeting Kit had changed everything. She would like to have told Janet about TD's Peter Pan notion. She would have understood. But Moira was not concerned at present with her own past, or with Janet's.

Janet realized that it was she who was fascinated by the coincidence of Neville and his son, not Moira. It would mean little at present to the young woman. There had been good reason for the affinity she had felt with Moira right from the beginning but it was *her* life that it had touched, not Moira's.

Moira was polite. 'How strange that you should have met his father, but I suppose it's a small world, as people are always saying. I do feel quite relaxed about Dennis now. I'm sorry if I bothered you with all my silly talk about feeling guilty. You've been very kind.'

'And you must come over to Deepden as soon as we are back from Zurich,' Janet said as she got up. 'Remember to bring Kit too. He came once, ages ago, and loved it.'

When Tom called for her in the car to take them back home Janet said nothing about the strange way life caught up with you.

230

Moira was now confidently waiting for her soul-mate to declare himself, and she hoped it would be soon. Moira had been the catalyst for her to put her own chequered past with Neville, which she had thought she had forgotten, to rest at last. In the end he had not held up her young life, and it seemed that Moira's might not be held up either.

Whatever she and Moira had in common had impelled father and son to love them, and no more must be said. She had moved on long ago, and now Moira would do the same.

But before she slept that night another memory came back. She could not so easily forget the boy Tristram, eight years old when she first saw him, an intelligent little boy, who might have become slightly less ruthless than his father. She prayed he had never suffered anything on her account; it was rather she who had suffered – as he had – from Neville's self-centredness. Relationships with clever men always used to involve inequality, unless the men fell in love with geniuses like themselves, which they rarely did. If every advance in women's freedom took something away from their children, how much the more might they have suffered in the past from paternal selfishness?

The object of Emma's unrequited passion had been a donnish one too, a man not unlike Neville, quite happy to have an affair with her but never committing himself to anything long-term. And so history had repeated itself the other way round.

Nowadays, many television dramas and novels told you that women could live just like men, which usually meant they could be promiscuous with impunity. Some women doubtless could, though not all men were promiscuous, and why should any woman after a certain age want to imitate a quality that led to an unsatisfactory sort of existence? In my conclusions I am no longer in advance of my times! Janet said to herself with some surprise. Age has caught up with me, and the present age has run on ahead.

She articulated this to Tom the following day over their snack lunch. It was the children she was worried about, she said.

'No wonder, the way things are going on,' he replied, to her surprise. 'They will discover morality for themselves when their lives wind down.' Tom, of all people, to actually agree with her! But unlike me, he has led a blameless life, she thought.

20

During that autumn, whilst Kit was getting to know Moira and
sharing some of his mental life with her, almost ready to take his
courage in both hands and share all his emotional life too, Vicky
and Graydon were enjoying each other's company more and more.
Graydon, being essentially an old-fashioned American puritan was
amused, a little shocked, but also fascinated by his new girlfriend,
and the tales of her convent schooldays. She said little about her
father, who had been a dreadful man, leading her long-suffering
mother a terrible dance, but she was quite happy to listen to
Graydon on the English class system, about which she knew far
more than he did, having made it her business early in life to leave
her allotted place in it.

He found her remarks amusing and they had quite a long discus-
sion after she told him that co-education was good for girls' social
life but not for their work or their emotions. For boys, she stated,
it was of course entirely beneficial. Vicky was also, in the words of
one of her dead mother's preferred novelists sparing of her favours
with the American, realizing instinctively that the rest of her life
was in balance.

Graydon admired her competence at work and in such practical
matters as cars and food. He even liked her rather hippy way of
dressing which was never overdone but enhanced her gypsy looks.
Yet he knew he had to return permanently in the spring of the
following year to the States and he had to make up his mind
whether to ask Vicky to accompany him.

Vicky took care not to flaunt her knowledge of painting and the
theatre and was enjoying going to musicals and fashionable exhibitions with him. He found her in truth an unusual ornament on
the business scene. Frieda Ingersoll, who was half-American

herself, observed the rapprochement between her old friend and her useful personal assistant with some amusement. Vicky had summed up Graydon well as a non metropolitan American, and Frieda feared she would lose her to him.

During that autumn too, Moira and Kit visited Deepden and enjoyed a tramp round the fields and lanes and woods.

'Those two suit each other well,' said Tom after they had gone.

In mid-October leaves were still on Blackwich trees, though they were descending daily. On days when the plane-trees in Blackwich were still green and gold against a cloudless blue sky, Anna wished they would stay like that for ever but on days when it rained steadily she felt impatient and longed to have the birth of her second child over and done with.

Christina had been prepared for the interloper as far as was possible. She liked to play with Moira, and Kit, who was acting as locum at a practice near his flat in Brickley, got on well with her too whenever he had the time for a short visit.

'We are both honorary au pairs,' Moira said.

Martin was still very overworked. He still dreamed of his old plans, had not given up his idea of owning a vineyard but for the time being abandoned the idea of France. If he ever did make the big change, the problem would naturally be financial. In spite of the costs of Hall House he was not paying a mortgage and if they ever did give the house back to Tom he would have to live on less income in earnest. He had not said anything to Anna about any of this, but she guessed his thoughts. He knew she would have quite enough to do for the next few years with two children, and they were both happy where they were. It was just that he could not help wondering whether it would be a good idea to stay for the rest of their lives in London. He worked long hours, took the obligatory trips abroad, attended the conferences and meetings but only tolerated an administrative burden that seemed to grow bigger every year.

Soon they would have another child. Just as when her first child was expected Anna had deliberately not asked to know the sex. She really did not mind. It would be a December baby and she had toyed again with the idea of having the birth at home. Her mother and father had once again offered to help; they would pay for a private midwife, or a maternity nurse for a few days; this was the fashion among the better-heeled inhabitants of Blackwich, but Anna declined the offer. She would not mind having someone to help a bit with Christina and the house but Martin had booked a week's leave from the office when it was necessary. He had insisted that some of his work could be done from home; he had just acquired a new more up-to-date PC and enjoyed working on it in the privacy of his own home.

Even Kit opined that a quick hospital stay for a second child was probably a good idea, the local hospital having recently improved its maternity services. A second baby was usually the least troublesome birth of all. Vicky and Moira would be in the house when she returned and he was there for emergencies, so she need not stay for long. Janet was disappointed that Tom's and her offer was not taken up but it was Anna having the baby, not herself. Her sixty-eighth birthday would fall round about the projected date of the birth and she was beginning to feel, if not old, at least older.

She did so much hope that this second child would have the swift, easy birth she herself had had with the child's mother, thirty-four years earlier. In a suitcase she found some old Viyella nighties that had apparently escaped her last clearing of baby-clothes. Anna, who had worn them as a baby, might like them this time. No! Epidurals and Babygros had replaced gas and air and romper-suits and Viyella. Janet put them back in the case but had not the heart to throw them out.

There were still almost two more months to go before the date when the new baby was expected, and it was at the beginning of November that Emma telephoned her parents in some distress.

Part Six

UPHEAVALS

21

That very morning Janet had said to Tom: 'They all *work* so hard. Too hard!'

'Emma's job is very responsible. She often takes work home, as I used to,' was his reply.

'But think of all the work involved with bringing up a toddler – and a new baby on the way! What one woman could do both Anna's job and Emma's without help from other people?'

'Usually other women,' said Tom. 'Nannies, or any sort of child-care: child-minders, nurseries – are work for other women, aren't they.'

'Often women who have children of their own. I suppose they don't find it so hard if they're being paid for it. Martin is usually home by seven o'clock but I well remember those long rainy after-noons playing with Emma when I was pregnant with Anna and just longing to put my feet up to read a book, or relax – or just think about something else.'

'You've always grumbled about chores,' said Tom, 'but if I remember rightly you wrote those stories for children in the evening not long after that. What became of them?'

'Oh, don't you remember? I gave up after two or three rejec-tions. I wasn't cut out for writing for children. I think you have to be more childlike in a way to succeed in that market. I was more interested in a sort of literary way in childhood. You'd say theory rather than practice.'

'You went back to that part-time teaching job for a term when Anna was only about three, didn't you.'

'I'd forgotten that, but I didn't have time for longer hours till they were both at school. You know, I think Moira is the sort of person who really could write for children. But she has a full-time

237

job working for them, and with them, in the libraries. She works just as hard as Emma in her office, I'm sure.'

'What about Vicky then? Always on the go – and a wonderful cook.' Tom liked Vicky.

'No children, though!'

'Don't the younger generation make you feel quite tired?' Tom asked.

'We did just as much ourselves, but we didn't make a god of work. At home I always wished I were a good gardener and a good cook and could sew and knit and make Blue Peter models. Anna isn't good at any of these things either. If you stay at home with children such talents do help.'

'You read them stories and brought them up to read them too, and listen to good music, and you took them to the opera and the theatre when they were older.'

Tom was tone deaf.

'Yes, I enjoyed all that part,' replied his wife.

The phone rang later that evening.

'Oh, damn,' said Janet. 'I wanted to watch the news tonight. I hope it's not Greta Allott. I always feel I have to cheer her up.'

But it was Emma and she plunged straight in.

'Lydia is getting married!' She sounded shocked, indignant. It took Janet only a few seconds to realize what this would mean. The Pimlico maisonette: Emma would have to find someone else to share it, and women with good enough incomes to afford that mortgage, never mind the down payment, were rare.

'Tell me all about it, love.'

'She came in yesterday night – there wasn't time to ring you then, and she sat down and said in a cool sort of voice: "Well, darling, you'll be the first to know Gordon and I have decided to get married!" '

'Gordon?' enquired Janet.

'Gordon Hodgson – her boss. He's retiring at Christmas, with a gong, I suppose, and he wants to leave London and live in his place in Dorset. She's apparently been going out with him for ages. In fact last week I thought I saw his BMW outside in the square and guessed he must have given her a lift home.'

'He must be over sixty at least if he's about to retire! Is he divorced?'

'He married when he was middle-aged, but his much younger wife died two or three years ago. He has two sons. They must be teenagers. They're away at school. Lydia mentioned this to me once. Then last night, she said: "He wants us to marry at Christmas. He's kept his house in Dorset and we shall live there".'

'Must have pots of money, apart from the job.'

'He has a house in Wandsworth too. I talked to him at a cocktail party a year or two ago. She's going to stop work.'

So Lydia had taken what was offered and made her choice. Being Lydia, she would not have agreed to his proposal unless the consequences were favourable to herself. How uncharitable I am! thought Janet.

'Perhaps they are in love.'

Emma only replied: 'Hmmm'. She thought Lydia wanted admiration more than love.

Janet had always considered Lydia Carter a secretive, selfish young woman – pure prejudice, she knew, but Emma had unintentionally conveyed this. Her daughter got on quite well with Lydia but they had hardly any social life in common and kept to their own circles. Janet had noted Lydia's "good taste" in furnishings and decoration. All this must be a terrible shock for Emma and would entail an unpleasant upheaval.

'The thing is, I've been thinking – done nothing else since. I'm going to find someone to share for a while in the New Year.'

'We can help. I mean, if you don't find anyone to share immediately . . .' We could well afford it for a few months, she was thinking. Tom gets the rent from Martin. 'Or you could have a room at Hall House.'

'I wouldn't hear of it – well, I mean not permanently.' Emma's voice sounded firmer. 'I can quite afford a smaller place for myself eventually. But I thought of Paula immediately – you know, Paula Talbot. I know she wants to move and she could afford a few months whilst Lydia and I put the flat on the market, so I asked her this evening and she says she could come in January when Lydia's gone. Of course we might sell before that.'

'Well, that sounds quite a good idea, love, but Lydia could have given you more notice!' Janet sounded indignant.

'I think she's been wangling it for months and he only settled it yesterday!'

'Yes, I remember you said in summer that she was always out. Was it always with him? Why didn't she bring him to the flat for a drink or something, then you might have been warned.'

'Not Lydia's way, and I think she was treading carefully, to give him the impression he'd have to make an effort!'

'I do hope she's not in at present.'

'Oh no, out celebrating I suppose. I wasn't invited.'

'Well, it's not a sin to get married!'

'Of course not, Mother. I'm delighted she's got what she apparently wants. She never mentioned him as anything but her boss. It's just the flat. Only three months' notice isn't much when you share a mortgage. But Paula will pay me as long as she needs to stay and then we shall have to see a solicitor and the mortgage people about selling the lease.'

'Your father wants a word.'

Janet handed the telephone over to Tom. Never one to let her feelings show, Emma had sounded quite distressed when she began the conversation but seemed to have cheered up a bit as she went on talking.

Tom did not bother making soothing noises but was prepared to give advice about selling the lease and buying somewhere smaller with her own mortgage. He had always thought the maisonette a risky business though he had not told Emma so. She was level-headed and would be therefore even more annoyed when circumstances were beyond her own control. He could certainly help her financially now, just as he was helping Anna. Emma realized he might say this but was prepared for it. She had recently been thinking on quite other lines but had formulated an idea only in the last few weeks and had not mentioned it to anyone. Lydia's bomb-shell was just the thing to enable her to make up her mind.

'I just wanted to tell you both about Lydia and get it off my chest,' she said to her father. 'But you're not to worry about me, I shall manage, and Paula will certainly tide things over for a bit, I'm absolutely sure about that.'

Janet felt indignant on Emma's behalf .They had all thought Lydia Carter enjoyed her single life too much to want to marry, and she had never given any indication she might do so. She was a year or two older than Emma, probably forty next year. Gordon Hodgson must be what they used to call a catch.

Emma, having got it off her chest and hoping she had also soothed any anxieties her parents might have, rang off.

'I bet *Lydia* doesn't agonize for long about giving up work,' Janet said to Tom as they got ready for bed. 'Can't you just see her in the country entertaining on a massive scale? She's clever and will do everything *comme il faut*, except for letting her friend down.'

'Well, you wouldn't want our Emma inheriting two adolescent boys, would you,' replied Tom. 'The chap will get his money's worth, I don't doubt.'

'Mm. "Lady Hodgson".' said Janet and took out her Trollope novel, which seemed a suitable epitaph to the evening's news.

Vous savez bien que l'amour, c'est avant tout le don de soi!
(You know quite well that love is above all the gift of oneself!)
                    Jean Anouilh (Ardèle)

Kit knew he was falling in love with Moira but he still had not realized that she had been attracted to him pretty well from the moment she had set her eyes on his. Their friendship had deepened all through the summer and autumn and the beginning of winter, Moira discovering how much more there was to her friend than a pair of beautiful eyes. There was a very good brain too. The reality for Kit was that he simply loved knowing that she was in the world, and liked being with her more than with any woman he had ever known.

'He adores her,' Anna told Martin.

For Kit the transition to being lovers must happen soon and yet he was a little apprehensive about changing their relationship.

They were baby-sitting for Anna and Martin one evening in November and had been listening to a late Schubert CD when Moira, who had risen to her feet to find another one she wanted to hear, suddenly said: 'He makes the world so beautiful and yet he knows it's perilous. Was it as unusual in 1828 to create music like this as it would be today?'

She was thinking: a composer, a poet, an artist of those times knew already how strange the world was, probably all people knew by then that their earth was just a tiny planet going round its own little star, the sun, in one of many galaxies, the Milky Way.

'They didn't know when Schubert wrote that sonata that our galaxy existed among living and dying galaxies in their billions, did they? They didn't know the universe – or universes – might be unending? Right to the edge of time. Yet what a pitifully short time poor Schubert had – or any of us have.'

There were tears glittering in her eyes.

'He created something timeless in the middle of time,' said Kit, and he stood up and took Moira's hands in his. He did not kiss her at first, but she shut her eyes, feeling his strength run along her every nerve, every muscle, of her body. Kit felt her warmth and softness pliant against him. As if by one accord, still holding hands, they stretched out their arms sideways looking as if they were both standing crucified face to face. The strange feeling of certainty came to Moira that she had had in her dream. Then he wrapped his arms around her and she put her own around him and for a time they went on standing quite still and silent.

'Another leap of faith,' he whispered, and kissed her.

When the others returned Kit went up to the eyrie with Moira for the rest of the night.

Janet was almost as impatient for the arrival of Anna's baby as Anna was herself. By the time he or she arrived, Anna and Martin would have been at Hall House for three years. Anna said it seemed much longer to her, but to Janet it was like last week. Only the changes in her granddaughter proved that time had passed. Christina had begun to talk early, and when Martin brought her over to Deepden one Saturday afternoon in November, to give his wife a rest, Janet noticed many new words. At seventeen months old the child already understood simple commands and had made her first two-word sentence on the very day her grandmother had last seen her, taking great delight in saying: 'Dropped it!'

This afternoon Martin told them: 'She woke from a nightmare a few days ago screaming "Mind! Mind!" She'd been frightened of the noise of the vacuum cleaner some time ago but Anna had said recently: "You don't *mind* it now do you?" Well, she clearly did, for the fear in her nightmare made her use the very same word to express it!'

Better was to follow this afternoon at Deepden when Christina came out with her first three-word sentence. On a table in the hall there was a broken lamp with the shade removed. Tom had promised to mend it but when the baby saw it she said in a clear voice: 'Daddy fix it!'

'Well, well! The child has the right idea!' said Janet. Martin said modestly that he was always 'fixing' things at home. Janet did not doubt it.

To Janet such progress – and in her own home – was like being given a prize. Tom showed his granddaughter a cup when they all went into the kitchen for tea.

'Break it?' Christina said hopefully. Obviously she had been told not to 'break it' by Anna. All this fascinated Tom too, the evidence of a little mind trying to join ideas together, not just use words.

'Anna thinks she's going to be an electrician,' said Martin, tucking into a scone. 'She's always telling us to put in a plug!'

'Well, perhaps she'll be more dextrous than her mother and grandmother,' said Tom. Janet remembered Emma imitating real actions like ironing and sweeping. How much one thought one had forgotten – and then suddenly it all came back.

'She'll be fitting the tape into the recorder soon,' said Martin complacently. 'She calls it "Music dance"!'

'Music dance!' said Christina looking round for the machine.

'We'll have it in a minute,' said Janet. 'Nice music on the CD player.'

How she adored the child. It was quite amazing to find that what everyone had always told her was true: a grandchild was one of life's greatest blessings.

'She always bursts out with a roar of laughter when Dora comes into the room,' Martin said to her, taking another scone.

'Dawa! Dawa!' shouted Christina.

'Granny hasn't got a cat.' Martin said to her.

'I love cats. We shall get another soon, I hope,' said Janet. 'I think we decided we'd find it harder to go abroad if we got another – they don't like catteries and I was upset when the last cat died. And two of ours through the years were killed on roads.'

'The roads are not too busy here.'

'True. I suppose I used to think of a cat like a baby. Anna's the one who has the cats now as well as the babies!'

'We shall soon have to be very careful what we say,' said Tom.

'Talking about road accidents – the child will imitate us. Do you remember, Jan, we used to have to spell everything out in front of Emma so she didn't catch on?'

'I remember b-a-b-y s-i-t-t-e-r, when she never liked us going out at night.'

She was thinking: I fear some wars that kill babies even more than roads do. You can usually keep an eye on roads. I used to fear the whole world on Emma's and Anna's account, I loved them so. You miss that especial closeness when they leave childhood. What sort of world will Christina grow up into?

She had said as much to Tom last night and he had replied that as people got older they no longer feared as much for themselves but more for the youngest generation.

'One day she'll certainly understand the new world better than we do,' he said now. 'I keep returning to that thought.'

'How's the satire?' Martin asked him politely, now removing the sugar-bowl from the table. Christina was excessively fond of sugar and was trying to reach it from her high-chair.

'Coming along.' Which was what he always said.

'How's Moira?' Tom asked him when they went back into the large sitting-room. Janet had already got out some music tapes for children which she had found at a stall in the market town. She heard Martin's reply as she took the little girl on her lap and listened to 'The wheels on the bus,' an action rhyme that was new to her.

'She and my brother have recently become seemingly inseparable!' Martin answered with a grin. 'Anna always said they were made for each other. When Kit can get away from his locum job he comes over regularly. I see him moving to Blackwich one day.'

Christina soon slid off her grandmother's lap and began to jig up and down to the music.

Well, that was good news, she thought.

Martin, who never usually said much about his brother, added: 'We think that he's writing a book as well.'

'Moira might be helping him,' suggested Janet.

'Well, she's certainly got him going!'

As the days drew in Anna was very busy with Christina, whose name they often shortened now to Chrissie. Only heavy physical weariness in the afternoons allowed Anna to believe she would soon be the mother of two children. Chrissie was very tiring. Anna had found two responsible girls from the local high school who lived nearby and who, during September and October, took the child out in the pushchair for a walk after their school day finished. Chrissie loved these two and learned some new words from them. Her favourite walk was to one of the ponds on the heath, and Anna could put her feet up for an hour or two.

Now that the clocks had been back for some time it was too dark for that. Anna never arranged for friends to call on her free afternoons but since they were over now for the time being, she was at home, unless one of her many friends with offspring had invited them both for tea. This happened on a sort of rota; it was a relief to have the company of another adult for an hour or so.

Occasionally, Lucy Hall would call in after work, having collected Edward from the child-minder. He was at school until half-past three. Lucy was probably even more tired than she was.

'I wish Edward could have a sister or brother,' Lucy often said wistfully. 'But it's not very likely. Who wants to take over a single parent with a child?'

Emma said Lucy was better without Edward's father, Noel. Anna agreed with her sister about Noel, who had fathered the boy and then done a runner. Lucy had been unlucky, but on the other hand she did have a child, and could one day resume her old career. Better no father than a rotten one. Anna's branch of the church liked to preach both chastity and contraception but was against abortion.

One afternoon in late November Lucy called at half-past four. It was already dark and had been dank and cold all day. In the kitchen Chrissie was busy arranging pans and talking to the pebbles she put in them. She was joined enthusiastically by Edward.

'I'm sure Sarah and Kate could take him out in the New Year. I'll ask them. By then the days will begin to get longer. They could collect him from the minder, if you introduced them to her first. It would give you an extra hour or two.'

'You might feel even more tired yourself in January!'

'If I am they could take them both – shall I ask them?'

'Well, thanks. What date exactly is number two baby expected?'

'Christmas Day! But Chrissie was late – our family's babies usually are.'

They parted. Anna wondered how many pan-banging afternoons like this her own mother had lived through. It was always a pleasure, once she had put Chrissie to bed and prepared a meal for herself and Martin, to hear first Vicky, and then Moira, return, and they often put their head round the kitchen door to say 'Hello'. Martin could be home at seven on good days and she savoured the evenings when there was no sound from upstairs and they could be alone together, discuss their day, eat a simple supper and then read peacefully.

'How much longer though?' Anna would ask him, and she felt it was a pity in a way that such peace could not possibly last very much longer. It was to last for even less time than she expected.

22

Janet, who had enjoyed the birth of her own babies and had not worried about Anna before Chrissie was born, was now more anxious because the first birth had not gone as smoothly as it should. The belief that worrying would remove danger was superstitious, but she could not help it. She resolved, however, not to let anyone but Margot know about her apprehension. She said nothing to Tom who did not share her worries, or at least did not utter them. If Anna was not worried, and was well prepared, there was nothing they could do. Martin was the one who could do the worrying. Anna had been to further natural childbirth classes and Martin reported that they had done her good.

Janet voiced her disquiet to Margot, who had recovered from her lumpectomy. Having trained as a doctor, she explained that natural births always had an unknown element of risk but that they would look out especially for any repetition of the first problem.

'They whisk them in for a Caesar if they are at all worried! Such is the climate of litigation surrounding every blasted procedure,' she added.

'We offered them a private midwife, but Anna says it isn't necessary.'

'It's up to your daughter to do what she feels best.'

Janet accepted the truth of this. It was Anna who was having the baby, not her.

'You thought you'd let them go once they were adults but you find you're always emotionally involved.'

'That's the penalty of motherhood! I still feel the same about my son,' said Margot sympathetically. 'The anxiety doesn't seem to be quite so bad on grandchildren's account. Have a second cup?'

Janet had had a strange dream. It must have been thirty years ago and she was standing near the window in the room that Tom had then used as a study. Someone behind her – who? – threw a crate of birds out of this window. The crate fell down, but the birds flew up. She saw that they were a large owl and a baby owl and they flew back to the window which was now shut and came to look in through the glass of the pane. The little owl was very clearly delineated, and in the dream she knew it was a male owlet.

What on earth had made her dream this ? It was a strange dream and one she could not help feeling was an augury. Her dreams always came in clusters and the very next night she found she was back in her repeated dream, at home in the north in the snowy landscape. This time, in her dream, she got off the little maroon-coloured bus and it chugged stodgily away. She was alone and she walked down the lane to the liver-coloured drive. Just a lane, just ruins, she thought in the dream, but before she could see these ruins, she woke up. The feeling around the dream remained with her all next day: a long ago winter, darkness coming on, the sound of the wind – and the expectation of someone who was about to meet her. . . .

She would occasionally walk, or if she was delayed take a cab, to the halt at Hookden where every half an hour there was a train for London. Once there – it took about half an hour if you were lucky – she would visit one of her favourite art galleries, her favourite bookshop and the London Library. The outing did her good. It was so easy to become stale, with the constant round of routine: buying food for meals, cooking them and clearing up after them, not to mention tidying up and washing clothes, all of which, however little you liked doing them, were essential if you were not to slip into chaos. Once outside and on the train, she would allow herself the luxury of observing other people or the scenes through the window, allowing her mind to wander. She tried to avoid sitting near any acquaintance who might have decided to choose the same day for a London visit. The train did not pass through Blackwich so she did not expect to see old friends or neighbours.

This morning, two weeks before the expected arrival of Anna's second baby, Janet had decided to go up to town. She was held up for a few minutes on her walk to the halt by meeting the girl who delivered their newspapers, who told her she was leaving to go to a technical college to take a diploma in health.

'I hope to go to university to study psychology,' she told her with that curious upward lilt of the young that Janet could never get used to. Every statement the girl made, and she was a nice girl, sounded like a question. When at last she finally escaped Janet hurried along to the train with 'I'm going to London?' echoing in her head.

She was going to spend a day browsing in a bookshop, buying one or two books for presents, and maybe some for herself with the money she was earning from her coaching, if she could find any from the long list she kept of books she must read. This list had grown over the years to fill many pieces of paper and many files. If she lived until she was 500 she'd never have enough time to scratch the surface of past masterpieces, never mind keep up with the endless avalanche of new books.

Janet just made the train in time without running, and sat down to look out of the window and let her mind wander.

She saw a woman on a platform who looked a little like Vicky Winterbon, and found herself thinking about her. How old was she? Probably forty. Less than forty years ago people had thought women were on the shelf at twenty-nine, and even graduates accepted it was their duty to get married. The French had had the expression that a girl who was unmarried at twenty-five had put on her Saint Catherine's cap: *'coiffer la Sainte Cathérine'*. Was that the same saint who was broken on the Catherine wheel? It had been worse for her own mother's generation. It was not that they all wanted to be married so much as marriage being the only way they thought they might find love, never mind have children.

From what Emma had told her and from what she had guessed from talking to Vicky herself, she sensed that as a girl and young woman Vicky had taken many emotional, even physical, risks. She suspected her to have come from a poor family with ill-suited parents, which would account for her ambition and her earlier escape.

Vicky was a gambler who had learned sense, after risking her reputation. She sensed too that Vicky had had an authoritarian father, most likely a bully. Anna had told her that Vicky now had a new boyfriend who appeared to make her happy and no less carefree than formerly.

She hoped that if Vicky did settle down with her new man it would not be too late for her to have a baby, if that was what she wanted. Vicky seemed to her to come from the sort of family where sex was the great unspoken, making it all the more exciting.

Whatever she had had to put up with in the past, Vicky gave the impression of being herself now. What a good thing that Kit Macdonald had not chosen her. Whatever her animal magnetism, Vicky was quite the wrong sort of woman for him. She needed a solid comfortable type, one who admired her sparkiness and her capacity for hard work.

A young intelligent woman who gave in to her sexual desires no longer needed quite the same courage that had once been necessary. With a mother like Nora Lister she had needed a certain amount of courage herself to do what she wanted. Just too late for her, the pill had put an end to that necessity and many young women now slept around before they settled down. Promiscuity might in the end do a woman less harm than being involved with the wrong man for years.

I am quite possibly mistaken, she thought, peering out of the window to see which station was coming up now. You can never know the truth, even about your own children. She had been full of theories of free love without enough courage to put them into practice until she met Neville, who had been dead now these fifteen years. Did she want to wrench up and into the air all the long pale roots the years had buried? Not really, but it was still true that how people conducted their lives in their twenties affected them for the rest of their lives. Only much later did they realize that love, or lust, in one's twenties often had to be paid off in one's mid-thirties. Then, they might want to settle down, and have children, and might discover it was too late. Customs changed and educated women got married much later than their mothers' or grandmothers' generation, but Nature did not essentially change, however much her 'clock' was interfered with by clever bio-scientists.

Moira knew that, and Moira could not be more different from Vicky. Moira neede to love someone who not only loved her but who realized the importance to her of that inner life of dreams, and Moira would also want a child. The world of work was still seen differently by women; they liked money of their own but had not expected to have *two* jobs: the 'homekeeping' and the outside work. Single mothers needed even more money and support. Independence too needed money, as Emma, husbandless and childless, had found, and she had a good salary. She had always under-rated money herself and that had been foolish of her, she realized now, even if she had managed to save from her own earnings.

All this cogitation got Janet to London Bridge. The train filled up and she fished in her bag for the shopping-list she had made earlier that morning. Books of course: she needn't put them on a list! Something for the coming baby too? She could give Anna the cash to buy that in Blackwich . . . A Christmas present for Chrissie – ah yes. What should she buy? Little girls did not wear velvet dresses any longer for winter parties, or stiff taffeta, or silk summer frocks like crumpled pink roses, did they? Emma's first party dress was still somewhere in that trunk in the cupboards of Deepden House basement. She really must stop keeping things: hoarding them, Emma called it.

Janet stepped off the train at Charing Cross and walked across to Trafalgar Square. On the Strand she noticed a hearse pass, flow-ers heaped upon its roof. A young black man standing at a bus stop crossed himself. What a strange mixture of lives you came across.

Moira was up in her room early one Friday evening in the first week of December, the day after Janet's day in London. She was listening to a Brahms *Liebeslieder* waltz coming up the stairs from Anna's bedroom where Anna was resting with her feet up. Moira recalled with amusement how both Anna and her mother egocentrically enjoyed hearing their favourite music in someone else's presence, maybe wanting the listener to see them as people to whom this music meant a lot because they were this or that sort of person.

There must always be a difficulty with such people, in that when they played music with others in the room, their thinking about the reaction of others to their reaction to the music might get in the way of the music for its own sake. Was she being uncharitable? Both Anna and Janet were musical.

She had said all this to Kit who was always now in her thoughts. He was very musical, really listened objectively, gave all his atten-tion to the music and did not want you to like it because he did.

Kit felt the same as she did about most things, especially about the so-called conflict between love and independence, marriage and feminism, children versus careers. He believed it was a luxury to have these problems when so much of the world population was starving or being massacred. He was above all extremely concerned with the welfare of children everywhere, and he did believe that the more you educated women, the better would be the lot of their children. It was just that you could not have everything all at once, and too many material goods upset the balance of people's lives just as much as did too few.

His feelings rather resembled Anna's religious position. Moira was sure that, like his brother, Kit was a man who would always do more than his share of looking after children. He might enjoy discussing abstractions, as she did herself, but he was a practical man.

Moira was expecting him to call in later and stay over the weekend but traffic was bad between his surgery a few miles away and Blackwich.

She heard Vicky's car stop on the lane at the bottom of the garden and then she heard Anna talking to Chrissie. Perhaps she might offer to give Chrissie her bath, before Martin returned. Anna found bath-time rather tiresome these days with all her extra weight. On Fridays Martin, unlike most people, always returned a little late, for he liked to tidy up the week's jobs before the weekend. She was just about to go down the top stairs to call Anna when she heard Anna call her from the bottom of the staircase.

'Moira, can you come down a minute?'

She ran down the stairs and found Chrissie on the landing in her slippers, pulling a toy dog, the bane of Dora's life.

'I think the baby has started! I'm going to call Martin. He'll probably be on his way. Could you take care of Chrissie for a minute?'

'Of course.' Anna stopped talking for a moment and Moira could see she was waiting for a contraction to pass. As soon as it had, Anna said: 'It's early days but I think I'll have to go in . . .'

'If Martin isn't back, Vicky will take you, I'm sure. I'll go down and ask her – I heard her come in – and I'll give Chrissie her bath and put her to bed. You go and try Martin's number.'

Anna nodded and Moira went on, taking the child's hand: 'Come on Chrissie, let's go and find Vicky, shall we?' She found a discarded cardigan on a chair in the bedroom and put it back on the child.

Chrissie made no fuss at this unexpected turn of events.

They went down to the basement together. Vicky had only just got in but Moira said calmly:

'Anna thinks it's started and she ought to go in to the hospital.

252

Martin's not back yet. I wondered – when she's tried his number again – if you might take her in yourself in the car and I'll stay with Chrissie and tell Martin as soon as he gets back?'

'Right. Good thing I filled her up this afternoon – you never know. I'll have it ready. I'll come up and see her.'

They all trooped upstairs again. Anna was seated on her nursing-chair looking rather pale but otherwise in charge of herself.

'It won't be just yet,' she said, 'going by the intervals.'

'Kit's coming over too,' said Moira. 'Do you want to wait a bit longer?'

'No,' replied Anna, then she took her daughter on her knee, saying: 'Moira can put you to bed for a treat! You can have a lovely bath but you can watch a video first on Mummy's television.' She didn't say: Mummy has to go out.

'Bob the Builder?' enquired Chrissie. 'Bob the Builder – he can do it, he can do it!'

'I'll try him again.' Anna took the phone up once more.

Vicky was calm.

'It won't take long to get you there. We can ring from the hospital. It could be a false alarm.'

'I don't think so!' replied Anna as the answerphone repeated its cheerful message down the line. 'It was meant to arrive on Christmas Eve. It's two weeks early! I never expected this!'

Moira led the little girl downstairs to the kitchen where the television was kept. Anna came down in a few minutes, Vicky carrying her overnight bag, which she had more or less got ready. Chrissie didn't take much notice of the departure. She was an adaptable child and was used to Vicky and Moira as baby-sitters.

'Friday's child is loving and giving,' said Vicky to Moira.

Chrissie had been told, as far as one could explain to an eighteen-month-old toddler, that she might have a new sister or brother for Christmas. What this might mean to her was evinced in her response which was always: 'Chrissie pull it?'

'As soon as he comes in I'll tell him, and I'll stay here and get Chrissie to bed. Kit will be coming round sometime this evening.'

'Uncle Kit might help to give you a bath,' said Anna to Chrissie.

Moira could not wave them goodbye as Vicky and Anna made their way down the lawn to the gate at the bottom of the garden, where Vicky parked her small car on the lane. This might have been a bit too unsettling even for Chrissie Macdonald, as it was not her mother's usual way out of the house. Moira had every confidence in Vicky's driving. It was a good thing both Anna's tenants had been in the house.

Moira was too occupied keeping Chrissie happy to worry too much about Martin's return. It was about half-past seven when she heard the key in the door. They had watched 'Bob the Builder' and she was just drying the child from her bath.

'Let's tell Daddy something nice,' she said, not leaving the child alone for a minute. She came down the stairs with Chrissie in her arms, all damp and rosy.

'Martin,' she said, 'Anna's gone into labour. Vicky took her to hospital about six o'clock in her car. Anna tried to get hold of you.'

'Is she OK?'

'Yes. It was rather sudden. I think . . . she's sure it'll be born tonight! I'll be here to baby-sit. Have you had anything to eat?'

'The train was late. There was a hold-up at London Bridge,' he replied, putting down his brief-case. 'I'll grab a sandwich once I've located Anna.'

'She said you're not to worry. Kit's probably arriving any minute. Chrissie will be fine with us.'

Martin said: 'Good night Chrissie. Daddy has to go out again. See you in the morning.'

'Bob the Builder?' said Chrissie hopefully.

'OK. I'll you ring here when there's any news. Perhaps you could let her mother know, then it won't be too much of a shock.'

'We'll wait up till we hear!'

He was off and out with a wave and she heard his own car start up from the kerb where he had been lucky to get a parking-place.

' 'Bye 'bye Daddy!' shouted Chrissie.

Moira returned to tidy the bathroom with Chrissie's 'help' and then, for a great treat, they watched 'Bob' once again. She put the child into her cot with all her furry animals: two lions, three teddy bears and a mouse. Chrissie was amenable, too sleepy to make a fuss, for it was far past her bedtime. Moira made all the good-night noises – this was not the first time she had helped with this partic-ular task – and left the door open to the landing so that a little light was seeping through. Then she telephoned Deepden.

'Janet? Moira here. Anna's in labour. Martin's with her. He'll let you know as soon as we can. She thought it better to go in.'

'I had a feeling this one would be early rather than late. Well, all we can do is wait,' said Janet. Moira heard her shout: 'Tom! It's begun!'

'I'm here looking after Christina,' said Moira.

'Give Chrissie my love in the morning. 'Bye then.' Janet rang off.

When Moira looked in a quarter of an hour later Chrissie was fast asleep. She was just going downstairs again to tidy things up when she heard Vicky shouting up the basement stairs:

'All's well. Martin's with her. The nurse is sure it'll be very quick this time!'

'Thank goodness. Chrissie's asleep.'

'I'll make us a quick meal.'

The front doorbell rang and Moira remembered that Kit was to come tonight; she had almost forgotten in the busy-ness of Chrissie's bedtime rituals. Well, why not all eat together? It was time Vicky and she shared a meal with Kit.

'Oh, Vicky, that would be lovely. Look who's here! Can you cook for three?'

'Sure can!'

Vicky greeted Kit on the doorstep.

'Anna's in labour,' she told him. 'Martin's with her. I've just got back. Give me a quarter of an hour and there'll be omelettes for all.' She disappeared down the stairs.

'I've put Chrissie to bed. It all happened so quickly. Martin didn't get back till half-past seven,' said Moira, coming down the stairs. Kit smiled and kissed her as she reached the last step.

'A good thing you were both here.'

'They're going to telephone here and to your mother when it's over, though I suppose it might take all night.'

'Second babies are usually fairly quick – the second is the easiest birth – even better than subsequent ones.'

Moira reminded herself he was a doctor.

'Perhaps by midnight, then? She said it had been niggling her all afternoon. I thought it would be nice for you and me and Vicky to eat together,' she added.

'A very good idea. How is the Quiet American?'

This was their ironic name for Vicky's boyfriend whose hearty laughter they had sometimes heard pealing up from the basement.

'Not here tonight.'

'May I stay over—?'

'Of course.'

'Saturday tomorrow and I'm free till Monday morning, but I've promised myself to work at the book on Sunday.'

Vicky called up then and they went down to her flat in the basement. Moira remembered that very first time, when she had eaten a meal with Kit, having helped Vicky to make it. It did seem ages ago.

After they had eaten the omelette, and a pudding which Vicky produced, saying: 'One of my Christmas ones – I've made a lot,' and drunk the red wine that Kit produced from his bag, Vicky spoke.

'I have an announcement to make,' she said. 'As it's a special day I thought I'd get ahead of the next news!'

They waited, glasses full.

'Well,' said Vicky with a grin, 'Graydon has asked me to marry him! And I have agreed.'

'Oh, Vicky. Congratulations!' Moira kissed her. Kit got up and kissed her too. 'I hope you'll be very happy. Where will you live?'

'In America. He's going back to the Big Apple in March. His family live in Michigan but we don't know yet where we shall live. I shall join him once I've got my visa and Frieda has found a new secretary. I haven't told anyone but her yet – she's already on the look out. We shall marry over there.'

'A toast!' said Kit and stood up. 'To Vicky!'

'To Vicky! We shall miss you terribly. However will Hall House manage without you?'

'I've been very happy here,' said Vicky, serious for once. 'It seems like I've lived here for ever, but it's time to move. I've always fancied the idea of the States and I've no close family left in England now except my old Auntie Orla. Graydon says we'll often come over.'

Vicky had been determined to marry, and this American might be just right for her.

'You must introduce him to us. We can cook for you for a change,' said Kit.

Just then the telephone on the wall rang and Moira jumped. Too much was happening tonight. Kit went to the wall. Would it be Martin? It was. Kit, mindful of their eagerness for news, repeated his brother's words:

'A boy – ten minutes ago – she's fine – eight pounds two ounces! Congratulations both of you. She wants to come back tomorrow? Right. Shall we wait to let you tell Chrissie. OK. We'll say there's going to be a surprise. Anna wants a word with Moira – here she is.'

Moira seized the phone.

'Oh, Anna, how lovely. I'm so relieved. Yes I will – of course – she'll see you tomorrow. Yes, we'll keep an ear cocked – (frantic hand signals from Vicky) – Vicky sends her love. Yes I will. 'Bye then – Vicky, she says thank you for taking her. If Chrissie wakes I must tell her Mummy sends her love, and she'll see her in the morning. I said we could get Chrissie up – she wakes about seven.'

'Martin will wait with her till after breakfast and return with her,' said Kit. 'He'll telephone Tom and Janet and my mother.'

'We must drink to the baby,' said Vicky.

'I'll sleep next door to Chrissie, in case she wakes,' said Moira. 'They still have a bed made up in the small room.'

By the time Moira had crept upstairs to check Chrissie and returned to drink another toast, and they had washed up it was well past midnight.

'The baby was born at half-past ten,' said Kit as he locked up and joined Moira upstairs. 'That *was* quick!'

'*You* can sleep in my room tonight,' said Moira. 'I must not be distracted from my vigil!'

BIRTH

On Friday 11 December 1998 to Anna and Martin
Macdonald of Blackwich, London, a son, Nicholas Thomas
Martin.

'At least he made it by Friday,' Janet said, 'Also he won't have to work too hard for a living!'

Two children at Hall House now. Anna would find life with a toddler and a baby fairly punishing.

'Nature gives you the energy at the beginning. It's when you have two children under three that you find you haven't thirty seconds to sit down!' she said to Tom.

23

How different from Christina's birth had been the birth of the baby they named Nicholas, soon shortened to Nicky. Anna was triumphant. By Christmas he was carrying on as he had begun: no trouble, far less crying – so far – than his big sister had indulged in, and a mother who knew much more about a baby's routine. Indeed, for two or three weeks Anna was to feel so euphoric that she stated she wouldn't mind having more babies immediately if their births were as easy as his, and if a baby was as good as Nicky.

On the morning of her mother's swift return with Nicholas Chrissie had showed a lively interest in her brother, pronouncing him: 'Chrissie's baby'. She was allowed to sit down and hold him and insisted on Dora too being introduced to this new person. The toddler trailed after her mother for the first few days but was, however much more interested in the large pretend steering-wheel bought for her by her father just before he collected his wife from hospital. He attached it to the kitchen wall and she played for hours, and with Martin, who diplomatically concentrated his attention upon his first-born. Moira played with her too that weekend and on other weekends, and sometimes Uncle Kit joined her. Moira enjoyed taking her for walks to the village, and the two sixth-form girls who had looked after her before, kept up the routine after school and during the holidays.

All in all she received a good deal of attention. Nicky's presence did not appear to disrupt her, for Anna found time to tell her stories and allow her to help whenever Nicky was asleep, which was mercifully quite often. She also liked to watch him having a bath. She would not remember a time when she had had no brother.

Anna's joy over the new baby was obvious.

Vicky went up to announce her own news to Martin once Anna had settled in with the baby.

'Date not fixed yet for my farewells,' she said, 'Sometime in February or March, we think, when Graydon's back here again for a few weeks, but I thought I'd better give you notice before we both leave for good.'

'Oh, I *shall* miss you,' said Anna.

'The others know. I told them the night I got back from leaving you in the hospital.'

Later, she said: 'You might make a nursery or family room down in the basement when I do leave.'

Anna was glad for Vicky, but did confess to Martin how sorry she'd be to lose such a helpful tenant. How different from last Christmas was this one. The Walkers, with Emma, drove over from Deepden just for the day, Emma having actually suggested she stay a few days with them in the country.

'She's hatching something,' said Janet, but forbore to enquire too closely, for she enjoyed having Emma around. Kit and Martin's mother said she'd come over in the New Year when things were established. Kit had to work over Christmas Eve this year but came over for the dinner, which he helped to cook, Moira having offered to make the Christmas dinner.

Vicky wanted to stay with Graydon in London for a day or two before he went back to the States for several weeks and was sorry she'd miss the Hall House celebrations. Before they went away to a country hotel for a few days, Vicky having decided to show him more of her native land, Martin invited him to meet the family. Graydon reported that Ms Ingersoll was 'real upset' that she was going to lose her secretary in a few months.

'Still, what's a guy to do?' he groaned.

'Sure, I'm sorry about it for her sake but Vicky's going to have a new life with me.' They all liked him, and Vicky looked extremely cheerful.

Emma was still angry over Lydia's defection but Paula had moved her things in as soon as Lydia's had been packed up; the flat would soon be on the market.

Anna had a brainwave. She and Martin had been thinking about Vicky's suggestion of a family room in their basement.

'We could offer the basement to my sister for a little time at first, couldn't we. Once Vicky's gone across the pond, of course, and we don't know exactly when that will be. I don't mean a long lease, for I'm sure Emma wouldn't want to stay here for too long, but when she does sell the maisonette and Paula goes, why not tell her she can have our basement?'

'Vicky will be off as soon as Graydon can arrange it,' replied Martin. 'He's very keen on marrying our Vicky! But eventually I would like to make over the smaller room down there for Chrissie and Nick and have the bigger one as a family room. Everyone round here does that with these old houses.'

When this offer was made to Emma she said she was grateful and might take them up on it, but not for very long. Her new plans, about which she had still said nothing as yet to any of the family, might come to fruition earlier than she had imagined. Six months at most, until possibly next winter, might tide her over.

'It all depends on selling the flat,' she said aloud, thinking: it depends too on negotiating with my present employers.

Janet knew wild horses would never drag anything out of Emma until she was ready, as she well remembered from her childhood. Emma went back to Pimlico on 2 January 1999 but she did not feel like writing her New Year diary that year. Graydon returned to New York soon after, and Vicky made her plans for packing up her life in the near future.

Kit and Moira spent their time together whenever possible. She did not want him to lose precious hours for writing, but she sensed that his time with her helped him to relax and see things in perspective. He did not tell her then, but later, that she had also given him the impetus to continue. Her intelligent questions had spurred him on to explanation as well as analysis. He wanted to write for the intelligent non-specialist, and Moira was a good sounding-board. He didn't want to cut into too much of Moira's free time either; as well as her daily toil at the library she helped quite a lot in the garden and with Christina; like him, she also needed time alone to think.

He knew that she was writing too, even if not the kind of writing he might help her with. He often told himself he had something like the life of a stable married man who was at the same time a war correspondent, lucky to have a combined woman friend and lover who understood his absences. His locum work was tiring and time-consuming, but for the time being he needed the money.

Moira would one day tell him that their mutual love had prepared new seed-ground for her own ideas. Yet she was still not quite sure that marriage was the best state for two writers. As long as she had ambitions to go on writing her poems, she was hesitant about being able to give enough attention to domestic life. She was devoted to Kit: it was not any lack of love, rather some atavistic notion that marriage was one thing for a woman, another for a man. Living together was one thing, marriage quite another. Once his book was finished to his satisfaction, she had to decide whether to accept their being together for good as man and wife.

Would she be doing the right thing?

In the beginning of his life, Nicholas had taken only two weeks to adjust himself to the routine of a more or less four-hourly feed; he was much more regular in all his habits than Christina had been, and at the age of three weeks, once he had been fed at midnight, slept through the night, often until after six in the morning. Anna could hardly believe it, for he was also putting on goodly amounts of weight. The health visitor said she was exceptionally lucky, which made Anna feel, as her mother would have done, that things could not possibly continue so well. She had been too lucky in almost everything recently. People were always saying so, and it was true. Lucky in her husband. Lucky to have Hall House. Lucky with the tenants. Very lucky with little Nicholas. She had not perhaps been so lucky at Chrissie's birth, but she had forgotten all that, and Chrissie was a marvellous little girl. Anna even sighed over her good fortune.

'It's your fear of *hubris*,' her husband said, not being subjected himself to any such fears.

Hall House life was undergoing a subtle metamorphosis and would soon change even more. Vicky would have gone and Emma would come to live with them for a time. Anna was convinced that one day Moira would soon disappear to live with the man her friend Lucy called 'Martin's handsome brother'.

Once he had returned after his paternity leave, part of his ordinary holiday entitlement, Martin was extra busy at work that year, and there were days when Chrissie was cross, or Nicky was awake and needed entertainment of a kind after his afternoon sleep, or both together. Some days the helpful girls had too much homework, or she had to go out to the shops for some forgotten item. It at least gave her the chance of some fresh air and exercise, as she did not drive.

She wheeled the roomy old pram into the kitchen so she could watch over the baby, feed Chrissie her tea in her high-chair, and prepare the next meal at the same time. The little sloping plastic chair that Janet had kept for thirty-six years was fitted into the big pram, and once Nicky could sit up in it and take an interest, at about nine weeks old, she felt he was part of the family, not just the baby. These days she would sometimes telephone her mother, who so well remembered the sort of life Anna was leading.

Soon Nicky would begin to teethe and might lose his cheerful outlook on life?

But soon, too, spring would come, and he would be christened? Then it would be summer.

Life with children was so much easier in summer. The busy days sped by for all of them.

Janet often wished that she could see more of her grandchildren, and do more for them.

She put on the radio news on 20 March and heard that NATO had intervened in Bosnia. She remembered the impotence of the United Nations over Srebrenica and all that she had seen on the television that July almost four years ago. Some things could never be forgotten or forgiven, and more horrors were always being perpetrated, but at least something was being done. Fighting in Kosovo was fierce and it was not in fact until her grandson was six months old that the place was more or less sorted out, and the settlement ratified by the UN.

One day Serbia might confess what it had done and take responsibility for it. Bosnia was still a problem.

Nicky was to be christened on 21 March, a Sunday, after matins. Emma told them Lydia Carter was to marry the now retired Gordon one Saturday in April. In Pimlico, with her old friend Paula, Emma was still waiting for a positive response to the sale of the joint lease.

'I'm invited to the wedding in Somerset – three weeks on Saturday,' she told them. 'I thought, why not? I mustn't bear grudges.'

Janet agreed.

When the day came, Emma travelled by train with two other Civil Servants, with both of whom she had worked.

They were quite amusing about their old boss, but she found the wedding itself rather gruesome. She was interested to find in pride of place in her copy of *The Times* on the Monday a full marriage notice:

> The wedding took place on Saturday 17 April at St Giles' Church, Coptum Magna, Somerset, of Miss Lydia Henrietta Carter, eldest daughter of Colonel and Mrs Gifford Carter of Hedges Manor and Sir Gordon Q. Hodgson, CBE of Angel House, Bishops, Exeter.

There followed a list of the bridesmaids, including a Daisy and a Louisa, nieces of the bride. Well, that was that.

Soon I shall have quite a collection of Births and Marriages, thought Emma.

Vicky was to leave later in April to fly to the USA with Graydon. The week before her departure, a party was organized by the Macdonalds and Moira, which all the Walkers and Frieda Ingersoll attended. They were agog to see the formidable therapist, who turned out to be not unlike Vicky, a tall jolly-looking woman without the dark-brown curls, but with a large grey bun instead.

'What a pity you won't be here for the Millennium celebrations,' Kit said to Vicky. 'But we must see you in the next century!'

This was one way of saying goodbye for the present, but he and Moira together had added: *Fondest love* on their card. Moira had never enquired of him exactly what his relations with Vicky had been.

'Well, she won't miss much with this bloody Dome!' said Ms Ingersoll. The squat tent was not yet up but rumours of its future contents changed daily. 'What a scandalous waste of public resources!' she went on. They all agreed.

'I suppose it's better than making war,' said Janet to Tom, under her breath.

The final farewells to Vicky took place a few days later, one April morning. Emma and her parents had said goodbye at the party, Emma promising to write regularly to her old friend.

Vicky's goods had been shipped and her little car sold. She took a photo of Anna and the children before she got into her taxi to Heathrow. She had a lump in her throat.

'I shall come back to see you all!' she cried.

There was no time for sadness; Chrissie demanded a game and Nicky needed a feed. Moira and Martin had made their farewells early that morning before going off to work.

Janet had wondered aloud to Tom whether Vicky would want a baby. Was Frieda Ingersoll the kind of therapist who thought a woman's problems were solved through maternity? Many therapists forty years ago had been of this opinion.

'I think Ms Ingersoll is more New Woman circa 1979,' Tom replied.

'But Vicky isn't!'

Tom was angry with the government now, even this new one, which had begun in such a wave of optimism, in his opinion misplaced. He was becoming nostalgic himself about the past, that 'past' which people under fifty kept telling them had been so dreadful. Janet had never been able to help feeling sad about the passing of time and now there were the deaths of so many of the people she had admired.

'Old people can always be played for comic effect,' said Tom, 'if they dislike the present and harp on about the past, so we'd better be careful or we'll be like your mother. She was lamenting what had become of England, the world, and morality thirty years before she died. They say that all women become like their mothers,' he added.

But when he sat down to his writing it seemed to him that many matters in our present consumer and celebrity society were qualitatively worse, when he made allowances for his own age and for all the pleasant things more people could now enjoy – easier air travel, better coffee, central heating, cheaper wine.

'Everything comes with a price tag,' he said to Martin on a visit. Martin thought it strange that his father-in-law should so care about paying for things when he was so generous.

'It was Great Uncle John's money that paid for us, so it didn't count,' Anna reminded her husband. She too could not forget the people in the world who were cold and hungry, or at war, or lived under tyrannical governments. One day, might all lament the new present and fear what the future might hold? Martin was more sanguine, not as worried about the world his children would inherit.

Tom told Anna he was putting all such ideas into his satire.

'I'm more interested in political solutions than your mother is,' he stated.

'Dad's an old Marxist,' said Anna.

They had many lively arguments about it.

MARRIAGE
Wilbraham–Winterbon

In New York on 1 May 1999 Graydon Stuart, son of Warren (decd) and Shirley Wilbraham of Michigan to Teresa Victoria formerly of London, England, daughter of the late Brian and Kathleen Winterbon.

'She didn't waste much time, did she!' said Janet.

Anna was following a 'garden life' that summer of 1999. The garden at Hall House was spilling over with roses which began to bloom as early as mid-May and then at least once again, some of them twice, before winter. Visitors that summer were left with a vision of pink: Chrissie in a bright-pink cotton dress, Anna's hall full of roses, even little Nicky using up his sister's old baby-clothes. By his sister's second birthday, Nicky, who had not yet begun to teethe, was sitting up straight in the old pram with an alert smile on his face, or surrounded by toys on a rug on the lawn. Chrissie's birthday was celebrated by the usual gaggle of children and parents invited by Anna. All went well apart from some hysterics over a burst balloon.

'Now that Vicky's gone I wonder how long Moira will stay,' said Anna the same evening to Martin. She answered her own question. 'It will depend on Kit, I suppose. He hasn't been over for a few days. I do hope they haven't had any disagreements. I know he's writing every free moment.'

'My brother is still worried about finding an agent who'll find him a publisher,' said Martin. 'He told me last week that he must get one interested before he comes up to the home stretch with the book.'

'I'm sure Moira's doing her best to advise. She said publishers always say they've never had such a difficult year as the present one to take on new books.'

'It's a question, I think, of the *right* publisher – he's confident it will be taken, but he needs an agent. In spite of appearances my brother was always a bit of a loner, and now he's in a world he's not too familiar with.'

'Is it holding him up with Moira, do you think?'

'He wants to leave his locum job but he needs money – an advance – if he's going to shack up with Moira.'

'Why?'

'Because I believe he wants soon to be a full time writer and that means 'downsizing' – and probably moving away from London. He doesn't want Moira to feel she has to keep him, but on the other hand she can't leave her present work unless she can find a similar job elsewhere – wherever they go, eventually.'

'She has a good job that she enjoys.'

'He knows that.'

'I know!' said Anna excitedly. 'If Moira speaks to my mother about it, Mother will have a word with Dad. He knows a lot of academics – he was one for a time, after all, and she could ask him to seek advice from an expert. His old colleagues who've published in the political field would know where to find an agent, I'm sure, if Kit had some of the book ready . . .'

'No harm in trying. Tell Moira to have a word with your Mum, then.'

Moira, saying nothing to Kit at first, was thus prevailed upon to speak to Janet, who had a word with Tom who agreed to arrange to meet his old – now Emeritus – professor of Third World studies at LSE. Tom told them not to build up any hopes but to ask Kit to send him a synopsis and two or three chapters which he could hand over to the professor. Kit was touched that they had all rallied round; his priority had been to finish the book, but he knew Moira was still anxious to find an agent before he finished his second draft. It took a week or two to set up Tom's plan, then Kit had the requisite chapters ready, having already toiled over a synopsis.

'Professor Fordyce took the TS,' Tom reported, 'and he's going to give me a ring asap. He wouldn't recommend any project he didn't think highly of – agents are as precious as publishers, but it's quite similar to his own field.'

'Hooray!' said Anna one morning to Moira, who was on her way out. 'Tell Kit that Prof Fordyce will telephone him with the name he needs!'

'The proposition seems to me sound,' said Fordyce on the phone to Kit the next afternoon.

Kit held his breath.

'My own agent is willing to consider you for his list – just make an appointment with him. I've forwarded to him all you sent to Tom Walker, but it's a good idea to take another copy of it all with you.'

Kit expressed his sincere thanks.

'My pleasure – not often one reads a truly original idea! Tom tells me you were a medic for Mothers and Children in various trouble spots.'

He chatted on for a few more minutes and then gave Kit the agent's details, ending with: 'Show him you're a practical type.'

He doesn't want me to waffle, thought Kit.

A week later, Anna saw Kit running upstairs to Moira's eyrie. After a few minutes they both came down together, both looking pleased. Oh, thought Anna, if she's got engaged she'd look more excited so it must be The Book. It was.

'The agent is very keen and is sure he can sell to a decent publisher who'll give him a large advance,' said Moira, eyes sparkling.

'No promises, of course, but I'm very cheered,' said Kit. He looked tired. No wonder, thought Anna, and then secretly wondered whether, when the book was finished and definitely accepted, they would get married.

Perhaps they didn't believe in marriage. They were partners already, but she was sure Moira wanted to live with Kit all the time, and for ever.

How complicated life was: homes and jobs and money and love. She went upstairs and looked on her two sleeping children. *Her* life was no longer complicated, just busy. Just now she was a bit worried about Emma, who had not yet sold the maisonette. Paula was paying her a decent rent. Half the mortgage was Emma's responsibility but she also had to be sure that Lydia had paid up to date. Lydia's husband could perfectly well have offered to buy her out and then sell, but they preferred Emma to have all the chore of the sale.

'I do hope Emma will sell it soon!' Anna kept saying to Martin. The basement would be ready for her move whenever she needed it.

'It just depends on a sale,' said Emma, 'And . . .' but she did not finish this sentence.

Anna was worried that her sister would not be able to sell at a price approved by Lydia, and waited to see what would come about. Emma did not seem too worried. She still had a secret. Of that Anna was quite sure.

Emma and Lydia did eventually sell the lease of the maisonette for a reasonable sum and each paid off her share of the mortgage. They made a profit, though Lydia still grumbled about the price. She had not seemed to want to prolong the haggling, however, and Emma left the rest of the negotiations to the solicitors and mortgage brokers.

She now had a month in summer to organize the moving of her possessions. Paula had decided to go home for a time to her own parents, who lived near Blackwich, the minute Emma had to move out. It had all taken longer than they had expected, but once the deal was done everything happened in a rush. The new tenants were to take over the week after all the last traces of Emma's Pimlico life had been sorted and packed and mostly put into storage for the time being. She took some clothes and a few of her most treasured personal possessions to the Hall House basement, telling them she was already looking for a small flat of her own.

Then she went on holiday, to a French friend in the Auvergne, promising she would be back in September.

'I shall have to travel round for my work during parts of October and November,' she added.

She seemed on the one hand in no hurry to find anywhere and yet, on the other, also certain she would not be staying in the basement much beyond Christmas. Anna was rather sad throughout

August to see the empty basement but Martin promised that as soon as Emma had found somewhere else he would convert it to a playroom and family room. Little Christina loved playing there.

What was her daughter holding back? Janet too was baffled by Emma's lack of real communication, but Tom was certain they would soon hear whatever it was she was planning or plotting.

'She's not a baby. She's very level headed,' he said.

'She'll find somewhere, and she needs a holiday.'

They would all be together in a few months to celebrate the New Year – the looming Millennium. That was the main thing.

The eclipse happened on a bright sunny August morning, and although places near London were to have only a 96.5% totality, the earth did slowly go dark.

Janet, watching on the Deepden House lawn with Tom, saw the crescent shape of the leaf shadows on the lawn fade away and there was a sudden silence where there had been a little birdsong.

People had been told not to look directly into the sun so Janet took several photographs with her old camera, shutting her eyes and moving it to where the sun had recently been. Everything then went slightly colder, and it was quite dark for about ten minutes. After about three quarters of an hour the sky became slowly lighter, and then the blue came back.

She found she had tears in her eyes. Friends confessed later that tears had misted over their eyes too. The sun – the only presence that kept our little earth alive! Without it, nothing. There might be, somewhere in the universe, billions of other stars, many of them maybe also surrounded by planets, but they were not our concern. We had just *our* sun to keep us alive. Everybody felt quite proprietorial: '*Our sun*.' Nothing like our earth, might exist, nobody exactly like us, perched as we were in our special history. How precious the earth was! It was the same feeling as they all had when, several years ago, for the first time, photographs of the earth from the moon had been shown, the earth so beautiful, all in swirling colour.

Janet and Tom put on their French television channel to watch continental reactions, and found them much more interestingly presented than by the domestic BBC. A whole band of land from Normandy to Alsace was in complete darkness, then apparently it swept over to Munich, and so onwards. . . .

'British commentators spoke as if the eclipse happened only here, to us!' Janet said to Margot later.

Unfortunately her photographs did not come out.

24

Emma returned from her holiday at the end of September to stay in the Hall House basement. One day in October she rang her parents from work saying she'd like to come over to Deepden the following weekend, if that was convenient. Janet was delighted and said they looked forward to having her. On her visits to Deepden, Anna was now usually accompanied by husband and children, and there was then certain chaos and noise, with the accompaniment of the kind of baggage unavoidable when babies travelled. It would be a change to have the unmarried daughter on a quiet and peaceful visit.

Emma had supper with them both and chatted pleasantly, but after supper, while they were drinking coffee, she said:

'I suppose I'd better tell you now. I couldn't decide whether to write or just let it slip out casually, but here goes!'

Janet waited, her heart beating fast. The ridiculous idea entered her head that Emma was about to go into a convent . . . or was getting married – no, it would not be that. Perhaps leaving to live in New Zealand?

'Well, put us out of our agony!' said Tom, filling his pipe.

Emma said quickly: 'I've given in my notice to the CS. I've got a new job – just what I wanted – and I'm going to live in Norwich . . .'

She looked a little flushed.

'Oh, darling!' said Janet. 'How long have you been thinking about this?'

'Well, if you're sure,' said Tom, 'you've a very good position where you are.'

'Yes, I'm sure. I was thinking about it even before Lydia decided to get married. I've always loved the work I do with historic build-

271

ings, and the National Heritage people advertised this wonderful position away from London – same salary – to do pretty well what I have done before, but I'll have more responsibility.'

'But what about a flat?'

'Not just a flat! I shall be able to afford a *house* now. Houses in Norfolk, even in Norwich, are nothing like as dear as in London. I've decided to live in a village not far from the city centre and I can drive into work. I've found the house!'

'When will you move?'

'At the end of February. I'll have worked out my notice by then and they'll transfer part of my superannuation.'

'What about all your things?'

'They're all in store in Norfolk!'

'Well, well,' said Tom. 'This calls for a drink.'

'I didn't want to tell you till it was all settled. There was quite a strong field, but I got it!'

She looked gleeful.

Tom went to the cabinet and took out some whiskey left from their Irish holiday.

'We'll have champagne another day. Have you told anyone at Hall House?'

'No, nobody. I wanted you to know first.'

Janet got up and kissed her and Emma hugged them both.

'I know it's the right thing to do,' she said. 'It's not as if I was leaving for the Antipodes!'

'I feared you might be!' said Janet.

'It really is a wonderful job. A lot of work – churches as well as land and estates. I shall have several staff working for me.'

'Congratulations, love,' said Tom, and they lifted their glasses. Janet thought; she's an independent spirit. This move is the best thing for her.

'I found this little house in a village only five miles to the south-west,' Emma said. 'No chain, and I've paid the deposit . . .'

'We'll talk about money tomorrow,' said Tom. 'There's still what I put aside from the rent I've been getting from Hall House. It's your turn now, if you need a bit of help you must ask.'

'No, I've got back all you gave me when you sold our old Blackwich house. My share's grown – the lease went for half as much again as we paid for it!'

They went to bed, Janet relieved but still a little apprehensive; Tom, once he had in his measured and rational way considered his daughter's new plans pleased. He told Janet he felt quite excited for her.

Emma was relieved she had got it all off her chest, and looked forward to telling the rest of the family when she returned to Hall House.

'I'm so pleased for Emma,' Moira said to Kit on hearing the news. Kit too had had fantastically good news from his agent Bill Lieberman. A prestigious publisher with a branch in New York had expressed 'great interest' in Kit's almost finished opus. Lieberman had told him they had an excellent editor over there, and this had spurred Kit on. Now he had only the final chapter to write.

Janet felt that the eclipse that summer had been a kind of turning point for them all. Nicky would soon have his first birthday; how the year had flown! She could not get used to this speeding up of time. Anna was firmly dug into life with a baby and a small child; nothing unforeseen was going to happen at present to her and Martin, her mother hoped.

The trials and tribulations of babyhood were much the same as in the past; what differentiated them was not the passing of time or the changes in the world but the temperament of the children. Emma had been an easy baby but more of a puzzle as a child, whereas Anna had been an infant screamer but an outgoing and popular child. Anna's Chrissie, like Anna, had been less biddable, more tomboyish, and Nicky was more like his Aunt Emma, who was soon to embark upon a new life.

Airmail letters from Vicky and Graydon arrived regularly. They were touring the States until he might settle where his firm needed him most. No definitive destination as yet.

'Americans move around all the time,' Tom said.

Emma rarely thought of Lydia, now 'Lady Hodgson', and never mentioned her unless it was to do with the lease. Her new country-house life must be quite a change.

When Kit's book was accepted – or perhaps once it was published – would they take off together? Even Martin seemed uncertain what his brother was going to do. Moira was keener for him to finish the book than devote himself to her.

'If they can both put up with being second to each other's projects, it will be a successful partnership!' opined Janet.

In early December she had a call from Moira asking if she might come over for the day at the weekend.

'I want Kit to be left in peace on his non-locum days,' Moira said, 'and I feel like a chat.'

Moira had never seen Deepden on a really wintry day. So many days in winter now were mild in the south of the country. She walked from the halt sniffing the cold air, which reminded her of Ilkgate. When she arrived she found Tom had built up a log-wood fire in the sitting-room before he went up to London to one of what Janet called his 'research sessions'. Moira was more talkative than Janet had ever known her. After lunch and an exchange of news, she said:

'Kit wants me to marry him and I have been wondering whether I really should. People just ask: "Do you love him?" as if that settled it! I do, and I know he loves me, but having once upon a time lost what I never asked for in the first place, I suppose I have become more superstitious – frightened – of taking a risk.'

'How would *marriage* make any difference?' Janet asked as she drank her coffee, thinking: my own children never asked my advice – and I know perfectly well what difference marriage makes! If I don't I should!

'Is it the public acknowledgment of your life together that makes the difference – or is it the fact of actually being a married woman?'

'It's the latter,' said Moira. 'I'm not a conventional religious believer, but I rather think that if I marry at all I'd rather marry in church, just to have the *words* said. We could just live together, but Kit wants to *marry* me!'

'That makes you suspicious!'

'No! It's whether, if I live as a married woman I'm the sort of person who will be able to put someone else first. You see, my writing is just as important to me as his is to him, but I can't live on it, and we have to eat. Kit will want to go on writing too, but if we had children he'd have to work at something else—'

'Certainly if you went on living in London,' Janet interrupted.

'Yes, but by himself he could probably manage to find time and have enough money. By myself I think I'd leave the the library and make do on less money, if I could – take a part time job, perhaps, live in a shack in a cheap part of the country. But I know he wants us to be together and I know how much children take up your life, so I feel I must act as devil's advocate.'

She was quiet for a moment, then she said:

'I used to wonder, when I was – attached – to Dennis, what if I never met anyone else ever who loved me as much as he did?' Janet waited, then Moira said; 'Do you know, his name for me was Isolde!'

'Did you love . . . Tristram?'

'I thought I did at first but not as much as he loved me. Kit and I are equals, and I'm frightened I might mess up his life. He's made the big decision to concentrate all his energies on writing, to 'improve the world'. Who am I to get in the way? I don't see myself as an amanuensis. I know that if Kit promises something he will carry it out.'

I promise we shall share *all* the household duties, Kit had said to her. You need not expend your soul on the dusting.

'If he is to be working at home, there is no reason why he shouldn't share, but men are more ruthless about putting their own work first, or they just don't realize all that needs to be done.'

'I don't want to clip his wings.'

'I have the feeling he'll help you as much as you help him. It isn't an amanuensis he wants – it's an inspiration.'

'I don't want to stop him working abroad again, but he might want to—'

'Go for it, Moira. He won't want a "wife" to look after him, he's not that sort of man. He needs to love and be loved in return – not necessarily someone to take over the mechanics of living.'

'He is an unusual man, you know; he's not aggressive, hates conflict, but he must have been brave to court the dangers he did in Africa and the Balkans. He was frightened, he told me that. I just can't be sure that I'm the right person – right *wife* – for him. Perhaps a woman, you know, like Vicky would be better for him – to cook, and be sexy when he falls out of love. I'm not that sort of woman.'

She didn't sound very convinced. Moira was really not a cynical person.

'Well, why do you think he didn't ask Vicky to marry him?'

'He didn't love her. He *was* attracted to her, he told me . . .'

Vicky had seen that Moira would be better for Kit.

'And he loves you, and he wants you. Not such a difficult decision for you, I don't think!'

Moira inspected the patch of pale skin under her watch. Summer had almost faded.

'Forget the past,' said Janet gently. 'This man lives in the real world, even if he worships you, which I'm sure he does. He's free and you are free to make up your mind. Believe me, you are quite good enough for a hero!'

'I *do* want to marry him – I hope for the right reasons – and I do want children. So does he.'

'Kit can perfectly well do part-time work, just as you can, and you can both write and both bring up a baby, so long as you find somewhere cheap to live and don't spend all your income living in London.'

I wish Tom's Great Uncle John had left *me* the money for deserving causes. I'd have given some of it to Moira and Kit, she was thinking. Moira was underplaying her own love. Her feelings were requited but she could not quite believe in herself. Janet remembered when Emma was about thirteen she had come out with: 'Why should people fall in love? It's not necessary!' For marriage, love was necessary, she thought: a necessary but not a sufficient condition, unless you were such a romantic that you did not connect romantic love with daily life. As – like his father – Dennis Whittaker had obviously been.

Moira smiled. 'Kit makes me feel alive,' she said, 'but he gives me time to myself.'

'What could be better?'

'Love must have brought me luck. Two of my poems have been accepted for a literary magazine!'

'And you don't feel in doubt about *that*?'

'No, I'm more confident about my writing than I am about my capabilities as a wife.'

'Kit can leave his locum job if the book does really well and you can have a different kind of life if you leave London for some nice unfashionable spot. There are still public libraries everywhere.'

If not for such a good post as the one you have, she thought. If they didn't want children, Moira could still stay where she was and live in Anna's basement with Kit when Emma left. But Kit would certainly not want that.

After tea, when Moira had gone, Janet thought about all that she had said. She had so much in common with her, but Moira was more far-seeing. Kit loved her deeply.

She saw that when she went to Hall House for Nicky's first birthday party. Moira had been at work but had come in just as she was helping Anna to put the children to bed – a lengthy process.

'Kit is to come over soon. He's finished the second draft!' Anna announced, as she was drying Nicky on her lap in the bathroom.

At two and a half Chrissie was imperious and strong-willed, but usually kind to her little brother. Nicky was a dear little boy, solemn and merry, if not as jolly and noisy – or naughty – as his sister had been at his age. Christina was at the bathroom door and saw Moira on the landing.

'Put me to bed, Moira!' she commanded.

'We have a present for your brother,' said Moira. 'From Uncle Kit and me.'

'What is it, what is it?'

'It's a set of bricks'

'Can I play with them too?'

'What's all this?' said a male voice. Chrissie pranced out.

'I'd better go' said Anna, and left Janet to finish drying her grandson.

They were all in Chrissie's room where she joined them.

Kit had his arm round Moira.

'Congratulations on more or less finishing your book!' said Janet. 'I wish Tom would finish his. He's downstairs.'

'We'll clear up,' said Moira. 'Kit is to cook for us all tonight.'

It took another half an hour before the bedtime story was finished and each child in bed, Chrissie clutching and talking to a fire-engine, one of her brother's presents. When Martin was back he went up to say goodnight to his daughter. Nicky was already asleep. Emma had returned home too, and over dinner they discussed the coming Millennium party. After watching the fireworks, they would all see in the New Year at Hall House, together with other friends who had decided not to go into central London, and who were not famous enough to be invited to the party at the Dome.

There was plenty of space to sleep the nine of them who were round the table. Janet remembered that Moira's bed, brought down it seemed aeons ago from the north, was a three-quarters size. Kit looked tired after many late nights' writing, but he talked to Tom about the agent and the book, and constantly brought Moira into the conversation.

'God, I do hope he gets a contract soon for the book and they can get away and make a life together,' said Emma afterwards when her mother had come down to her basement to see the photographs of the house she was buying in Norfolk. 'I quite like being here, more than I had expected, but I wouldn't want to stay too long. Martin and Anna are definitely going to turn all this into a playroom and family room. They'll have some peace without all the rest of us.'

'Won't they have to find more tenants?'

'Martin's just had a rise in salary and as long as they stay here they'll manage – perhaps just one new tenant when Moira's gone.'

'Do you think they'll stay here for good?'

'Who can say? Not forever, I don't think. I bet Martin still wants his vineyard.'

'Oh, they won't go to France to live, will they?'

'Apparently the English are producing quite good wine now. I think he'll look round in England, they won't move for some years. Don't worry, Mother!'

Janet knew many young families were moving away if they could work from home for at least part of the time. Kent and Sussex and Suffolk beckoned, not to mention Norfolk. The two went back upstairs to join the others who were still discussing the Millennium.

Janet was thinking that nothing was ever completely settled when you were young. Or even when you were old, like her and Tom? There were always surprises, welcomed by those in their thirties but perhaps to be less and less welcomed when they too aged.

She looked across at Tom, who was chatting to Martin, feeling relieved that, as far as life could ever settle you, they seemed at present to be 'settled down.'

LAST WORDS

NEW YEAR'S EVE 1999

The Millennium will fall on the morrow, 1 January 2000; Christina at two and a half years old and Nick at thirteen months will not remember it.

Emma says it is not the real millennium until the following year. She says you must wait for 2000 years to have passed. There has been quite an argument in the office about it.

She is leaving her job at the end of the following week. She and the removal van will be travelling to Norfolk a few days later, and Tom will be on hand to help with the unpacking and the carrying. She will finish furnishing the rooms only when she sees something she really likes; she has quite enough furniture to be going on with, and most of the rooms have already been repainted to her taste, and the sitting-room sanded and polished.Once she is unpacked, before her new work starts in February, she will add a few finishing touches to the paintwork, put up new curtains and buy more rugs. It is an early nineteenth-century cottage in a pretty village with a windmill. Two rooms downstairs and three up, a modernized kitchen and bathroom and a small garden. The smallest room upstairs will be her study with her computer and new steel files. She has already been shown over her office in the centre of Norwich.

At eleven o'clock on Millennium night Vicky telephones from New York where it is six o'clock in the evening. She tells them she and Graydon are to live in New England. She is thrilled, and so is Graydon. She is looking forward to being his secretary – he is about to set up a business of his own.

June Barraclough

*

Lydia does not telephone.

Janet rings up Margot Denton who is staying with her son and his family.

'One thing children do is make you live in the present,' says Margot. 'Happy New Millennium! Are you going to the Dreadful Dome? I might take Toby.'

'We can all see it from the car a mile or so away,' says Janet.

Insider reports of it are not ecstatic and Janet does not think she will visit. Her grandchildren are as yet too young. If Tom wants to go, she'll wait until the anticipated crowds have thinned, and accompany him later in the year. Nobody knows how long the government intends the monstrosity to remain.

She wishes her old friend all the best for the New Year. So far there has been no recurrence of the cancer and Margot feels sure she is in the clear.

Janet hands over the telephone to Martin and Kit, who want a word with their mother in Cambridge, and then Tom phones his old aunt's residential home. He is told they are all asleep but have had a 'lovely party'. His aunt is ninety-six, and will see the next century.

At midnight, as Big Ben sounds on the television sets and radios, Janet goes out with the others to the front of the house to watch the firework display laid on by the council. When it appears to be finished, the rest of the inhabitants of Blackwich, and of London, and of England, light up their houses and gardens in similar fashion. Janet thinks, at the end of this millennium year, Nicky will be two – and I shall be seventy.

Tom hadn't wanted a fuss for his own seventieth, but she might just accept one!

Kit and Martin are letting off a few rockets in the back garden, having a few hours earlier produced a sparkler parade for Christina and her brother. Anna makes sure Dora, locked indoors, is still happy.

Tom kisses Janet and says: 'I have known you for two centuries.'

282

In the garden, Kit has his arms round Moira.

'I love you so much,' he says, 'whatever happens to my book, you *will* marry me, won't you?'

'Will you want a wife whose mind may sometimes be elsewhere?'

'I hope it *will!*' he replies. Moira thinks, if I am self-disciplined, pottering at home is probably more likely to provide soil for ideas than the professional work I do here. Domestic tasks can actually lead to creativity, though in Kit's case they might not. There is a world of difference between noting down the sound of a bird, the look of a cloud, shaping and reshaping a few lines for days and days, and Kit arguing the details of the case for a cut in global expenditure on arms.

But now, in the garden, on the eve of the Millennium, Moira takes her leap of faith. She kisses him.

'I love you, Kit. Yes, of course I will.'

'I shall love you for ever,' he whispers.

Champagne is opened in the kitchen and fizzes satisfactorily.

The New Year is toasted.

The Millennium is toasted.

Kit and Moira, quietly announce their decision and are toasted. They will welcome the new Millennium in bed.

'Our mama *will* be surprised' Martin remarks to Anna. 'She is wont to say of my brother: "Your father always thought he'd marry Penelope!" Penelope is a nurse he knew years ago.'

'Well, your father is to be proved wrong.'

'Thank goodness.'

1 January 2000, Blackwich.
Emma's Diary

Not much time to write today and I am a little tired from the late night, but I thought I had better register the New Year and my imminent new beginning. Next year, will be the real millennium, and I shall be writing my diary in Norfolk – DV as Mother would say.

I'm so glad that I am leaving the Service – the job with EACH – East Anglian Church and House Heritage – really excites me. I start in late February. I do know I have done the right thing, and I'm thrilled, if a little apprehensive. I believe Anna will be quite sorry to lose her tenants when I go, and eventually Moira leaves. Dad says Hall House has gone through various metamorphoses, and now it will be just what it was meant to be: a family house. I suppose they *may* get another tenant for Moira's room when she leaves, but once Martin has converted the two rooms of Vicky's basement to his family room and the children's playroom, perhaps they'll have another child. Anna and he will have a nice child-free sitting room by then, though knowing my sister, I feel sure children will infiltrate that too.

I write here for the record that my niece Christina (Chrissie) is already a bossy extrovert, and my nephew Nicky a gentle, quiet boy. I often wonder what will happen in future to us all, to the children and their parents, and to Mother and Dad, as this new century toddles along, sometimes jerking ahead, occasionally slowing down or seeming to stop, in the way babies – and time itself – are apt to do.

I know Mother would still like me to find a partner, but I think they are pleased about my job and not too sad about my leaving London. One day soon they'll be able to have holidays in Norfolk. I shall have a spare bedroom and there's a B and B in the village.

MAY 2000

MARRIAGE: Mr and Mrs James Carruthers of Melbourne Australia, Mrs Cora Macdonald of Cambridge, and all the family at Hall House, Blackwich, London, announce with pleasure that Moira Emsley and Dr Kit Macdonald tied the knot on Saturday 6 May 2000 at the Friends' Meeting House in Blackwich.

Special love from Deepden House, Hookden; Norwich; Ilkgate, and Boston USA. Congratulations from the London staff of the MA and MR foundations, the staff of the Childrens' Libraries Bickdon, and all at Hall House.

All the Macdonalds and Walkers, and a large number of Kit's old Across Frontiers Rescue and Mothers and Children charities, including many young children, came to the party afterwards in one of the beautiful old buildings on the heath. Bridie Banks and Aurelia Smith and her family, came down from Ilkgate, and there was a contingent of child readers from Moira's libraries.

Moira and Kit left London in June to live in rural north east Essex, strangely enough not far from Vicky Winterbon's old village. They brought many books with them, sold the motor scooter and acquired an old car and two cats. Kit is working on another book and Moira is collecting poems for a slim volume of poetry at the same time as she works part-time as a peripatetic county librarian with a base in the nearest little town. She can even be home for lunch.

Lydia, now Lady Hodgson, has taken to marriage like a duck to water and in Somerset presides over both Sir Gordon and what is usually called a Lovely Home. She has no desire whatever to work. There is quite enough to do keeping up the Queen Anne house to the standards which Gordon requires. Nor does Lydia evince any inclination to have babies. It is by now in any case a little late, and her husband, with two grown-up sons, shares his wife's disinclination to add to his progeny. They have a pleasant life with many long trips to far away places. Lydia is content.

Emma's diary
*New Year 2001 – the *real* new century.*
Wymondham Cottage, Norfolk

I wonder what will be in store for us all this year? My mother is very glad that Milosevic is to be tried in The Hague.

Dad has had a cataract operation.

Kit Macdonald's book, *The Fourth World*, appeared in the autumn. It made a stir. He is still researching another, but I have the feeling that possibly one day in the distant future he will revisit one of his old stamping grounds, for there will be no shortage of terrible wars.

Moira is bringing out her poems under the title: *Parish Skies*. Who said: 'through the particular the artist remakes the world'? Well, that's Moira for you.

Vicky Wilbraham communicates frequently from Boston: 'Thank God Graydon was not in New York that dreadful day last

September,' she writes in her large upright hand. I was touched when she confided she was finding it impossible to conceive and was embarking on IVF. 'I remember acting in Richard the Second at Drama School,' she wrote, 'and I've always remembered his words: "I wasted time and now doth time waste me." I don't say such things to Graydon, but I can to you. Wish us luck. If IVF doesn't work, we may adopt.'

Christina will be four in summer. She has been at nursery school for the last six months. Nicky will go part-time when he is three. Anna will take a part-time job once they are both at school, she says to 'balance her life'. She has her eye on a local gallery. Marriage may have clipped Martin's wings but I believe he still wants to buy a vineyard, not in France but in Kent. He is sniffing out the possibilities, having realized that Anna doesn't want to live permanently in France.

When the children are grown up she may change her mind and move, but there's a long time to go before then. They go to SW France for their summer holidays, have already been twice to the coast near Bordeaux and, according to my sister, the children loved every minute of it.

They rented a cottage in Kent last Easter and will go there for school half-terms as long as they are in London. One day they might all move to live near the hypothetical vineyard. It will depend on how much money he will be able to put into the scheme, and also on which secondary schools they want for Chrissie and Nicky. Dad would make a tidy sum now on the sale of Hall House, much of it thanks to Martin's improvements, and Anna and Martin's share would go towards the purchase of vineyards. . . .

Emma says leaving London was the most brilliant career move she could have made. Her life has been transformed. The slow pace of East Anglia has relaxed her and she is much happier. Her new career in charge of EACH suits her talents. She is The Boss; the county is vast and beautiful and she is able to drive on uncluttered roads. She is editing a guide to the pre-1700 windmills and churches of S W Norfolk. The Walkers and the Martin Macdonalds have already visited and Emma is looking forward to having Christina and Nicholas to stay with her without their parents – once they have reached the Age of Reason.

Will Janet and Tom continue to settle into old age? Janet writes regularly to Moira who replies at length. Janet and Bridie still correspond too. Having read Janet's reviews of 'time slip' stories for children, both Moira and Bridie have told her to write one of her own. Janet has taken their advice and begun to write a saga in which people from her own family history take on life and meet across the generations and the centuries.

Tom is just as busy as ever. He has not yet put the final touches to his satire which still has the title *Disunited Kingdom*, but he plans when it is finished to send it to the agent he found for Kit Macdonald.

He and Janet are both delighted that their grandchildren may one day live nearer Hookden. It is such a pleasure when they come to stay in the cottage nearby rented by Martin and Anna. Each time they see them all the children have grown and changed.

Janet's anxieties have not faded away but Emma's move out of London has allowed her to relax, and to accept that adult children do not need parents to make them happy, and that not all women need children, to complete their lives.

Possibly she has surrendered something?

Possibly she has just grown old.

BIRTH On Christmas Day 2002 at home in Spire, Essex, to Moira and Kit Macdonald a son, Robin Charles.

Moira and Kit share looking after little Robin. Kit finds child-care a useful corrective to global anxieties. Not that they will ever disappear.

Whatever happens to the grown-ups, the future will belong to Christina and Nicholas and Robin, as it belongs to all children.

What kind of earth will they inherit?

How long even will our old familiar world exist, turning and turning round the sun?

Janet believes that the words of Marvell which he applied to love apply to the whole of life:

June Barraclough

But at my back I always hear
Time's wingèd chariot hurrying near:
And yonder all before us lie
Deserts of vast eternity . . .

Andrew Marvell

There are no true endings to all these stories.